MISFITS
DEBTORS
DRUNKARDS
THIEVES II

TIMOTHY SCOTT

MISFITS DEBTORS DRUNKARDS & THIEVES II

INFILTRATORS

TATE PUBLISHING
AND ENTERPRISES, LLC

Published by Tate Publishing & Enterprises, LLC
127 E. Trade Center Terrace | Mustang, Oklahoma 73064 USA
1.888.361.9473 | www.tatepublishing.com

Tate Publishing is committed to excellence in the publishing industry. The company reflects the philosophy established by the founders, based on Psalm 68:11,
"The Lord gave the word and great was the company of those who published it."

Book design copyright © 2013 by Tate Publishing, LLC. All rights reserved.
Cover design by Ronnel Luspoc
Interior design by Joana Quilantang

Published in the United States of America
ISBN: 978-1-62510-448-9
1. Fiction / Fantasy / General
2. Fiction / Fantasy / Epic
13.04.29

DEDICATION

This book is dedicated to my father, who taught me to work and serve, and to my mother, who spent many hours stimulating my curiosity and imagination. And also to my wife, who supports all I do.

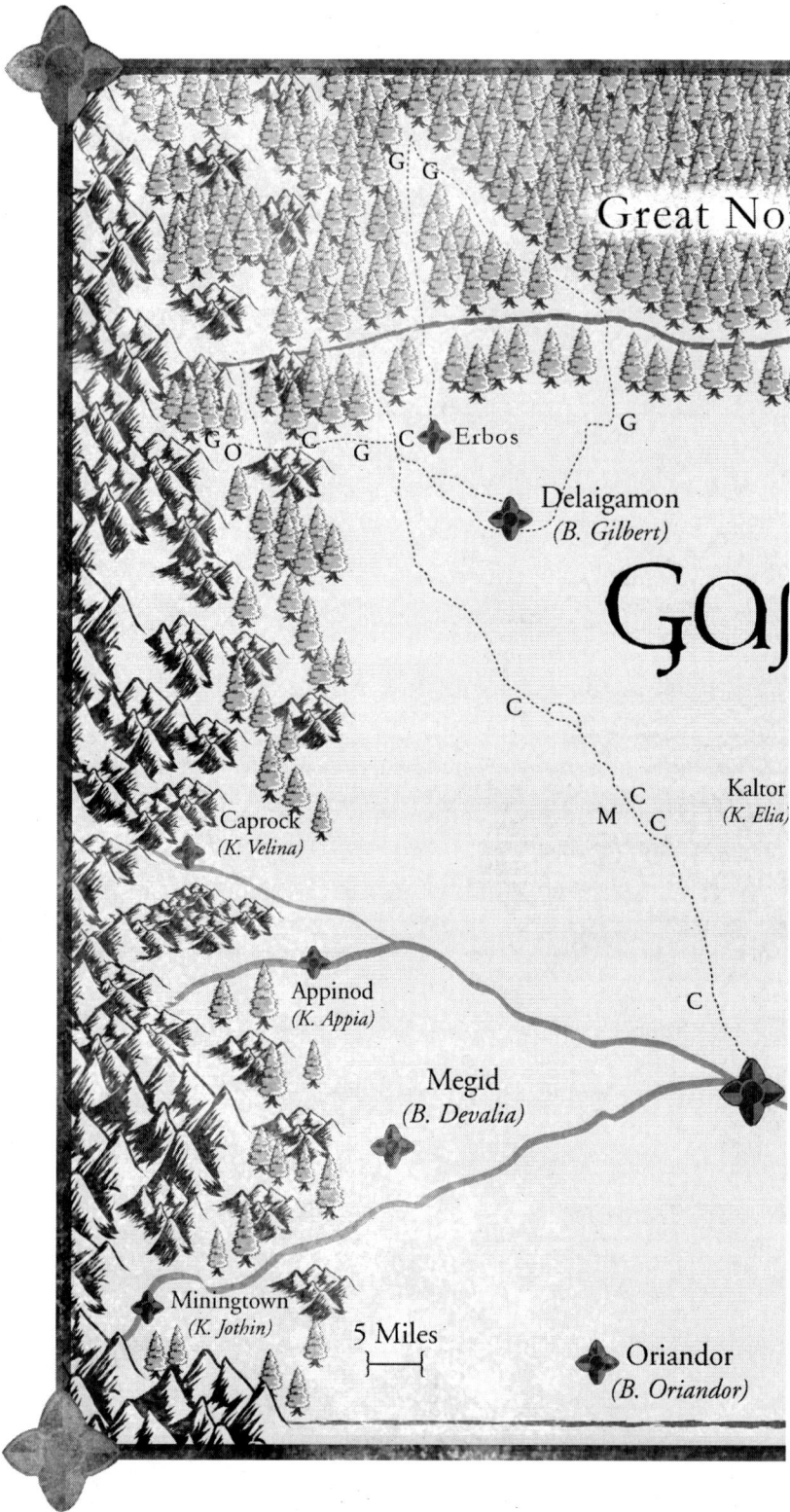

rth Wood

Merian's Crossing
(K. Merian)

Elm Hollows
(K. Vorenius)

MALIUS

Copelia
(K. Vandor)

Dewland
(K. Megina)

Caginor
(K. Cagor)

Brondar
(K. Galia)

Greenland
(K. Brigton)

Whispering Willows
(K. Rathios)

Sartena
(K. Miatona)

Gamalius
(D. Eviola)

Bright Home
(B. Gardoney)

Dedit
(K. Deditia)

Davinor
(K. Larid)

Helestia
(V. Nolinas)

Longmeadow
(K. Garrett)

CHAPTER 1

Baron Gardoney thought again of the brief message from Baron Gilbert about the Rogue's Squad. The courier from Gilbert to Duchess Eviola passed through on his way to the capital Gamalius. Because he was the ranking baron under the duchess and tactical commander of her armies, the courier stopped to show him the message.

His son's squad had decimated the first band of goblin raiders with no loss of life. By now, the second ambush should have been intercepted and they should be heading to the east to stop the third. He hoped they were as fortunate with the second attack.

Having Andolar as the magician for the group was a constant source of worry for him and made it much harder to concentrate on what he needed to do. The boy would be the prime target for every goblin, and his attitude could easily make the others not want to help him.

Gardoney looked again at his position on the map and thought about how quickly he could get north. His camp was north of the capital Gamalius in an open field—and was properly ditched and fortified—a useful training exercise for the recruits and refresher for the seasoned troops. He was working the troops hard to get them into condition for a war.

Nothing could ever really prepare those men and women for war, except experiencing it for themselves, but he did what he could to help them survive. Knowing he wouldn't succeed with them all was another source of worry, but having so many veterans from the last war in the army would help the recruits learn faster and better. He had already decided to move further north in the morning to get closer to the goblin kingdom. That would allow him to support Gilbert quicker in case of a full-scale invasion. King Durp of the goblins must be planning to invade, or he wouldn't be using fake bandits to strike into the duchy. He examined his motives again to make sure he wasn't moving north just to be in a better position to help his son.

At least Andolar had some good people around him. Petrion was a skilled young ranger and not bad in a fight for his age. Gardoney still believed he was innocent of the theft charge, but there was no way he could know for sure. Berinda wasn't as good in technique as Petrion but was a lot tougher overall. Because of her continual brawling, she was used to finding a way to keep fighting even with serious injuries. Of course, that required her not to lose her temper and do something stupid. Lecik wasn't nearly as good in a sword fight as the other two, but without him, they wouldn't have anyone that could use a bow with any real skill. He was essential to keeping the goblin archers from having a free shot during their battles. They were lucky Berinda picked a fight with him. That made Lecik look enough like a criminal that they could throw him in with the others.

Gardoney shook his head and refocused his attention on his plans to move the army north. He quickly finished his message to the duchess about his intentions.

"Dathin," Gardoney called to his aide. "Get this message on the road to the duchess immediately. And tell the officers to meet here in one hour because we're moving out in the morning. Let the sergeants know too so they can get the men starting breaking down the camp."

"Yes, my lord," Dathin replied with a salute. "Do you want me to tell them where we're going?"

It was a not so subtle request for advance information, and Gardoney smiled at the man who had been his field aide for the past three years. Before that, he had been a sergeant responsible for a cavalry unit. The baron was going to have to make him an officer soon no matter how much he hated having to train a new assistant. The man was too good at unit command to leave him in a staff job for long, but getting more insight into overall battle strategy was good for unit commanders.

"We're heading north," Gardoney told him. "We need to get closer to the goblins. I think war is on the way, and we wouldn't want Baron Gilbert to have all the fun."

Knowing the direction of travel would allow the men to stage the equipment and supply train on the north side of camp. It was a small gain in time but showed his aide was thinking about overall strategy. Gardoney passed the message to his aide with a smile. Maintaining an attitude of confidence in front of the army was one of many things his father had taught him during his early years. The man had been a skilled fighter and someone the troops admired. He could have lived a lot longer if he had thought ahead a little more. That training he received from his mother. She was always showing him how much effort could be saved with a little planning. She applied that to her own life so well that Gardoney didn't realize until years later how thoroughly she had instilled those virtues in him.

Dathin was a thoughtful man too, and Gardoney tried to cultivate that quality in everyone that served with him. Those that were the best became officers. Dathin would find his way to a high-officer position if he managed to survive. Gardoney wished he could have sent him with his son. Unfortunately, he was too well established in the military to be pulled out and made part of a group that was supposed to be operating without official permission.

Haslan, the thief, could provide at least some of that seasoned experience and forethought to the group. He was a careful planner who didn't believe in taking unnecessary risks. He was also used to finding creative solutions to a wide range of problems. He should be a big help to Petrion in setting up ambushes and in keeping the squad from being ambushed. Petrion's chameleon cloak would be an advantage as it blended into the background. The other enchanted items in the group would also help protect them. The extra strength Berinda's enchanted headband would give her would make her even more devastating in a fight. Hopefully she wouldn't use her advantages on the other members of the group. She was definitely a bully.

Gardoney found himself wondering if he could get some cavalry to the site of the next ambush before it took place. It was possible, he decided quickly, but was not what needed to be done to win the upcoming war. Andolar would have to take his chances like everyone else in the military.

The baron stopped himself again and dragged his attention back to the route of travel he would use moving north. The main road was an obvious choice for speed and ease of travel, but there was always the risk that Durp could have paid informants hanging around the major roads. However, supplies could be easily purchased in the towns along the road to augment what he had. More supplies meant more time they could stay in the field. There were enough stocks of food in the north to last for several months, but if he had to wait to collect them, his options for a quick thrust into the goblin lands would be reduced. On the other hand, if the goblins were planning a thrust of their own, a supply convoy would be a very valuable target. Goblins weren't the only danger that supply convoys had to deal with. There were brigand groups operating in the duchy. Murmandun was one of several brigand leaders that had managed to evade law enforcement. At least they didn't have to worry about that particular brigand anymore.

Word had come to him two days earlier about the fight between the squad and Murmandun's brigands. The squad was lucky to come out of that battle alive. Based on the reports, three of the squad members had been seriously injured. Gardoney was very glad that Andolar hadn't been drawn into close combat. He was totally inept with weapons and could use only the simplest of spells to protect himself. The rangers that assisted them also suffered some serious injuries and had one killed.

They were all very lucky to have two healers along instead of the one that would usually be with an attack squad that size. The brother-and-sister healers, Korin and Florine, were also skilled in herbal medicine, which greatly added to their effectiveness. Because of their poverty and unpaid debts left by their father, they were used to getting by on very little.

Unfortunately, they were also young and could only use the simplest of healing magic. The healers still saved the lives of a couple of the rangers and probably at least one of the squad members. With the help of their healing, the squad was well enough to move out under their own power the day after the attack. The message from Gilbert said they had fully recovered from their injuries.

All of this wasn't getting him any closer to deciding on a route of travel. After a couple more minutes, he decided on a compromise route. He would stay far enough away from the road to avoid most watchers, but he would be close enough to pick up supplies by packhorse or wagon if he decided he needed more.

Judging by the sun, he had enough time to grab some supper before the officers' meeting began. Dathin wasn't back yet, so he set out on his own, except for the four guards that shadowed him, for one of the groups of new recruits. He would eat with them so they could get to know him a little better. That was another lesson from his father. A leader had to be accessible to the people below him, and they had to know their leader was concerned about their wellbeing. Otherwise, their morale and fighting would suffer because the person sending them into danger was a faceless, emotionless figurehead that didn't care if they lived or died.

Gardoney walked smartly across the compound, showing an energy he didn't really feel. It was another of the trappings of leadership. Thoughts of Andolar followed him as he walked.

CHAPTER 2

The rain cut loose with a fury that night, soaking them and their gear. Petrion found a grove of evergreens, and they found enough dry material to get a fire going. Unfortunately, the ground had a slope to it, and it was hard to find a way to lay that you didn't feel like you were ready to slide down the hill. Lecik wished they had stayed at the farm for the night. It would have been great to have a warm, dry place to sleep. They could have eaten their travel rations there as well as here. He sure wasn't going to eat Mattie's cooking again. He thought blisters were going to form on his mouth and tongue when he ate that first spoonful of stew. They ended up eating all of the bread trying to cool the fire in their mouths. Petrion and Haslan told about slipping over the parapet to dispose of their dinner. Korin had gotten rid of his too. The travel rations seemed better tonight. There were no complaints.

They had quickly packed up their gear and headed away from the farm, while Barth was heading off to alert the authorities.

Six more goblin prisoners were a nice present for Baron Gilbert, although one might not survive.

They were traveling just south of east on a direct course for Delaigamon so they could deliver a report to the baron. They had been discussing the third and fourth attacks and what they could expect when the wind picked up. Darker clouds moved in quickly, and they began looking for shelter. The rain hit an hour before they found a sheltered spot, and they were soaked through. Their waxed coats weren't enough to keep them dry.

There were pieces of clothing and armor hanging all around under the trees, drying hopefully. Haslan had gone to check on his shirt and found there was a water path down the tree that his shirt was absorbing. He wrung it out and hung it in a different place. Just about all of them had moved something already, as the rain found more and more ways through the trees. Haslan cooked, and Petrion took cleanup since they were not out on their normal scouting duties. Andolar was very pleased to be relieved of that duty for a night. Petrion instead gave him the job of composing the letter to Baron Gilbert.

"Well," Andolar called across to Petrion, "are we going to the area of the fourth raid or not?"

"We haven't decided yet," Petrion answered for the fourth time. "Why can't you just write around that part and come back to it later?"

"Because," Andolar said with exasperation, "I don't know how much space to leave since I don't know what I am going to have to say."

"All right, all right."

Petrion was starting to get annoyed as well. They originally planned on ambushing the goblins four times. Now some were of the opinion that they should only do three ambushes since the goblins might be prepared for them by the fourth. That group had the majority vote, with only Korin and Berinda against. Korin thought they should stick with the original plan because that was what they told everybody. Berinda thought it would be interesting to take on a bigger goblin force and turn the tables on them. She acted like she needed something more difficult to prove her abilities, and turning the goblin commander's retributive strike against him appealed to that urge.

Unfortunately, the five members that were for stopping after three ambushes were also split. Two of them wanted to call the job done and return. The other three wanted to use the time of the fourth assault as an opportunity to raid the goblin base camp. Andolar argued that their original job was to take out one group of raiders, and they had already taken out two and were going for the third. Lecik thought they had evidence enough for Baron Gilbert to mount an assault in force against the goblin base camp and so should stop raiding and join with the army.

Petrion argued that the base camp would be poorly defended after losing three groups of raiders. They could also have an enlarged fourth group getting ready to do a raid. It would be their best chance ever to take the base camp. Also, that fourth raid might deviate from the pattern since the commander would know it had been broken.

Florine thought they should do the most damage possible to the goblins, and that was what their real mission was. Haslan argued that the really good loot would be at the base camp. The arguments were already starting up again.

"Well, I don't plan on spending my entire life," Andolar announced, "traipsing around the countryside hunting goblins. We've done our share, so let's get going."

"And what happens if we haven't 'done our share,' as you put it, and the duchess sends us out to take the base camp?" Petrion countered. "They will be much easier to defeat now than after they have gotten replacements. And do you honestly think the duchess is going to let a usable weapon out of her grasp until she has gotten the most use possible out of it? Our group is a weapon in her hand."

That shut Andolar up. Being the son of a lord, he knew more about the duchess than the rest of them. If Petrion was right, they would be sent on other missions even after they completed this one. When he thought about it, he figured Petrion's observation was correct. He could tell by the looks on some other faces that they were coming to the same conclusion. The way they reacted to the news went from horrified shock to almost cheerful acceptance. Of course, he was planning on serving in the army, and that was the sort of life he expected. It was a lot more comforting being in a larger group though, especially with the duchess and baron directing the army. He wasn't nearly as confident about the squad's capabilities.

"Thank you for that comforting thought, Petrion," Andolar huffed, "I wish I had some of that wine, but I suppose tea will do. Does anyone else want something to drink?"

Five cups were raised, and Korin looked like he was debating. Andolar made his way to the fire and got the teapot. He started with Florine and worked his way around the group. There were several sighs of pleasure from the group as they sipped the hot drink.

"If we're stuck," he said after a couple of sips, "then we might as well join with the rest of the army and get more support for our raid."

"You are assuming that someone is willing to send the army across the border," Haslan said for the fourth time, "rather than just a small group of fake bandits. Besides, they must pay a human commander well to get his support. Especially if he is good at tactics like we think. Think of all the money we could pick up. He will probably have gems and jewelry just to cut down on the weight of his treasure. There might even be an enchanted item. Those bring very high prices. If we go in with the army, then the army will get everything."

"Yes, but our mission was to stop four raids," Korin said again. "That is what we told them we were going to do."

"We will be stopping, at least temporarily, all of the raids if we take out the main camp," Florine said in her "don't be so dense, brother" tone. "That was the real purpose of our mission rather than a certain number of attacks."

"All right, we'll just have to go with the majority," Petrion said. "That means we set the ambush for the third raid and then move into goblin territory for an assault on their main camp."

"You don't have a majority," Andolar quickly pointed out. "You only have three of seven in support of your plan."

"Well then, we'll go," Petrion said quickly, "with the option with the most votes."

"Yes, but we can combine against you into a 'don't go' group and still win four votes to three," Andolar said smugly.

"Fine, then we'll use my favorite way of deciding," Petrion said with some temper starting to show.

"And just what is that?" Andolar grouched back, "Flip a two-headed coin to get your way since you can't come up with a legitimate way?"

"No, I have a legitimate way, magician," Petrion said as he closed the distance to Andolar. "I am the leader of this party by appointment of the duchess, so I have the final say. We'll do it my way. That's the way it goes unless five of you decide that another single plan is best. Any objections?" Petrion was about two inches in front of Andolar's face.

Lecik admired Andolar's courage for standing there with Petrion glaring at him. The ranger was only a little taller but a lot bigger than the magician and in armor. Andolar probably had a lot of experience ignoring glares, considering what they knew about his past.

"That was what the duchess said," Korin told them as he hurried to diffuse the argument. "So I guess that's what we'll do."

Petrion looked at Korin and then after a deep breath walked away.

"Put that in the letter, Andolar," Petrion called over his shoulder, "and let me read it when you're through."

"Whatever you say, my lord general," Andolar replied sarcastically. "I live only to serve your wishes."

Petrion's look hardened again, but Andolar ignored him and sat back down.

Things quieted down for a while, except for the scratching of a pen across the paper and the drop of water. Lecik wondered what the others were thinking about.

"What if we are heavily outnumbered?" Korin asked finally.

"We don't let them see us," Petrion answered, "and then we get out of there as fast as we can. If they do see us, then we split up and run and meet back together at a set place on our side of the border."

The scratching of pen on paper was the only sound again for a while, with a stop only for a grump when a big drop of water fell on the page and ruined it. There were more drops getting through now. Andolar pulled his waxed cloak over his head and the writing board and started on a new sheet of paper with the old as a guide. It made it even more difficult to keep the lamp light on the paper. After about five minutes, Andolar was finished and handed the letter to Petrion with an admonition to keep it dry.

"Everyone listen and see if anything needs to be added," Petrion called as he started to read.

Baron Gilbert,

We are writing to tell you of our progress, to report some vital information and to tell you of a change in plans. Raid one of twenty-eight goblins was stopped with four goblins taken prisoner. Raid two of twenty-six goblins was stopped with six goblins taken prisoner. One goblin was killed on the wrong side of the border on raid two.

Attached you will find a map. In the area of the last raid, there is an *O* marked on the map. A man named Omnirus lives there and is a goblin trader. Included are some interesting things we found in quantity at his residence. We had an altercation but left on good terms. Also included is a bill of sale for all we received from him and the price. We didn't want any misunderstanding with the authorities about the legalities of our actions, and he seemed the type to report crimes that weren't committed. He has a strong box hidden in the cellar behind some boards. It contains silver and gold bars made from his metal shop in the barn, as well as more of the attached types of coins. We had not seen this particular type of coin before and thought it might be of interest to you.

We also suspect that Omnirus is involved in cattle thefts in the area, having matched hoofprints from his house with ones around the raided farm.

We will carry out the third ambush as planned but will not do the fourth. We expect either a change in pattern or overwhelming odds against us in the attack area marked *A* on the map. Instead, we will be crossing the border and attempting an attack on the base camp while all the troops are away.

According to the goblins captured during the first ambush, the leader is a human male named Churinius. The goblins have a camp of about two hundred people, and it is about twelve miles into goblin territory. It should be somewhere north and east of Omnirus' house.

We do not need a reply but will have a messenger wait overnight in case you want us to change plans. We suggest you randomize patrols after our third attack, expected the second week and the seventh day of fall, instead of waiting till after the fourth attack. We would also suggest that you send a large force to the attack area marked *A* to intercept any force coming from the goblins. Their attack pattern suggests finding the richest target in the area by human standards, but also one which is isolated and can be approached closely under cover.

R. S.

Petrion waited for a couple of seconds after he read the letter for comments, but when none came, he packaged the letter, bill of sale, map, and items into an oilcloth envelope so it would stay dry.

"Now who's going into town to deliver this?" Petrion asked.

Petrion had six volunteers, not counting himself.

"All right," Petrion said when he saw the hands, "now we need reasons for people to go into town. As before, I will make the final decision."

"Korin or I," Florine said, "need to go so we can pick up additional medical supplies at the herbalist's shop. Since I am the oldest, it should be me."

"You're only two years older!" Korin said back. "That's not enough to make a difference!"

"Start making a list," Petrion said quietly, "so whoever goes in can pick up the supplies."

"I can pass easily as a wandering warrior," Berinda got in at the next chance to speak, "and I can fit in well at the tavern where the person in town will be staying."

"And get into a fight and get arrested," Lecik added. "I can do the same thing as Berinda, but without the risk of violence."

"Sit down, Berinda," Petrion told her.

Berinda started for Lecik as soon as he spoke. Lecik wished he had held his tongue. He scrambled to his feet and started backing away.

"You just proved Lecik's point for him," Petrion continued. "You are no longer in the running. I said sit down! You will learn to control your temper, and there will be no more attacks on party members. You may be a good fighter, but I doubt you could take on the whole squad. Violence against another squad member is a crime against the squad and will be punished accordingly."

Lecik breathed a heavy sigh of relief when Berinda actually listened to Petrion. Korin and Florine also came to his defense. If he didn't learn to keep his opinions about that belligerent, overbearing fighter to himself, he was going to be in serious trouble one of these days. She might just accidentally forget to take off that headband before she attacked.

"I have all of the qualifications of either Berinda or Lecik," Petrion continued. "And I have the best chance of finding a camp that has been moved. In addition, I have my cloak which I can use to hide and escape if it is required."

"Using a major magic item," Haslan countered, "is a sure way to attract attention, and attention is the last thing we want on this trip. I, on the other hand, can fade away and escape as I have proved many times."

"And you could also," Petrion threw back, "lift some valuables that just happened to come within your grasp. Having a theft attributed to the squad would get all of us in trouble. And you can bet that Baron Gilbert will blame all of us if an unknown halfman who had been a visitor at a certain wine shop was accused of theft.".

"I could give my word that I wouldn't steal anything," Haslan pleaded.

"Halfmen don't travel as much as humans," Lecik said, "and are therefore more likely to attract attention. You could get in trouble even if you didn't steal anything. If someone saw a strange halfman in the room and later came up missing something, regardless of the reason, they would report you as the most likely culprit."

"Bigoted humans," Haslan snarled, "are always willing to accuse the poor halfmen even though there are more human thieves around."

"Point made though, Lecik," Petrion said, "Haslan is ruled out."

"Wait a minute, I should get another say in all of this," Haslan complained.

"Sorry," Petrion said, "but if everyone got to say everything they wanted to, the decision would never get made. That's two eliminated."

"How about if the two healers flip for which of them stays in contention," Lecik suggested. "If their reasoning wins out, only one will go anyway."

"Will the two healers agree to abide by that?" Petrion asked and received affirmative nods.

"It was Lecik's idea," Petrion told them, "so he flips. Florine, you call the toss in the air."

Lecik dug out a silver coin and threw it in the air. Florine called heads, and the coin landed with the head up. Korin and Florine came to look, and Florine let out a whoop when she saw the coin. Korin snickered on the way back to his seat when a large drop of water fell right on Florine's head. Florine glared at him, but Korin just kept smiling.

"That eliminates, Korin," Petrion told them. "That leaves Lecik, Florine, Andolar, and myself. How about you, Andolar? Aren't you going to give any reason why you should be the one allowed to go?"

"I was waiting till all of you finished talking," Andolar said in a smug voice, "because I have reasons which the rest of you will not be able to refute."

"Oh, really now?" Petrion said with sarcasm. "Let's hear them and see how many reasons we can get against you going. I know one already. You are a known drunk, and going to a wine shop and an inn seems like way too much temptation for a drunk to handle. If you get drunk, you might give away the mission or get into trouble."

Lecik could see there was really starting to be some tension there. Andolar had been doing some leading of the party, not from any want to, but just out of necessity. Lecik wondered if Petrion was a little jealous of the way Andolar handled the last two battles. They didn't need any more friction in the squad. The goblins were making enough trouble without them making it for themselves. Although when it came to someone watching himself, he really needed to watch his mouth around Berinda. Unfortunately, bullies rubbed him the wrong way.

"First," Andolar said with perfect poise, "I need spell components to be picked up just like the healers need medicinal herbs. I am the only one in the group who could go into a magic shop and talk intelligently with the proprietor. Since I am well versed with natural items, I can also talk more intelligently at a medicinal shop than anyone but the healers. I am better at hiding in a crowd than anyone but Haslan because of years of experience evading my father and brother's watchdogs. I can pass as a noble, magician, commoner, merchant, or any number of other professions except fighter. And finally, our contact is in a very exclusive wine shop. I know far more about wines than any of you and can make our cover story seem real. Haslan would be the only other one to have a chance of posing as a wine connoisseur, and he has already been ruled out as a candidate. Also, I have never heard of an influential person sending a halfman to buy wine. And I don't think *goblin trimmer* would be an exception to the rule."

"Goblin trimmer?" Lecik said in puzzlement. "What are you talking about?"

"That's our code name," Andolar replied.

"Our code name is *gobtrim nilrem*," Petrion said, suddenly enthused again. "If you can't remember our code name, then you have no business going into town. I guess that rules you out, Andolar."

"Not hardly," Andolar replied with a very self-satisfied grin. "It shows I am the best candidate. None of the rest of you figured out the significance of our code name. Code names are picked to be easy for the chooser to remember, while at the same time making it hard for an enemy to decipher its significance. Gobtrim nilrem is merely 'goblin trimmer' altered so as to be unrecognizable to an outsider. The first syllable of each word was made into the first name, while the second syllable of each word was made into the second name. To further confuse an enemy, the order of the letters was reversed in the last name. It is something easy to remember and with significance to the person creating the code. There could also be some problem with our set communication path. In that case, I have the better understanding with which to decipher cryptic communications, as well as to create them. And finally, if all else fails, my position in society would give me immediate access to the baron in an emergency without revealing our purpose to anyone."

Petrion opened and closed his mouth several times, probably thinking up and discarding arguments to counteract those of Andolar. Lecik was at a loss to figure out anything other than the argument Petrion already used. And Petrion's only other advantage, finding the group again, wasn't nearly as convincing as any of the arguments Andolar used. Andolar had sat there and let them put out all their reasons while he worked out indisputable reasons and threw them all out at once. The magician even let Petrion narrow the field to cut down on his competition. He wondered if Andolar could come up with something like that for most situations or if he really was the most qualified to handle the trip into Delaigamon. He would bet that last thing about the encrypted code name had been thrown in specifically to get them to show they hadn't understood it before he enlightened them.

He started trying to think of other times when Andolar could have maneuvered them into getting his own way. Other attempts might not have been as obvious as this one. Maybe this was the first time, and Andolar was still clumsy at it. Or the magician might possibly be trying to look obvious when he got his way this time so that his less obvious attempts would look like mere coincidence. He was getting a headache. That line of thought could go on forever with plots and counter plots. Still, it would be a good idea to keep his wits about him when dealing with Andolar in the future.

"Now the next question," Andolar said when he saw the opposition silenced, "is if any one person can pull off all the things that need done without arousing suspicion. Magicians, healers, and wealthy merchants seldom travel without an escort. Showing up as a stranger with one of those identities without escort might be enough to arouse suspicion and interest. I could play it up that my escort was quartered in poorer surroundings as befits their status to explain being alone. That would work anywhere but at the gate getting into town, and I could have a different story there. A single fighter escort would still enhance the image and make the story more believable. Wealthy people also are not inclined to purchase basic supplies such as travel rations and arrows. I would have to work several different characters within the same area of town, and that also is likely to arouse interest. The fighter escort would again take care of that problem. Then I believe Petrion's equipment needs some repair work, and that would be best handled by the person using the equipment."

"That is sound reasoning," Haslan said grudgingly. "I think you should listen to him, Petrion. And I think you should be the fighter to go. Berinda would be the next best if you decide you need to stay with the squad. You have the size to be intimidating as a single guard needs to be, and Berinda looks like she has seen a lot of action. In a situation like that, looks are as important as ability."

"We were only supposed to send in a single person, but I think I have to agree with Andolar and Haslan," Petrion said after a few moments of silence. "I will accompany him, and the squad can move ahead while we are getting supplies and delivering the message. Then I can get us back together with the rest of the squad."

"You know the area better than I do," Andolar told Petrion. "When do you think we should break off from the rest of the squad?"

"Tomorrow morning," Petrion replied. "We'll head southeast to the city, while the squad continues due east. We'll meet where you cross the road north of Delaigamon. We should reach Delaigamon about the middle of the afternoon. We can deliver the message and collect our supplies before the shops close for the day. Then we can leave at first light when we're sure no reply is coming from the baron."

"Hey," Haslan called over to where the two were sitting talking, "what happens if he isn't there when your message arrives? We won't know if it was actually delivered to him. Only that we gave it to the contact."

"We just have to assume that if Quilonia gets the message, it will get into the baron's hands," Petrion told him. "If we don't get an answer, the letter lets him know we are going ahead with our plan. If he isn't there to receive the message, then he'll have to go along regardless. It's not as if the entire realm hinges on what we're doing. We are just a small assault force out to take care of some goblin raiders. We have provided him with all the important information we had. Where we hit the goblins matters very little in the overall picture."

"Yes," Haslan said solemnly, "but if enough little things are out of place in the big picture, the picture is still ruined. Small miscalculations and slight changes in pattern can ruin the best of plans and strategies."

"You're right, of course," Andolar said, "but I think our part in the big picture is to delay the start of hostilities by disrupting the raids. If the current goblin plan falls apart, then they may have to regroup for a while. Baron Gilbert could do the job just as well or better with a thrust from the army."

"I'm not sure he could," Petrion speculated. "One odd thing about the goblin tactics is they seem to be trying to provoke us into violating the treaty. That doesn't fit any pattern of goblin activity I've ever known or even heard about. They act like they want a war to start but want it to look like we started it. Goblin leadership typically doesn't go in for the political niceties of wanting to show they're in the right. They only care about the end results of the actions, and if pulling something underhanded helps the cause, so much the better. There has to be more to this than what we know. And until we do know, I don't think we or our leaders will want to give the goblins what they are trying to get."

They were quiet for a while as they thought about what the goblins were up to. They were getting ready to go into goblin territory soon, and goblins didn't take prisoners except maybe to use as slaves. He would hate to be one of the spell casters because the goblins always killed them immediately. Fighters they might keep alive, giving at least some hope of escaping. That need for legitimacy had to feed into the goblin commander's response to losing his raiding parties. It would be terrible if they completed their assigned mission and still left the duchy in worse shape than it was before.

"Maybe the raid into goblin territory really isn't the answer then," Lecik put his thoughts into words. "If they are looking for a reason to attack Gamalius, then our crossing the border would give them that reason."

"You're forgetting why we were chosen for this mission Lecik," Berinda countered. "We were picked because we were expendable and because we have absolutely no ties to the legitimate government. Petrion is the only one who has even seen service in the military, and he was cast out in disgrace."

"And you can bet," Andolar added, "that the duchess will have the papers to corroborate that you escaped from confinement if they are needed. She will easily be able to claim that they kept it quiet to keep the public from losing faith in the jail system."

"Besides," Haslan sighed, "it would take more than a week at best, using the roundabout methods of communication we have available to us, to get any new orders from the duchess. As far as we know, we are doing the job she wants done. She even told us we might need to cross the border."

"Right," Berinda said with conviction, "we do the job we were sent for, which is to stop the goblin raids."

"Everyone not on watch needs to get some sleep," Petrion said as he stood and pulled some of the larger pieces of wood out of the fire. "We have a long day tomorrow and probably several more after that."

Everyone rolled up in their waxed cloaks to stay as dry as possible and tried to get to sleep on the sloping ground. Lecik saw Petrion pull on his waxed cloak and then his enchanted cloak on the way into the woods before he faded from view. It was still odd to watch and made you feel like people were creeping up on you. He still remembered Petrion walking right into the camp with a horse and no one knowing what he had done. They weren't very far from the goblin border. The boundary stones were only about five miles to the north through partially wooded territory. With those thoughts in his mind, he didn't manage to get to sleep for some time. It was Haslan's steady pacing that let his mind relax enough for sleep to take him.

CHAPTER 3

Few of the things left hanging the night before dried out. Fortunately, someone had the forethought to put an extra cloak over the pile of firewood so they could have a warm breakfast. Korin cooked as usual, and the memory of Mattie's cooking kept grumbling to a minimum again. Several people added different fresh foods to the list of supplies Andolar and Petrion were to pick up in Delaigamon. Magical and medicinal supplies took first priority, followed closely by arrows. Haslan added in climbing rope and smaller rope useful for setting traps. Haslan had some training in such things in previous years, and with Petrion's more recent experience, he thought they might be able to do something for an ambush along a trail.

They ended up giving two hundred eighty golds and two hundred silvers to the pair for front money and for provisions. They still had a good supply of travel rations but decided to purchase additional. It would be best to be prepared if something unforeseen, like large numbers of goblins, kept them from resupplying for a while. They planned on moving toward the border as soon as the ambush of the goblin raiders was completed. They would try to limit spell use so they could cross the border that night.

Petrion looked at the final list and thought two packhorses would carry everything but decided to take three just in case. The squad shifted their supplies to the other four packhorses to free up the necessary animals. Petrion and Andolar rode off into the rain shortly after it was light, leaving Haslan in charge of the rest of the squad.

What a scene that had been. Haslan wondered if Berinda was going to blow up when "that little thief" was put in charge of the remaining squad instead of her.

"Haslan has been spending a lot of time with me learning about wilderness movement," Petrion had told her. "Therefore, he is the most qualified to lead the squad to the meeting place."

Haslan thought even Berinda should see that her temper and willingness to get into fights had put her at the bottom of the leadership chain. She was still griping about not getting to go with Andolar into Delaigamon as well. She thought her battle scars gave her an intimidating look that would better serve than the mere size of Petrion. She was probably right as far as the lower-grade criminals were concerned. Real trouble would come from professionals, and professionals realized that scars meant you lost a lot of fights, were bad tempered, or both. Those characteristics could easily be exploited to get to the party money. The amount they were carrying was sufficient to tempt the professionals if they thought the mark was easy. Besides, from all indications, Andolar was a good-natured drunk and Berinda was a bad-natured drunk. Not a good combination under any circumstances.

They finally got everything ready, and Haslan had Lecik help him up. Before he could take the lead, Berinda headed off to the east. Haslan sped up until he was going as fast as the clerics could safely ride, but Berinda always kept the lead. He finally gave up and slowed the horses back to a walk.

Berinda was trying to show her prominence by riding ahead of him like she was doing the scouting for the party.

"Berinda," he called, "you need to take the rear guard position now."

She ignored him. She ignored him again when he called for her to come back and join them. She wouldn't even glance in his direction. Much as he hated to take the chance on an altercation, this behavior had to stop. The rest of the squad was focusing too much attention on what was going on at the front and not keeping good watch.

He didn't have enough force left to make her do what he told her, so he needed to show her how silly she was being in a way that didn't get him into a fight. He stopped his horse quietly, and Berinda was so busy ignoring him that she kept on riding. He motioned for the rest of the squad to halt and slid down to check his horse's leg. When Berinda was ten more paces ahead and the snickers started, he looked at the rest of the squad.

"The first person Berinda sees laughing," Haslan told them in a low voice, "or the first person who makes this out to be anything but a stop to check my horse will get to go best two out of three falls with her hand to hand this evening."

That really quieted them down fast. He took a quick look under the horse's belly to see if Berinda had noticed the rest of the squad was no longer with her. She was still moving on oblivious. Berinda was thirty paces ahead of them. Things had been rather quiet in the squad because the rain had everyone huddled into their cloaks. He still thought she should have noticed by now that the only hooves squelching through the mud were her own.

Haslan started working on the saddle straps, and since he had trouble reaching them, he had Lecik get down and help him. Berinda was fifty paces off now and still without a clue as to what was going on. Or maybe she did know and was going to the rendezvous whether they stayed with her or not. She went into a slight dip in the ground and disappeared from sight. Haslan stalled a couple minutes and then decided it was probably a wasted effort and had Lecik boost him into his saddle. He hated riding a full-sized horse. He couldn't even mount without help. He really needed to get a saddle rope attached to his saddle.

He fished around in his saddlebags and came up with some trail bread and jerked beef. Chewing that beef was like chewing leather, but it did quiet the rumbling of the stomach. A sip of water helped the chewing, and he took a bite of the trail bread to go with it. Everyone else took the opportunity for a snack, so he took it slow and easy when he started again. At least the rain made eating trail bread easier. It would be nice to have a few good meals of fresh foods when Andolar and Petrion got back. When they got to the edge of the dip where Berinda disappeared, they didn't see her, but with the rolling hills and her lead, he wasn't surprised. He kept everyone traveling on course but didn't see any evidence Berinda traveled that way. After a while, he decided she must have cut off on her own.

"I haven't seen any trace Berinda came this way," he told the other squad members. "I'm not as good a tracker as Petrion, but in these conditions, I think I would have seen something by now."

"I noticed you were weaving a bit," Lecik said with a laugh. "I was beginning to think you stashed some wine in that water skin."

"Berinda must have decided to desert," Haslan said with a touch of panic.

"Who knows," Lecik replied, "it might be the best thing that's happened to the squad."

"Yes," Florine snapped, "and maybe you'll get the job of defending the door against the goblins. A little close combat on your own might make you appreciate what she does in battle a little more."

"Hey, I do my share with my bow," Lecik replied sharply, "and I'm in as much danger as she is."

"She's gone, and I won't be able to find her," Haslan said with exasperation. "So let's not have any more quarrels in the party. We can't afford to lose anyone else. Oh no, what's Petrion going to say when he finds out I misplaced one of the squad members."

"Considering who you lost, he might actually thank you," Korin said to try and cheer them up.

Florine glared at her brother after that remark, and Korin ducked back into his cloak to avoid her gaze. Lecik apparently decided that might not be a bad idea and imitated Korin. Florine turned back to him for instructions. He didn't know what to do. Berinda needed to be found, but it would be a miracle if he found her tracks after the rest of them trampled over the ground. Well, if he couldn't find her, the only thing to do was continue on to where they were to meet. Petrion would be very upset, especially when he found out what was going on when she got away. He should probably try and get word to Petrion so he could plan for not having one of his fighters along.

"Lecik," Haslan said finally with a heavy sigh, "I need you to ride to Delaigamon and find Petrion. Tell him what happened. The healers and I will go on to the meeting place, and we'll see you there."

"Shouldn't you send one of the healers?" Lecik asked in surprise. "I'm the only fighter left in the group."

"I know, but I can't leave because I'm in charge," Haslan replied. "And Korin and Florine have no experience traveling across country. That leaves you."

"The group is already weak," Florine said with concern. "Can we afford to weaken ourselves further with goblins raiding?"

"Why don't we all go together?" Korin suggested. "Most of us could wait outside the city while one went inside to look for the others. That way, we also wouldn't have to worry about one group missing the other and spending hours searching for each other. We can watch the road while we check out the city. The baron said there were a number of inns close to Quilonia's Wine Shop.

We can't go to the wine shop without blowing their cover story, but we can look around the inns. They are planning on staying overnight anyway."

"Good idea, Korin," Haslan said after he thought on the idea. "I believe that will work without having to worry too much about someone else getting lost. We'll have to hurry though. Let's ride."

Haslan kicked his horse several times to get it up to a fast trot and heading in what he thought was the direction of Delaigamon. He hoped they wouldn't miss the city. The rain slowed to a drizzle after about an hour and finally quit an hour after that. They had been riding for several hours when they came to a main road. Haslan thought the city should be south, but he could have cut too far south which would put the city to the north. He decided to try south until he found someone he could ask.

They soon came upon a thin old man driving an empty wagon with a pair of horses. All of them looked like they were about worn out. Haslan stopped and hailed the old man.

"Excuse me, sir, but we've gotten turned around a bit in the countryside. Could you tell me which way Delaigamon is?"

"Sure," the man replied, "you didn't miss it by much. It's about two miles on down the road."

"Thank you, sir, may fortune be with you."

"Don't need fortune, just need to get the corn in."

"Then I wish you a speedy harvest."

"Thank you, young man."

They kicked their horses back into a trot until they came within sight of the city. A trot was all Korin could manage without falling off. It was not nearly as big as Gamalius. In fact, it looked like it was less than a tenth that size. They started angling toward the east gate of the city. They finally got to a grove of trees that looked like a common camping place for people who couldn't or didn't want to stay in one of the inns. They started setting up camp while Lecik rode into town with five of their gold for expenses. Now they would have to wait and watch the roads. If Lecik didn't find the others, they would move to the north gate before dawn.

"Florine, you gather some firewood," Haslan said to start the camp setup. "Korin, you get out some supplies and start fixing the evening meal."

"There isn't any firewood, Haslan," Florine said. "Everything that could be burned in the area has been used."

"Well," Haslan griped, "cut down a tree or something."

"This area belongs to the city, Haslan," Florine told him. "We used to help people who lived on the edges of Gamalius. You aren't allowed to cut down the trees, just pick up anything that's already on the ground."

"Well, the people who have camped here before have gotten firewood." he said with exasperation, "Where did they get it?"

"From the wood seller over there," she replied calmly. "What I was going to suggest was that if you ride over there and pay him, he'll bring us over some dry firewood."

"Sure, I'll do that."

How was he supposed to know how people bought firewood around here? Coal was burned most places where he stayed, and the price of the fuel was always part of the room cost. He hadn't had to pay attention to details like that when he lived at home either. His dad earned enough to afford a couple of house servants, and the servants took care of those details. Since they had been camping out, the wood had been available for the taking. And here city people were telling him how to get firewood. Well, they were poor enough they would have to go out and buy fuel.

As he rode toward the city, he saw several wood and coal sellers set up outside the gate. There was quite a crowd of minor stalls for goods in the area. He picked a wood seller at random and gave him two silvers to deliver some firewood to their campsite. There was a man with a heavy money pouch—but with too martial a bearing to be a merchant—in the area, trying to get some stupid thief to make a try for the pouch. Only an amateur would fall for that old trick. Haslan hurried back to the campsite before he saw anything else that might temp his fingers. He had been out of action for quite a while, and it got to be like an itch you couldn't scratch when you hadn't practiced your trade. Much as he hated to admit it, Petrion was right about him not going into the town.

The firewood arrived shortly after he did, and he wished he had asked for less than two silvers' worth. They had a large pile sitting with them in the camp. The wood seller must have thought they were staying for a week, based on the amount of wood he bought. He hadn't wanted to look stupid, so he ordered a certain amount rather than bargaining for a set volume of wood. Now he looked foolish to the two healers, but at least they were keeping it to themselves. They must be remembering what happened the last time they made a fool out of someone.

Korin fixed supper in a very subdued group, and they ate and turned in. Haslan had the first watch as usual. He felt better about watching here, since trouble was most likely to come from city people. He walked slowly around the camp in the dry clothes he pulled out. It was going to be a long night. He hoped it wasn't going to be an equally long day tomorrow

CHAPTER 4

Petrion rode out at a quick pace with Andolar beside him. Andolar looked like he was comfortable in the saddle again. He had quit using all the awkward riding positions people with saddle sores were apt to assume. He also wasn't limping around in the evening when he dismounted. They were moving about double their normal traveling speed so they could get to the city early in the afternoon. Andolar was leading the packhorses so he could keep his hands free in case of trouble.

Travelers were seldom attacked in Gamalius because justice for people who committed crimes against their fellows was generally swift and severe. Stealing would get you indentured to the one you robbed until you worked off the debt in whatever manner the person wanted. The more the value of the theft, the longer you worked. The robbed person could at their discretion accept a payment from the guilty person rather than making the person work. If they didn't want to keep a criminal around, then the criminal would work off the debt for the government, with the money earned going to the damaged person. Even if all the goods were recovered, such as in his case, there was a penalty exacted for having done the crime based on the severity. People who killed as a crime, or during a crime, were executed. In between those two extremes were various means of convincing criminals to seek a different profession. It wasn't the harshest justice system he had ever heard of, but it seemed effective enough in curbing the crime in the area. He wondered how much longer he would be working off his crime, and if his fiancé would be waiting on him when he finished his work.

He hadn't thought about Lydia for some time now. It surprised him when he realized how long it had been. That made him suddenly doubt if he was really in love with her. It could have been just physical attraction. When they were going out in the evenings, there were times when he thought his heart would burst from the feelings boiling inside him. Now that ranger seemed almost a different person. There was so much going on that he personally had to take care of that any other thoughts didn't have time to surface.

It was almost like the thought of her triggered all his feelings at once. The ache came back as he remembered the times they spent together and the plans they made for their futures. Maybe running into goblin territory wasn't such a good idea. If the duchess would reinstate him for what they had already done, then he could go back to Lydia and start making those plans all over again. They had destroyed two bands of raiders and uncovered a goblin merchant. Add another group of raiders to that and he had done quite a bit for the duchy.

The duchess was just as likely to send them out again. What was it he had said—a weapon for her to wield. He realized they had been gone for less than two weeks. It seemed like a lifetime ago. It was amazing how quickly you became used to a new situation and started reacting as if that was your whole life.

One part of his mind started analyzing his feelings, trying to determine if he loved Lydia as much now. The other part of his mind tried to silence the first with reasons why his thoughts had been diverted.

"Who was she?" Andolar asked.

"What?"

"I asked you who she was."

"Who are you talking about?"

"There's only one thing I know that can make a man look sad, wistful, and confused all at the same time," Andolar told him, "and that's a woman he's in love with. So I asked you who she was."

"Her name was Lydia," Petrion said with a heavy sigh. "We were engaged before I was arrested. I don't know what she's doing now."

"Not knowing is always the hardest part, but you can thank the duchess for keeping it a secret what you're up to. If the lady knew what you were getting into, she wouldn't sleep for worrying."

"How would you know?" Petrion said with some heat in his voice.

"I've talked to lots of people in bars over the years," Andolar replied calmly, "and the most heart-wrenching thing next to losing a loved one was having them going into danger. Besides which, my father risked his life many times while I was growing up, and I remember the feeling. My mother did also, and it drove my father crazy. And then one time, she didn't come back."

Petrion sighed and looked at the magician, trying to figure out what he was up to this time. Andolar seemed lost in thought about previous days with his mother and father. He supposed it wouldn't hurt him too much to be at least cordial to the magician.

"My parents were killed in the goblin wars," Petrion said finally, "and I went to live with an aunt and uncle. They raised me from the time I was eleven. I always wanted to follow the career my parents had when I grew up. Losing them only reinforced my resolve to battle the goblins until they couldn't threaten us any longer. That's why I made a special point of learning how to combat goblins while I was going through training. Of course, that's what most of the rangers want to learn. There are always a few though who are training to go down and fight with the High King in the war with the barbarians across the mountains."

"My mother was killed at the start of the goblin war," Andolar said, "but my father is still fighting them."

"If your father is a lord and in the army, then I've probably heard of him. He must be an officer."

"You've heard of him, all right," Andolar said with a smile. "You've even met him. Baron Gardoney is my father."

"The baron is your father!"

"Yes, wonderful, isn't it?"

"Wow, I can't imagine what it must have been like to grow up in the house of the highest-ranking baron in the duchy."

"It was mostly lonely," Andolar replied, still looking off into the distance. "He was always away working with the army or helping the duchess with administration. We got to stay with our parents in Gamailius during those times. He didn't have a lot of time to be a father to us. After our mother was killed and the war started, he spent even less time at home. He did try to spend his free time with us."

"My father wasn't around much either. He was in the ranger squads. My mother was a fighter in the regular army, and she was home more often. I went to stay with my aunt and uncle whenever they were both out on a mission. Then when they didn't come back, I stayed there permanently, at least until I was old enough to begin ranger training myself. I only ever remember hearing about one son of Baron Gardoney's though. How come I never heard of you?"

"For the last several years," Andolar replied, "I haven't done much for people to talk about, at least nothing good. Most people quit mentioning me out of concern for my father, I think.

They didn't want to cause the old boy any more pain than what I was already. It's been several years since I've been to Gamalius as well."

"I suppose most people don't like to bring up painful subjects," Petrion said. "Everyone who knows my aunt and uncle will be trying to avoid me as a subject now, or at least the ones with manners."

"I remember my brother telling me," Andolar said, "that another noble in the duchy made some disparaging comment about me in front of the duchess as part of a political maneuver to gain precedence over my father. It didn't work with the duchess, of course. My brother told me that father later demanded the man spar with him in the practice room the next morning. The man declined, but my father told him if he didn't, a more formal challenge would be coming. He didn't have much choice but to accept the practice session. The man left the city for quite a while after the sparring match and a visit to a healer. That probably had something to do with no one talking about me as well. There aren't too many people who are willing to go one on one with Father."

"I can sympathize with them," Petrion replied. "Your father beat all of us at once. I can't imagine what would happen if he was really mad at you."

"My brother told me that story to show me how much Father really cared about me," Andolar said thoughtfully.

They continued on in silence for several long moments, each lost in his thoughts.

"Wow," Andolar said with some humor, "it's bad enough to have a dark, cloudy day, without having dark, gloomy thoughts as well. Let's find something else to talk about. Do you think I will be able to sample some wine at Quilonia's?"

"I wouldn't be surprised," Petrion replied with his own forced laugh.

"Ah," Andolar replied, "now that's the spirit, or spirits, as the case may be. Maybe we should pick up the pace a bit more so we can have more time to relax. The horses will be having a good rest this afternoon and tonight anyway."

"All right," Petrion agreed, "let's head for the city."

The horses' hooves beat out the gallop as they flew across the countryside toward the city of Delaigamon. The beat of the hooves didn't stop the thoughts about his uncle and aunt, his parents, and mostly about Lydia. From the expressions chasing themselves across Andolar's face, he wasn't having any better luck avoiding gloomy thoughts. After a few miles, they slowed back to a walk. They got wetter riding fast in the rain. They walked the horses for a while to let them cool down, and the rain began to let up. They kicked the horses back to a faster speed, but one they could hold for hours. When they got to the city they could get a meal and some dry clothes. He had almost forgotten what being dry felt like. He knew it must be a good feeling.

The rain finally stopped entirely, and when it did, they were able to see the city in the distance.

"You should probably take the horses now, Petrion," Andolar said over the sound of the hooves. "I can't be leading them and stay in the role I'm supposed to be playing."

"Good idea," Petrion replied.

They both slowed down, and Andolar transferred the lead ropes to Petrion.

Without saying a word, they both kicked their horses up to speed and headed for the warm dry clothes they would get once they had a room.

They entered through the west gate, two wet, weary travelers, and made their way across town to the east gate. There wasn't much traffic in town, although it increased as they continued. It was probably because the rain stopped. The winding stone paved streets got them turned around several times, but they eventually came within sight of the east gate and saw Quilonia's wine shop. Andolar was looking over the nearby inns.

"Why don't we stay at the Golden Badger over there?" Andolar told him. "It looks like the best in the row."

"What makes you say that?" Petrion asked.

"It is clean and in good repair," Andolar replied with authority. "That means the proprietor cares about the place. There are also several horses from locals tied up outside, so it is a known and popular gathering place in the city. That means the food is probably good. That also means it's not too expensive since there are horses instead of carriages outside."

He looked at Andolar in surprise at how much he could tell about the inn just from looking at the outside. Of course, Andolar had spent quite a bit of his life finding out about taverns. Getting the feel of a city was probably as hard in its own way as getting the feel of the woods. From the lack of scars on his face, Andolar must be good at picking out quiet spots.

"All right then," Petrion said to the magician, "let's drop off the message and then go to the inn."

"The inn first," Andolar countered. "Wealthy people look after comfort first and business second. Therefore, we should be dry and cleaned up before we go to the wine shop. Also, with the weather like it is, the inn will fill up fast. I want to make sure we get a room."

"All right, all right. Lead on, my lord magician."

Andolar took the lead as they made their way to the Golden Badger. He spotted a stable boy out front and motioned him over.

"Are rooms still available lad?"

"Yes, sir."

"Excellent. Stable our horses please and then have the gear sent up to my man's room. He will know what I need and bring it to me."

"Pardon me, sir, but you have to pay before I stable the horses. It's more if you want grain for them."

"Is that enough to take care of the horses and grain?" Andolar asked the boy as he flipped him a pair of silvers.

"Yes, sir," the boy replied after deftly snagging the coins in the air. "I'll go get your change."

"Keep the change, boy, for being honest."

"Thank you, sir!" the boy called as he came to get their horses.

They both took their saddlebags and climbed to the porch. Petrion started to walk in, but Andolar elbowed him and pointed to the boot scraper set by the door. He was already using the one on the other side. Petrion knew he was out of his element here just like Andolar was in the woods. It left him feeling self-conscious and nervous.

"Relax," Andolar whispered as he started inside. "You'll give us away if you keep acting like that."

Petrion decided to pretend he was on parade and started after Andolar. Andolar walked to the end of the bar where the room tags were hung on the wall. There were only three left. The man tending the bar came when he saw them, wiping his hands on the bar towel.

"What can I do for you, gentlemen?"

"I require a room for myself with an adjoining room for my man here. Do you have one available?"

"Yes, sir. How long will you be staying with us?"

"Just tonight."

"That will be one gold, five silvers, sir," the innkeeper said, handing them the plaques for rooms 5 and 6. "The rooms are up the stairs and all the way to the back. The numbers are marked on the doors. Six is yours"

"Does the room rate include baths for both of us?"

"Uh no, sir, that would be an additional five silvers. Three if your man uses the common washroom."

"No, you better bring him bathwater as well. If you don't, I shall no doubt be dealing with the consequences for the rest of the evening."

"Very good, sir. I'll have the bathwater sent right up."

"Excellent. Now can you tell me where I could find a good restaurant close by?"

"We have excellent food here, sir, if you would care to try. Or if not, I can direct you to other establishments in the area."

"I suppose we'll try the food here," Andolar said thoughtfully. "Could you have a table ready for us in about an hour?"

"Certainly, sir."

"Oh, the stable boy will be bringing our things in soon. Could you direct him to my man's room? He can sort them out from there."

"I'll take care of it, sir."

"Thank you, innkeeper," Andolar said as he handed over the two golds and walked toward the stairs. "You have a fine establishment here."

The innkeeper was positively beaming at them as they left. They found their rooms and went inside to start taking off their wet and muddy clothes. Petrion was sure he would be up half the night getting his armor back into condition. He needed to pick up some oil while he was shopping. He hadn't thought to bring any along with them. He took off his armor and was leaning his sword against the wall when a knock sounded at the door. He opened the door slightly and looked into the hall. Two boys with a small bathtub and a large flat pan were waiting to come in. They came inside as soon as he finished opening the door. He noticed a couple of other boys already carrying hot water into Andolar's room. The person with the purse always got the best treatment he supposed. They took soap and towels out of the tub and set the tub in the large pan. They started a fire in the fireplace and then went down to fetch some water for him. They also brought up all the gear off of the horses.

It wasn't long before he was in the hot water and was enjoying being warm and clean. As the water started to cool, he decided it was time to get dried off and ready to go. He must have spent a half hour in the tub.

His armor was already showing some rust. He needed to get started on that soon. He dipped his chain mail in the soapy water and swished it around for a while to loosen the rust. He dried the armor with the towel and hung it up to finish drying close to the fire. He hoped they didn't get charged extra for all the rusty stains on the towel.

The fire warmed the room up nicely while he was taking his bath. A person could really get used to this kind of living, even if the price was high. After he finished with everything, he knocked on the door that joined the two rooms.

"Come on in," Andolar called. "The door isn't barred."

Petrion opened the door and went in to Andolar's room. This room was larger and nicer than the one Petrion was staying in. Andolar also had a larger tub and was still in it.

"I'm not getting out," Andolar said before Petrion even had a chance to ask. "At least not until my clothes are back from being cleaned."

"Cleaned?" Petrion said in surprise. "We can do that."

"Correction," Andolar said, "I can do that. These people clean garments, not armor. Besides…"

A knock interrupted their conversation.

"Come in," Andolar called.

"I have your clothes ready for you, sir, "the boy said to Andolar as he deposited the clothes on the bed and turned to go."

"Here, boy," Andolar called, flipping the boy a silver. "Share that with your friends now."

"Thank you, sir! I will!"

Petrion waited till the boy had gone and Andolar was drying off before saying anything more.

"You sure like to throw money around, don't you?"

"Not particularly," he replied, "but I do know the value of keeping people happy when they are doing things for you. And also of not breaking out of character to save a few silvers. How much are you willing to pay to make sure the mission succeeds?"

"A lot more than you are, I'd say," Petrion shot back.

"I'd say that too," Andolar calmly replied. "So if you're willing to risk your life for the good of the realm, then why aren't you willing to spend your money? Actually, it isn't even your money. That doesn't make sense."

"Not to you maybe, but that's because…because…because…you are right, I guess," Petrion said, ending up with a smile. "I guess even a blind boar finds a nut occasionally."

Andolar smiled back at him, and Petrion relaxed a little bit around the magician. Andolar finished drying off and started getting dressed. There were some high quality clothes packed away in his gear that Petrion hadn't seen until brought back by the servants. When Andolar got them on, he looked quite the young man of money. Petrion was impressed in spite of himself. He went back to get his sword. He also pulled on his chain shirt but left his shield. Finally, he got the package for Baron Gilbert while Andolar was finishing up. They started down the stairs together a moment later.

The innkeeper saw them coming down and rushed over to seat them. The inn crowd had thinned out significantly since lunchtime was well over, and the innkeeper showed them to one of the better tables not too far from the fireplace.

"What can I get for you to eat, sir?"

"What's available, good innkeeper?"

"We have beef and pork roasts turning on the spit, and we have corn on the stove. We can fix whatever the good sir wishes however."

"I believe I am rather hungry today. Why don't you fix me a medium-size steak well done, and I'll have the corn. I would also like some bread and cheese with the meal, and would you happen to have a three-twelve Machinon?"

"No, sir, I don't have one in stock, but I can get one by the time the meal is ready."

"Oh, don't bother. I saw a wine shop across the way. I'll just go over and browse around for a few minutes and find something suitable."

"Don't just stand around, fellow!" Andolar said to Petrion. "Order your dinner so that we can be off to the wine shop."

"Well, yes," Petrion said to the innkeeper, "I…uh…guess I'll have what he had. On second thought, you better make my steak extra large. I really am very hungry."

"Very good," the innkeeper replied. "We do have some excellent vintages here, sir, perfect for steak if I could show you the list."

"We might try one of those if we can't find something in the shop," Andolar replied to the innkeeper. "But I really must have a look at that shop. That's why we're here after all."

"You came to purchase some wine?" the innkeeper asked.

"Yes, so I might as well go over while dinner is being prepared."

"Very good, sir."

Petrion was wondering why the innkeeper looked like he just lost his best friend when Andolar brushed by him on his way out the door. Petrion hurried and caught up with the magician as he started over to the wine shop.

"I committed a minor breech of etiquette there," Andolar whispered to Petrion as they crossed the street between a pair of wagons. "I should have let the innkeeper come over and get the wine so he could make some profit on the sale."

"Huh. Why do you care if an innkeeper makes a profit?"

"We are eating at his establishment, so he is entitled to make a profit on all food and drink used in the inn."

"Considering what we're paying him," Petrion replied, "I wouldn't think he would be disappointed in his profits."

"An innkeeper or any other business man is always disappointed in his profits, especially when they could have been more."

"I suppose so."

As they reached the door to Quilonia's, Petrion stepped ahead and opened the door for Andolar. Then he had to close the door and clean off his boots again. This bodyguard-servant job sure had a lot of things you had to remember. No wonder most fighters stuck to the army even though the pay was worse. A clerk immediately came over to help them when they entered the shop. Petrion saw Andolar gazing around the room in awe at the selection of wines. There were a lot of bottles and casks here, and Petrion could see more rooms in the back.

"Can I help you, sir?" the clerk asked.

"What? Oh excuse me. Are you Quilonia?" Andolar replied.

"No, sir, but I'm sure I can help you get what you need."

"No, just go and fetch Quilonia, and I'll discuss what I need with her."

"I'm sorry," the clerk replied, "but she's busy with another patron right now, but I'm sure I could find what you are looking for."

"I believe I shall find a different shop with which to contract if the proprietor can't spare the time."

Andolar started back toward the door, and Petrion wondered what was going on. He was making funny hand signs too, and Petrion decided his head was muddled around somehow. The hand motions got frantic by the time Andolar neared the door, and Petrion finally realized what he wanted.

"Wait, sir." Petrion said as he jumped up to stop Andolar. "His lordship sent us all this way to find this specific wine shop. He might be disappointed if he found out we left without even speaking to the proprietor."

"Hump. I don't know. How long till the mistress of the shop is free to discuss business?" Andolar asked the clerk.

"Just a minute, and I'll go see," the clerk said as she hurried across the room and up the stairs.

"What changed her mind about getting Quilonia?" Petrion asked when the clerk left.

"Why, you did of course," Andolar replied with a smile. "When you mentioned 'his lordship,' you changed my position in her eyes from a moderately wealthy merchant to a personal attendant for a high lord. Only a high-ranking lord would have a servant as wealthy and overbearing as me and with a guard, besides. That worked very well."

Petrion saw now how the subtle play had worked on the clerk's imagination. Andolar really did play the role well. He just wished the magician would inform him a little better about what his part in all of it was to be. He wasn't that good at coming up with stuff quickly when it came to acting.

"Back into character now," Andolar whispered when he heard footsteps on the stairs again. "If she offers a seat only to me, remain standing behind my chair and between me and the door."

Two ladies were walking down the stairs conversing in a friendly manner, followed by the clerk who looked like she was about to bust with wanting to talk. The one lady was dressed simply but looked very good in what she was wearing. The second lady who was doing most of the talking was a bit overdressed, but obviously wealthy. It was a good thing Haslan wasn't around to see that jewelry.

"Ah thank you, Quilonia," the overdressed woman said. "You shall be able to have everything ready for the party next week."

"Oh, most assuredly," Quilonia replied. "We have everything you will need on hand, and I'll have it delivered on the morning of the party."

"Very good. Well, I must be going now. It was so nice talking to you."

"Go tell the lady's driver to bring the coach around," Quilonia ordered the clerk.

The two conversed for a short while longer until the clerk opened the door again for the lady to get to her carriage. After she was gone, Quilonia focused all her attention on them. Petrion felt like he was being weighed out to see how much he was worth. Andolar stood up well under the scrutiny. Petrion realized he never would have been able to pull off the role Andolar was playing. He had been practicing being a noble for his entire life. There were just too many little things he did which Petrion didn't understand. He realized suddenly that Andolar would have commanded more attention than all but a few people in the duchy if he came here under his own name. That was a sobering thought.

"What can I do for you, sir?" Quilonia asked.

"We are here to discuss a delivery of goods for Gobtrim Nilrem." Andolar said as he plucked an imaginary piece of dust off of his shirt. "Is there someplace where we can discuss the delivery?"

"Yes, please come up to my office."

"Thank you, Onviela," Quilonia told her clerk. "You can start storing the new shipment after you bring glasses of wine for the three of us from the top bottle."

"Yes, ma'am," Onviela said with a look of mild surprise.

"This way, sir," she said to Andolar with a slight bow.

They followed her up the stairs. Petrion decided she was probably about thirty-five or forty but still a very attractive woman in spite of her age. They turned right at the top of the stairs, and Petrion saw more rooms filled with bottles. Many of them were dust covered from sitting so long. They entered an office at the end of the hall, and Quilonia motioned for them both to take seats. She seated herself and then waited until the clerk set a tray with three glasses of wine on the desk and closed the door.

"Help yourselves, gentlemen," she said motioning to the wine.

She was waiting for them to take the glasses, so Petrion took his and sipped a bit at the wine. He had never cared for the taste. He looked over at Andolar, and the magician was studying the wine in the light from the window. He then smelled the wine before taking a sip and holding it in his mouth. When he finally swallowed, he let out a sigh of pleasure.

"You are too kind to poor travelers, ma'am," Andolar said to Quilonia. "A Raginor and a three-oh-three, if I'm not mistaken."

Now it was Quilonia's turn to look surprised. She took a polite sip and then got down to business.

"You said you had a delivery you wanted made, my lord?" she questioned.

"Please, good lady," Andolar said without the haughty overtones, "I am but a nameless adventurer, not a lord. Yes, we have a package that we need delivered."

Petrion dug out the sealed package that contained the notes and items. Quilonia took the package and hefted it. The items were wrapped so that they wouldn't jingle, so the only impression she got from lifting it was that it probably contained some metal.

"I'll see it is delivered immediately," Quilonia told them.

She placed the package in a drawer and pulled out an envelope. She took a paper out of the envelope and quickly wrote in a date. She was very perceptive to be able to pick up on Andolar being a noble. Then on the other hand, maybe Andolar let enough hints drop so she would be sure to know. He thought the magician was probably a good-enough actor that he could convince people he wasn't a noble if he chose to.

"We will be leaving early in the morning," Andolar told her. "We are not sure if a reply will be necessary or not. If it is, we are staying at the Golden Badger. We will assume there is no reply if we don't hear from you."

"Very good."

"Well, we have taken up enough of your time, ma'am," Andolar said as he rose to leave. "Thank you very much for the wine."

"I hope to see you again as a patron," Quilonia replied, standing to shake his hand, "after your nameless-adventuring days are over."

"I would like that," Andolar replied, finishing the last of his wine and setting down the glass. "If you would like to share some wine and some dinner this evening, I would enjoy the company."

"Thank you, I would."

"Good day, ma'am."

"Good day, my lord."

They walked down the stairs and back across the shop. Petrion heard her calling for the clerk before they left. They made their way across the now crowded street and back to the inn.

"A very interesting lady—Quilonia," Andolar said wistfully.

"Yes, I noticed that you two seemed to get along very well."

"She reminds me of the times before I became so much of a drunk that my old circle of friends didn't want to be around me anymore."

"I hope dinner is ready when we get there, I'm starving."

"I am hungry as well," Andolar answered. "I suppose I should skip the wine. I better not risk it. Besides, it will ease the inn-keeper's feelings."

They entered the inn and took their seats. The innkeeper seemed disappointed that he didn't get a wine sale. It was probably a high-profit item for him. Maybe Quilonia's shop was why so many good inns were in this part of town. They talked about inconsequential things until a serving boy with their dinner arrived and then devoted their entire attention to alleviating their hunger. Petrion thought the food was excellent, and Andolar looked like he was enjoying his as well.

"We can probably do our buying at the same time," Andolar said quietly around a mouthful of food, after checking to make sure no one was near. "I can go to the magician shop and herb seller's while you pick up arrows, sling bullets, and food supplies. Pick up a couple more daggers for Haslan as well. He might lose one, and I don't think we asked for any spares in Gamalius. He's been using mine fairly often."

"All right," Petrion replied, "and I'll get the rope too. It should be in the same area of town."

They went back to serious eating after that, and soon had their plates emptied. Both sat back with a sigh of contentment at their full stomachs. Petrion picked up a bit more bread and cheese to nibble on while they talked. He was really full, but the cheese went well with the fresh bread. This innkeeper had a really excellent cooking crew. When the innkeeper saw they were finished, he went back into the kitchen and came out with a fresh apple pie. Petrion's mouth started watering all over again.

"Could I interest you gentlemen in a piece of pie," the innkeeper asked, "while I go tally up your bill?"

"Yes, my good man," Andolar replied, "and would you have some cream for it?"

"Oh course, sir. I'll send one of the serving boys out with it immediately."

"Thank you."

"I thought I was full, but the apple pie looked too good to pass up," Andolar told him.

"My thoughts exactly," Petrion replied.

"There is a problem though," Andolar said seriously.

"What?"

"How are we going to be able to move around to shop after all of this food?" he concluded with a smile.

Petrion was still chuckling when the serving boy dropped off large slices of pie covered in cream and picked up their dinner plates. They both picked up their forks and took a bite. The pie was every bit as good as it had looked and smelled. Petrion was finished with his sooner than he would have believed possible. Andolar was only about half done and was savoring each bite as he took it. Petrion wished he had room for another slice, but his stomach already felt like it was going to burst. He contented himself with sips of tea while he waited on Andolar to finish. The innkeeper bustled around behind the bar until Andolar put his fork down and then came over to settle the bill.

"That will be six silvers for the two dinners with dessert," he told Andolar.

"Please give two extra silvers to the cook, one to the serving boy, and keep one for yourself," Andolar said, giving the innkeeper a gold piece. "You have a most excellent establishment here. I believe we shall eat dinner here as well, the food was so good."

"Thank you, sir," the innkeeper replied. "Is there any special time you would like to have a table ready?"

"No," Andolar replied as he got up to leave, "I have some more business to attend to, and I'm not sure how long it will keep me."

CHAPTER 5

Petrion felt more like a nap than a shopping trip after lunch. He ate more in one sitting at the inn than he had in some time. He would have to have a late supper if he ate.

Andolar asked the innkeeper some general questions about what parts of the city were the best for different items before he exited the building. Then they walked to the stable where the stable boy saddled Andolar's horse. Petrion put the packsaddles on two of the packhorses and then saddled his horse as well. He would have to practice so that he could play the lord one of these days. They headed west into the main part of the city. They traveled together for a while, but eventually Andolar cut down a street to the left toward an herbalist while he continued toward the stores that sold general supplies.

Petrion took both packhorses with him because he would be picking up most of the bulk in goods. Andolar hadn't wanted the third horse. He decided that if things got too heavy he would pay to have them delivered. It took Petrion two hours to get all the supplies. Prices on many things were higher here than in Gamalius, but on others, the prices were less. He ended up spending twenty-two gold and forty-three silver by the time he finished.

After loading his purchases, he went to the metal worker's section of town and found a blacksmith to mend his shield and armor.

"Been in some fights?" the blacksmith asked as he worked on the shield.

"Some, awhile back," he replied.

There was no way to disguise the damage from a professional. The hack marks in the edges of his shield were especially noticeable. Only a sharp-bladed weapon swung with intent to kill did that kind of damage. After he finished the shield, the blacksmith replaced some weak links in his chain shirt. He also had oil for the armor. After the armor was finished, Petrion decided to get his sword sharpened. A professional job was always better. After an hour with the blacksmith, he started for the inn. The repairs to his equipment had cost him another five gold. His half of the money was going fast.

When he arrived at the Golden Badger, he paid the stable boy a silver to move the stuff into the secure storage space. He picked up two gross of arrows because he didn't want to come up short again. They were using about fifty arrows in each battle, and they were likely to need a lot more on their trek into goblin territory. The stable boy was inquisitive about the arrows, so Petrion told him his master's archers liked the arrows from a certain fletcher here the best. Therefore, every time one of them came this way, they were supposed to come back with what they could carry. That seemed to satisfy the boy, and Petrion went inside. When he entered the inn, he saw Lecik sitting at a corner table having a drink. Petrion made a hand motion to stop him when he started to get up and made his way to the innkeeper. The proprietor was much less cordial to him than he was to Andolar.

"That man in the back was asking after you and your master," the innkeeper said. "I told him you were out, but he wanted to wait. Do you know him?"

"No," Petrion said, "but my master was making several purchases today. Maybe this man is supposed to deliver one of them. I'll go check, and thanks for the information."

Petrion worked his way to the table where Lecik was seated. From the expression on Lecik's face, whatever brought him to town was bad. He took a seat.

"What is it?" he said quietly.

"Berinda deserted."

It took Petrion several seconds to compose himself. Finally, when he thought he could control his voice, he resumed the conversation.

"When and why?"

"She left this morning. We were riding along, and Berinda was mad about not getting to lead the squad. She wasn't paying any attention to the surroundings, so Haslan decided to halt the squad and let her make a fool of herself by riding on ahead. We waited around for a while, but she never came back. When we rode out again, she was nowhere in sight. There was no way we could find her trail in the rain, so we came here. Haslan and the healers are camped east of town. Haslan sent me to tell you."

"Great, we've lost one of our fighters with the biggest battles still ahead. That means I'll have to hold the door, and you'll have to shoot it out with the archers alone. It's hard telling what we'll have to do at the goblin encampment."

"Hey, it's not my fault. Haslan's the one who ran her off."

"And you weren't glad to see her go?"

"Well, I suppose I was a little."

"I think she knew that," Petrion said in a low voice. "That's probably why she left. She's too much of a glory hunter to miss an opportunity like this unless she was very upset."

"Well, you could have put her in charge."

"I know. Knowing I'm partly to blame doesn't help either."

Andolar walked in while they were talking. He acted like everything was perfectly normal.

"Ah, you found us," he said loudly. "I was afraid you wouldn't when I realized I hadn't given you the name of the inn where we were staying."

"Uh yes, I did. There aren't that many inns on this end of town."

Andolar sat down with them and was quickly and quietly filled in on the details. He thought for a while, like the rest of them, about what they could do.

"Do you know," Lecik said, "I would almost bet she came to Delaigamon? She's probably around town somewhere."

"That's a good bet," Petrion replied, "but there is too much town to search and hope to find her. I really can't believe she would desert the squad."

"Maybe she didn't," Andolar said suddenly.

They both stared at him a couple moments, waiting for him to explain.

"Maybe she became 'separated' from the squad," Andolar told them, "and made her way here to try and link up again. She's not a very good tracker. So if she was separated from the group, she would come here where she knew we would be."

"That's a nice thought, but a little far from reality," Lecik said with sarcasm.

"I know," Andolar replied, "but someone with an ego like that can justify almost anything. Trust me, I know."

"That's not a bad thought," Petrion said. "She could have come to town and found a tavern. After thinking for a while, she could decide she hadn't done anything wrong. She would have to find us eventually but could stay where she was for now to avoid blowing our cover story."

"The problem is which tavern is she at," Andolar sighed.

"That's easy," Lecik told him. "Find the taverns with lots of fights, and you'll find Berinda participating. She had a bad reputation among the caravan guards. I heard about it too late."

"Lecik and I," Petrion said, "will go check around and see what we can find."

"I think there is a certain concoction I can get made here that could be of some help," Andolar said. "It's a sleeping powder that can be made from common ingredients. An old apothecary told me about it some years ago as he was mixing it up for my teacher. He had an old wound that pained him sometimes, and the powder eased the pain and helped him sleep. I'll go out and get it together and then come back here. If there's a problem getting her to be reasonable, come and get me."

"My man here isn't sure that you are the sort of guard I need," Andolar said for the benefit of the innkeeper in a louder voice. "I'm tired of the conversation right now. Why don't you two go off and talk about it for a while. I'll decide later what to do."

Petrion went upstairs to drop off his freshly oiled armor. When he came back down, Lecik got up, and they went out. Petrion picked up his horse from the stable. Lecik's horse was tied to the hitch rail in front of the inn.

"Which of the taverns in town have the most fights?" Petrion asked the stable boy.

"I don't get around that much," the stable boy said while looking a question at them. "I have heard about the Fighter's Home tavern in the armorer's district. I've also heard guards talk about the Great Bear, which is by the coppersmith's, and the Lost Home, which is just inside the western gate."

"Thank you, boy," Petrion said, flipping him a copper coin. He was getting almost as bad as Andolar throwing money around

They mounted up and started riding toward the west gate without saying a word to each other. There was a rough tavern just inside her most likely entrance to the city. That should be the place. If she wasn't there, the patrons would be able to direct them to the next likeliest location. He hoped she didn't get into serious trouble before they could get her out. Traffic was heavier on the streets, so his trek across town was much slower than before.

They got to the Lost Home tavern after about a half hour. Petrion got down and went to the door. Berinda was sitting in a back corner over a drink. He gave Lecik a thumbs-up signal and then motioned for him to stay outside. He crossed the tavern to where Berinda was seated and pulled out a chair at her table.

"I like to sit alone," she growled at him without looking up.

"I thought you might like some company from a friend."

She looked up then and without any pleasure. He was surprised by the look. He always treated her fairly and tried his best to include her in the group. He had even helped her back into the group after the trouble with Lecik.

"I wondered if you might like to come over to our inn on the other side of town," he told her.

"I'm comfortable here. I'll catch up with you in the morning. Now leave me alone and get away from my table."

"We need you to come with us," he said with forced cheerfulness. "There's some good ale. I'm sure you'll like it."

"I don't want to leave," she said in an ugly voice. "Take yourself out of here, or they'll be carrying you out. I may have to stay with you as part of my job, but I'm on my time now. I don't have to socialize with you."

"You will come with me now," he told her in a low voice when he realized the friendly approach was getting him nowhere. "You are not on your own time until I say you're on your own time. Now get outside, get your horse, and get going."

Suddenly he found himself facing the ceiling in his chair rather than Berinda. She must have hooked the front legs of his chair with her foot and pulled. Petrion shook his head to clear it and got slowly to his feet. His back was sore where he landed on the chair.

"You cheap little—" Petrion started and then, with difficultly, got control of his temper.

Berinda was smirking at him from across the table, trying to goad him into throwing a punch. He could still claim she started it with the chair, and Lecik would back him up.

"I don't want to fight you," he said finally. "We have more important things to do. Now get up and get moving."

"I like it here," she replied.

"I know," he shot back, "but you'll have plenty of time to crawl back into the gutter later."

"You rotten thief," Berinda snarled as she kicked her chair back.

The people in the room started clearing a circle around them, and he could hear wagers being placed. This situation was getting worse by the second. Petrion stepped back quickly to keep space between them. He glanced toward the door and saw Lecik looking in with a sympathetic expression on his face. Lecik turned around while he was watching and disappeared toward the street.

"What was that you said?" he asked Berinda when he realized she had been talking to him.

"I said it's too late to run. It's time you learned who the best fighter is, and I'm going to teach you."

"You are going to take off that headband, aren't you?" he questioned her quietly.

If he had to fight her with her increased strength, he would be lucky to get out without serious injuries. Petrion thought about pulling his sword but knew that would get him into worse trouble. Fistfighting was frowned upon, but sword fighting was a good way to get thrown in the dungeon. Fortunately, Berinda took off her headband and tucked it into her belt pouch. She tied the pouch tightly to make sure it didn't come off.

"I don't need it for you," she spit out at him.

"This is crazy," Petrion said as he circled out of range.

"This is justice," Berinda replied. "The only justice I'm likely to get. Maybe next time you'll think twice before you insult me."

"I didn't insult you," he told her.

"Come on, you two," someone called from the crowd. "We didn't get out of your way just to see you dance together."

"Maybe they're going to kiss and make up," another one called.

Petrion knew they were trying to goad him, but it wouldn't work. Then maybe, judging from Berinda's expression, it would. She was closing the distance on him, and the circle wasn't dropping back any more. He stepped away from the human wall, dodging a quick left to get some room in which to fight. He would just have to beat her so he could get her out of here and back to the Golden Badger. Petrion tried to remember everything Gardoney taught him.

Berinda stepped in to hit him, but he stopped her with a straight left to the face. He wished he had on his chain mail to protect his chest and stomach. Berinda had hers on, so he would be forced to focus on her face. She came in again and blocked his left out wide and landed a left into his stomach. Some of his breath came out with the punch.

She was strong despite the fact she was smaller. The smaller size of her fist didn't help either. It put more force in a smaller area than a man's fist did. Still, she had been drinking, so she would wear down from the blows before he did. She ducked under the right he threw, but she had to back up a bit to keep from giving him an easy shot with his left. The weight of her armor would slow her down. That might even things up for the extra protection it gave her. She was trying to crowd him again, while he was trying to keep her back with his left. He feinted to the body and swung his right at her head when she dropped her right to block. Her left arm took his right out wide, as the body feint failed to work. Her right came in for an open shot at his chin, rocking his head back on his neck. The punch really hurt.

She tried to follow with a left, but he blocked and landed a left of his own. Unfortunately, she ducked her head back, and the blow was only glancing. He started throwing his left at her face again, because if he could keep her at a distance, he would win. She knew it too and took the left, coming in to close with him.

That was what he was waiting for. Instead of dropping back like he had, he took a right in the stomach to catch her arm and turn her around. In a clench, he had the advantage of size and strength. Her speed and boxing skill wouldn't help her. He had one of her arms pinned behind her and the other held by his arm around her waist. She tried to stomp his foot and head-butt him at the same time, but he got his foot out of the way. Her head just bounced off his chest. He was expecting that maneuver. It was one of the only ways to break out of a situation like that. She tried it with her left foot the next time, and he got his foot out of the way again. She hooked the back of his left foot with hers when he took his weight off it and jerked his foot forward while throwing her weight backward. He fell and released her so he could try and break his own fall. She landed right on top of him, knocking some more of his breath out. She swung her head back again when she hit, just in case his head happened to be under hers. Fortunately, she hit his chest again. She scrambled away before he could get hold of her again. He got up carefully to try and keep her from getting in any punches. She still managed to land one good one, but he was on his feet again.

This fight wasn't going very well for him. Still, he had seen her tricks and could compensate for them. He was bigger and had a longer reach. She was in close when he got up and started sending blows into his stomach. Petrion landed a hard right to her ear and knocked her sideways and off balance. She awkwardly dodged his following left but stepped into his next right.

Berinda hit the floor hard but was on her feet again quickly. He absently noticed the betting was no longer favoring him by much. He was glad to hear that he still had some advantage. That last punch had to have taken some of her energy. His stomach and ribs were getting very sore in spite of his conditioning.

She tried closing again, but he used his reach to best advantage, keeping her away. He landed three long lefts that rocked her head back. After the third shot, she collapsed toward him. He heard a combination of cheers and groans from the crowd as he caught her.

As soon as he had his arms around her, she came alive again. He was suddenly falling backward because of a leg behind his and a good solid push from what he thought was a dead weight. She held his arms as he fell, so he couldn't do anything but hit the floor on his back. Her knee was in his stomach when he landed, and his breath exploded violently out. He tried to suck some of it back in, but he couldn't seem to find any. He vaguely heard some applause as he fought for air.

Petiron managed to make it back to his feet on the third attempt. The first two were interrupted by punches to his face. He was still having trouble breathing and could hardly find the energy to move. He tried to throw a left, but she slapped it out of the way and hit him in the stomach again. He did manage to get her solidly in the head with an elbow before she got away. The elbow opened a small cut on her cheek. She stepped back in and landed two more blows to his stomach and one to his jaw. He tried to swing, but his arm seemed like it weighed a hundred pounds. That was odd. The ceiling was where the wall should be.

Andolar returned from the herbal shops and was sipping some tea at the same table he had earlier. He was tired and was enjoying sitting quietly. He visited four herb sellers before he found everything he wanted. He had almost ten pounds of sleeping powder put away in the room after doing the mixing. A good sleeping powder could be a very effective weapon against the base camp. He kept two small vials of the powder and put them in a sleeve pocket before coming down to the common room. Lecik came bursting into the inn while he was on his third sip. Andolar looked at him in annoyance, and Lecik immediately slowed his pace. Everyone in the place was staring at him, and the last thing they wanted was to attract attention. Lecik looked embarrassed. He walked over to Andolar and leaned over to talk to him.

"We found her on the other side of town," he whispered. "Petrion went in to get her, but she decided it was time to show off her abilities again. You'd better get down there."

"What?" Andolar said loudly enough to carry a few tables. "My man is involved in a brawl? I shall take this out of his wages and put him on patrol duty when we return home. How dare he disturb my evening! Lead the way, fellow."

Lecik led him outside, and the stable boy quickly saddled his horse. The crowd on the road was starting to thin as evening approached, so they made a relatively quick passage across the city. They tied their horses at the hitch rail of the tavern and walked to the door.

Andolar quickly scanned the interior and spotted Berinda sitting alone at a table in the back. She had a cut on her cheek that bled some and some swelling starting in a couple places on her face. It took him a while to find Petrion, leaned back on the wall unconscious. His face was bruised up badly. A large man shouldered his way past them and into the tavern without any kind of apology. This really was a fighter's tavern.

"You better let me go in," Lecik told him. "That's a really rough crowd in there, and you look like a magician or rich person, neither of whom they will like."

"You're right about the rough," Andolar replied, "but I think the sight of you might provoke Berinda into another round of boxing. There's no way I can carry you guys out of here by myself. You better wait here."

"All right," Lecik replied, "but I don't think they're going to like having you in there."

"Well, there have been a lot of places where people didn't want me. I still got into most of them."

With that, he opened the door the rest of the way and stepped inside. He immediately assumed the exaggerated walk of a person who has had too much to drink and made his way to the bar. There was some grumbling and shoving as he got closer.

"Get out of here, puny. Only fighters drink in this tavern."

"Yeah, go find yourself a tavern that serves milk," another yelled. "That's your drink."

He pretended not to notice they were talking to him until one of the fighters grabbed him by the arm.

"We told you to get out. You're not wanted here. If you don't leave, we'll have to throw you out."

With a crowd for cover and some drinks in them, these men would be willing to do a lot of things they wouldn't normally consider. They were already coming together like a mob. Andolar was scared but continued playing the part.

"You don't want me here?" he called out quickly to try and get control.

He got back a chorus of nos and a few less-polite comments. He straightened up and looked over the crowd.

"I bet shou ten shilver pieces I can change your mind," he said in a drunken slur.

"I'll take five of that," someone called.

"I'll take three."

"I'll cover the other two," followed quickly.

A chance for some easy money had bought him a short reprieve.

He counted out twelve silver pieces on the bar to continue looking like he was drunk. The three who agreed to cover the bet counted out their ten and were already considering who got the extra two silvers, getting more of their focus off of hurting him. When all the money was there, he turned back to the crowd that was looking on in anticipation.

"Les do it by vote, I'll go first."

"Sure thing," one of the others in the bet said. "All in favor…"

"Not so fasht, my good man," Andolar slurred. "I get to ashk since it is my presence we are debating."

"All right, boy," the man replied. "Do it so I can throw you out of here before you pollute the air anymore."

"Well, how rude," Andolar said as he turned back toward the crowd.

"All right," Andolar said loudly enough to be heard across the room, "we'll do it by vote."

"Everyone in favor of my shtaying, come over here and have two drinks on me," he said drunkenly while holding up three fingers.

The room was silent for all of two seconds before everyone started crowding around the bar. The three who lost money stood there stunned for a few seconds longer before deciding that they might as well get something out of it and joined the others reaching for drinks. Andolar managed to get three of the twenty-two silver pieces on the bar before the bartender raked them into his apron. He was slapped on the back in congratulation so many times that he was going to be permanently bruised. Maybe that was the intention, since they voted he could stay. That one guy he bet with was coming around for an extra slap when Andolar turned so he couldn't. The man just shrugged, grabbed another mug of ale, and went back to his seat. Andolar managed finally to grab two mugs.

He held them in one hand as he turned slowly around and dumped in one of the vials of powder. He quickly had the vial back up his sleeve with no one the wiser. Another slap on the back made him slosh out some of the contents.

Andolar walked across the room to Berinda. She was one of only four or five who hadn't gone to the bar.

"Why don't you get your boss over there," she told him when he got close, "and get out of here."

"But we need you in the group," he said as he sat down.

"Like I told him," she said pointing a thumb at Petrion, "I'll meet up with you in the morning. Tonight I'm on my time, and I'll do what I want."

"Great, so am I. I'm tired of running around all over the place without any time for fun. Hello, serving maid," he called out, "over here when you get a chance."

It took her a bit, but she eventually made it. Berinda had almost finished the ale he'd brought her by then. The sleeping powder was slow acting, but he would still need to keep her drinking to make her passing out seem natural. He gave the serving maid four silvers.

"Bring us a couple pitchers of good ale and keep the change."

That got him a smile from her and a quick curtsy.

It wouldn't hurt to have the barmaid on his side. The owner was already smiling with the increase in sales. He probably wouldn't want his extra profit put in jeopardy. He caught Lecik looking in from the door and motioned for him to get Petrion out of the corner. Hopefully, Berinda wouldn't notice. In the mood she was in, all Lecik would have to do was breathe to get in a fight with her. If she decided to come after him, he was running. They weren't going to be carting him out of here like a piece of baggage.

The ale came, so he stood to pour for them and at the same time blocked Berinda's view of Lecik and Petrion. He took his time, sloshing some out on the table so she would think he was pouring slowly because he was drunk. When he sat back down, Lecik was just leaving with Petrion draped across his shoulder. The first two pitchers passed quickly, with Berinda downing nearly all of the drink. He was just about to order some more

when the combination of alcohol and sleeping powder over-
whelmed her and dropped her head to the table. Lecik was back
inside and standing at the far end of the bar in a crowd. After
waving him over, Andolar got up to leave. He didn't want to
be seen having a part in carrying her out. That might start the
fight he was trying to avoid. He had to leave three golds with the
owner for his bill even though the actual cost should have been
less than two. He saw some hostile glances on the way out, but
many were enjoying the free drinks and laughing at the three
who lost money. He made it out of the door without incident and
heaved a sigh of relief.

Petrion was sitting on a bench in front of the tavern, holding
his stomach. He was a lot stronger and better trained than Lecik,
and she had still beaten him. Fairly severely too, considering the
difference in the way they looked. Lecik came out with Berinda
draped over his shoulder, and Andolar helped him get her across
the saddle of her horse and tied in place. They had to help Petrion
into his saddle too. Petrion was groaning, and Andolar and Lecik
were panting by the time they finished.

Andolar led the small procession across town, looking like a
man who'd retrieved a couple of guards that drank too much.
They stopped at the Golden Badger, and Andolar sent the stable boys to get their stuff out of storage and loaded onto the
packhorses with Lecik's help. Lecik was going to the camp and
then return to the inn, so he took the supplies with him. That
would save time in the morning. They still had two and a half
days before the next raid, but they wanted to be early for this one
in case the goblin commander planned an unpleasant surprise
for them.

Andolar finally made it back to the common room and saw
Quilonia seated at the table he had been using. Maybe something
good would come of the evening after all. It would be great to
have her for company.

"Hello, Quilonia," Andolar said in greeting as he made his way to the table. "It's good to see you again."

"Thank you," she replied with a smile. "Please join me."

Andolar sat down, feeling much better about life in general and his in particular.

She insisted on selecting their meals at the inn, although he won the argument on who was to pay. It was one of the best meals he had ever eaten, and they shared bites back and forth. He tried to stump her with a wine selected for the meal, but she merely laughed good-naturedly at his attempt, told him exactly which wine it was, and complimented him on his choice.

Lecik had thankfully decided to go out and eat when he saw that Andolar had company. Andolar's knowledge of literature and art was good but several years out of date. Quilonia talked about some of her recent favorites when he asked. The current play in the city was an old favorite, so he was able to participate more in the discussion of it.

It was almost closing time when Quilonia finally insisted she had to go so she could open her shop in the morning. Lecik had turned in, using Petrion's room, several hours before. They had talked the entire evening away, and Andolar couldn't remember a recent evening he enjoyed more. She never once tried to pry information out of him about what they were doing. She did tell him there was no reply to the message.

He walked Quilonia to the door of the inn, trying to find the right words to say good-bye.

"I can't remember when I've had a nicer evening," he told her finally.

"Why, thank you, sir, I enjoyed the evening as well."

He hadn't been able to tell her his name, and that made things a bit awkward. She compensated for it by using *sir* as she would a name. The innkeeper about choked the first time he heard Quilonia call him sir. Andolar supposed there were few people she would want to be so formal with. Andolar saw his value in the innkeeper's eyes go up another notch.

"You must call on me again when you are next in the vicinity, good sir," she said as she put her hand on his arm for a moment.

He covered her hand with his own and stood by the door with her for a moment, looking into the night before answering. When he looked down, he saw her eyes starting to tighten. She probably thought he was going to brush her off.

"I would like that very much," he said as he squeezed her hand again. "I wish it could be tomorrow, or I guess it would be later today."

She smiled again and stood on her toes to kiss him on the cheek. He obliged by leaning over a bit to make it easier for her. He started whistling a spritely tune as he watched her go and got a last wave before he turned and made his way to the stairs.

He had spent quite a bit of their money over the course of the day. He had nineteen gold and a handful of silver left. Oh well, money well spent, he supposed. And he had really enjoyed at least part of his stay in Delaigamon. He would have to return here sometime in the future—if he ever had a future. He had managed to forget for the evening what they were getting ready to walk into. He just hoped they would be able to walk out again. Those thoughts followed him for some time after he got into bed, and he was thankful for the late hour and the glass of wine to help him sleep.

CHAPTER 6

Lecik was up before light the next morning and dressed shortly after. His pounding on Andolar's door was finally rewarded with a groan of "I'm coming." He heard Andolar try the hall door first and then finally work his way to the adjoining door.

"What is it?" Andolar grouched.

"It's time to get ready and go."

"Time to go," Andolar groaned. "It isn't even light outside yet. You can at least wait till morning to go waking people up."

Andolar started back to bed, and Lecik caught his arm. He ignored the glare Andolar sent his way and merely stood there waiting till Andolar huffed and started getting ready. After watching him for five minutes, Lecik gave up on ever getting the magician to hurry and went downstairs to get their horses ready. He hurried through the common room, ignoring the people who were up early cleaning the place, and made his way to the stable. There was a stable boy up, but he went ahead and saddled his and Andolar's horses. Saddling Andolar's horse got him a dirty look from the stable boy, who was probably counting on a little extra spending money from the magician. Andolar still wasn't out when he finished, so he walked the horses to the front of the inn and tied them. He went inside and saw Andolar sitting at a table looking like he had been up getting ready for an hour. Lecik knew he was badly rumpled from his hurried dressing and now felt self-conscious. He made his way to the table and leaned over to Andolar.

"We need to go," he told the magician. "I have the horses ready."

"If you think I'm leaving before breakfast," Andolar said with a smile pasted on his face, "then you can just try and have another thought. Oh by the way, I ordered breakfast for you as well. You might as well sit down and eat. You don't want to waste our money, do you?"

Lecik sat down with an annoyed look at Andolar. The magician merely ignored him and sat easily in his chair, waiting on his breakfast. It was only a couple minutes later when a serving boy came out with plates of bacon and eggs. On his next trip, he brought out bowls of bread and melon chunks. Lecik decided that breakfast before leaving might not be a bad idea.

He realized he was right about breakfast after the first bite. There was cheese mixed in with the eggs. That was a very tasty combination. The melon was excellent as well. He ordered seconds while Andolar was only about half done with his first plate. He finally quit after he had almost finished his third helping. Andolar was just finishing up his breakfast as well, so they were ready to leave. He thought Korin was a good cook, but the chef at this inn was phenomenal. It was too bad he went out to eat the night before. He couldn't believe the worthless drunk could walk into a strange town in the afternoon and have a date for the evening. And she was a wealthy, intelligent, attractive lady of good standing in the community. He couldn't say two words to a woman without messing up at least one of them.

Andolar left six silvers to cover the breakfast and finally got up to leave. The magician shook his head when he saw the horses ready to go. He rode to the stable and flipped the stable boy a silver coin even though he hadn't done anything. Lecik frowned at the magician, but Andolar acted as if it couldn't possibly matter to anyone what a lowly fighter thought. Lecik glared at the stable boy, but the boy smirked at him and turned away. When he looked back around, Andolar was headed for the gate, expecting Lecik to follow. Andolar didn't allow him to catch up and ride next to him until they were outside the city proper and into the outlying merchant area. Lecik tried to speed up a couple times, but Andolar always maintained the same distance ahead. Finally, Andolar let him catch up.

"Is my lord finally going to allow his lowly servant the privilege of his company?" Lecik asked sarcastically.

"Can't you play a simple role for a few hours without taking it personally?" Andolar said with exasperation. "I have to keep up the appearance that I am a man of money and influence. We shall hopefully be coming this way again, so we have to maintain appearances. And I thought Berinda was the hothead!"

With that, he kicked his horse on the ribs and started off to the campsite. Lecik sat there for a second, thinking about acting like Berinda. The mere thought was enough to scare him. He galloped to catch up with Andolar before he reached the camp. The sun was about halfway past the horizon when they arrived. Korin had breakfast ready. Everyone else was packing the camp.

"Planning on staying for a while?" Andolar asked, pointing at the pile of firewood."

"If you have a problem with that," Haslan replied, "then next time you can stay in camp sleeping on the ground and nursing hurt and drunk fighters."

"She isn't drunk," Andolar told him, "at least not only drunk. I gave her some powder that put her to sleep so we could get her out of there. She's should wake up before too much longer, but she'll have a bad headache. I picked up some extra in case we get a chance to use it against the goblins in camp."

"That's a good thought, Andolar," Petrion said as he rolled over and got stiffly to his feet. "Put it in the pack saddle. Haslan or I would have to be the delivery person, and most likely Haslan."

"Don't think I'm walking into the middle of a goblin camp to put them to sleep," Haslan told them. "A disguise works in some surroundings, but I'm built awfully small compared to the size of a normal goblin. They also have a tendency to pick on the smaller goblins."

"Good point," Petrion replied. "At least we'll have plenty of sleeping powder to get Berinda out of bars."

Petrion wasn't favoring his ribs like he was the night before, so the healers must have helped him. His face was still bruised. It looked like Berinda was bruised up more than Petrion now. It was petty of him, but he was glad Berinda was able to beat Petrion. Petrion was considerably larger and stronger than he was. That meant Berinda was actually a good fighter, instead of proving he was pathetic. She had busted him up three times now, and it was starting to bother him more than he would admit to anyone but himself. He shouldn't mind because neither she nor Petrion could come close to his ability with the bow. It was all a matter of where your talent was and what you worked at the most.

Florine was elected to wake up Berinda. They decided that since her injuries were minor, she could do without healing. Maybe the pain would convince her that beating up her fellow squad members was not a good idea.

"I would be most obliged to all of you," Andolar said as humbly as he could probably manage, "if none of you would mention to Berinda about the sleeping powder. She should think she got drunk and passed out if no one tells her otherwise."

No one said anything for a while. Florine finally shook his head to indicate she wouldn't say anything. Everyone else was enjoying seeing the quick-witted magician suffer. Berinda could swat him down without really trying. Korin followed his sister's lead, and Petrion said yes as well. Lecik finally agreed, more from not wanting to see anyone else suffer through Berinda than from any good will toward the magician. Haslan was the only one left, and everyone turned to see what he would do. It only took one, and Andolar was starting to sweat.

"I suppose I could agree to that," Haslan said at last. But before Andolar could even start a sigh of relief, he continued. "But I think, for the good of the party, you should let me carry one of those enchanted daggers."

"You already have an enchanted sword. I don't think you need another enchanted weapon."

"Yes, Andolar," Haslan replied, "But those daggers are more heavily enchanted than any other weapon in the group. And you do have two of them. Since you don't know how to fight with both hands, you can only use one anyway. You also don't use them as thrown weapons, so there really is no reason for you to have two."

"Yes, but I might drop one and then be defenseless without the other. I need the extra enchantment of the dagger to have even a remote chance in combat."

"But you are supposed to stay out of combat, Andolar," Haslan told him, "and use your spells from a safe distance. You haven't used a dagger in combat yet, while I have used them several times."

"These are very precious to me," Andolar said when he saw his current line of defense wasn't working, "and I don't want to give them up."

"Yes, I know," Haslan told him, "they belonged to your mother. Do you think your father, Baron Gardoney, would want you to keep them when the party would benefit from giving one of them up? Besides, I'm not asking to keep it, just to borrow it for a while. You can have it back when our mission is finished."

Lecik looked up in shock when he heard Andolar's father was Baron Gardoney. He saw Korin with a shocked expression too, but apparently everyone else had known. He figured Andolar was an unwanted younger son of a minor knight. Instead he was the son of the second-ranking noble in the duchy. He couldn't remember hearing how many children the baron had.

"Petrion," Andolar turned to the squad leader, "you can't let him do this. It's thievery."

"Actually, Andolar," Haslan replied, "I believe the correct term is extortion."

"Whatever it is," Andolar pleaded, "it's illegal and shouldn't be condoned. You should order him not to tell for the good of the squad. Having your magician beaten to a pulp wouldn't be good for any of you."

"Yes," Petrion mused, "I could probably do that just as I could order you to give up the dagger for the good of the squad. However, if I sit here long enough, I believe both problems will work themselves out without my having to do anything. Those are my favorite kinds of problems."

Andolar sighed in defeat and took out the dagger he had hidden inside his shirt. He stroked the hilt for a second and then handed the dagger to Haslan. Meanwhile, Petrion walked to a packhorse and retrieved a spare dagger for Andolar to have in case the worst happened. Andolar almost didn't take the blade, but then his good sense got the better of him and hid it inside his shirt.

"Just remember that I expect to get that dagger back," Andolar told Haslan, "and not a look-alike dagger either."

Haslan assumed such an innocent expression that Andolar looked like he was ready to take the beating rather than let the thief use the dagger. Berinda, who was sitting up, convinced him not to say anything more about the matter. Lecik blamed him not at all. He was very likely to lose the dagger and get the beating if he pressed the subject now. Florine moved away from Berinda after she woke in case there was an outburst. Berinda was too busy holding her head to worry about who was around her. Florine went to a medicinal pack and poured a bit of some powder into a small cup of water. She managed to convince Berinda to drink the water. She also relented on healing and used her magic on the fighter. The cut on Berinda's cheek closed, and much of the swelling went down.

Between the magic and the medicine, Berinda started getting back to her normal loud, obnoxious self. Petrion might have to monitor that powder to keep Berinda from getting a dose of forced sleep every day.

"Berinda," Petrion said in a cold voice, "this is the second time you've assaulted someone. If you take the first swing at anyone else, I'll bring you up on charges of mutiny. You know what that means."

Mutiny during time of war could be grounds for execution. That seemed to get through to her a little because she frowned and acknowledged with a nod of her head.

Korin called out that breakfast was ready, breaking the tensed mood.

The rest of the squad got breakfast, and they were soon on their way toward the next ambush area. They should arrive in the afternoon. They had discussions on what other things they could do to get the odds more in their favor. They all remembered Baron Gardoney's warning that they could be ambushed on the third attack.

"We should probably find the most likely target today and stay there tonight and tomorrow night," Petrion suggested. "That way, I can obliterate most of our tracks and there will be no way anyone could see us coming in, unless they started for this area right after the first raiders didn't make it back."

"This attack should tell us something about the enemy commander," Andolar mused. "If it is a normal attack, then he is not all that careful with his command. If it is a tougher attack, then we can probably assume that he's very careful."

"Why would anyone care if he's careful or not?" Berinda asked.

"Individual goblins don't matter a bit to Durp," Petrion replied. "But taken as a whole, the number of goblin warriors he has is the amount of power he has. No ruler, not even one of goblins, wants to see their power leeched away, especially by a foreigner. If the commander starts losing, then Durp may think he's not worth his wages or even that he's working for the duchess. And if he takes too many losses, then his job is probably gone and his life as well."

"The duchess would never condone that kind of strategy," Andolar said with assurance.

"You never know what someone will try until they are desperate," Haslan threw in. "I've seen many a person that people thought good turn into something else entirely when things didn't go their way."

"Not all people are like that," Korin said.

"If they aren't," Haslan returned, "then they haven't been desperate enough yet."

Korin was about to continue the argument, but Florine rode close and put her hand on his arm to stop him.

"Besides," Petrion said to get the discussion back on tactics, "it doesn't really matter what the duchess would do. It's the kind of strategy Durp would like to pull off, so he will believe the duchess would do it as well. We all figure that everyone else thinks like us. If there is a larger force, then the commander has lots of available soldiers, which means he is in good standing with Durp. If there is no attack, then his position is not so secure."

Haslan moved his horse up beside Petrion's and started discussing traps. Petrion must have asked Berinda to move to the back because she jerked her horse's head around and waited till Lecik got there to start moving again. He felt like he ought to say something to her but figured whatever he did say would be wrong. She acted like she was still feeling some of the affects of the sleeping powder or the drink.

"Did you know that Andolar was Baron Gardoney's son?" Lecik asked her finally, settling on what he hoped was a neutral subject.

"Baron Gardoney's son!" she replied in shock. "You've got to be kidding."

Andolar turned long enough to give them a disgusted look and then turned around and ignored them.

"No," Lecik said while trying to look friendly, "I'm not kidding. Haslan broke the news this morning before you woke up."

Lecik could have kicked himself for that comment. Here he had been trying to stay away from sensitive subjects and just walked into the most sensitive. Berinda didn't seem to be heating up though. She just looked thoughtful. Maybe he had escaped retribution this time.

"I wondered why the baron took such an interest in the squad," she said at last. "It must have been because we were going out with his son."

"I don't think it was that, at least not entirely," Lecik countered. "If he was that worried, he wouldn't have sent his boy out in the first place. It must have just been his interest in seeing us succeed."

"You may be right," Berinda said as she winked at him. "He wouldn't have any real interest in a drunken bum like that."

Lecik was so shocked by the wink from Berinda that he almost missed the look Andolar threw at her. He chuckled along with Berinda at Andolar's discomfort. Apparently, she hadn't forgotten Andolar's lordly attitude either.

"He's nothing like his father, is he?" Lecik said after the chuckles died down.

"The baron is an excellent fighter," Berinda said, agreeing with him, "and Andolar has neither the strength nor inclination to match him there."

"He does have a certain commanding presence though," she said in a voice meant only for him. "He picked up that much from his father. He just uses different methods. You should have seen him control the tavern last night. Fighters have an almost inherent dislike for magicians and rich-society types because too many of them look down their noses at the ones who protect them. He walked into the room and changed the intent of the crowd from violence to grudging acceptance."

"You seem to respect him," Lecik said quietly. "Why's that, since fighters don't like magicians."

"He beat me in a fight."

"When did he ever beat you in any kind of fight?"

"Last night when he came into the bar and slipped something into my drink," she replied with a laugh.

"How did you—" Lecik got out before he could stop himself. If she was fishing for information, he had just bitten on the hook.

"I didn't have enough drink to put me on the table. I remember I was feeling a bit different as well. I don't remember ever just dozing off at the table when I had too much to drink."

"But that doesn't count, he tricked you."

"That's what all battles come down to in the end," Berinda told him. "Tricking your opponent into giving you the opening you need to strike. He tricked me into believing he was drunk and harmless, and so was able to attack me."

Lecik let out a hard laugh but choked it off when everyone in the squad looked at him to see what was so funny. Andolar glared at him, figuring he was the butt of some joke. Berinda sat beside him smiling, probably figuring she was about to find out what was so funny. It was his third try when he finally managed to tell her.

"Andolar gave one of his enchanted daggers to Haslan so the thief wouldn't tell you he'd drugged you at the tavern," Lecik said finally when he got his laughing under control. "Andolar was afraid you would give him a boxing lesson that he wouldn't be walking away from."

"I'll have you know that I only hit people who deserve it," Berinda said as she widened the distance between them.

Well, of all the things to get upset about, that was not the one he expected. Oh well, at least she hadn't decided *he* needed another boxing lesson.

CHAPTER 7

The clouds were starting to thicken again, and it looked like they would be getting more rain soon. Petrion had them increase the pace slightly so they could get their scouting done quickly. He also motioned Berinda back to the front, and he dropped back to talk with Andolar.

"We're going to need to stay at the place of the assault for most of two days," Petrion informed Andolar. "What disguise do you think you should use?"

"If we use the bandits-in-hiding plan again," Andolar replied, "we will be holding the family hostage for two days. That will cause problems and ill feelings even if we do beat off a raid for them. We could use the eccentric-magician routine again, but I dislike leaving behind an obvious trail for someone to follow. The only other thing I can think of would be a merchant caravan. We have several well-loaded pack horses but really too many guards for the goods we have."

"The merchant idea does have merit," Haslan said, riding up, "and the large guarding force is not unheard of for small valuable cargos such as gems, jewelry, or," he said, twirling Andolar's dagger, "enchanted items."

"All right," Petrion said, "then that is the tactic we will use. Andolar will be the merchant, and the rest of us will act as guards."

"Petrion," Andolar interrupted, "you can act as the merchant for enchanted weapons as well as I. Then I could be one of the guards."

"That might be better," Haslan said. "That way, we won't have to come up with some strange explanation of why the merchant knows spell casting. It will have to be the enchanted-arms merchant though, if you are paying even a junior magician for added protection."

Petrion sighed heavily. He didn't like responsibility any more than Andolar apparently did. Giving up control of some of the decision making for a while appealed to him. It let him get away from making all of the little choices while still letting him decide the setup for the battles.

"Very well," he said at last, "I'll be the merchant and you can be the guards I've hired. Arms merchant is an occupation many retired fighters decide on after getting out of the service. I'm young for the job, but merchants my age are not entirely unheard of. And as an ex-fighter, I can still scout the area. Maybe, if it's raining, we can use that as the excuse to stay on for a couple of days while setting up a defensible position. It's a good thing the houses are built for defense."

"We can thank the goblins for that," Andolar told them.

"Yes," Petrion replied, "I know. During the Great Goblin War, every house had to be constructed to hold off raids until the military could respond. And many a military group that found itself outnumbered and in danger of extermination fell back to a house until relief forces could arrive. The farmers, herders, and woodcutters helped us win the war in more ways than just supplies."

They finally arrived in the attack area after several hours of riding and started scouting for likely targets. He was glad the treaty allowed no houses to be built within five miles of the new border. Having houses close to the border would make stopping an attack almost impossible. It would also allow the goblins to cross the border, hit, and be gone while it was still dark. Maybe that was why the duchess hadn't objected to that part of the treaty. Her people were able to use the land but not to build on it. Spots close to the cutoff line were popular—as long as things were peaceful—because of the extra grazing and woodcutting possible. The rule against building also included plowing and cutting trees that had a diameter in excess of two feet. If he remembered correctly, the duchess hired woodcutters to cut everything that was close to, but still less than, two feet in diameter as soon as the treaty was signed. That had thinned out the forests considerably and left plenty of wood for the people who would settle. Every year, the ranger patrols were tasked with marking the trees in the area that were getting close to two feet across.

They found a burned-out farm shortly after entering the attack area. It was the second since leaving Delaigamon. Petrion was glad they didn't have to defend the house. There were trees growing all around where the house had been, and a wooded gully with a high bank was only about fifteen paces from the house. It was an ideal location to attack. Most people living close to the border opted for the greater security of not having trees close to the house. The ones who did leave trees generally cut off all limbs that could block a shot from the roof of the house. These farmers had done neither. He hoped someone else might profit from their mistake, because they surely wouldn't.

By late afternoon, when they reached the far edge of the probable attack area, they had four likely targets for the next raid. Much of the original forest was still in place in the area, giving easy access for the goblins to most houses. This was an area annexed by the duchess after winning the war and was not developed as well as some of the areas that were under human habitation longer. All four houses were built with defense in mind. There was really nothing to set one apart from the others though as the most likely recipient of the attack.

One of the farms looked a little more profitable for the goblins, a different farm had the best approach, and a third appeared to have less people than the others. Since all of the houses were reasonably wealthy, and all had decent approaches, they opted to go to the house with the fewest people. He was definitely going to watch the border on this one. That meant another long night without sleep. If they could get to the chosen house early in the day, he could change his sleep schedule.

They reached the final decision and started for the house just as the rains came. They could see the edge of the storm sweeping across the woods toward them and grabbed for their waxed cloaks. Andolar was the only one who didn't get his cloak on before the rains hit. He packed it in the middle of his blanket roll. For being so smart, the magician lacked a lot when it came to plain, old common sense. At least it was a gentler rain than before. Combined with the last rain though, it would quickly swell the streams and turn the paths into mud.

"You know," Korin called over the sound of the rain, "the goblins may not attack if the weather is bad. They might wait until things clear up. Bad weather keeps people inside their houses where it will cost them more lives to get them."

"If we were just dealing with goblin bandits," Petrion called back, "then I would agree with you. I don't think a military commander would care to disturb his schedule just for the convenience of the troops."

"This rain will play havoc with archery," Lecik yelled from the rear. "A wet bowstring is almost useless."

"We'll have to modify one of the plans we discussed for combat without bows," Petrion called back.

Andolar finally retrieved his cloak. Petrion turned around and hurried the pace toward the farmhouse. The rain started to increase in intensity shortly before they arrived. He tied his horse to the porch and went to the door. A man with a crossbow met him at the door before he had a chance to knock.

The man was large but not fat and was covered with black hair. It was only absent where he shaved his face. The hair on his head was plastered down from wearing a hat all day. His nose was too large for his face, and his eyes were darting around, looking to see if they were going to cause trouble. The crossbow he held was steady though and pointed right at Petion's stomach.

"What do you want here?" the man asked Petrion.

"Sir, I'm an arms merchant," Petrion replied. "I was traveling with my escort when the rains hit. I wondered if we might purchase meals and a place to stay and dry out for a day or two."

"Not packin' much for a merchant," the man observed as he kept the crossbow trained on Petrion's stomach.

"No, sir," Petrion told him. "I do business in enchanted weapons. They cost so much that I can't afford to have many with me. When we're traveling, we keep them out for added protection. I thought the baron might be in the market since there have been so many raids of late, but he said all his money was tied up in bringing new recruits into the army."

"That baron, he's smart," the man said with a chuckle. "You can equip an awful lot of recruits for what you have to pay for an enchanted sword."

"Yes," Petrion said, "but a well-equipped fighter of rank is more valuable than many new recruits in a battle."

"Well, I expect we could argue this for most of the day," the man told him. "I suppose you can all bunk in the barn. There's more trouble than just goblins around, and I'm not sure I trust you yet. I'll bring some food down after bit."

"Thank you, sir," Petrion said with a slight bow. "How much do we owe you for your hospitality?"

"Won't charge you nothin' for the barn," the man replied. "Meals for your group will be two silvers. Meals for your horses will be two silvers a day. We have fresh hay and oats in the barn. I'll have my wife start fixing you something if you're staying."

"Let's see, from the rain were getting now, it will probably be about two days before things are all right to travel again. That would be six meals and two days for the horses."

He dug into a money pouch and came up with a gold piece and six silvers and handed them to the man.

"Thanks for your hospitality," Petrion said after he handed over the coins. "Do you keep a watch for trouble, or do we need to?"

"We try to watch, but you might want to keep your own anyway."

"All right," Petrion replied, "that sounds like a good idea. We'll head for the barn and get dry."

They led the horses to the barn, which was remarkably well kept. There were five horses already there, so it was quite crowded. Andolar got his horse unsaddled, pulled out dry clothes, and went into the loft to change. Everyone else started removing the packsaddles from the other animals. While they were working, Andolar started forking hay into the horse stalls. Petrion looked up in surprise and saw he wasn't the only one. Lecik added some oats to the feed troughs.

They had stuff stored away within a half hour. Everyone climbed to the loft to select a sleeping place. Petrion took some oil along to use on his armor and weapons.

"You know, Petrion," Lecik said as he hung his bow on a nail, "we could maintain some level of arrow fire from here. They have a hay door up here. I could stay out of the rain. Then I'd just have to compensate for the water the arrows picked up on the way to the target."

"That's a good thought," Petrion replied, "but it would require us to split our force. We'll have to discuss it some more."

Lecik shrugged his shoulders and started laying out his bed-roll. Petrion was close behind. Andolar was already resting comfortably in the hay. He had naturally picked the best spot. You could always count on Andolar to look for as much comfort as was available. Of course, he did that as well. He just wasn't nearly as good at it as the magician. He laid back to rest till the owner brought their food. He hoped it was better than the last farm. That woman, what was her name, was almost as bad a cook as Andolar. The other woman must have done most of the cooking, or those people would be starving. He laid his head back for a few minutes to rest.

❖

Berinda decided to do some mild exercise while they were waiting for the meal. Everyone else was taking the time to rest. She had been afraid the enchanted headband would hurt her physical development by enhancing all her activities. Fortunately, it didn't affect her natural strength. She checked it out by doing some unaccustomed exercises one day to see if her muscles stiffened up. They had. She had gone to too much trouble building up her body to let it waste away because of an enchanted item. With a battle less than two days away, she needed to be in peak form. She was injured by the goblins the last time and had no desire to repeat the experience. If she lined up her body better when she shield-slammed, she shouldn't have that problem again.

Petrion had finally explained how to counter what the goblins were doing. The ranger couldn't believe she wasn't taught the flying-goblin trick and how to counter it in battle. He apologized for not telling her more about goblins and how they fought. After this battle, they were going for the base camp. That would be a real test of her abilities. The last engagement was more of a brawl.

She had been exercising for twenty minutes when the farmer came in. He waved to her when she looked around, and she waved back. It couldn't hurt to be friendly with the farmer after all. She yelled for everyone to wake up for the meal.

"The missus wants all of you to come inside for supper," the man told them. "She said it didn't make sense for us to carry food all over the place when you could eat where the food was. Bring your bedrolls as well. I guess you can all sleep on the floor in the house."

Haslan quickly climbed back up the ladder, having been the first to start down for mess call. They quickly collected the things they needed, brushed the hay off their bedrolls, and followed the farmer to the house in the rain. There were pegs driven into the house under the porch roof for the cloaks. She could smell the food cooking as soon as the farmer opened the door. At least it smelled good. She was the third one of the squad to enter the house, and found a bare spot on the floor to drop her bedroll.

The house was clean and neat if somewhat sparsely furnished. She figured they weren't as wealthy as they appeared but rather had planned for a future when they would be able to afford more. They would likely lose everything when war broke out. Well, the goblins wouldn't get them on this raid with her here. If the rest of them could keep the archers pinned down, she could hold off the fighters.

The woman making the meal was not very old, but thick from childbearing. There were several things she was working on laying around the house, including a very nice quilt. Her light-brown hair was damp with sweat from cooking, in spite of the cooler weather that had come. Both of them had hands roughened from work.

They all picked up plates from the table, but Petrion motioned for them to wait until all of the family had a chance to get their food. The man nodded to Petrion in thanks for the courtesy.

It was amazing how easy it was for Petrion and Andolar to lead these farmers around. They fell all over themselves when someone they thought as being of quality treated them as equals. Her parents were like that. They were poor tenant farmers eking out a living on a small plot of ground that belonged to a large landowner. They groveled to the lord of the land they worked. They groveled to the freeholding farmers that traded in the same town they did. They groveled to just about anyone.

Her fighting started at the age of seven when some boy told her that trash like her didn't belong in their school. She was beaten severely that time and many times after that until she got the hang of fighting. Her parents were called to the school regularly to get her. There hadn't been any quit in her even then. She kept trying to fight until she couldn't stand up. By the time she was eleven, there were only two boys and no girls in the school who could best her. The boys were thirteen and fourteen, and even they didn't start fights with her because it wasn't worth the pain.

Not long after that, she heard about schools for people who wanted to study fighting to get into the army. She went home and asked her parents to enroll her. She could tell they didn't want her to and told her she had to have recommendations to get into a school like that. They said if she got them, she could go. She had her recommendations from the school she attended and from the landowner as soon as she made her intentions known. They were as eager to get rid of her as she was to leave.

Admission was a foregone conclusion. She was accepted at the fighter's school in Gamalius. She immediately started plotting her path to fame and fortune as she fought her way through the school. She was thirteen. Never once had she been back to visit her parents, and their letters stopped coming after two years without a reply. Now her future was finally looking better again. After all the troubles with the military and her security jobs, she was about to give up on making her way as a fighter. Then a perfect chance came her way for money and notoriety. One of these days, she would go back and show them all. She had plenty of time to make good; after all, she was only nineteen.

Berinda looked around the room and saw that while she was lost in thought, everyone else had grabbed something to eat. Feeling slightly embarrassed, she made her way to the table. The food was quite good. She noticed several squad members taking tentative first bites before getting down to real eating. She quit after two helpings and then went on the porch to finish exercising before going to sleep. Lecik came out shortly after she did and stood watching her for a while.

"Berinda," he said at last, "can you show me some more moves that I can use against the goblins if I lose my sword? I would also like to do a little sword work with you, if you don't mind. My bow is going to be mostly useless for as long as this rain continues."

"Be glad to help you," she answered him, "as soon as I finish warming up. A good muscle-stretching warm up helps you avoid training injuries. You can start by doing these with me."

They warmed up for ten minutes and then went to more serious training. After a half hour of mock fistfighting, they switched to swords. Petrion and the healers came out shortly after and started weapons practice as well. The porch was getting crowded, so she and Lecik moved to the side to rest. They traded off partners several times so everyone got as much work as possible against different opponents. After an hour of weapons practice, they headed to their beds. Practicing by lantern light was a bit more dangerous. When they entered the house, Andolar and Haslan were already rolled up asleep on the floor. Petrion woke Haslan when he went in to get him to stand first watch.

CHAPTER 8

For a change, Korin used the early morning hours of the day for weapons practice instead of cooking. Berinda wasn't as good a teacher as Petrion, but she was better than Lecik. They took turns walking around the farm to check the night. They had a timetable for the attacks, but all bets were off on this one. It could come at any time or anywhere. They breakfasted with the family as the sky began to lighten, and Korin went with the farmer to the barn. Feeding horses was better than sitting around waiting for an attack.

"Have you been having trouble with goblins around here?" Korin asked the farmer.

"Some in the last few weeks."

"The boss is worried about what's going on in the countryside. He's afraid we're going to walk into an ambush."

"Well, he should be. From all accounts, there are about thirty goblins in the bandit party. As good as they're doing, they may have drawn a bigger following by now. Hopefully, one of the bar-on's patrols will catch them and wipe them out soon. Until then, nobody is safe."

"We'll be careful."

Korin walked back to the house in the light rain. Everyone was sitting around going over their equipment. Korin decided his armor could use some oil. Lunch time finally came, and shortly thereafter, Petrion headed for the border. Now the waiting was going to get really tedious. He knew they wouldn't receive word about the goblins until at least the next day, but he still found himself constantly scanning the area for Petrion. They continued to set watches during the day. Apparently, the family could sense the rising tension in the squad because supper was a very quiet affair. The family probably figured they were worried about their boss. Korin was looking at the clock on the wall every twenty minutes after lunch. Now, after supper, he was looking every five minutes. Andolar finally got up and walked out when the tension and the pacing got to be too much for him to concentrate.

The lady of the house brought out some apple cider after a while. The squad members grabbed a glass. Andolar even came back in.

The children were served last. They had four children, ranging in age from three to nine. The couple was probably in their late twenties or early thirties from the size of their children, but they looked older.

Later in the evening, the man brought out a worn Battle game. Andolar perked up at seeing the strategy game, and soon was destroying anyone that cared to try him. Unfortunately, the quiet of the game added to the tension for everyone else.

Korin went to sit by the children and play with them. When Korin started a song with the children, everyone began joining in. The heavy mood finally began to lift. He had a reasonably good voice. Even Andolar was trying, but the ill use he had given his vocal cords over the last couple of years hurt him. Florine, as usual, never quite managed to find the note the song was supposed to be on. They all made up in enthusiasm what they lacked in talent. They played some group games after that.

The youngest two children eventually fell asleep in a chair, and the mother carried them to bed. The older two went reluctantly under their own power. Korin took a look around the parapet and then on the ground before turning in for the night. Haslan and Andolar were taking the first watch. They all had fun together. Maybe that was another way of bringing the squad closer. It sure relaxed the tension.

Petrion moved off slowly and kept to streambeds, whenever possible, in spite of the rising water. The ground was muddy enough to hold prints for a long time if the rain didn't keep coming to flatten them down. The rain would make hiding easier in some places and harder in others. It would mask his sounds effectively in the heavy forest with its thick carpet of leaves. If he were in the mud though, his prints would point him out even as the cloak hid him. They might be able to see the area under him where the raindrops did not hit if they were looking closely. He angled to the west so he could leave his horse well out of the way of any goblin troop movement. The dark clouds and rain would cut visibility severely. The cold water would also impair the heat vision of the goblins. After almost two hours of riding, he came to an area where he hoped he could safely leave his horse while he went scouting. He tied the horse and moved off a short distance where he could still see the horse but would not be stumbled on if someone found the animal. He leaned up against a large pine tree, wrapped his cloak around him, and went to sleep.

When he woke up the first time, it was still light. When he woke up again, it was full dark. There was no way he could tell what he was doing on a night like this. The clouds were so heavy that he couldn't see anything. He decided to give up on scouting. He was likely to injure himself falling over or into something in the dark. Sleeping was as good a way as any to pass the night, so he laid his head back down. Sleep wouldn't come this time, so he thought of ways to attack the goblin base. It seemed unreal that they would later this day stage a seven-person invasion of the goblin nation. If they were discovered, they would have to flee and hope they could outrun the goblins.

Even if they did get through safely, what were the chances they could defeat the goblins at the base camp? It was much more likely that he would scout the camp and find it too well defended for them to attack, and they would sneak back across the border with a report on the goblins. They would need to move right after the attack if they were physically able. That would give them the best chance of surprise. He wondered what the reaction would be to the second goblin patrol not coming back.

The next attack was scheduled for the far-eastern area of the Barony. That meant the goblin troops for the larger raid should be past the squad's entry point when they entered goblin territory. Of course, Churinius could have changed the attack plan already. Then the goblins could be just about anywhere. Somewhere in the early hours of the morning, he dozed off again.

The third time he woke up, it was already light outside. It had to be at least a half hour after sunrise. He had sat for what seemed like hours, thinking about attack plans, until he dozed off. Now he was late getting on the trail. The rain was still falling, but only lightly. He hurried down the slight hill to where he left his horse. It was eating contentedly on the small grassy area Petrion found between the trees. He cleaned the water off his horse as best he could, saddled it, and stored his gear fast. He was getting ready to gallop when he realized the goblins might have left watchers at the border to see why their raiders were being ambushed. If he left a clear path, then he would be letting them know. They might go back and have the camp prepared for attack or come down to attack them. He started his horse south, keeping to a streambed to hide his tracks. When he was about a quarter mile from the border, he started cutting to the southeast.

He rode the horse slowly across the woody terrain, looking for a trail and keeping watch for an ambush. He took extra time searching for tracks when he crossed streams and rocky areas, in case the goblins had the same idea he had. This was a nervous business. The goblins crossed the border during the night but then waited somewhere in Gamalius until time to move on to the attack. That waiting place would have to be outside the range of the patrols at the border, but not so far south to get into more heavily traveled areas.

He finished crossing the expected entry area without finding any indication that goblins had passed. He rode a little further to make sure and then turned his horse back toward the west. Angling to the south was out of the question because he might actually bump into the raiders. That would be deadly.

He headed straight across the barony. He moved even slower this time because he couldn't afford to miss the tracks again. He took extra time at all the streams and gullys.

Time was getting away from him quickly. He still couldn't tell what time of day it was because of the heavy clouds. To make matters worse, the rain started to increase. After another half hour of searching, he came to what he thought was the goblin trail.

Petrion dismounted and carefully followed them south for a while to make sure and finally found a full print in the mud along the stream bank. They were goblins, and they were taking extra care to not leave a trail that could be followed. The goblin commander could be thinking that the army was finding and destroying the patrols by tracking them from the border.

When he was sure of the tracks, he hurried as fast as he could safely go back to his horse. He walked the horse to the east for a half mile and then kicked him to a gallop to the south. The goblins weren't going to attack the house they camped at. They were attacking the one with the best approach. If he remembered right, the goblins could get all the way to the barn without being seen. They could attack the house from there or from another concealing point about thirty paces away. A narrow gully carried runoff water into the stream, providing a good approach. He pushed his horse as hard as he could. It might have to be left behind.

The horse was laboring when the farm finally came in sight. As he galloped the horse into the farm's yard, he saw the squad members ducking into their attack positions.

"Everyone out here now!" he yelled.

The squad members got up and ran to him.

"Goblins are coming, but not here," he told them when they arrived. "They will be attacking the farm that had the best approach."

"That one's the furthest east," Haslan moaned. "It will take us awhile to get there."

"Then let's get packing!" Petrion called out.

"Korin and Florine," Petrion said, handing out assignments in a quieter voice, "you get everything out of the house. Andolar and Lecik will get the saddles on the horses, starting with the packhorses. Berinda and Haslan get the stuff stored on the horses as they are saddled."

"And here," he told Lecik as he started toward the barn, "take my horse with you. Don't put a saddle on him. He's had a rough morning."

The horse was heavily lathered and breathing hard.

Petrion hurried to the house and saw the family watching the excitement from the door. He went over the story he had concocted again as he hurried toward the house.

"There are goblins in the area," he told them. "I spotted fresh tracks this morning as I was circling back to your house. We'll try to warn the people."

"Are they coming here?" the farmer asked with concern.

"No, sir, they looked like they were heading more to the east. I think they'll probably attack a few miles east of here from the direction they were traveling."

"We need to send for the guard," the lady said, "they will be able to stop them."

"The goblins will be done and gone by the time someone could ride for help and return," her husband told her. "What we need to do is gather up people to go over and beat off the attack."

"We're going to head that way," Petrion told them as Korin and Florine came running out of the house with their arms full of gear. "We'll help them if we can. Try and organize some help from the neighbors."

"I'll start gathering people up," the farmer said. "I'll start with old Enok. He has three boys old enough to ride for help. One can look for the army while the others help get people together. I'd better get my spear and crossbow."

His wife looked anxiously after him as he went to get his weapons. Petrion went inside the house to pick up the last few things. He almost collided with Korin as he made his way back out the door.

"I have the last of it," Petrion told the two.

"We still have to get the arrows off the roof," Korin told him. "We had extras up there."

"Just hurry," Petrion said urgently. "We may be too late to help them as it is."

Petrion hurried to the stable to help load the packhorses. Korin and Florine soon joined them with the extra arrows. It seemed to be taking forever. The horse he rode earlier looked like it was going to be fine for the run to the next farm. The other horses were stomping their hooves and moving around, catching the excitement from the squad. They finished loading before the farmer had his horse saddled. They gave a quick wave and were off to the east.

Petrion felt time pressing on him and leaned into the horse to help it move faster. The horse stretched out to run.

They were making good time in their rush to the farm. Maybe they would make it before the goblins got there. It would be a very close thing whichever way it went.

He saw Andolar galloping hard to come even with him and waving, while the pack horses charged along behind. The magician yelled something and pointed back over his shoulder. Petrion slowed, turned around, and saw only three squad members. Berinda and Lecik were in sight, but some distance behind. Haslan and the healers were nowhere to be seen. He thought about just waiting for the others to catch up but decided the others might miss them in the rain. He called himself several kinds of fool as he kicked his horse into a gallop back the way they had come. He had ridden for several minutes without checking on the squad.

"Wait here," he called over his shoulder.

Haslan came into view in the distance, but not the healers. He should have known the inexperienced riders couldn't keep a fast pace. They could have been hurt trying. He sent Berinda and Lecik to wait with Andolar and motioned for Haslan to join him. He let the thief's horse dictate the speed they were traveling.

"What were you doing?" Haslan asked with some annoyance as he came even.

"Being stupid!" Petrion answered. "I'm not perfect you know. Have you seen the healers?"

"I tried to keep them and you in sight for as long as possible, but I ended up losing sight of both groups."

"I hope they don't miss the tracks."

It took another five minutes of backtracking to find the healers. They were still on the trail of the squad at least. Korin was covered with mud. Florine had a lot on her, but nothing compared to Korin. He must have fallen off his horse. They were coming along at a pace that bounced them around. Korin looked like he could fall again any second. Petrion waited for them and then turned his horse around and let the healers set the pace. Korin looked terrible.

"I'm sorry, Petrion," Korin said. "I tried to keep up, but the horse bounced me off when we crossed a creek. Florine had to ride after the horse. I sprained my arm when I fell and had to heal myself."

"It's not your fault," Petrion said in anger.

He might have jeopardized the entire attack by those few minutes of carelessness. If he wasn't in such a hurry, they would be farther now. When they came to a shallow stream, Petrion allowed time for Korin and Florine to get down and wash off some of the mud. He tried to clean their horses.

"Go on, Haslan," Petrion told him, "and tell the others we're on the way. We can't afford another delay looking for someone who's looking for us."

"Sure, Petrion," Haslan replied as he started his horse.

"And tell them to eat something if they're hungry," Petrion yelled after the thief.

Haslan waved to show he'd heard and kept on riding. The healers were hurrying as much as possible, but he was still unhappy at the delay. Every minute made it more likely they would be too late. He still took time enough to have Korin make sure he had no additional injuries. Korin was lucky not to have broken bones from falling off a moving horse.

Petrion suddenly had to struggle to hold in a laugh. This was much too serious of a situation for laughter, but the way Korin looked trying to clean off the mud all over him suddenly struck him as funny. He finally pretended to be checking his saddle, so he wouldn't have to look at the healer.

"We're ready," Korin called from beside his horse.

"Let's go," Petrion said as he mounted without looking at the healers. "You set your best pace."

Petrion rode just behind the healers so he could see how well they were handling the ride. He could also hide the laughs he was trying so desperately to control. The healers were looking back occasionally to find out what the strange noises were behind them, but so far, he had managed to have a straight face whenever they turned. The constant inquiring looks were making the situation worse.

"I'm just going to ride ahead a little bit and look around," he told them.

He kicked his horse into a gallop and buried his face in the horse's mane to keep the laugh from sounding out. When we looked up again, he was closing rapidly on the rest of the squad. He waved to them and then turned and motioned to the healers to come on. They formed their standard traveling order and moved out as fast as the healers could bear. They were bouncing and swaying, and Petrion turned around to keep the laughs from coming again. When he looked back the next time, Andolar was trying to give the healers some advice on how to ride better. They were moving at a good speed but still far below what he could do on his own. He came to a decision and moved back beside a packhorse Andolar was leading to get two extra quivers of arrows.

"Haslan, come to the front," he called back. "Can you find the farm again?" he asked the thief when he caught up.

"It shouldn't be any problem," Haslan replied. "We just have to follow the line of houses at the edge of the settled region till we get to that one."

"Good. I want you to lead the squad on at your best pace while I ride ahead and scout the area. I'll have to scout on foot to remain concealed. Follow my tracks if you can. No, scratch that. I'm going in from the south, and you should come in from the north. When you're a mile from the house, take extra care. Don't rush into the attack even if you see or hear signs of a battle. If you can, attack from the north. That will bottle up the goblins so they can't escape as easily. We really don't want any getting away from us this time to alert their camp."

"Sure, boss," Haslan said with a smile. "Don't get into anything you can't handle. We'll be there as soon as we can."

"Thanks," he said as he took off at full speed toward a battle.

"Where are you going?" Berinda called as he rode past.

"Scouting," he called back over his shoulder, not caring if she heard or not.

CHAPTER 9

Petrion quickly lost sight of the squad. He was wearing down horses today.

If he remembered right, there was a small grove of trees where his horse wouldn't be visible a couple hundred paces southwest of the house. He would leave the horse and go in on foot. He started angling southeast to approach the grove from the south. He kept close watch for smoke in the direction of the farmhouse. It was wet enough that the outside wouldn't burn, but if the goblins got inside the house, they could set a fire easily. Heavy smoke would be a sure sign he was too late. He wasn't watching the surrounding area as closely as he should but instead relying on his speed to keep him out of trouble. He hoped it worked.

After several frantic minutes of riding, he arrived at the grove and quickly picketed his horse. The animal wasn't concealed well, but he didn't have time for more. He started for the farm at a run.

This farm was mostly for livestock, but there was a tended field to the east.

The rain was still coming steadily, so he didn't bother carrying his bow and arrows. He got his shield on under his cloak as he ran. He sighted the farmhouse and two barns as he made his way through the widely scattered trees. There was no one visible. He caught himself slipping from tree to tree instead of relying on his cloak to shield him from view. Berating himself for yet another silly mistake, he started running again.

He could see smoke coming from the chimney but couldn't see the front to tell if anyone was outside. He heaved a sigh of relief when he realized he beat the goblins to the house and started around toward the front. That was when he saw the goblins moving in behind the barn. Several had bows out in spite of the rain. He had to slow to a walk and went to the back of the house, which was closer. Goblins were already closer to the front than he. Moving faster than was safe, he reached the back of the house and a rear window.

"Hello the house," he called as loudly at the closed window as he dared.

"You have goblins coming in to attack," he said when he heard someone moving on the other side of the window.

"Who are you?"

"No time for questions," he told the voice. "The goblins are moving in. If the door and windows aren't barred in the next few seconds, you'll be asking your questions of them."

He heard some low-voiced conversation in the house and then suddenly the sound of bars being slammed into place. The goblins apparently recognized the sound because they abandoned quiet and charged the house shrieking. Petrion heard the impact when they tried to force the front door. The front windows would be next then the other windows and cellar door. He had to move or risk discovery.

"Thanks, stranger," the voice said again at the window. "Move over where I can see you, and I'll let you in the window if you're human."

"Too late," he said. "They'll be here in a few seconds. You better bar this window as well."

"You can't survive out there with all those goblins."

"I have an enchanted item that hides me," he told the voice. "You worry about keeping them out of the house. Help is on the way if you can hold out. Get someone on the roof if you haven't already and lock down the cellar door. They'll get around to those soon. The goblins have archers ready to shoot. And make sure there aren't any other places they can break in."

Petrion's heart still sank when he heard the window bars put into place even though he ordered it himself. He regretted not being able to use the protection of the house, but the goblins most likely would be here before he could find something to stand on and get through the window.

The goblins were starting to pound on the front of the house with something. If the farmers braced the door, it should take some time for them to break it down. It was time for him to get out of there and warn the squad.

He had waited too long to move. Goblins came around both sides of the house at the same time and were spread out, so he couldn't sneak between them. He hadn't counted on that. Petrion ducked his head quickly to make sure the goblins couldn't see his face.

There was no way he could outrun the goblins with his armor on. It would just be a matter of who gave up first. He decided he might as well try though because things were going to get unhealthy here. He could break between them when they got closer and then count on the cloak and the rain to protect him from arrows until the goblins gave up the chase.

"Look, new boot for Durn," Petrion heard in Goblin.

With a further sinking in his heart, he turned his head slowly while keeping his head down and looked at his foot. His cloak had hung on the top of his boot, and the boot was showing. *No help for it now*, he thought as he drew his dagger. When the goblin reached for the boot, Petrion swung his arm out and jammed the dagger into his neck.

Suddenly with his cloak open, he was visible to the goblins. The sudden appearance of an armed human in their midst stunned the goblins momentarily. He left the dagger and drew his sword as the goblins quickly adjusted to the situation. He managed to thrust into the shoulder of another goblin before they overcame their surprise. That still left him with eight goblins to deal with for now, and they were already calling for help. Rangers were feared by the goblins, and Petrion's cloak marked him as a powerful ranger even though he wasn't.

A crossbow bolt coming at point blank range from the window glanced off a goblin helmet, disorienting him for a moment. Petrion was trapped against the side of the building, engaging two goblins with swords and another with a spear. Two archers dropped back to get a better shot at him over the heads of their comrades. The goblin with the spear got the point past his shield, but his armor stopped the blow from penetrating until he could get a swing at the shaft. The goblin jerked the spear back rather than take a chance on losing the point. He was totally on the defensive, fighting three opponents. He had to get out of here now or die against the back of the house. He heard answers to the calls for help from the goblins in the front. The people in the house were doing what they could with bows to stop the arrow fire, but their shots were mostly ineffective.

A goblin knelt down behind those in front of him, and Petrion got ready for the old flying-goblin attack. A goblin came running up to the fight and yelled "Duck!" just before he got there. This was a favorite goblin tactic against taller people. It had also been covered in ranger school. The center and leftmost goblins ducked to let the flyer go over their heads. The one on the right attacked.

Petrion used the break to deliver a blow to the head of the goblin on his right. The blow wasn't perfect since he was trying to do several things at once. But it knocked the goblin down. The flyer he deflected into the building with his shield as he took a step to the right. Then he kicked the center goblin in the head. The goblin made a perfect target, and he fell backwards over the kneeling goblin. Petrion almost fell over the downed goblin as he continued the movement to the right.

Petrion's shield was toward the archers as he moved along the back of the building. His forehead broke off an arrow that sank into the wood in front of him. That would leave him with a bruise. He almost started laughing hysterically at being worried about a bruise when he was about to die. He managed to stop himself before he lost the little bit of concentration left to him.

He had to keep moving or he would be trapped. He kept his sword in front of him like a spear as he ran alongside the building. He had to jump a spear thrust into the wall in front of him and almost lost his balance again when he landed on the muddy ground. Another spear grazed the back of his leg.

He finally reached the corner of the building and knocked the goblin coming from the other way, sprawling. Size and weight advantage were great things to have sometimes. So was having a large shield to lead the way. He started a sideways run toward the front of the house. It was slower than a straight run, but it let him keep his shield where it could help deflect the arrows that would come his way from behind. He just hoped the family would let him in the front door. The end of the porch was empty, but goblins were closing quickly from behind. A goblin spear flew between him and the building while he was running. Two arrows hit heavily into his shield, and another streaked past his eyes. Two inches closer, and he would be dead. Another arrow slammed into the side of his leg as he tried to stop.

His feet slid in the mud, and he ended up at the front edge of the porch. He looped his sword arm around the corner post to stop and then used it to pull himself up. The goblins on the porch were busy with a bench trying to break in the front door and hadn't noticed him yet.

One behind him stopped quicker than he did and attacked while his shield was out of position. He was hit on the sword arm by a short sword, mashing his arm into the post. His greave held, but his arm was partly numbed by the hit. Petrion got his arm out of the way before the next swing, which left the goblin's sword stuck in the post. He got back to his feet and away from the edge before another could swing at him.

The porch goblins were chanting a cadence to time the blows of the bench against the door and missed the sounds of combat. Petrion charged across the porch to get to the door before the goblin archers could get a shot at his back. He ran full speed and shield-rammed the massed goblins. The entire group went rolling across the porch, and he had to fight for balance at the sudden stop. The nearest goblin saw him just before impact, and his eyes went wide as plates at the sight. It was funny how much detail you picked out at such times. His shield arm began to throb from the impact. He hoped he hadn't broken anything.

The height of the porch slowed the goblins, giving him back a little of the time he lost on the corners, but two were already heading toward him. A quick push on the door showed him it was still barred. He got in the doorframe, using the thickness of the walls to help shield his sides from the attackers.

"Human at the front door!" he called, hoping the people were brave enough to let him in.

The two goblins reached him but were too quick to come on the attack. He attacked high right on the spear wielder and then shifted the attack lower mid swing to cut into the goblin's ribs. The goblin's ribs stopped the stroke from killing, but he dropped back to try and keep blood loss from finishing the job. The second goblin had a sword but was no match for the ranger. Petrion swung his sword across in front of the goblin, and the goblin moved back enough to let the sword pass. When the sword reached the center of the goblin's throat, Petrion converted the swing into a killing thrust. His arm still wasn't responding the way it should. The thrust sliced along the edge of the goblin's throat instead of going into the center. It still managed to cut the great artery in his neck.

Some of the goblins with the bench were getting up, and four more had climbed onto the porch when he heard the bar being lifted. The door opened suddenly, and he ran backwards into the house so they could slam the door. An unfortunate goblin managed to get his hand on the edge of the door and lost two fingers as the two men slammed it shut. A woman was nearby to drop the bar as soon as the door closed and had it seated before the next goblins hit.

Petrion sank to the floor and gulped air as fast as he could. There were three men, two women, and four children staring at him in disbelief. He looked down at himself and saw he was heavily splattered with dirt mixed with some spatterings of blood. Luckily, most of the blood belonged to goblins. He had an arrow that he hadn't noticed stuck in the shoulder plate of his armor. Apparently the arrow that hit his leg hadn't penetrated his greave either. There were about a dozen arrows, mostly broken off, sticking out of his shield. It was funny that he only remembered two. Two of the broken shafts had fresh blood on them. That goblin apparently had good reason to be scared of being hit with his shield.

He put his sword down and slid his shield off the other arm. He got out a bandage from his belt for his left leg where the spear wound was dripping blood on the floor.

"Hi," he finally said into the silence. "It's nice to see all of you.

Either his words or the renewed banging at the front door brought them to their senses. One of the men braced the door with a chair and then picked up the goblin fingers and threw them into the fire. The other men climbed the ladder to the loft and went onto the parapet. The younger of the women hustled the children into a corner of the room, while the other brought some water and cloth over to clean him up. She started on the wound on the back of his leg. It was stinging badly, and the wound cleaner she dabbed on it didn't help. He bit his lip to keep from yelling. She threaded a needle to stitch the wound closed, but he stopped her.

"I'll have to get back in the fight," he told her, "and the stitches would probably pull out and make the wound worse. Just wrap it good for now."

The water was nice and warm, so he cleaned his hands and face. He pulled off his right greave while continuing to work his sword arm to get the feeling back. He was lucky not to have lost the use of the arm because the greave had all but given way under the blow. There was a small cut through the metal and a shallow cut to match on his arm. The woman worked on that next. When his cuts were tended, he pulled the arrows out of his shield and pounded out the dent in the greave as best he could with the pommel of his sword.

He had fought his way through the goblins and come away with minor wounds. Reaction from the fight was starting to set in, and he had to clamp his teeth down tight to keep from giggling or screaming, he wasn't sure which. He didn't need these people thinking he was any crazier than they did now. Of course, the battle was far from over. The raiders were still out there. He had done in two of them for sure, and the one missing the fingers was probably gone as well. There had been no time for him to get an accurate count of their numbers while fighting.

The door was starting to show some damage but would probably hold for several more minutes.

"Do you have any windows leading into the cellar?" he asked them.

"No," the man replied.

"Then get the children into the cellar. Keep the doors to the other rooms open," he told them, "so we can see if they start working to force one of the windows. And thanks for the bandages."

"Thank you," the man said, "for risking your life to warn us. If the goblins had found an unbarred door, we all would have died within seconds."

The man was probably in his early fifties and was as hairy as the one at the last house. The only difference was the top of his head was as bare as an egg. He more than made up for it with his beard though. It was bushy and halfway down his chest, with just a few places of the original brown color showing in the gray.

From what he could remember from the last frantic moments, the other men in the house bore a hairy resemblance to the old man. The woman working on his arm was heavy, but not really fat. The children were probably hers since they looked between six and ten years old. The younger woman looked to be in her early twenties and was very pregnant.

"Help should be arriving soon," he said in a quieter voice. "We found goblins tracks and started to rouse the countryside. The rest of my group should be here before too long. I came ahead to warn you. Your neighbors should be here sometime after that."

"Are you in the army then?" the older woman asked.

"No," Petrion answered her, "I'm an arms merchant. Having goblins running loose in the countryside is very bad for business. It's also bad for a merchant's health. We figured we better try and get rid of them while we could."

"That leg wound is still leaking," the woman said after she finished dabbing at his forehead. "Are you sure you don't want it sewed up?"

"Just try and wrap it a little tighter," he told her, "and I'll have a healer take care of it later."

As the door started to weaken, Petrion looked over his gear carefully before getting ready to go back into combat. He had to loosen the strap on his right greave to get it back on his swelling and bandaged arm. He heard one of the men on the roof yell that he'd got one. He was thankful the goblins wouldn't be able to burn them out because of all the rain. That would end the defense very quickly. It would also destroy everything of value. The goblins were generally reluctant to use fire until after they pillaged a place.

"Stand behind me with the spear," he told the old man, "and take out any that happen to get past me. Don't try and thrust past me to get a goblin. I could move in front of the thrust. Keep in contact with the guys on the roof so that everyone knows what's going on. The goblins will get around to trying the roof eventually."

He moved behind the door, just out of range of where it would swing open. The bar was cracked, so the door would swing instead of splitting or falling inward. He might be able to use that to help him.

"Let's move that table over here," he called to the man, "and put it so the door will only open about two feet."

He leaned his sword and shield against the wall and hurried to place the table. The bar was about to give way, and being without sword and shield when the door opened could end the fight quickly. He slid his arm through the shield straps and picked up his sword. Both his arms were aching badly, but he could use them. He quickly switched his sword to his shield hand and unfastened his cloak, tossing it into a corner. He didn't want it damaged. Then it was time to wait.

The bar was still holding, but he could see it weakening. *Thud. Thud. Thud.* The sound was almost maddening.

"Well hurry up and break," he whispered to himself.

He had hurried since he found the goblin tracks, and now this little delay was about to drive him crazy. He took a couple of deep breaths to calm his nerves. Battle was a thinking business. He couldn't afford to have his concentration waver.

The bar finally snapped, but the door didn't swing open. Petrion flipped the remaining little piece of the bar out on his side using his sword and waited for the next hit. The door flew open when the bench hit it, and the goblins tumbled into the room. The table moved back several inches from the force of the blow but was still holding the door partially closed. Petrion thrust quickly with his sword and took the lead goblin in the side. A backhand swing smashed the head of another into the door while opening up the back of his head. Two down quickly, but the others wouldn't be so easy. The remaining goblins on the bench scrambled out of range and let the ones ready for battle engage. Arrows started hitting the door, and some were coming in.

"Push the table up farther," Petrion called, "so that the arrows can't get into the room."

If he could engage them one at a time, he could keep killing them.

A goblin with a sword stepped into the doorway as the farmer started shoving the table. Another one with a spear worked behind him. Petrion blocked the spear thrust with his shield and knocked the front goblin's sword out wide with his. Then he swung down hard on the spearhead and knocked it into the front goblin's shoulder. The spear flipped out of the goblin's hands and fell in the doorway. Petrion cut the sword goblin on the sword arm and then the shield shoulder to put him out of the fight. The goblin archers shifted to get a clear shot at him, so he moved partway behind the door. That let the goblins into the edge of the room. Another pair of goblins came on the attack, and Petrion was back defending himself against spear and sword. Other goblins began working with the bench to break open a window.

That combination of two goblins was hard to fight. He finally got lined up where he could swing down on the spear shaft at the same time he was swinging at the sword goblin's head. His enchanted sword cut the shaft and continued into the goblin's shoulder as he tried to get out of the way. He jerked the sword free to an accompanying scream from the goblin and thrust over his head into the throat of the other. He finished off the front goblin with a short thrust to the chest.

Arrows started flying around him again, and he was forced to keep his shield high to stop them, leaving himself more open to the close attackers. Archery was always uncertain in the rain, but the goblins decided that some damage was better than none. The next goblin pair worked him back from the door a little, allowing a second sword goblin to get close enough to engage, with the spear goblin supporting from behind.

Petrion saw a pair of goblins kneel behind the fighters just before the flyers came in. When he heard *duck* shouted in Goblin, he turned his shield so the edge faced out and thrust with it. One of the goblins took the shield edge right in the throat and fell into the house gasping for breath. The second goblin managed to react enough to get his hands on the shield. The edge still shattered his nose and laid him out on the floor. The goblins in front were bent over, and Petrion slashed down hard on the backs of their heads. The blow struck through the leather helmet of one of the goblins, but the angle was wrong to hit the other.

He pulled on his sword, but it was stuck. He was trying to do too many things at once but didn't have any choice. He kicked the table forward to distract the second goblin as the third thrust his spear at Petrion's exposed side. His armor and the turn he started took some of the force away, but the spear pierced his mail and sliced a bad wound in his side. He jerked his sword with attached goblin into the house and threw his weight against the table and door. The older woman was running over with a bandage for his side. Dizziness and nausea hit him like a wave, making him glad for the door against his back.

The old man made sure the goblins on the floor were dead and wedged the table to help hold the door closed. Two goblin bodies kept it open enough for others to get through, but the opening was narrow, making the entry more dangerous. They would want to force the door before attacking.

"How many are left out there?" he called up to the roof.

"Near as we can count," one of them yelled down, "there are ten to fifteen of them left."

About 50 percent losses. They could very well decide to retreat rather than continue the attack. How long they fought usually depended on what their commander would do to them if they came back without victory. The attack stopped for a moment, but the men on the roof said the goblins were still there. Petrion pulled the two bodies into the house using a goblin spear. Then he used the spear as a bar for the door. He had to use the door for support again when he was done.

The woman working on his side told him to stand still.

The door was badly damaged and would fragment soon, giving the archers an easy shot into the house. He would have to stand in the doorway in arrow fire and fight the goblins. If he moved to use a wall for protection, the goblins would flood inside.

"Pile that fire wood behind the table," he ordered the women.

One ignored him and told him to hold still again so she could work on his side.

The goblins decided not to give up on the attack and started banging against the door and both front windows. It would only be a matter of time until they could attack the room from several points. Petrion called for one of the men on the roof to come down and watch a window. He was right. The fellow was as hairy and almost as bald as his father. The old man was already guarding the other window. Petrion would have to hold the door again. Ten to fifteen goblins were left. He hoped the squad arrived soon. He hoped he could stay on his feet till then.

CHAPTER 10

Andolar, for all of his riding experience, wasn't used to riding in bad weather. Riding for him had been for pleasure and so was not conducted in the rain. He couldn't keep his stupid waxed cloak shut enough while he was riding to stay dry. Well, at least he wasn't bouncing around all over the place like Korin and Florine. They were swinging a bit to the north so they could attack the goblins from the north. Lecik figured they were maybe two miles to the northwest of the farm. Soon they would turn due east for a while and then south to the farm. After covering about a half mile, they came upon a clear track of many booted feet beside a streambed heading just east of south. The boot tracks were smaller than normal human but nearly as wide. Lecik got down and looked at the tracks, which had mostly filled with water.

"I think the goblins made these," Lecik said finally. "It was a large group with small feet, and the goblins are the only ones I know who would be leaving that trail in this weather."

Haslan motioned for them to follow the trail. Lecik remounted and resumed his place at the back of the squad. Andolar jerked the lead rope on the packhorse string to get them to follow. That was another riding experience with which he was unaccustomed, and he had the rope burns to prove it. Haslan picked up the pace for a short while. Shortly after they slowed again, Lecik rode to the front and told Haslan he thought they were getting close to the farm.

Andolar started tensing up. The plan was to move in on the farm slowly so they could determine the situation before attacking. Haslan motioned for a halt, and Andolar wondered what was going on until he saw Haslan trying to listen. Andolar picked up the sounds then. Even after his short time at fighting, he recognized the sounds as the sounds of battle. Metal was ringing against metal. Andolar could feel his pulse quickening as they rode. He didn't like being exposed. When they went riding into the farmyard, every arrow would be trained on him, according to his father. And if there was one thing his father knew, it was goblin battles. He jerked on the lead rope of the packhorses to pull them into line.

The sounds were growing clearer. They could here heavy thumping. Someone was pounding on something. He hoped Petrion was still alive. He couldn't imagine being in the squad with Berinda fighting for leadership all of the time. That would make life even more miserable. It would also take away some of his buffer against attack. Anything that kept him out of combat was a good thing. He finally spotted the side of a building through the trees. They were getting close. He looked to the front of the squad to see what orders Haslan had, when Haslan suddenly rolled out of the saddle.

"*Ambush*!!" Haslan yelled as he fell.

Andolar looked around in shock to see goblins moving from concealment among the trees. They were coming from both sides in front of the group. He saw a goblin archer aiming at him and suddenly remembered what was likely to happen. He rolled out of the saddle and hit the ground hard. The next second, he was rolling away to get out from under the hooves of his horse. The horse had two arrows in its side and was rearing and flailing its hooves in pain. Andolar swallowed hard when he realized those arrows were meant for him. His horse screamed and bolted in the direction of the farm. Andolar was rolling away again as the packhorses stampeded past. In the confusion, he crawled and got his back against a tree.

A quick glance both ways showed Berinda and Korin were fighting to his left, and Lecik and Florine on his right. He didn't see Haslan anywhere. That thief could melt into his surroundings in the blink of an eye. He looked across the way and saw a goblin pointing an arrow in his direction. He dove away from the tree and heard two hits behind him as he landed on the ground. A glance back showed an arrow and a sword stuck in the tree where he was just sitting. There were goblins between him and the front of the squad, so he ran toward Lecik and Florine. Several arrows flashed around him as he ran. One even grazed his left buttock, making him let out an involuntary yelp of pain.

Lecik had one goblin down but was engaged with two more. One had a sword and the other a spear. Florine had a spear-wielding goblin facing her. They had a tree close behind to help cover them, and Andolar dashed into the small protected space. One of the goblin archers put an arrow into the tree beside him, so he prepared a fire-dart spell. His hands were covered in mud when he looked down, and he quickly wiped them on a somewhat clean spot on his shirt. Another arrow struck the tree behind him as he worked. He ducked to present as small a target as possible and reached for one of his small lumps of coal. He focused intently on his magic to release the spell properly and had the satisfaction of seeing the goblin archer fall from the burning wound in his throat. His group was definitely drawing most of the arrow fire from the goblins. Lecik had a cut on his cheek, and four arrows sticking out of his shield. Florine had six or seven arrows in her shield and one in her side. She must have taken time to cast a healing spell because Andolar didn't see any blood flowing from the wound. The goblin in front of Florine jerked twice suddenly and fell forward with a pair of daggers sticking out of his back. Haslan joined them, retrieving his daggers as he passed the goblin body.

"I finished one of the archers out there," Haslan told them, "but they spotted me and I had to run."

"Glad to have you with us," Lecik replied.

The pressure against Lecik eased up with Florine able to engage one of his goblins. He started beating his way through the goblin's defenses. Andolar took a second to glance toward the front and saw Berinda fighting three of the goblins. There were two down already in front of her. Korin was trying desperately to keep another one from killing him. They were lucky Haslan noticed the ambush before they were all the way in it.

Andolar saw three goblin fighters coming toward them, and there were still four archers out there causing trouble. Three of them were firing at him. He cast a sleep spell and had the satisfaction of seeing all three of them collapse to the ground. Lecik finally dropped the goblin in front of him with a second hit to the head and moved to double up on the remaining goblin. The other three arrived before they could finish that one off. Haslan slipped off again to who knew where, and now Lecik was overmatched and trying to keep two swords and a spear away from his vitals. One of the goblins on Lecik looked like the leader because his trappings were fancier. Andolar shot a fire dart into the goblin in front of Florine and finished him off. Three daggers in quick succession flew at the goblin wielding the spear against Lecik, and two of them struck home in leg and arm, sending the goblin down screaming in pain.

Now it was two against two again, but the goblin on Lecik was managing to hold. When he looked over to see how Berinda and Korin were doing, he saw Korin on the ground unconscious with his hands on his side. Berinda was still engaged with three, so she must have killed one. She had her back close to a tree and was standing over Korin to keep him from being slain by the goblins. He didn't see the fourth archer, and that worried him greatly. He scanned the area carefully to locate him. He finally saw him by the sleeping archers. He had woken one of them and was moving to the second. Andolar cast his last spell and put the two archers to sleep while they were trying to wake the others.

He saw Haslan again, and the thief was trying to stop a sword-wielding goblin that was heading toward the sleeping archers. Andolar moved to the side as if he was going to engage the goblin on Lecik. The leader glanced over to see what he was doing, and Lecik gave him a minor cut on his shield shoulder. Andolar looked around to try and find something to do. Haslan was trying desperately to stay alive against the goblin fighter. Berinda had a leg wound but was managing to hold off the three goblins at once, even though guarding Korin was hampering her movements. The sword of one of the goblins went flying as he watched, and the goblin ducked and ran to retrieve it. Lecik and Florine were dueling about even. He let out a wild yell and charged the goblin attacking Haslan.

The goblin looked around to see who was coming and turned slightly to face him. Haslan only needed that second of hesitation from the goblin to bury both sword and dagger into the goblin's stomach. The goblin collapsed groaning and slipped into unconsciousness.

Andolar ran back to help Lecik and Florine while Haslan went to help Berinda. He tried the yell trick again on the goblin leader and almost got sliced on his knee as he skidded to a stop. He pulled a piece of trail bread out of a pouch and started mumbling as he ground it between his fingers. That broke the goblin leader's concentration enough to let Lecik finish him with consecutive cuts to the arm and stomach. Florine's goblin turned to run but had his head crushed with her morning star in spite of his leather helmet.

He looked toward Berinda and saw Haslan drop one goblin from behind, and Berinda finish another with that devastating overhand swing of hers. The third became a dagger target as he tried to escape. Florine moved quickly to help Korin, while Haslan went to make sure the sleeping goblins didn't wake up and run away.

Korin regained consciousness with the first cure spell from his sister and smiled to see her bending over him. Florine cured Berinda to repair the wound to her leg. Korin reached for the arrow in his sister's side, but she stopped him.

"Haslan," Berinda said just loud enough to carry to the thief, "you stay back with Korin and make sure none of the goblins get away to the north. Everyone else come with me."

She hurried toward the farm without even a glance to see if they were coming. They heard a loud crash, followed by the ringing of swords that cut off almost as soon as it began. Then the pounding was the only sound to be heard again. Andolar checked behind them and saw Korin coming. Haslan was nowhere in sight as usual.

They approached the house the same way the goblins had, using the barn to shield them from sight. When they reached the back of the barn, Berinda peeked down one side and Lecik down the other. Korin caught up with them. Berinda motioned for him to stay put, apparently trying to keep him out of combat, which was where Andolar desperately wanted to be.

"We're going to hit the group by the window," Berinda whispered to them.

Berinda took the healers and Lecik around the right side of the barn to attack the four goblins at the side window.

The goblins saw the squad members charging and turned to fight before the squad could reach them. Each of the squad members faced off against a goblin. Korin swung his morning star to keep the goblin back until someone could help him. The goblins screamed for help as soon as they saw the fighters, but the one in front of Berinda died from a split head before he could complete the scream. Florine also managed to deliver an incapacitating blow while her goblin was fumbling to drop a bow and draw a dagger. Lecik was too busy helping hold off the goblin in front of Korin as well as his own to press home a quick attack.

More goblins came from the front of the house during the brief exchange of blows. Berinda and Florine took position against the three from the front. No sooner had they arrived than four more came from the back of the house. Two men on the roof fired crossbow bolts at the goblins and managed to wound one of them. Nine against four wasn't very good odds though. Korin moved into the center of the triangle to be able to cure at need, leaving the other three to attack. Three goblins dropped back to use their bows while the others attacked. They never got the chance to release an arrow.

The men on the roof shot at the archers and drew their attention, and before the goblins could return fire, Petrion ran in among them.

Andolar almost let out a cheer when he saw the ranger—bloody and battered, but alive. He had bloodstained bandages on his leg and around his waist. Petrion attacked from behind, and only the last goblin even realized he was there. Some of the fighter goblins saw him though and decided the odds were not in their favor. They broke and ran.

Instantly, goblins tried to head for the best escape. Two of them were cut down as they tried to disengage. Another, whose back was to Petrion, ran right toward the ranger. In three passes of the ranger's sword, the goblin was on the ground with a fatal stomach wound. Berinda followed two that were running together and cut them down from behind. The fourth goblin chose the north and ran toward the barn. Andolar turned to duck out of his way and almost stumbled over the thief. Haslan allowed the goblin to close to twenty feet and then started throwing his daggers. The goblin blocked two with his small shield and a third missed. The fourth struck him in the leg, causing the leg to collapse. Haslan ran toward him, and the goblin dropped his sword and held his hands out wide in surrender.

Andolar was just starting a sigh of relief when screaming from the house had him flattening against the barn. When he turned around, he saw two men and a woman on the parapet jumping up and down and screaming for all they were worth.

Petrion collapsed to the muddy ground, and both healers ran to help him.

Andolar sagged against the barn to catch his breath and enjoy being wet, filthy, sore, and alive.

CHAPTER II

Florine let Haslan cut off the end of the arrow with the enchanted dagger and then gritted her teeth as he prepared to pull it out. She and Korin both had only a single healing spell left, after Korin had flushed Petrion's side wound and closed it with a healing spell. That left her with the worst wound. She had managed to cure the wound before the goblin fighters closed with them but didn't have time to pull out the arrow. She screamed in spite of herself when Haslan pulled out the arrow and almost passed out. They told her she was lucky the point had gone clear through. Otherwise they would have had to cut it out of her. Petrion inspected the point for poison but didn't find any. The pain eased suddenly as Korin finished the chant of the spell. She looked down and saw the wound was almost closed and chanted her final spell to complete the job.

The farmers were standing around in the rain trying to look serious while at the same time being overjoyed to have beaten the raiders. They thought they wouldn't survive the attack. Florine had been doubtful for a while herself. There were nineteen goblins in the ambush party and another twenty-seven in the raid on the house. The farmers were praising Petrion so much that it was starting to get on his nerves. It had gotten on Berinda's nerves a lot earlier.

Berinda wanted to talk about how she held off three goblins while a goblin archer was using her for a target. The rest of the squad had already heard the story twice. The farmers cut in with stories about how Petrion held off an attack by almost thirty, including archers. He wounded two outside in his desperate run to get into the house, then several the first time they forced the door, two more when the door had given way again, and finally four in the battle outside. Berinda looked like she was almost smoldering at being upstaged by the ranger. Petrion looked weak, worn, and just glad to be alive and didn't want to be reminded how close death had come. They would have to get him to tell the story of that outside fight someday. It must have been terrifying.

Andolar rode in with the string of packhorses. He had left right after the battle to collect them before they got too far away. One of the pack horses was missing. He got wearily down from Korin's horse and came over to where the others were gathered around her. Florine hoped he would take some of the attention away from her because being stared at was making her self-conscious.

"My horse was dead about two hundred paces south of the house," Andolar told them. "He was hit by four arrows. One of the packhorses apparently couldn't stop in time and fell over my horse when it died. He broke one of his front legs, and I had to put him down. The things in the packsaddle weren't damaged at least."

"We'll have to load the remaining horses a little heavy," Lecik said, "with two of them down."

"You can have one of ours," the youngest of the farmers called out. "We would have lost him anyway if you hadn't come along."

"Thank you for the offer," Petrion said as one of the older men elbowed the one that had spoken. "We may have to purchase one of yours if the loads on ours look to be too heavy."

Florine saw the farmers relax a little bit and realized that the price of a horse would be hard to come by, especially with trouble on the border and the extra preparations that were needed to handle it. They would probably leave most of the goblin goods behind again, and that would more than offset the cost of a horse. The farmers didn't know that, especially since Petrion was supposed to be a merchant. Haslan walked off to check the ambush goblins for valuables. Lecik was doing the same with the ones around the house. Petrion told the farmers they had better start digging a grave. The men all walked down to the barn, grabbed shovels, and moved to an area about a hundred paces northeast of the house and started digging.

Andolar, Korin, and Petrion made use of hot water the women provided and got the worst of the mess off themselves and their gear.

The other farmers from the area came in a group about an hour after the battle was over and stood around in the light rain listening to stories. The work on the grave stopped as they recounted different phases of the fight. Petrion went to retrieve his horse and had them start packing to go.

Haslan and Lecik collected about four hundred coppers, thirty silvers, and four golds. Haslan added the silver and gold to the squad money supply without asking anyone what they thought. The loot of the battle seemed more important to them because of the cost. No one disagreed with what he had done. They were battered but loaded and ready to go by the time Petrion returned with his horse. Some of the farmers were still talking about the battle. Others were looking through the supply of goblin weapons and pieces of armor for things they might like to have. The people who lived here would probably be doing a brisk business among their neighbors in goblin gear.

"Petrion," Haslan said as they got ready to mount, "there are about four hundred coppers still here as well as a bunch of arms and armor."

Petrion looked at the crowd discussing the glory of the last battle and finally seemed to see what he was looking for. He must have spotted the man they stayed with because he was heading toward him. The man was packing his horse to leave. Florine saw Petrion had the sack of coppers.

"Excuse me, sir," he called out.

The man looked around and saw Petrion coming and then looked around to see whom he was talking to. When he realized Petrion was talking to him, he answered.

"What can I do for you, master arms merchant?" the man asked.

"I have something here I want you to take home with you," Petrion told him, "and some things over there as well that I think you might need."

Petrion looped the strings from the pair of sacks containing the copper pieces over the pommel of the man's horse and guided him and his horse to where some of the goblins were still lying. He reached down, wincing a little from the side wound, and grabbed a pair of swords and daggers. He placed the blades in a large sack that was on the porch. Then he added a couple of the goblin bows and three partly filled quivers of arrows to the sack. He handed the sack to the man and then gave him a couple of spears.

"What is this for?" the man asked.

"You were hospitable to us," Petrion answered, "and I'm afraid you're going to need these things. Unless I'm badly mistaken, the goblin wars are about to start up again. This wasn't just a band of goblin raiders or brigands. This was a planned attack. Learn to use those and quickly. Get the defenses of your place in order as much as you can. It would help if you all weren't so isolated.

Maybe you could move together for a while so there will be more of you around in case of trouble."

The man looked down at his shoes for a while before answering and looked uncomfortable giving the answer. The others had stopped to listen as well.

"You make good sense, but it's harvest time. None of us can leave the fields, or we won't have the food to make it through the winter. We have to bring in our crops, or the goblins won't have to come down to kill us. Besides, if a goblin army comes down, it won't matter how many of us are together."

"The goblins send out raiders instead of large armies most times," Petrion said angrily. "This little group of ours could destroy any of your houses. What do you think a band of fifty goblins would do to your farm and family?"

"Same thing they did to Nealy's place over by us," the man replied. "Didn't change the situation then, and doesn't change it now. These places are ours, and we'll keep them or die trying."

Petrion just shook his head and walked to his horse. Haslan had already moved his horse over by a chopping block so he could mount. The rest of them got on their horses and headed them toward the northwest and the main goblin encampment. The farm folk cheered them as they rode off, and Petrion turned and waved back at them. They had no spells and were in need of more healing. A day at least would be needed to recuperate from the battle. A day they did not have. They would cross the border into goblin territory that night and should get to the goblin camp not long after, depending on how fast they rode.

They rode slowly to conserve what energy they and their horses had left. Berinda was still sulking at the front of the formation about being upstaged by Petrion. Lecik acted like he was glad she was at the front because it kept as much distance between them as possible. Petrion seemed oblivious to any tension and rode along lost in thought. Haslan rode from the back to the front to talk to the two fighters for a moment and then returned to his place beside Lecik. After he talked to them, Berinda and Petrion both began studying the surrounding area with more care. Florine heaved a sigh of relief. Being ambushed once was enough. They might not survive a second such attack.

Florine wondered what the border would be like. Would they see patrols of goblins going by and have to thread their way between them? Or worse, would goblin ambushes be waiting for them no matter which path they took? Having arrows flying around her was a new experience. She couldn't imagine how Andolar must feel, having been the main target. He got out of his saddle just in time. She took time out from studying the country to look forward to where he was leading the packhorses. He must be feeling just like she was because his head kept darting from side to side as he inspected the trees and bushes they passed. They were all very fortunate it was raining during the ambush. She sat there for a couple of seconds after Haslan called and saw Andolar roll off his horse and dodge the pounding hoofs. It had taken an arrow hitting her shield to bring her back to her senses enough to dismount and seek other squad members. Lecik was already on the ground defending against two goblins. More arrived the same time she did. Another couple of seconds delay and she would have been cut off and probably killed.

She broke off her recollections and started scanning the surrounding countryside again. That freeze up in battle was worrying her. Death came quickly for people who couldn't react in tight situations like the ambush, and she didn't want to end up like most of the duchess's force had at the start of the last war.

A leaf-covered limb off the trail moved suddenly, and she was off her horse and on the ground. A squirrel ran across the limb and higher into the tree. She looked around quickly to see if anyone noticed and saw Lecik on the ground with his bow ready and Haslan gone.

"Squirrel," she said quietly, pointing into the tree.

Lecik fired at the squirrel, probably because he was as scared as she was. The arrow hit the limb the squirrel was walking on with a loud *thunk*. The squirrel retreated behind the tree, and the rest of the squad was on the ground looking for an enemy. Andolar was scrambling for all he was worth toward a tree while trying to get out his dagger. Everyone was really on edge. Petrion checked one of his horse's hooves after he sheathed his sword, acting like that was what he intended all along. The others remounted, and Lecik had to help Haslan up. For some reason, it made her feel better to know that everyone else was as tense as she was. It made her feel somewhat justified in her feelings.

The day started darkening as they traveled, and her dread increased with the amount of darkness. It was unnerving to think that people could be out there who could see you clearly in the dark because of the heat of your body. Petrion turned from the direction they were going and led them into a group of close growing trees and dismounted.

"We are about four miles from the house now," he said, "and as near as I can figure about two miles from the border. We should also be somewhere around a mile and a half away from the path the goblins took on the raid. This should be a relatively safe spot to stop."

"I thought we were going straight across the border to take out the camp," Korin said.

"I thought of something else that might work better while we were riding along," he told them. "I'm going ahead and scout the border, but I should be back around the middle of the night. Keep only one person on watch at a time. The fighters and thief will take the turns. Spell casters, use every minute for sleep to recover your strength. We have to be at our best when we hit the goblin camp."

"Won't we lose the element of surprise if we don't follow up the attack now?" Andolar asked.

"I think it might actually give us more surprise if we delay our advance by a little while," Petrion answered. "I was thinking about it last night, and then thinking back to the ambush setup today made me think my idea was right. See if you can find any flaws that I haven't thought of. The goblin commander, after he finds out he has lost a troop, sends out a heavier detachment with an extra ambush party in case anyone follows them from the border. He might very well have stationed guards along the border as well to see when and if they come back. They would also be able to warn him in case a return attack is launched. He has probably heard about the loss of his second band of raiders by now. That's another reason he may have people watching the border.

"I intend to find those goblins if they are there. I won't kill them because I don't want to alert him. They should send someone back to report that their raiders didn't return sometime before morning. Any remaining border guards probably won't be expected back to their base camp soon, so we won't be alerting the camp like we would if an expected border messenger didn't arrive. We will move out as soon as the spell casters are ready in the morning and take out any remaining border guards. Then we'll move on the base camp. The commander should think that we are content to pick off his raiders. That's another element of surprise in our favor. He also may dispatch more people out of the base camp to support the future raids."

"You have taken into account," Andolar immediately threw in, "that this is all supposition based on what you think the enemy commander will do based on the information you think the enemy commander has. And that this is all based on you understanding what a total stranger will do based on a few, small details that we know about him, such as his name, that he plans his raids, and that he reinforced a raiding party."

Petrion looked embarrassed about having come to such a solid conclusion with so few facts. He looked to be trying to come up with some reply when Andolar chimed in again.

"Of course, none of the rest of us knows anything more about this guy than you do, so your guess is as good as any. I also figure it's best to be as prepared as possible. Finally, I side with you because I'm for anything that delays us from going into an area where there will be hundreds of people wanting to kill us. So I shall bid you all good night and retire to my bedroll."

Andolar got down from his horse and started stripping the gear from its back. The rest of them followed Andolar's lead since there didn't seem to be much else to do. Florine was very tired besides. Spell casting, especially to your limit, could leave you as drained as a few rounds of boxing with Berinda.

Soon everyone but Haslan and Petrion were bedded down. The two of them started breaking out some rations. Haslan seemed to be the only member of the squad with an appetite. Petrion was packing some extra food for his journey to the north. The sight of Haslan eating made her stomach growl, so Florine got out of her bedroll and made her way to one of the food packs. Everyone else gradually drifted over as well, and Haslan came back for seconds. As soon as they finished, those not on watch drifted back to their bedrolls.

Haslan began walking a random guard pattern around the camp, and Petrion turned and started walking toward the border with his cloak pulled around him. His leg and side wounds were still causing him problems. It was a mark of how tired Florine was that she hadn't noticed when the rain stopped. She turned over and started thinking about what they could expect from the next day.

CHAPTER 12

Petrion left the camp on foot to avoid the complications of finding a place to hide a horse. It would cost him some speed in an emergency, but probably wouldn't cost him time since he would have to walk almost a mile anyway. Since he would be scouting in his leather under armor, the exertion wouldn't be quite as bad. It would be full dark when he got to the border. The clouds were finally breaking up, so he would have a chance to spot goblins. If he hadn't had the light of the moon, he would have waited till morning to go. As it was, he would need to be very lucky or very good to find goblins at night, unless of course they helped him by moving around and talking a lot. It would help that he knew approximately where the goblin raiders had crossed. Any border guard should be placed in that area.

He was very fortunate that his cloak hadn't been damaged in the fight. Maybe the enchantment strengthened the material of the cloak. He wouldn't scout well at night without it. Of course, if the cloak had been destroyed, he wouldn't be out losing sleep again. He wished there was another ranger available to help. Unfortunately, he was the only one around in trouble.

Oh well, no sense moaning about what might have been. He tried to pick up his pace, but exhaustion soon had him back to a fast walk. His leg and side still ached too. If he sat down tonight, he would be asleep in no time. His mind kept wandering back to his fiancée. He tried to imagine what she was doing now. She could be trying to see him in prison. She could also be engaged to Nacker and setting wedding plans in motion. His mind was able to create many scenarios between those two extremes. The type that seemed to occupy his mind the most was where she grieved for him as if he were dead and tried to get on with her life. He had come close to making his death more than imagination several times during this mission. He had come close several times that day and more were coming. He tried, somewhat successfully, to turn his mind to possible goblin camp attack setups.

He was almost on top of one of the white border stones before he noticed them. The white-painted rocks were strung out in a long straight line along the border. He would bet that the duchess had to pay laborers a goodly salary to get them to freshen the paint each year. If he remembered his history right, this area was where the goblins tried several times during the first year of the treaty to move the boundary. Finally, after being caught and embarrassed a few times, Durp had given up. The treaty had provisions which required the offending party to compensate the other for any violations. He wished he knew how the duchess managed to collect from the goblin king for treaty violations.

East was the direction the crossing point should be, so he started that way. If the goblins were there and quiet, he could search all night and not find them. Not finding goblins wouldn't assure him that there weren't any around. He used an alternating pattern of movement, northeast and southeast, to cover an area about one hundred paces wide. Hopefully, if goblins were watching the border, they would be within that area. The minutes went by without result, and his alertness flagged. It had been too rough a day for him to come out scouting during the night. He had a long walk back to the camp ahead of him after checking the border.

He figured he had covered about a quarter of a mile along the border and probably about three times that much distance walking. At the worst, the goblin crossover point should have been no more than three quarters of a mile from where he started. They sent almost a double-strength attack force against the farm. Did that mean that the commander had plenty of troops to spare, or had he used his remaining two parties of raiders to make the third attack?

There had been a scenario that they had not considered. Two groups could have made all the attacks in an alternating pattern. It worried him that they had completely missed a likely possibility in their planning. They had all gotten sick of talking about possibilities. For a while, he had continued to prod the discussions along but had finally given up when he started thinking there was nothing left to discuss. How many places had they blinded themselves because they had a set idea of the situation? Maybe they could come up with something new if they really thought about it for a while.

He shook his head to clear it. He was focusing too much attention away from looking for goblins again. Stumbling across one would not be the best way in the realm to find them. His legs were worn out, and he stumbled and almost fell over a tree root because he hadn't lifted his foot high enough. He sat down next to the tree and pulled some travel bread and jerky out to chew on. He sat facing the tree and ate under his cloak to keep his body heat concealed. Water helped loosen the bread so he could chew it. The food and the room at the inn in Delaigamon would be great to have right now. He would even put up with Berinda and Andolar together to get back there. He could almost feel that bed.

Petrion got quickly to his feet as he felt himself beginning to nod off. Daydreams about relaxing in a soft bed were an easy way to get taken by sleep. He continued eating while he resumed walking to search for goblins. He stopped periodically where he couldn't be seen and carefully took another bite or drink.

After a half mile along the border, he was wishing he waited till morning to scout.

The whisper of goblin voices came to him unexpectedly and was just as suddenly gone. He had been ready to quit. He caught only snatches of conversation in Goblin, so they were some ways off and talking louder than they should on patrol. They were probably confident in the dark that they could see the enemy long before they could be seen and heard. He was close to the border stones, so he began working his way north. There were only two voices from the goblins so far, so he could attack or hide as he chose. He watched the landmarks closely so he could find the exact spot again in the daylight.

There was no fire, so the goblins were there to watch for the raiders, who would have been returning to the border not too long from now if their raid was successful. Petrion decided he would wait to see the reaction before he returned to his own camp. He moved carefully to avoid making sounds that would give away his presence.

He saw the goblins finally, sitting beside a tree close to the border with as clear a view as possible to the south. There were a half dozen of them. His ideas for options were reduced to find-ing out as much as possible then getting out before they realized he was there. Four of the goblins were awake and patrolling the camp. True to form, the goblins weren't taking their guard duty very seriously. Every time they passed one another, they stopped to talk for a while. Most of the talk centered on the good living conditions at camp and about the new prisoners they were hoping the raiders would take. That surprised Petrion. Everyone had thought the people at the farms killed. No body counts had been taken that he knew of, so Baron Gilbert didn't know that the goblins were taking people prisoner. Goblins many times abused and mutilated the bodies of the humans they killed and generally fired the buildings. People didn't usually bother trying to identify what was left in the building. Some rangers had nightmares about finding bodies after the goblins finished with them. The more time they had to work, the worse the people looked. Prisoners were generally only taken so that the goblins could get more time to work on them. He wondered if they had changed tactics there as well.

He remembered suddenly what the first goblin prisoner told him about humans in the camp. He hadn't thought about a permanent group at the time and hadn't told anyone about that piece of information. It was another place where he had overlooked possibilities. He fumed at himself as he continued to move in.

Petrion closed to within fifteen paces of the goblins and decided to stop. He could hear them clearly from this point, and the odds of him being detected were slight. He stood behind a tree and held his cloak so only one eye was uncovered when he looked out. They would be able to see the heat from his face if they happened to be looking in his direction, but the area of heat would be small enough to pass for a small nocturnal animal. Their discussion centered mostly on food and getting back to camp. They did confirm that there were prisoners in their camp and also that they were not treated well. He almost changed his mind about initiating an attack when he heard some of the stories of abuse they were telling.

He noticed that as the night continued, their conversation was more sporadic and they spent more time looking south. Finally, two of them picked up their gear and headed to the northwest. Petrion flattened himself against the tree as they ran past and then marked their direction in his mind for future use. The remaining goblins woke up the two that were asleep, and then another goblin left at a run for the east. He must be going to warn the next raiding party. That meant the commander hadn't needed to combine two of his raiding groups to make the larger raiding party. Or that there was a relief party stationed nearby to go find out what happened. Or that he just wanted to run in that direction or maybe ten other things. He was still coming to conclusions too quickly.

The remaining goblin that had been awake lay down for his turn at sleep. The other two goblins took guard positions. The first took over the watch to the south. The second goblin stopped where he must just be able to see the first. He would be the runner in case of news. Petrion would have to deal with him in the morning before the squad came within visual range. He eased to the west and started working his way back to the camp. His weariness returned in force as soon as the tension wore off. Maybe they could wait till noon to move out. The thought of his bedroll was enough to get him to jog again for a little while. It was a definite change, when dealing with goblins, for the human to be able to see the goblin best at night.

It took him most of an hour to make his way back to the camp, and he saw Lecik on guard when he arrived. He called to let the archer know he was back and then, without a word, went to his bedroll, which was ready for him. He mentally thanked whoever had set his stuff out. He laid his head on his saddlebag and fumbled for the blankets. He was asleep before he got hold of them. Lecik took time out from his patrol to cover the ranger.

⚜

Andolar made sure he had his spells firmly in his memory and wished he had someplace other than his saddlebags to place his mother's spell books. There were several interesting spells in the books, and he wanted to practice using them. He really needed a set of traveling spell books as well.

His mother's spell books had all the notes, material ingredients, and concentration clues needed by a beginner to learn the spell. A traveling spell book would have the words of the spell with maybe a few notations on trouble spots since the caster already knew all of the other things.

For the coming battle, he would probably use his sleep spell more than the fire dart. In an open battle, he decided he was more likely to want to take down several goblins for a limited time rather than a couple goblins permanently. He wished he were able to use spells from the second level of mastery. If he had practiced instead of drinking himself silly for those years, he would be casting them already. He supposed he should be thankful he retained any of his spell-casting ability. Opening another spell book, he looked over the web spell again and tried to commit it to memory. He could remember the words, but could not invoke the level of power necessary to impart the needed force to the spell. He had gone through these same feelings years before when he was trying to use spells of the first level of mastery. It should come in time if he kept practicing.

Petrion was still asleep. The ranger came in during the night and went to sleep without a word to anyone. Andolar wanted to go over and wake the ranger to find out what was going on. At the same time, he wished the ranger a good long sleep so that they wouldn't have to go. Hopefully, surprise would be on their side this time. Haslan was getting better in the woods, so that would help. It was Haslan who suggested that he wear clothes that would blend well with the woods. The fighters had too much metal about them to conceal, but he could hide if necessary. He was for anything that lowered his chances of being attacked.

He went back to reviewing his sleep spell. There was no sense waking the ranger until all the spell casters had recovered their mental energy. He could feel his energy getting back to full strength. The mental effort to cast spells was, he reflected, similar to physical exertion. Except you learned after a while how much energy a spell took to cast and could then gauge after a fashion how many more were possible.

The fighters and the thief were checking their gear. Andolar felt a stab of jealousy when he saw the thief checking his mother's dagger for nicks. He pulled his gaze away and focused on his spell book. He almost put the book away, but he reminded himself that the least error could be devastating. It was amazing that he hadn't done himself any permanent damage during his drunken years. He suddenly realized that he never wanted to be under the control of alcohol again.

He finished his studying in spite of the noise and activity. Lecik and Berinda were mending and patching the squad's armor and weapons. Petrion's was finished. Lecik put a lot of work into repairing the arrow hole in Florine's armor. Berinda was working with wire, pliers, and spare rings on Korin's chain shirt. Most of the damage to the metal plates in the armor would require the attention of a blacksmith, although the fighters could use the hammer to bang out the worst dents. Berinda wired a small plate onto Korin's chain shirt at the place where the arrow had pierced it and the external plate. It would give some added protection in what would be an obvious weak spot to an opponent. Their gear hadn't been this badly damaged during the battle with the brigands.

The noise finally woke Petrion, and after a quick breakfast, he outlined what he had seen. His plan for dealing with the border guards was to circle out on foot to pick up the one in the back while the squad moved forward toward the close guard. Petrion would also keep an eye on the other two goblins to make sure they didn't escape. He figured they would either run, in which case the fighters on horse could run them down. Or they would hide, in which case the squad would get close to where they were and attack. They were all hoping that having a magician along would keep them from trying arrows. He hated being the blasted target for everyone all the time. It was almost enough to make him put on armor and pretend to be a fighter, except he couldn't move in armor.

Andolar envied healers' ability to use armor and heavy weapons. Casting his form of magic took too much study to allow work with armor and weapons. Armor was a hindrance to concentration, and spell ingredients would be harder to get at. Fine targeting control also suffered because of armor getting in the way of free movement.

Healer magic, according to the lectures given by his former teacher, drew partly on the resources of the patient's body unlike his magic. Healers didn't have to worry about targeting either because they touched the recipient. Both types of magic were physically and mentally exhausting.

Lecik nudging him in the ribs brought him out of his thoughts and back to the business of getting ready to leave. Petrion had apparently been discussing possible attack and defense patterns on the goblin base camp. Why he needed to listen to that, he had no idea. He carefully schooled his features though to reflect interest in what Petrion was saying.

"We will leave here as soon as everything is ready to go," Petrion said. "From the looks of things, that will be almost immediately. Haslan, do you have the sleeping powder Andolar procured for us?"

"Yes, I have a large pouch stored with my gear," Haslan replied. "I also have a couple more pouches in my saddlebags. I have more room since my clothes don't take up space like yours do."

"All right," Petrion continued, "I'll take the rest. We will use some of the places we have been as regrouping spots in case we have to run for it. The first spot where we should try to regroup is the border crossing. Don't wait there more than a few minutes. It's too close to the enemy. If you're closely pursued or need to move on from the border, come to this grove. Ride on rocks, streams, or sand whenever possible, so the enemy can't follow you. If some of us don't arrive here within a day, then go to the Golden Badger in Delaigamon."

"What happens if someone goes down or gets captured?" Korin asked.

"If you can't get to them without being captured yourself," Haslan answered, "then keep going. You aren't going to do anyone any good if you get caught too. If goblins are pursuing you, then you keep running."

"That's the way you have to work it," Petrion added. "We will keep our horses some distance from the goblin camp. If we are forced to run, get to the horses. If you get to the horses, then take them all if you are pursued. They won't do the ones left behind any good, and we don't want to give them to the goblins. If you get cut off from the horses, then try not to head directly south. That is the direction they will expect you to go, and you will likely be caught before you can cross the border. Can anyone think of anything else?"

"Everyone make sure you have enough supplies in your pack to last for a couple of days in an emergency," Lecik said.

"Good idea," Petrion told him. "Keep a little food and water with you when we attack the camp. Everyone check your saddlebags to make sure you have everything you need to get by for a while in there as well."

"Sorry, I can't," Andolar said. When he had everyone's attention, he continued. "There's no way I can fit a couple hundred soldiers into this saddlebag."

A couple people chuckled, and everyone went back to checking their goods. Andolar, Haslan, and Florine went to the food packs for extra provisions. Lecik grabbed a couple quivers of arrows to tie behind his saddle. Haslan stored away a couple daggers. Andolar grabbed a bag of sleeping powder after he picked up his extra food. Finally everyone was ready, and they mounted their horses and headed for goblin territory.

Petrion set an easy pace for the trip, and Andolar saw Berinda fidgeting at the front of the party beside him.

"Why are we going so slow?" she asked at last. "We want to get there before winter sets in, you know."

"We have to conserve our horses now," he answered calmly, "in case we need them for speed later."

Silence prevailed again after that. When they were about a half mile from the border, Petrion dismounted and went ahead on foot. He was wearing his chain shirt this time, so he would have to be careful about noise. Petrion called for Haslan to come to the front of the squad.

"I think I should lead since we are going into combat," he heard Berinda tell Petrion.

"I think we may be going into an ambush," Petrion replied, "so I think Haslan should have the job since he detected the last ambush."

She conceded with poor grace, big surprise, and took her place alongside the thief. Petrion started jogging northeast. Haslan gave him a ten-minute start before following. He maintained the pace Petrion set, and soon they came within sight of the white border stones. Petrion was sitting on a log and waved to them as they approached. Haslan kicked the horses into a trot and pointed the squad at Petrion.

Before they reached the ranger, they saw three goblin bodies on the ground. Petrion had them on the human side of the border in a small gully where they wouldn't be visible from the goblin side.

"They were in the same formation as before," Petrion told them as he mounted his horse. "The one by the border never looked back to see if the back goblin was still there. I killed the one in the back and then moved up and finished off this one.

The goblin that was asleep woke up but didn't make it out of his blankets."

Andolar heaved a sigh of relief because he avoided being a target for a while longer. Petrion heard the sigh and smiled at him. Berinda looked upset that she hadn't been able to take part in the killing. Petrion smiled at her too.

"I think you'll have ample opportunity to show off your abilities soon," Petrion told Berinda.

She just huffed and turned her head. That widened Petrion's smile even more.

Petrion started them off again, this time to the northwest.

As soon as they crossed the border, there was a change in the forest. There were many more trees, and the visibility was a lot less. There also wasn't as much grass, but ferns and briars were common. They had to be careful of the legs of the horses. Many of the trees were giants hundreds of years old. A thick carpet of old leaves on the ground muffled the steps of the horses.

According to the first goblins, the base camp was that direction. Petrion rode in front about a hundred paces and looked to be following tracks on the ground. Andolar hadn't seen anything remotely resembling a track until they came to a muddy spot where a few goblin prints were visible. Petrion didn't seem to be having any trouble though. He could follow the trail at a trot on his horse. Their basic plan was to close the distance to the goblin camp, hopefully avoiding any goblin patrols. When they got close, Petrion would dismount and use his cloak as he led them the rest of the way in.

When he sighted the camp, he would signal the squad to stop and survey the situation on foot. The ranger would then report back, and they would make the final assault plans. Or flee if the odds were too great.

Andolar wasn't sure whether he wanted there to be a small group because of the limited danger or if he wanted a large group so he wouldn't be involved in another battle. The worst scenario was a medium group that they thought they could take. A glass or two of wine would go very well now. He was thinking that just about any wine would go good with fear. The woods were remarkably noisy. Birds occasionally flew up, and squirrels scampered around in the trees. They passed a few clearings where grass was growing in the midst of the woods. Petrion always scouted them in advance in case they were home to goblins. So far they hadn't seen any goblin houses.

After one such clearing, Andolar looked to the front of the party and saw Petrion's horse with no sign of Petrion. He must think they were closing on the camp. They had been traveling for many hours now and at a rapid pace. It was getting late in the afternoon.

Andolar felt the now-familiar boiling of fear in his stomach. He could have avoided all this if he hadn't become a drunk and gotten himself thrown out by his father. Then again, knowing his father, maybe he couldn't have.

He searched the area carefully and tied the lead rope of the packhorses to the pommel of his saddle so his hands were free. He put his leg over the rope so the rope couldn't hold him in the saddle. He saw the other squad members making sure their weapons were loose and ready to grab on short notice. He added Petrion's horse to the string of packhorses when they reached it. Haslan continued moving forward.

Andolar noticed small marks in some of the trees and realized Petrion was marking his route for the thief to follow. That comforted Andolar to know that the best goblin killer among them was going to be around when the battle started. Petrion would have discovered that ambush set against them the day before.

The day before. It seemed more like a week since the last battle. It was amazing what your nerves could do to your sense of time. With Petrion traveling the trail ahead of them, they didn't need to worry about ambushes. Well, it helped him a little at least to think of it that way. You had to take what victories you could, no matter how small.

When Petrion suddenly appeared at the front of the squad, everyone almost attacked him. Petrion seemed to take it all in stride and closed the remaining distance without comment.

"Have you found the camp?" Haslan asked.

"I believe so," Petrion answered. "The tracks of the goblins I was following continue to the northwest, but it looks like there is a clearing in the woods more to the north of here. I could see smoke rising when I got a little closer."

"Are we going to attack?" Korin asked with a mixture of fear and anticipation.

"I don't know yet," Petrion replied. "I need to check out the situation. What I want you to do is move slowly to the north. Try and find a good spot to conceal the horses and wait for me. Don't get too close to the clearing. I'll go scout the camp and meet back with you. Make sure you post guards so you won't be surprised. It's about four hours after noon now. Get yourselves something to eat. I should be back within an hour. That will still give us plenty of time to attack in the daylight."

The ranger swirled his cloak around himself and faded into the woods again. Andolar saw Haslan trying to follow the ranger's progress for a while before he gave up and led the squad north. They moved slowly to keep the noise down. At least they didn't have to worry about raising a dust cloud after all of the rain. He looked back and saw Lecik watching the rear. They had left an easy trail for the goblins to follow, but goblins on foot couldn't catch them.

They still hadn't found a good hiding place for the horses when they saw an area to the west that looked a little lighter. Figuring it might be the clearing, Haslan started working his way back east to find a suitable spot. He was beginning to think they would never find something when they came to an uprooted giant of a tree.

They took the horses to where the roots had pulled a massive section of dirt out of the ground. They dragged some of the broken limbs over for additional concealment and to form a crude corral for the horses. There was a small amount of grass where the sun could now reach the ground, and the horses made the most of it. Haslan told them to give all of the horses some of their packed grain. That might give them some extra energy for a run.

"Looks like we're about a tenth of a mile from the goblin camp," Lecik said, looking toward the clearing. "We have a reasonable field of view here, so we should be able to see anyone from the camp coming before they could get close enough to hurt us."

"A tenth of a mile is a long way to run if they outmatch us in battle," Andolar said with a touch of panic.

"Andolar," Haslan said, trying to sooth him, "we aren't going to attack if we think they can overwhelm us. Besides, if we have to run, you and I will probably have a head start on the others since we stay in the back."

Lecik didn't look too happy about that pronouncement, but Berinda acted as if she didn't care. She was probably ready to take on the whole bunch by herself just to show everyone how good she was. They only loosened the saddles on the horses so they could get out quickly at need. They would tighten the saddles before they left on the raid, just in case.

Haslan was already breaking out some food. Andolar and the others joined him in some cold trail rations. All of the good food was gone. They had plenty of trail rations. He had three days' rations in his saddlebags and another in his belt pouch. He had a water skin over his shoulder, although the chances of coming up short on water now were slim.

"Hello, the camp," Petrion called in softly, "I'm coming in and don't want to get killed doing it."

"Come on in," Haslan said quietly, "we're just having something to eat."

Petrion had a hard look on his face when he entered the camp. Everyone seemed as taken back as he was by the expression on the ranger's face.

"Are we that badly outnumbered?" Korin asked.

"What," Petrion growled, "oh, no. We should be able to defeat them with a little bit of surprise. I don't think there are more than forty of them in the camp."

He spit on the ground like he was trying to clear a bad taste out of his mouth.

"What's the matter Petrion?" Korin asked him.

"Korin," Petrion said after a slight pause, "goblins are filthy creatures that have no business being alive. What they do to people they attack is nothing compared to what they do to prisoners they take. Men, women, and children are treated exactly alike when it comes to labor. I didn't see a one of them that didn't have lash marks on their backs. They all looked like they were starving as well. They hardly have any clothes left at all between the lash and the labor. I never saw people before who looked like walking dead. The women were the worst. They cringed and cried every time one of those filthy goblins came by. I saw one dragged by her hair screaming into what must be the goblin's barracks. Her screams went on for a long time, and the goblins guarding the prisoners laughed at them. A clean death from a sword is too good for vermin like that, but it's what they're going to get right now."

He pulled his sword out and swished it through the air a couple of times.

"What does the camp look like?" Haslan asked. "How do you want to go about taking it?"

"Everyone come here," Petrion told them as he cleared a spot on the ground.

He grabbed a few rocks and sticks to use to model the goblin camp.

"On the southern side of the camp," he began while placing the objects, "is the goblin barracks and the commander's shack. Right here, across from the goblin barracks is the slave pens. There is a small horse corral with a single horse beside the shack and what looks like some kind of covered cellar a little to the north of the shack. The slaves are all out working. There are cook fires in the center of the camp tended by some of the women prisoners. It looks like they are about ready for a meal. On the west side of the camp are the sheep and cattle pens. The cattle are grazing north and west of the camp and the sheep east. The northeast part of the camp is a garden tended by the slaves, mostly the boys. There are guards placed all around the area, but the heaviest concentration is to the south. There are four guards on the south, one each on the east and west and two to the north. There are also two guards in front of the commander's shack. Guards are also stationed with the prisoners. Three are with the cattle, two with the sheep, and two watching the people in the garden. There is also a sentry post in a tree farther south that houses a lookout. I didn't see him until I was on the way back. I think I can point him out to Lecik, and he can make sure he doesn't give us any trouble. The guards in the south are within sight of each other, so as soon as we attack one, the alarm will be given."

He gave them all a chance to look over the setup and think about the strategy for taking the camp. Andolar didn't have any ideas.

"Are they likely to kill the prisoners as soon as they are attacked to keep them from fighting?" Andolar asked.

"I have no idea," Petrion answered. "It's a possibility. On the other hand, they went to a lot of trouble to bring them here. It could be that the slaves are valuable to them."

"Is there any place where we can pick off a guard without the others seeing?" Haslan asked.

"Not that I could tell," Petrion answered. "It seems their commander has tried not to have any weaknesses in his defensive formation."

"Could you slip into the camp and put Andolar's sleeping powder into the food pots?" Korin suggested.

"It's possible, but I think the meal will be over by the time I could get back," Petrion replied. "We would have to wait till breakfast time tomorrow to try it."

"We shouldn't sit here any longer than we have to," Haslan added. "One of their patrols could find our tracks."

"What did you have in mind, Petrion?" Berinda asked with a trace of animosity. "You've seen the camp. Surely you have a plan you're just waiting to tell us."

"What I thought we might try," Petrion said, ignoring Berinda's sarcastic tones, "is to have Lecik take out their far sentry. He might go down without the others noticing. If he falls from the tree—or if Lecik misses—they will notice, and the battle will be on. Haslan can work his way northeast to the side of the camp and try to take out a guard or two there. I will go to the easternmost of the southern guards and take him out when the rest of you start in. With luck, we can take out several of them by surprise."

"You placed eighteen guards," Andolar said. "What makes you think there aren't a whole lot more in the barracks?"

"The barracks looks to hold about forty goblins," Petrion told him. "If they rotate through the beds, then half again as many could be in the camp. I figured they had about half of their total number on guard though, rather than a third."

"Another big assumption?" Andolar said with a raised eyebrow. "What happens if there are sixty instead of forty?"

"We take them out and rescue the prisoners," Petrion replied vehemently. "No one deserves to be in a situation like that."

"That's too great of odds," Haslan said with concern. "We are hard-pressed to deal with twenty or twenty-five of them in a straight-up battle. Forty is likely beyond our ability. Sixty will be deadly, surprise or not. You're talking about odds of nine to one."

"I have an idea we could try," Korin said timidly.

"What is it, Korin?" Petrion said encouragingly.

"How many doors and large windows are there in the goblin's barracks?" Korin asked.

"Only one door," Petrion answered. "There are small windows with firing crosses on them all around the building. The building also has a parapet."

"So they have a fortified stronghold to defend," Andolar said. "And you want us to attack it while they have the strong point."

"Can you get on the roof, Petrion?" Korin asked. "And are the windows big enough for a goblin to get out of?"

"Yes and no," Petrion answered. "There is a wood pile next to the building that would provide easy access to the roof. The windows look like they were made to keep people from being able to use them to enter the building. Now what do you have in mind?"

"Well," Korin said, "here's what I thought we could do. The raid can go off as planned except for your part. Why don't you take all of our oil flasks and use them on the barracks? You can pour some out by the doorway. That will trap the goblins inside. You can also throw some down from the roof to get the inside burning. You'll have to light them quickly to keep goblins from using the door as an escape route."

Petrion jumped up and gave Korin a big hug.

"What an idea!" he said. "They haven't prepared for a surprise attack from within their camp. If I can keep the barracks from emptying, then we only face about twenty goblins. We can take twenty goblins any day of the week. Florine, go get the oil flasks. I'll use some to soak the doorway and the roof. Then I'll fix the others to light and throw into the building. Lecik will hit the goblin in the tree once the fire has distracted them and then move to the sentries with Florine. Berinda and Korin can go with them and fight with them or on their own. I'll try to join Haslan on the east side of the camp once the barracks is burning good. Andolar, you stay with Haslan and sneak in on the east. That way, you can support whoever needs you the most."

Florine handed Petrion the pack full of oil flasks. They wouldn't be having a lamp at night, not that they had used them that much anyway. Petrion and Haslan took several of the flasks and traded the stopper for a torn piece of cloth. After it was repacked, Petrion slung the pack on his back and made sure his cloak still closed in the front. He also made sure he had flint, steel, and tinder.

"Well, if there's nothing else, let's go," he told them. "The sooner those vermin are dead and the people free, the better."

Everyone grabbed what they needed and climbed over the limbs that held the horses. Petrion led them toward the goblin camp. When they were three hundred paces from the camp, Petrion stopped them and took Lecik on ahead. Petrion kept his cloak closed, so Lecik had trouble following him. When they had gone a ways, Andolar saw Petrion appear and point out a tree to the archer. Lecik nodded and moved carefully to a concealed position where he could shoot at the goblin. Petrion worked his way back and then dispersed the squad to their individual assignments. Florine, Korin, and Berinda moved only a little ways forward, keeping low. Andolar realized that if an alarm was sounded before Petrion had a chance to light the barracks, they would be running. Haslan led him to the east side of the camp, moving from tree to tree, until they lost sight of everyone. Petrion went directly to the camp.

They kept out of sight of the guard posts. They had a long way to go before the battle started. Haslan slowed as they got closer. He only moved when all the guards were turned away and moved only to the next tree. He finally had Andolar stop when they were about a hundred paces from the camp and seventy-five from the guards. Haslan continued moving forward until he was only about thirty paces from the guard, and concealed by some low bushes. By staying low and having on clothes that blended into his surroundings, Andolar hoped to remain unnoticed. He could see the sheep grazing in the open area just ahead of him. Two goblins were standing guard over the three prisoners who were watching the sheep. Andolar couldn't see much from this distance, but the prisoners were moving very slowly. He wondered how Petrion was doing.

CHAPTER 13

Petrion hurried toward the goblin camp. He wanted to attack quickly in case there were more in the barracks than he thought. He used the widest gap between guards to cross. It was lucky for him that the ground was still wet from the rains. Otherwise, he would have been raising a dust cloud. This way, he just had to watch for really wet spots where he might squish loudly. He also had to be very careful of his armor to keep it quiet.

When he finally got into the camp, the ladies were no longer tending the food but were cleaning up after the meal. Petrion saw them scraping every bit of food they could into bowls, probably for the prisoners. From this distance he could see the bruises and cuts covering their bodies. A goblin walking from the commander's shack to the barracks went out of his way to kick the bowl out of one lady's hands. He laughed as he watched the woman scrambling for the scraps on the ground. He waited until she was almost finished and then knocked the bowl out of her hands again. It was all Petrion could do to hold in his temper as the goblin went laughing into the barracks. He hoped the goblins were slowly roasted to death rather than killed by the smoke. Even that would be an easier death than they deserved.

Petrion made it across the camp to the woodpile without any of the guards noticing that he passed. He climbed carefully onto the roof. The roof had only a slight slope to the back of the building and was made of planks.

The ranger opened his cloak enough to get his shield out below the level of the parapet. He sat the shield on the roof and put his pack on top of it. Petrion scanned the area quickly, but no one noticed the movement. When he felt safe as much as possible, he stood up again.

He carefully made his way across the roof toward the door, easing from one position to the next. There was a lot of loud chatter coming from the building. A pair of women went inside, and Petrion was forced to listen to the vulgar comments of the goblin soldiers.

There was a door from inside the barracks to the roof that was shut. He expected that but reminded himself to keep an eye on it.

As Petrion walked across the roof, he tried to place his feet where the rafters would be. The roof still squeaked several times on his walk, and each time, it sounded like an alarm going off in his ears, but no one came to investigate. He stopped above the front door and waited until the women left, taking piles of bowls with them.

Looking at the parapet over the door, he could have hugged the builder even if it was a goblin. There were two murder holes cut into the bottom of the parapet, so that defenders on the roof could attack anyone trying to force the door. The women even had the courtesy to shut the door. He kept waiting for something to go wrong. So far, everything was working perfectly.

He had twelve flasks of lamp oil and another ten with wicks to throw. He opened six of the regular flasks and started their contents pouring down the side of the building next to and over the door. He decided to light off the front door before oiling the trapdoor in the roof. He struck his flint and steel as quietly as he could and soon had the tinder glowing. When he had it burning, he lit the wicks on the ten breakable flasks. He suddenly realized that all the remaining flasks were sitting above the doorway where the flames might hit them. With a heavy swallow for a disaster avoided, he moved the flasks three feet from the edge. Then with a smile for what the goblins inside were about to suffer, he threw the first of the lighted flasks onto the step and stepped backwards.

The flask burst and lit off the whole oil-soaked wall. The flames were shooting up five or six feet above the roof, and Petrion had to move back further from the edge. He took four oil flasks along with one of the lit ones to the trapdoor. He heard cries of alarm below, and smoke was starting to rise with the flames. He dumped the four flasks on the trapdoor. Dropping back about five feet, he waited until he saw the trapdoor start to move before he threw the lighted flask. That section of the roof went up in flames and, from the cries below, some of the goblins as well. The trapdoor dropped shut.

He hurried back across the roof, not caring about the noise now, and picked up two of the lit flasks. An arrow flew past his head, and he flattened himself on the roof as a couple more flew past. He had become so involved in burning the building that he forgot to stay hidden. Now they knew where their enemy was. He wondered if they would wait for him to come down or come up after him. The fire at the front was dying down. The logs were still too wet to burn well, but the door was burning. They should try to open the door soon.

No sooner had the thought crossed his mind than the door swung open. When it did, he sent two flaming missiles through the door to shatter on the floor inside.

Murder holes. He liked that name. The flasks splattered more goblins inside the barracks. The wood floor and furnishing would burn very well. He laid down on the roof and slung a lighted flask deep into the barracks. A couple of arrows were shot, but his arm was already out of the way. He tipped two flasks over by the murder holes and let the oil add to the flames below.

With five flasks left, he crawled to the trapdoor and used his sword to flip it open. The ladder was burning and some nearby bunk beds. He got choked on the smoke but still managed to throw two more flasks into different areas of the building to increase the conflagration. Three flasks left. The goblins would be getting desperate.

He crawled back to the door and threw a flask down to break just inside the doorway. Flames filled the doorway again, and he heard cries of panic. One goblin came running through the flames with his clothes and hair on fire. Two of his fellows got him knocked down and the fire put out, but by that time, he was no longer moving. He saw smoke pouring through the roof in several places, including where he was crawling. He started coughing again. It wouldn't be long till he would have to leave or join the goblins in their fate. He couldn't see what was going on around him. It was just as well, because if he could see them, then they could see and shoot him. The front of the building was totally engulfed in flames. His fingers were burned as some of the flames came up through the roof. He backed up quickly to get closer to the trapdoor and away from the flames. He heard the sounds of goblins banging on the windows, trying to fight their way free. He also heard the sound of furniture being moved. Smoke was rising through much of the roof around the door area. He wondered how the internal support beams were run. If one of the main beams burned enough to break, then he would be roasting in seconds.

He decided it was time to cause a last bit of trouble and leave. He waited until the flaming furniture had been moved and other things stacked under the trapdoor before throwing a flask on the stack. He flipped the burning trapdoor closed with his sword and threw the last flask on top of it. Now all he had to do was get off the roof before it caved in. He wrapped his cloak around himself and slowly stood up. He could see a battle raging between his squad and the surviving goblins and the human commander. Old Churinius was going to taste some steel before this day was over, and Petrion was sure it was going to be bad for his digestion. He was worse than the goblins. He hadn't been brought up in a society that idolized cruelty like the goblins had. He had seen a better way of life and rejected it.

All of this thinking wasn't getting him off the roof. The screams from inside the barracks had stopped finally, a sure sign that the roof was an extremely bad place to be. The goblins were focusing on his squad, so he went to where he left his shield, grabbed it and his pack, and climbed down the woodpile to the ground. It was time to give Churinius his late supper.

⚜

Haslan watched the barracks building, until suddenly the front door burst into flames. The sound caused the guards to turn. The guard closest to the barracks died watching the flames with a dagger and sword in his back. He really liked that dagger of Andolar's. The enchantment allowed it to penetrate armor easily.

Cries of alarm immediately sounded, and he dodged quickly behind a tree as an arrow cut through the air where he had been. One of the guards by the sheep had seen him. The guard to the southeast of the camp was busy trying to keep Florine from caving in his head with her morning star. Haslan hurried toward Florine and away from the goblins that knew where he was. Hopefully, Andolar would remain under cover until he was not in danger of having to fight. A second goblin joined the one attacking Florine, but two quick arrows stopped him. Lecik was good with that bow. He must have gotten the one in the tree if he was moving on to other targets. The other goblins from the camp were converging on the shack of the commander, who came out to take charge of the battle. He was wearing plate mail and using a hand-and-a-half sword.

Haslan went past the burning barracks and saw Berinda and Korin joining Florine. He was getting ready to plant a dagger in the goblin on her when her morning star crushed his right shoulder. The goblin flew to the side, unconscious before he hit the ground.

He saw one dead goblin on the side where Berinda had come from. He decided to go the other way and see if he could come up behind some. He still didn't see Andolar. Haslan wandered if the magician would stay out of the fight entirely. The best thing Andolar could do was to prevent goblins from escaping. Haslan would be in a similar position soon. Three goblin archers were covering the roof of the barracks, which was now almost totally in flames. Haslan saw an oil flask explode in the doorway as he worked his way to the garden fence. A goblin came running through the front door with his clothes on fire. He tried rolling on the ground but was unable to get them out.

The slaves were standing around, staring stupidly at the flames and the battle going on around them. He saw Andolar then. The magician was starting the people moving toward the south with the flock of sheep. Haslan thought it was silly to saddle themselves with the sheep, but then he decided the sheep could probably move faster than those poor people. He saw close up what Petrion had been talking about when he chanced upon a woman's body beside a half-dug grave. There were several graves at the edge of the garden already. The people with the sheep were moving now. One went to get a sack and grab what he could of the produce in the garden, while the second started the sheep to the southeast. The people in the garden saw what was going on and started grabbing food as well. It quickly spread to all of the slaves. Those with the cattle and those cleaning dishes joined the exodus.

Haslan put a dagger into one of the goblins by the barracks because he tried to cut off the people's escape. The other two had gone to the commander, who was calling something out to the goblins. If he was going to stay in this part of the country, he was going to have to learn to speak Goblin. Petrion taught him a couple dozen or so words that he could use to help him hide among them. Most of them were threats. The goblin he skewered with a knife was moving to attack him. His next two throws were misses. At least this goblin didn't have a shield. That made the battle a little easier. It also helped that his only weapon other than the bow was a dagger. Haslan actually had an advantage of reach over someone.

Andolar came running up with dagger drawn and distracted the goblin long enough for Haslan to insert his short sword between his ribs. The goblin had naturally assumed the human was the greater threat. It was helpful sometimes being a halfman. Andolar smiled at him.

"At least I'm getting good at being a decoy."

"Right you are," Haslan replied. "Just don't get in a situation where you have to follow through with your bluff."

Andolar drifted to the west, and Haslan made his way past the burning barracks to the commander's shack. The burning goblin had finally died near another one.

The battle in the front was finally joined. Berinda, Lecik, and Florine formed a triangle with Korin in the center. The goblin commander was standing back watching the show and, from the look of him, trying to decide whether to run or not. Haslan suddenly saw Petrion fade into view behind the man and deliver a massive overhand swing. The commander must have heard footsteps or been warned by instinct. The stroke that was aimed for his head hit his shield shoulder instead, slicing through the heavy armor and into flesh. The four remaining archers turned on the ranger but fell to the ground asleep before they could shoot. Andolar hurried over to make sure they would never wake up.

Berinda finished off two of the goblins in front of her. One of the blows had come from that nasty overhand swing she used to drive an opponent's sword into their own body. That enchanted headband really increased her strength. Lecik had finished off another of the goblins, but Florine was totally defensive against two and taking hits. Korin was doing his best to keep her in the fight. Haslan had already seen him use two of his healing spells. Things were in the favor of the squad now though. Petrion was one on one with the commander and managing to stay alive. He wasn't really on the offensive though, even though the man no longer had the use of his shield arm. Berinda, down to two opponents, finished one and then quickly killed the second with an overhand swing that sheared off his arm. Korin came out, and the goblins were fighting one on one. Berinda's strength allowed her to thrust through the goblins shield and into his stomach. Her sword stuck in the goblin and the shield, and she took a couple of seconds freeing it.

Petrion was fighting a defensive battle. His enemy would continue to weaken, so all the ranger had to do was keep him fighting. The man was good with a sword though, so Petrion had his work cut out for him. Haslan used the opportunity to slip behind Churinius and drive an enchanted dagger into his back. Churinius screamed in pain at the thrust. The dagger made easy work of the armor, and Haslan left it there to work around in the wound.

Petrion used the distraction to swing at his leg hard enough to cut through the greave. He immediately went back on the defensive. Churinius was losing blood from two major wounds now and wouldn't last much longer. Time was on Petrion's side, and he was working to hang on. Lecik and Berinda killed another goblin each at about the same time, and the fourth quickly died as he tried to run. The squad moved to surround Churinius, but the fighter collapsed from loss of blood before they arrived.

Petrion walked over to give Korin a slap on the back.

"That was an excellent plan, I would say," Petrion told him.

Lecik and Andolar cheered the healer, and Haslan decided to join in as well. They had destroyed the goblin base camp with the odds substantially against them. Haslan looked in the distance and could still see the prisoners moving south. He hoped they split the herds and scattered so the goblins couldn't pick them all up at once.

"How are we fixed for spells?" Petrion asked.

"I only used a single sleep spell," Andolar said.

"I appreciate the timing on that," Petrion told him with a smile.

"I used two," Korin said, "and Florine used none."

"Excellent," Petrion said. "We are in almost top condition for the trek home. If we ride through the night, we should be across the border by morning. We really should try and take care of the prisoners. I think we should follow them. At the speed they can manage, it will probably take till tomorrow evening or a little more to get back to safe territory. If they run into a patrol, they won't have a chance."

"Thanks, Petrion," Korin said. "I hoped we would do that. Those poor people need every bit of time they can get."

"Haslan," Petrion called, "start checking around for anything we might be able to use. I think we'll take this guy's armor and see if it can't be modified to fit either Lecik or myself. Plate mail is hard to come by and dear to purchase. We'll load everything onto Churinius's horse to take back to where our horses are waiting. Let's hurry. I have no idea where the nearest goblin patrol is, but the smoke from that barracks will be visible for several miles."

Haslan found some papers and a book in some strange language in the shack. There was also a small coffer with a little silver and gold. They found ten silvers on the goblins that hadn't been caught in the fire. The roof on the barracks crashed down while they were working. Haslan took the papers and the book to Petrion and to Andolar, but neither could read the language. Petrion told him to store the documents along with the rest of their items on the back of the horse. The plate mail had a gash in the shoulder and a puncture in the back but was still in reasonably good condition. It could probably be modified for Petrion or Lecik. It could also be sold to someone, and they could split the profits. The fighters would never agree to that. It was hard telling when they might find another. If it should be enchanted, that would definitely be the end of any thoughts of selling it. The plate mail would add to the load for the horse, but it should be used to carrying the rider and the armor. Haslan gave the bag with the silver and gold coins to Lecik so he could tie them to the saddle. Petrion also decided to take along Churinius's sword and dagger on the chance one of them might be enchanted.

The proceeds from this attack were not what Haslan expected. The goblins must have been allowed to keep and then spend all the money and valuables they looted from the farms. The livestock was being held to feed them, so they hadn't been able to make a profit on that either. It was an unusual situation for a bandit leader or for a mercenary captain. They generally demanded and got a much larger share of the treasure. The goblins had hit a large number of farms, and the goods should have been worth a lot. The goblin king must have taken most of the valuables from the raids. That was not an unusual situation at all.

Maybe they should talk to those farmers about keeping some of the livestock as a finder's fee. After all, they were the ones who liberated it. Korin and Petrion would never agree to that. Andolar probably didn't care enough about it to make it an issue. Florine would side with her brother. He didn't know which side Berinda would come down on, but he was already badly outnumbered. Oh well, better luck next time.

Korin was headed out to the garden, probably to see if there was anything worth taking along for food, while the others were looting the bodies. He evidently found some things he liked because he started filling a bag. The farmers were long out of sight when they finally had everything packed and ready to go. The barracks was sending a dark cloud of smoke into the air, and everyone within a few miles would know something had happened. Haslan had lost one of his daggers and decided that while everyone else was occupied, he would look for it again. It wasn't the enchanted dagger, thank goodness. Baron Gardoney and Andolar would be after him if he lost that. He found the dagger finally. It was stuck in the cloak of a goblin. He slid the dagger into his boot and started back for the squad. Petrion and Lecik were still fiddling with the armor, so he decided there was time for a closer look at the commander's shack. He checked carefully for loose boards, hollow posts on the bed, and anything else he could think of as a possible hiding place. He even got a stool and tried the ceiling of the shack, thinking Churinius might have hid the treasure high since he was living with short people. No luck at all.

"Haslan," Petrion called, "we're ready to go."

"Be right there," Haslan called back.

"Andolar," Petrion yelled, "we're ready to go. Hurry up or we'll leave you for the goblins."

"I'm coming," Andolar yelled back. "You wasted a half hour and yell at me for half a minute."

Haslan chuckled at the exchange and took a last quick look around as he made his way out of the shack. He felt he was missing something obvious here. It was like an itch he couldn't scratch. He finally gave up and went outside to where the squad was waiting with the loaded horse. Andolar was making his way across the compound from the garden.

Haslan saw movement out of the corner of his eye, and when he turned, he saw a goblin attack force bearing down on them with a human in plate mail leading. The commander's shack blocked the view of most of the squad members, and Andolar wasn't paying any attention. No, this wasn't the commander's shack!

"Run! This isn't the camp of the raiders. The raiders are coming from over there," he screamed pointing to the west.

He saw Andolar gaping in astonishment at the sight of a horde of goblins coming at a run. Or maybe it was at the figure in the polished armor leading the goblins.

"Run!" Haslan yelled again.

The man on the horse left the goblins and charged toward the squad. He was riding a fully armored warhorse. The horse and man both towered over the goblins.

Haslan finally realized what was wrong with the goblin camp. The money had been the first clue, but it hadn't been enough to bring what was wrong to his mind. The barracks was the giveaway, or at least it would have been if he were thinking. There was no way it could have housed the goblins they found here as well as the raiders they had killed. This place must be a supply dump for the main camp, placed here because there was grazing for the livestock. Or maybe just to spread things out in case of attack. The real goblin raiders were coming now to wipe them out.

CHAPTER 14

Andolar looked up in horror at the approaching mass of goblins. The armored man on the warhorse looked even more dangerous. He was charging directly toward the squad. Petrion swirled his cloak around himself and faded from view. The healers started toward the horses at a run. Korin already had his hand on the bridle of the commander's horse and kept hold, taking the horse with him.

"Everyone run," he heard Petrion's voice calling.

"Grab the saddle," Lecik called to the healers, "and get the horse running. He'll pull you along."

Korin caught the pommel and yelled to get the horse started.

"Grab on, Florine," Korin yelled as the horse started to pull him.

She grabbed the pommel from the other side and was almost jerked off her feet as the horse started trotting. The horse was very large, and they were having trouble hanging on and keeping their feet out from under its hooves. It looked like they were taking ten-foot leaps with the horse running between them. Lecik and Berinda were following as best they could on foot. Lecik was stopping every few steps to turn and release an arrow. So far, none of the arrows were effective against the armored man. Two arrows were in the man's shield. Andolar wondered who the man was. Maybe, from what Haslan yelled out, he was the real Churinius. Andolar wanted to use a fire dart on the man but decided against it. He really couldn't do much more than injure the man slightly, and that wasn't worth giving away his position to do.

He was too far away to catch up with the squad members, so he decided to go east. The goblins hadn't seen him yet. His clothes would easily blend into the background at this distance, while the armor of the fighters showed up clearly in the late sun. He dropped low and hurried as best he could toward the northeast and the garden. The tall corn plants in the garden should hide him from view till he could reach the safety of the woods. Working his way across the garden was torturous as he tried to hurry while disturbing the plants as little as possible.

When he reached the far side, he broke into a bent over run. He reached the trees, found a large one, and slid behind it. He peeked out just enough to see. He was fifty paces from the clearing. The goblins soon came in view. They were running full out to the southeast chasing the squad. He breathed a muted sigh of relief that he had apparently escaped their notice.

He settled down to wait until it was clear. He had to get away from the goblins before nightfall, or he would be plainly visible to them. He wished there was rain coming down again to hide his heat. The goblins would surely search the area around the camp. The safest way he could go would probably be the way the goblins came from. He didn't want to move further from his group, but he couldn't think of a decent alternative. When the last goblin disappeared from view, he waited a few moments and eased out of the trees.

He crossed the open area again and reached the garden without incident. Then he saw a goblin straggler moving among the bodies and ducked quickly into the plants. The goblin saw him and motioned for him to come. He must be nuts. Andolar readied his fire-dart spell. The sleep spell would be a surer take down, but it was slower, and he didn't want an outcry. The stupid goblin was waving a dagger in the air even though he was far out of range. That goblin was really acting strange. Andolar was just about to cast the spell when the goblin pulled down his hood. He saw Haslan standing there and waving to him. That dagger he was waving around must be his mother's. How was he supposed to be able to recognize a dagger from this distance? At least now it looked like he would have company for his escape. He wondered how the others fared.

⚜

Haslan didn't have a chance to run. The only horse was already gone, and that was the only way he would stay ahead of the goblins. He scrambled behind the building to block their view. Haslan quickly settled on a plan and crawled to where goblin bodies were laying out of sight of the approaching force. He unfastened a cloak from one and pulled it over himself. He hoped the dead act would work until he had a chance to complete his disguise. He kept the hood of the cloak pulled out enough to see what was going on. The man on the warhorse was quickly closing the distance on Lecik and Berinda. Berinda was pacing Lecik. With her gloves, she could run as fast as a normal person without armor. She could easily outdistance anyone but the goblin commander. He wondered if this was Churinius. He certainly looked more imposing than the last one. He was in his plate mail, riding his armored horse and carrying a large assortment of weapons including a lance.

Lecik was pausing to shoot arrows at the commander to try and slow him down. If he didn't manage it, then even the healers would be run-down. Churinius quickly closed the distance and couched his lance to take the fighters. Even if he missed, it was likely his horse wouldn't. The steel shoes on that heavy horse would be worse than maces in the hands of fighters. The commander was fifty paces away before Lecik managed to put an arrow into him. It went through his breastplate and stuck in his shoulder. From the amount of arrow sticking out of the armor, you could tell that it hadn't penetrated his chain shirt very far if at all. Lecik and Berinda had to turn and face the charge or get speared in the back. The only thing someone on foot could do against a mounted lancer was to wait till the last second to dodge. The mounted warrior was lining up on Lecik. That arrow must have hurt him some.

Haslan saw a sword sweep out from close to a tree as Churinius rode by and then saw Petrion behind the sword. The sword took the horse across both legs below the armor and sliced cleanly through one of them. As the horse went down, Churinius went flying over its head. He shined and sparkled in the dappled sunlight as he arched through the air. The sound of his impact was clear even to Haslan. Berinda ran to attack him while he was on the ground. Petrion lost his sword and ran after it. The goblins were within a hundred paces of the fighters, and Lecik turned his attention toward them.

"Run," he heard Petrion call in the distance.

He must have said more because he was gesturing with his hands, but he was too far away for Haslan to make out the words. They were about seventy-five paces from him now and looked small in the distance. Berinda ran but toward the man instead of away.

The goblins were starting to run past Haslan on the way to the fight. He clenched his teeth to keep from yelling as first one and then another goblin stepped on him. They didn't even respect their own dead. When the last was gone, Haslan got up and followed them. He picked up a helmet to complete his quick disguise and a stray arrow in case he needed to play dead again.

Haslan looked toward the unfolding battle again. Lecik was moving away but was firing arrows to try and help the others. If Berinda had just ran instead of glory hunting, they might have gotten away. Now she was in a hot fight with Churinius, and he looked to be winning in spite of his wounds. She managed to get a good cut on his side while he was down, but he still fought back to his feet. Petrion joined her. He was the only one who had a chance of getting away from the goblins after they closed. Churinius was handling them both easily though and waved the goblins on after the other squad members rather than have their help. Haslan slowed further and looked around quickly for witnesses. When he saw there weren't any, he used the arrow to play wounded while he walked closer.

"You two may join me if you desire," Churinius told the two fighters.

"I'm the leader of this outlaw band," Petrion replied, "and none of my people are taking orders from you."

"Well," Churinius replied, "maybe they will after you are dead."

Churinius stepped up his attacks against Petrion and just defended against Berinda. Haslan was only ten paces away, but the battle was flowing so much that he couldn't get behind Churinius. There was no way he was going to take him on from the front. Churinius deflected one of Petrion's thrusts out wide and then swung his blade across at throat level. Petrion had to jump back to avoid being sliced down. Berinda tried to close and deliver a thrust, but Churinius stepped in and knocked her off balance with his shield.

Haslan looked to see how Lecik and the healers were doing. The healers were out of sight now and should with a little luck get away.

Lecik had delayed too long. Haslan saw him stumbling along with an arrow sticking out of his shoulder and another in his leg. He couldn't seem to keep moving in a straight line, so he was badly injured or poisoned. The goblins closed on him quickly. They were about a hundred and fifty paces away when Haslan saw a pair of goblins tackle him and then one drove a sword into his back. Haslan turned away as the goblin started jumping on Lecik's body in victory.

Haslan looked back to the closer fight rather than look at Lecik. The fighters weren't faring well against Churinius. His sending the goblins ahead hadn't been a boast but a surety that he could handle the situation. Berinda looked like she was still untouched, but Petrion had a cut along his sword arm. As he watched, Churinius feinted a thrust to Petrion's left side and then changed directions after Petrion moved his shield to cover. Petrion tried to deflect the stomach thrust wide with his sword, but the goblin commander's sword pierced Petrion's armor and made a long gash down his right side. He was wounded badly and losing blood.

Petrion tried to overwhelm his enemy with attacks before the wound took him down, but Churinius was equal to it and more. He deflected every blow while still keeping Berinda from getting in a good swing. Finally, as Petrion's attacks slowed, he delivered a hard overhand cut. Petrion ducked back to avoid the blow but was too slow. He only got partly out from under the swing meant to crush his head, and the point of the sword caught his face after slicing through the edge of his helm. It left a cut from forehead to chin across his face and through his right eye. Haslan gasped as Petrion dropped unconscious to the ground.

Berinda used Petrion's fall as best she could and thrust hard with her sword. Churinius got his shield between them, but her thrust pierced the shield and carried through to his side. He looked down in surprise for a second and then at Berinda smiling up at him. Churinius slung his shield out hard while Berinda's sword was still stuck into it. The headband gave Berinda extra strength, but not extra size. She wasn't braced to pull against Churinius. Berinda had to let go of the sword or go along with it.

Churinius was bleeding from the shallow gash in his side, but he had a sword and Berinda didn't. Berinda dove to tackle him before he could bring his sword into play. The goblin commander didn't try to use the blade of the sword though. He simply used the fist the sword was in to strike her in the head. She flew backwards from the blow and lay still. He rubbed his fist with his shield hand and pulled out a couple of clothes to slow the flow of blood.

Churinius was still moving relatively well, so Haslan gave up on killing him with a thrust to the back. He wouldn't last a minute in close combat with that man. Instead, he stumbled closer and held a piece of the arrow against his shoulder. The commander looked across to where Lecik was laying with goblins around him and shouted a curse at the goblins. Haslan understood at least some of that little speech about the goblin's ancestry and intellectual ability. All the goblins standing there took off running after the others, probably hoping to lose themselves in the crowd.

Churinius turned around and saw Haslan in his goblin disguise coming slowly toward him. The commander said something to him in what sounded like Goblin, and Haslan figured he was being told to finish them off. He had to duck a blow from the commander's fist and back quickly away to avoid being hit when he pulled out his dagger. He put the dagger away when the commander shouted something he couldn't understand. He must want them alive. Haslan almost made a major mistake by pulling out a clean neatly rolled bandage but caught himself and grabbed a piece of rope instead.

His actions seemed to satisfy the commander because he nodded his head and walked toward Lecik. He looked back once and said something threatening as Haslan was tying Berinda but moved on when Haslan bobbed his head again. Haslan did a poor job tying the fighter, hoping she might wake. Then he went to check on Petrion.

It would take healing to keep Petrion alive. His cheek was laid open, and his teeth showed through the side of his head. His eye was ruined as well. The commander stopped briefly at Lecik's body and then continued after the healers. He must be happy having taken down three of the five people he saw. Maybe Churinius would find the goblin that killed Lecik and kill him slowly.

There was no way he could carry or even move the fighters. The only horse in the area was lying dead on the ground. At least Petrion managed to cut off pursuit of the healers. He should have just left Berinda to be killed. Of course, he couldn't because the duchess had ordered them not to lose any of the magic items. Magic items! That was it. After checking to make sure the goblin commander was still moving away, he went to Berinda and took the headband. He quickly fastened it around his own head. He found Petrion's sword and put it back in the sheath. He hated to move the ranger, but he would surely die or be captured if left here. The problem was that even though he did have exceptional strength, he had the arm length of a halfman. Finally, after trying several different things, he managed to crawl under Petrion's body and stand up with the ranger on his back. The man's armor was poking him in several places. All the metal these fighters insisted on wearing was a real pain at times. Petrion's arms and legs were dragging on the ground.

He hurried as fast as he could to the goblin camp and put Petrion down close to the still burning barracks. He figured that would be the least likely place for him to be stepped on for now. He bandaged the ranger's wounds as best he could, but the wound in his side was still leaking blood. The bandage on his face was becoming soaked too. Haslan checked for a pulse in Petrion's neck and found a weak one. He wouldn't last out the day, even if Haslan stayed to care for him. He took a couple of sticks and placed them close to his body to mark the place and then covered him with his cloak. Petrion faded from view and looked just like the ground around him.

Haslan ran away from the camp after he finished with Petrion and went to where Lecik was lying. He didn't figure there was any hope, but he owed it to the fighter to check. He also needed to retrieve Lecik's bow and arrows if he was dead. He reached the body quickly, but could see goblins coming back in the distance. He didn't see any horses with them, so the healers must have gotten away. The healers were cut off from him now, so Petrion was as good as dead. The man had probably sent goblins to chase them clear to the border. At least some of them had gotten away. He hadn't seen Andolar either, so the magician may have made good his escape. The only way he could get one of the fighters to the border was steal a horse, and stealing a horse would mean leaving the fighters lying alone. Berinda would be captured, and Lecik and Petrion were dead. Petrion managed to convey the impression they were outlaws while the goblin commander was slicing him apart. Berinda deserved whatever fate had in store for her. If she hadn't been glory hunting, they all might have gotten away.

Haslan didn't bother to check for a pulse when he reached Lecik. He had several stab wounds in his back. Haslan wished there was something he could do, but the goblins would be coming back. He grabbed the bow and the quiver that contained the enchanted arrows. Only two were left.

When he turned back to the camp, he saw Churinius in the distance. It would only be moments before he saw that Petrion was missing and started looking for a small goblin with an arrow wound. Haslan darted quickly through the trees to get plenty of them between Churinius and him before the commander discovered the missing body. With luck, he would think the fighter had awakened and escaped. He might also have seen the cloak Petrion was wearing operate and search for him in the immediate area. Haslan didn't intend to be around to see. He would go back and get Petrion's cloak and sword and get out of here.

He could hear Churinius yelling something in Goblin from where Berinda was by the time he reached the edge of the camp clearing. No doubt he would be sending a group to take possession of the camp and start the rebuilding process. They would find Petrion's body and that would be the end of the mystery. It would be easy to find a goblin body to lie close to Petrion's with an arrow broken off in his chest. He hurried across the open area till he was concealed by the remains of the barracks. He grabbed one of the goblin bodies lying in front of the commander's shack and dragged it to where Petrion was. As he put the body down, he saw movement in the garden.

He concealed the motion of pulling a dagger while watching the movement out of the corner of his eye. Whoever it was didn't hide very well and was bigger than a goblin from the size of the disturbance. It was Andolar! He stood up and motioned for the magician to join him, but Andolar just ducked further into the brush. He held up the dagger he had borrowed. Finally, he took his hood off when he saw the magician preparing a spell. This was better than anything he could have hoped for. He ran as fast as he could to reach the magician and grabbed his arm to pull him along.

"Give me the healing potion," he ordered the magician.

"What are you talking about?" Andolar asked him.

"I haven't got time for your games now, magician," he said angrily. "Give me the healing potion your father gave you or I'll take it off of your body."

Andolar stopped and looked like he was ready to cast a spell as soon as Haslan made a move. If he kept fooling around, the goblins would be there before they could get away.

"All right, I'll tell you what's going on," Haslan said as quick as he could talk, "but get the potion out while we're running toward the barracks."

He suited his words to actions and started running toward Petrion talking in a voice low enough that Andolar had to keep up to hear.

"I have Petrion stashed over by the barracks, but he's unconscious and badly injured. I saw your father give you the belt thing that night we left. If we give Petrion the potion, he'll surely come back to consciousness and be able to get us out of here. The goblins are coming, and if we don't hurry, they'll get here before we get away."

By the time they reached Petrion, Haslan had finished the abbreviated story and Andolar had retrieved the potion. Haslan found Petrion and pulled the cloak back. Andolar gagged at the sight of Petrion's face and dropped the potion. Haslan picked it up and turned Petrion's head so none of the liquid would spill through his ruined cheek. That meant keeping the cut side of his face pointing up where it could be seen by the squeamish magician. Haslan checked for a pulse to make sure he wasn't wasting the potion, and almost decided he was too late when he found one. He removed the stopper from the bottle and gave it to the ranger. Nothing happened.

"You idiot," he said to Andolar, "you gave me the poison potion. Get out the other one."

Andolar was still retching, so Haslan detached the belt device and got the potion himself. He hoped it worked. As he poured the potion down Petrion's throat, he had the sudden thought that maybe he had given the ranger the right potion. He could already have died. He almost stopped pouring to save part of the potion but decided if he were wrong it wouldn't matter much anyway.

Then he saw the wounds on Petrion's face begin to close. Amazingly enough, even his eye healed back to almost its original state. It looked fine except for the scar running down the eyelid. Petrion opened his eyes and looked up. Then he reached for a sword when he saw the goblin cloak above him.

"It's me, Petrion," Haslan said urgently. "We have to move now. The goblins are coming back."

Petrion got unsteadily to his feet with Haslan helping, and then Haslan got Andolar up. The magician looked surprised at the sight of Petrion's face. For that matter he was surprised as well. He didn't figure a potion was strong enough to repair damage of that sort, but maybe it worked because the wound was fresh. Petrion was favoring his side, and Haslan saw through the rent in the ranger's armor that the wound had not completely healed. The potion must have expended almost all of its magic on the face wound. Where was a healer when you needed one?

The side wound was not bleeding at least. Petrion leaned on Andolar as they moved across the camp. Haslan peeked around the barracks to see where the goblins were. Some of them were making a stretcher for Berinda out of spears and cloaks, so they were planning on keeping her prisoner at least for a while. He'd like to see her have to get out and work as a farmer. Another group of the goblins were down on hands and knees searching the surrounding area for the ranger. Apparently, Churinius had noticed Petrion's cloak. Sneaking out of here might not be so easy. Another group was coming toward the camp. Haslan ran to Andolar and Petrion, dragging the cloak behind him to obscure their tracks.

Andolar was making to the northwest without being told. Apparently, the magician had at least a bit of common sense. Petrion seemed to be regaining some of his strength because he was moving under his own power. He was still being careful of his side. They were already outside the camp and almost to the trees by the time Haslan caught up with them.

"Good choice of direction, Andolar," Haslan commented when he caught up.

"It was the direction I was heading when you spotted me. I figured it would be the only direction they might not look. Now what are we going to do? The goblins are out in force between us and the border no matter which way we go."

"Is Berinda dead?" Petrion asked.

"No," Haslan answered, "and what a pity it is too."

"What did she do to you?" Andolar asked.

"She got Lecik killed. He tried to help Berinda out with his archery when she wouldn't run, but the goblins caught up enough to get an arrow in him. They ran him down and killed him."

Andolar looked shocked at the news. Petrion didn't look surprised.

"Florine and Korin apparently made good their escape to the south," Haslan continued, "because the returning goblins didn't have any horses with them. Berinda was knocked unconscious after you went down, and it looked like they were taking her with them."

"Churinius did try to recruit us," Petrion said. "I thought about playing along, but he probably wouldn't have believed me if I did say I'd follow him. So does anyone have a plan on how to get Berinda back?"

"Get her back," Haslan said in disgust. "I think she deserves to stay where she is. I got her headband and Lecik's bow, so we don't have to go in and get her."

"The odds are too great anyway," Andolar added. "They were too much when there were seven of us. There's no way we can take them out with only three."

"I agree," Petrion said, and Haslan and Andolar sighed in relief, "a fighter, magician, and thief can't get them out. But a goblin, returned prisoner, and invisible man might be able to pull it off. Let's get someplace safe and see what we can come up with."

Haslan and Andolar looked at each other and then at Petrion in horror. There were scores of goblins in the group that came after them, not to mention the commander who had beaten their two best fighters after being thrown from his horse. Petrion didn't say anymore, just focused on walking deeper into the woods away from the goblins. After a while, he started to hide their tracks better. The goblins were bound to have trackers among their numbers just as the humans had the rangers. When they had come about a mile, Petrion called a halt at a shallow trench in the ground. They would have to lie down to remain unseen, and there was no water in the area. It was almost dark though, and all of them were tired.

"This is a terrible camping spot," Haslan said in disgust after Petrion told them they were stopping for the night.

"Exactly," Petrion replied. "The goblins are likely to try staking out and searching all of the good camping spots in the area. None of them would even think of this as a camping site. We can rest here while we keep watch. There should be enough supplies between us to last for a couple of days. Now Andolar and I are going to sleep while you keep watch, Haslan."

"All right. I suppose you have a point."

Petrion lay down and was almost immediately asleep. Andolar wasn't far behind.

They were on top of a shallow rise with scattered trees around. Haslan stayed in the shallow place most of the time but got up to look around occasionally. After night fell completely, he leaned against a tree. Anyone that saw him should think he was a goblin. He started getting sleepy and dug out some trail rations and started chewing on them. They weren't so bad as far as rations went. They were certainly better than that one farm lady's cooking. His watch passed quietly as he ate and thought about the plan Petrion had hastily outlined. Sneaking into the camp would be a good way to acquire some treasure. He woke Andolar up after he was on watch for about four hours and lay down to get some sleep. He was comfortably full, and visions of treasure were floating through his head.

CHAPTER 15

Petrion tightly bound up his side during the night. It still ached a lot, but it was much better than the open slash had been. He wouldn't have to worry about infection with the wound closed. He opened his pack and got out some blood restorative and pain killer that Korin had given him. Both of them tasted terrible. He also saw the bag of sleeping powder. The plan he had thought of began to be more detailed in his mind as he sat on watch, chewing on the hard trail rations. It wasn't very good food, but he would be wishing he had more in couple of days. He would have to teach Haslan more of the language if his plan were to work. They could take up this day learning and then implement the plan the following day. The enemy camp should have settled down by that time, but the scattered soldiers and fourth group of raiders probably wouldn't be back.

Now he had to think of a way to convince those two to go along with his idea. Andolar would be the hardest. They had enough sleeping powder to affect maybe a hundred goblins if they could get it into their food. The next problem would be getting rid of Churinius. Andolar could tear his clothes enough to look like a prisoner, and Haslan could disguise himself as a goblin. Haslan was smaller than most goblins, but close enough to pass. He could use his cloak to get in.

Once inside the camp, they could taint one of the meals with the sleeping powder. Andolar could move among the prisoners, if there were any, and tell them not to eat the food. They could also try and taint the officer's food. Andolar could use his spells to help clean up any leftovers. He and Haslan would use their weapons. Berinda would help if he could free her. The biggest problem would be the commander. There was no way he was getting into a stand-up fight with that killer again. Petrion hadn't inflicted a single injury on the man, and there were two of them attacking. Maybe he should ask Haslan for the headband.

It was getting light out, so he woke Haslan. The thief heard the stealthy movement and came awake on his own. When he saw Petrion, he took his hand away from his dagger. Petrion made another survey of the surrounding area. It appeared that they weren't going to be followed. Of course, the goblin heat vision wouldn't help them follow a trail at night. They would have to wait till daylight. Haslan woke Andolar up, and both of them got out some trail rations to eat.

"Take it as light as you can on the rations," Petrion told them. "It might be awhile before we get more."

"I'd prefer to carry it on the inside rather than the outside," Haslan replied as he took another bite.

"All right," Petrion replied, "but don't come to me looking for more when all of your food is gone."

Haslan dropped some of the food back into his pouch after that comment.

"How long do you think it will take us to get to the border?" Andolar asked.

"That depends on how long it takes us to plan and execute an attack on the goblin camp," Petrion answered.

"You can't possibly be serious," a stunned Andolar said. "Taking on that camp is suicide. Churinius could take us three out, and there are still a hundred or more goblins to deal with."

"Some of them should be at the other camp," Petrion replied calmly. "Others will be following the healers or looking for me. That means there will be fewer at the camp."

"Or more," Andolar countered. "The goblin commander wouldn't have left his base undefended, so there could be more than a hundred there."

"We'll get them with your sleeping powder. I have a bag of it, and I think Haslan has one."

"I have two bags," Haslan told him, "but they have to be delivered to be any good."

"With you posing as a goblin and Andolar posing as a prisoner," Petrion said," someone will have access to the food. Either a goblin or a slave should be tending the cooking."

"So that's how you plan for us to get into the camp," Andolar said. "The problem is if something goes wrong, both of you can escape. I'll become a real prisoner if that happens. I'll leave Berinda rather than chance joining her permanently."

"We aren't leaving anyone as a prisoner," Petrion told him earnestly. "I won't leave you to be a goblin prisoner, any more than I'm going to leave Berinda."

"That's assuming you have some say in the matter," Andolar shot back.

"I can't pass as a goblin for long enough to pull it off," Haslan said with conviction. "I can't speak the language."

"That's why I'm going to spend today teaching you."

"I'm not going," Andolar said finally. "It will surely end in death or torture for me."

"If that's the way you feel about it," Petrion said with a sigh, "then go ahead. Of course, you won't have me along to find the goblins before they see you, especially at night. You can't find your way since you don't know exactly where we are. And finally, I could stir up a major goblin movement with my activities, and you wouldn't know it until they hit you. Haslan can't outrun a goblin, and you Andolar surely can't outrun a horse."

"Oh well," Andolar said, "I still think the odds are better. I'll just take my dagger back, Haslan, and get myself out of here."

"No," Petrion countered, "you won't. If you leave the squad, then you'll leave your enchanted items here for the rest of us to use. I can make you do that."

"You don't have a squad, Petrion," Andolar said caustically. "You have one dead, one captured, two missing, and two getting ready to leave. We are the squad, not you."

"Fine," Petrion said angrily. "Let me put it in terms you'll understand. You are both coming with me. We are going to rescue Berinda from Churinius. Anyone who does not follow my orders will be killed for desertion."

Andolar backed up to get some room from the ranger. He was a woodsman, but he was also a fighter. The magician wouldn't have a chance in combat. Petrion saw the magician reaching into a pouch.

"If you so much as say a word," Petrion said in a level voice, "draw out a component, or make a gesture, I'll cut you down where you stand. If you do get your spell off, I'll follow you and kill you. Even without my cloak and weapons, I'm more than a match for you."

"You have no authority to do that," Andolar replied with a glance at Haslan.

Andolar was looking desperately for a way out. Petrion was glad that Haslan hadn't taken the side of the magician. If Haslan sided with Andolar, then he would have to abandon his plan.

"Leave off, Andolar," Haslan said finally. "I'm going to see what Petrion has in mind before I tuck tail and run. We might be able to do by stealth what you'd need an army to do by force.

They should think Petrion ran for it if he is still alive since both healers took off for the border. And they never saw either you or I, so they won't be expecting us to show up at all."

All the bluster went out of the magician then. He just flopped to the ground with his head in his hands. Petrion knew Andolar was right about exceeding his authority, but he had gamboled that Andolar would give in. He needed the help of the magician to pull this off. Petrion intended to increase his force by freeing all the prisoners in the camp, and Andolar would be essential for that part of his plan.

"Andolar," Petrion said, "start recovering your casting ability."

"I am fully restored," Andolar said in a dead voice. "All it takes is time and rest"

"Haslan and I will start working on the Goblin language," Petrion said briskly. "This is going to be a quick course, so study hard."

"You can count on it, Petrion. My life is going to depend on it."

"What life?" Andolar said in the same dead tone as he pulled a small roll of paper out of his robe.

"Keep the headband for now," Petrion told Haslan while ignoring Andolar. "I think you might need it more than I do. Goblins tend to be hard on others who are smaller, and you're about as small as goblins come. The strength will get you some respect. Try and figure out a way to disguise your features."

"Lots of dirt and padding is the only thing I can think of."

"All right, let's start practicing."

He and Haslan worked hard through the morning on the language practice. Andolar started listening in on the practice after studying for a short while. When lunchtime came, they ate sparingly and moved closer to the main goblin camp. He had to scout ahead, and that made him worry about Andolar using the opportunity to escape. Taking a chance on that was better than taking a chance on being spotted. He stopped when he saw a small patrol in the distance. Eight goblins were in the forest on what looked like a standard patrol path. He must be getting close. He turned and worked his way back to where the others were hopefully following.

They were both still walking toward the camp when he reached them, speaking haltingly in Goblin. Andolar had quickly picked up on the language. He spent the afternoon continuing the instruction in Goblin. Haslan was getting good enough to at least pass as a goblin. Andolar was almost able to carry on a conversation. He must have a natural ability with languages.

"You're picking that up quick," Petrion said when Andolar showed he had mastered another string of words.

"It's not hard if you focus your mind," Andolar replied. "Learning magic spells is much harder."

"It's too bad you're not a halfman as well," Petrion told him. "Then you could pass as a goblin."

Andolar didn't appear interested in talking, so Petrion left him alone and continued the lessons. After another light meal, with loud complaints from Haslan, Petrion decided to go all the way to the camp to complete his scouting. Andolar and Haslan continued to practice speaking in Goblin. Just talking using the words they learned would make them more familiar with the language and able to call the words up quickly at need. And Goblin wasn't a very intricate language to learn.

He moved away from the camp with his cloak pulled close. He left behind all his armor except for the leather under covering, which he stitched together during language practice. He decided against leaving his sword though and took a dagger as well. Andolar gave him the other enchanted one since, as he put it, "Dead men don't need to carry daggers." He was apparently dealing with the situation by assuming everything was going to turn out for the worst.

The ranger wondered suddenly what the baron would say if Andolar was lost on a high-risk mission like this. He could be executed for losing men if it was ruled he acted recklessly, and he doubted he could expect leniency from the baron.

Petrion stopped to let a patrol go by. He could see a clearing in the distance. When he reached the path they used to patrol the camp, he could see a wooden structure in the clearing. He moved on after carefully erasing his footprints from the path.

When Petrion got to the camp, he was ready to agree with Andolar's assessment. From the size of the guard force, there could be hundreds of goblins. And it wasn't just an open camp. It was a wooden palisade. Sharpened posts were arranged in a rectangle that was around seventy paces on the short side and over one hundred on the long. They made a wall about ten feet high. The area around the fort was cleared back for a hundred and fifty paces. There were towers built into the corners and over what looked like two entrance gates. The gates were in the longer sides of the fort. The tower walls were five feet higher than the main walls. Goblin archers were stationed in pairs in each of the towers. Goblin fighters were guarding the gates and walking the walls on a parapet. This was a permanent fortification and base for striking against the human lands.

The commander must have good knowledge of siege and defense to have constructed this. Furthermore, he had to have extremely strong control of the goblins in his force to get them to put out this much work. He was smart enough not to try and use his goblin warriors as his hard-labor crew. The raids were making more sense now since Petrion could see Churinius was using the human prisoners for his main labor. He got money, damaged the human lands, and got free labor at the same time. He also gave himself time to fortify his position before the start of open hostilities.

Petrion could see human laborers under goblins supervision taking more trees out of the woods for further construction. Others were trimming and dressing the timbers. Another group was splitting some of the logs to make planks and shingles. There were close to thirty slaves working on the outside of the compound. They were in somewhat better condition than the ones at the other camp. Maybe they sent all the ones that caused trouble over there. There weren't nearly as many women as men in this camp. That suggested another reason for the other. It could have been used to provide a recreational area for his goblins. It sure would be nice to see Churinius turning on a spit over a low fire for a few hours.

He was approaching from the northeast, and one of the gates was on the northern side of the fort. The other was on the south. Northwest of the fort, human women and children were working a garden patch similar to that at the other camp. There was also some stock being tended by some of the older children. The only structures outside the walls were for the livestock. A cattle pen was north of the gate and a sheep pen to the northwest. There was a split rail fence around the garden to keep the animals out.

Petrion went to where the men were dressing the timbers. He followed along with a group of men carrying a log into the fort to get a look at the inside. The two men in front of him bowed to the goblin guards as they went in the gate. Petrion started to bow out of habit from trying to blend in and quickly stopped himself. Then he ducked low just in time to miss the string tied across the opening at human throat height. The goblins had rigged a little something to make the prisoners bow. He had to hurry just to keep from getting stepped on by the man behind him.

He saw the tower over the entrance had murder holes in the bottom. This commander seemed to know his business. Murder holes didn't look nearly so nice from this perspective. He moved to the left after he got through the entryway and saw the man behind him staring curiously at the ground as he walked. The man must have noticed the odd occurrences where Petrion's feet were hitting the ground. The ground inside the fort was hard-packed dirt, but there was a layer of dust on top where it dried after the rains. The man shook his head and apparently decided it was his imagination.

Petrion very carefully raised his head to look around the fort, keeping only a small opening in the hood of his cloak. Even with that precaution, he made sure no one in his line of sight was looking directly at him.

The area inside the fort was crowded. Judging from the stack of sharpened posts by the west wall, the fort was about to be enlarged. There were three of what looked to be barracks buildings, each about thirty paces long and ten wide. There was another building attached to the end of the three, which was probably the common room. There was a smaller holding area on the other side of the fort that looked like it was for the prisoners. The nicer building with four goblin guards around it was probably the commander's house. From the ringing of hammers, one of the smaller buildings was a blacksmith's shop. Two other small buildings had barrels stacked outside them, so they could be for general storage. There was another better-constructed building that was about the size of the goblin barracks buildings. It might be a training room or officer's quarters. The last structure inside the fort was a large horse corral, with six horses in it.

He looked back toward the gate to make sure no one was coming his way and saw bells attached to the string that was stretched across the fort entrance. He wondered if the string and the bells were added by Churinius after the last battle. That sudden fall from his horse had to have hurt, not to mention having seriously bent his armor.

Petrion decided to check the buildings to make sure they were what he thought. He went into the building connecting the barracks buildings because the door was open. Only a few goblins were in the room talking, but the tables would seat eighty to a hundred. Human prisoners were cleaning up from the last meal. This was apparently the main eating room, and it was tied directly to the other three buildings.

He looked into one of the connected buildings and saw it was a goblin barracks. It had bunks for over a hundred. It was almost empty. The second and third buildings were about a third full or a little more. He didn't get close to the commander's house. The guards looked too alert, especially considering they were goblins. The small building by the barracks was a storage building, but the door was barred and locked. It was probably a weapons repository. The second storage building was probably for food and drink supplies. There was a spring in the middle of the fort that had a short wall of stone around it. Having a source of water within the fort was an excellent idea.

He decided to try the larger nice-looking building before getting back out of the gate. The door to the building was closed, so he looked through the windows. After studying the inside as best he could, he decided the building was another barracks with cooking and eating area attached. But in this one, everything was sized for humans. It could probably hold twenty-five to thirty people. As far as he could tell though, it was unoccupied. So Churinius, if that was indeed whom they had seen, was planning on more human help for his endeavor. This man needed to be stopped and soon.

Things didn't look good. All told there were between one hundred and fifty and two hundred goblins in the fort in addition to the commander. He went out the gate with a departing work group, remembering to duck under the string. The stack of posts they were heading towards was close to the edge of the woods where the cutting was going on. Petrion stepped out to the side and waited till everyone was past. Then he headed into the woods to where Haslan and Andolar were waiting. He realized he hadn't seen Berinda. Oh well, there was no way he was going back to check. It was nearing sunset, and he wanted to be back with the others before dark. He passed between the two patrols without having to stop this time. It took him ten minutes of searching once he got in the general vicinity of the camp to locate where it was. It was really a good site.

"Coming in," he said softly when he neared the camp.

"Glad to have you back," Haslan replied. "What's the news?"

"Not good," Petrion said. "There are more than a hundred and fifty goblins, and the camp is a big wooden fort. They are holding somewhere around seventy human prisoners, counting men, women, and children. The commander appears to be there, but I couldn't get close enough to his house to see him or Berinda."

He expected another outburst from Andolar then, but the magician just sat quietly. Petrion looked again at the magician and saw in the dim light that his clothes were a ragged mess. His disguise was complete except for some dirt.

"There was a barracks for human troops, but it was empty."

"You did say he was trying to recruit you," Haslan suggested. "He's planning on getting some more human help."

"I don't think so," Petrion said, "at least not entirely. Now that I think about it, the place had a lived-in look to it."

"When do we go in?" Andolar asked.

"I'd say either in the middle of the night or just before noon tomorrow."

He realized suddenly that Andolar had spoken in Goblin. He smiled at the magician, but Andolar was staring off into the distance at nothing. That "I'm going to die" attitude was really unnerving. When Andolar turned to look toward the camp, Petrion saw welts and cuts on his back and legs.

"I figured they would notice right off if he didn't have the marks," Haslan said when he saw Petrion staring. "I was careful to make marks that would show now but not permanently."

"Then the earlier we go in, the better," Petrion said, getting back to business. "We'll get into the camp tonight and plan on knocking them out with breakfast. Do we have enough to do that many people?"

"From what the herbalist told me," Andolar replied, "each of those big bags should be able to do up to fifty humans. The more you use, the harder they are out. If you try to get fifty with one bag, then they'll go to sleep almost normally and be easy to wake up. A spoonful would put someone out within a few minutes, and they wouldn't wake up for several hours. If you use enough, it can cause death. We have four of the big bags. I had one with me as well."

"Haslan," Petrion said, "you take all but a couple of spoonfuls. You can hide them as padding in your clothes. Get the main goblin food supply at breakfast. I'll try and get some into the commander's food. Do you have a vial I can put some in?"

"Sure," Haslan said, digging out an empty potion vial.

"Is that how you saved me?" Petrion asked suddenly.

"Andolar had it from his father," Haslan said in explanation.

Petrion suddenly felt dread again, thinking about what he was doing to Gardoney's son. It was enough to make him reconsider. He decided to continue but to not start anything unless there was a very good chance of final success. Otherwise, he would get Andolar out using his cloak as best he could.

Andolar dug out the vial he used to hold Berinda's dose of the sleeping powder out of his stuff.

"This holds a one person dose," Andolar said as he handed it over.

Petrion filled both vials just in case, and Haslan took the rest. He saw that Haslan had rags wrapped around his hands to thicken them in the gloves.

Haslan stuffed the bulk of the powder under his clothes for more padding. He and Andolar started using dirt to complete their disguises. Within a half hour, they had everything stored. Petrion took all of Andolar's gear, except for two pouches the magician hid under his shirt. The first pouch contained the components to work his spells. He also hid a larger pouch of food.

"Won't that make them suspicious?" Petrion asked.

"Actually, I thought it would work just the opposite," Andolar replied. "If I was being recaptured by goblins, I think the one thing I would try to keep would be food."

It sounded like a good thought to him, so he didn't say anything more about it.

"Do you think we should go to the outer patrol first?" Haslan asked.

"Yes," Petrion answered, "because they probably have some kind of pass through set up. You don't want to suddenly appear at the gate."

"Well," Haslan said, "you'd better explain the fort to us. Then we'll head in and hope for the best."

Petrion sat down in the fading light and told them the setup and about the trip line at the gate. Andolar should be placed with the other slaves, and Haslan should be free to move around the compound. Petrion would enter the fort the same time they did, try and find where Berinda was kept, and then try and taint Churinius's breakfast. Haslan would get the powder into the morning food either by himself or using Andolar if he had to. Andolar was to warn all the people not to eat the food that morning and to be ready to attack and escape. They might need the help of the people before the morning was over. Petrion thought he might be able to break into the armory and get some weapons for them. He hoped that wouldn't be necessary. Breaking into the armory without being noticed would be very hard.

CHAPTER 16

They started moving south. If goblins brought in escaped slaves, they would bring them from the southeast. Petrion worked the area ahead of them, but they were moving too fast for him to do a real, thorough job. Hopefully, none of the goblins would be this far from the fort.

When they walked for about an hour, Petrion waited for them to catch up. Then he started them off to the northwest, staying with them this time. The first meeting would be tricky without heat vision. The goblins would expect Haslan to be able to see them as well as they could see him. If they came upon him suddenly, his disguise could be uncovered. Petrion started staying north of them, so he would have a better chance of spotting the goblins first. He still hadn't seen any lights when he heard the tramp of feet in the brush ahead of him. He slipped as quickly as he could to the south to warn Haslan. The goblins saw the thief and magician first though and called out to them.

"You stop, or we shoot you."

"I stop," Haslan replied. "Got slave back."

The patrol closed with him, and Petrion had to move quickly to stay out of their way. His armor, which he put on before leaving, jingled a little when he moved, but the goblins didn't react to the sound. They quickly circled Andolar and Haslan. If they attacked now, Petrion would be hard-pressed to keep them alive.

"Got slave back, sure," one goblin said. "Pog, give signal to gate."

Petrion heard some movement, and suddenly one of the goblins quickly slid open the panel of a lantern twice. An answering flash came from what must be the gate. *Naturally, the place wasn't lighted*, Petrion thought as he mentally kicked himself. The goblins had more of an advantage in the dark.

"You go to gate," the goblin said when he saw the answering signal.

Haslan started through them without saying anything more. His speech was a little higher pitched than the goblins, so even though he was trying to lower his voice, he was going to talk as little as possible. They walked straight toward where the light came from. Thankfully, the moon was shining brightly in the clearing. The gate was closed when they reached it, and four guards were standing outside.

"Me catch slave," Haslan told them. "You let us in. I put him away."

The biggest of the four guards walked over to Haslan and looked him over.

"I take slave in," the guard said. "You stay and watch gate runt."

"My slave," Haslan replied, "your gate."

"You stay at gate, or I bust you."

"You stay gate or I bust you," Haslan replied.

The guard took a swing at Haslan, but his workout time with Berinda paid off with dividends. He ducked under the clumsy swing of the guard and planted a solid right in his midsection.

The guard folded up on the ground. One of the other goblins ran to open the small door in the gate. Haslan delayed a bit, rubbing his knuckle, and Petrion took it for a signal to get through. He waited on the other side. The small door got them under the trip string. Haslan walked Andolar across the compound to the slave pen and shoved him inside after the guard opened the gate. Then he went into the eating area of the barracks complex and sat down at a table with his goblin cloak pulled over his head. There was some bread, and Haslan started nibbling on it. Petrion watched him for a while to make sure nothing was wrong and then went outside. His first stop was the armory. The door was still locked, and he would make a lot of noise trying to break it open. His only option was to wait until there was enough noise to cover the sound. He could have used Haslan for this. As a matter of fact, he could bring the thief over to pick the lock. No. Goblins would get suspicious of another goblin being around that building as well. And Haslan didn't have the cloak to hide him from heat-sensitive vision.

Petrion made a slow circuit of the camp while it was dark to get a better feel on how things were laid out. He also took the opportunity to get a good look at the commander's house. The house was the only lighted place in the camp, but the back was dim enough that any dust he raised wouldn't be visible. Unfortunately, the windows had cloth coverings on the inside that prevented him from seeing the interior. When he had satisfied himself that he had found out everything he could, he erased his footprints from around the window and started looking for a spot to spend the night. He found a spot behind the poles cut for the fort addition and composed himself for sleep.

Andolar fell when he was shoved into the slave pen and had to listen to goblin laughter and jokes behind his back. He almost replied to them, but that would surely be a suspicious thing to do. Knowing a lot of the goblin language had its bad points too.

The other slaves were laying close together for warmth at one side of the compound. He could just make out two slaves sitting on the other side. He went first to men in the group. After jostling a couple of them walking through, they were all awake. The complaints raised by the ones he kicked or stepped on woke the others.

"Everyone gather around," he said in a whisper.

Only three of them paid any attention to him. Unfortunately, they looked like they were ready to beat him to get him to shut up.

"My troop is setting up an escape for everyone," he whispered.

He figured it was best to make them think he had lots of help around. It would make them more eager to listen. He had the attention of seven.

"Are there any guards close enough to hear us talking?" Andolar asked.

"No," one of the men finally answered. "The guards at the entrance and at the wall are all they need. They can see us plainly in the dark."

"That's right, so don't move around very much while I'm talking to you," he whispered.

When he was sure they were listening, he continued.

"Pass this on to everyone. Do you have any informers among you? If you do, let me know who they are so we can keep them from knowing what's going on."

All of them whispered that none of them would betray him. They were all eager to hear the escape plan.

"Just after breakfast," he continued in a whisper, "we are going to attack. I am here to warn you not to eat the breakfast. I am a magician, and when the attack starts, I will be covering you. If any of you have military background and see a chance to help, do so. Before the attack, you have to act normally."

He paused after each sentence because the people were passing on his words as he said them so they didn't make any mistakes. Everyone was up now. He hoped the goblins weren't alarmed by the increase in movement.

"Do any of you cook breakfast for the goblins?" he asked them.

The men directed him to the women in the group and passed the word across as he made his way around. When he reached the women, two of them motioned him over beside them. Both were older women, probably around fifty.

"Are you the cooks?" he asked them.

"Yes, we cook the meals for the goblins," one of them answered. "We also fix our meals."

"In the morning, when you are cooking," he told them, "don't raise an alarm if a small goblin comes around where you are cooking. Help him if you can."

"All right."

"Do all the goblins eat at the same time?"

"Mostly. The ones who are going on duty eat first. The ones going on duty after them eat next. By then, the first ones have taken position and the ones coming off duty eat. It takes about an hour to feed them all."

"How much food do you cook?"

"We make three large pots of stew for the goblins, one for each group, a smaller one for the slaves, and a small one for the commander and his guard."

"That will be perfect. Have you seen anything of a woman fighter captured recently?" Andolar asked the woman.

"Yes," the woman replied, "Churinius has her confined in his house. The girls see her when they deliver the meals."

"Which girl delivers the meals?" Andolar asked.

"Whichever one we send," the woman told him.

"Could you have her deliver a message to the woman?"

"They couldn't pass anything to the woman," she said. "The commander would surely see it, and we'd all be in trouble."

"No, a carefully phrased verbal message."

"What is it?"

"Let me think for a moment. It has to be something she'd understand, but something that would not be recognized by Churinius. She should remember the tavern well. Does the commander know your names?"

"No. They just tell us what to do and whip us if we don't do it fast enough."

"Good. Here's what the girl should say. 'Andolar made this up special.' Do you think the commander would find anything wrong with that?"

"I don't think so. We can send Dania with the food. She's the oldest of the girls and will remember the best. She also fancies herself an actress, so she might pull it off a little better than the others."

"Dania," the woman whispered louder, "come here for a minute."

A girl of probably about eight crawled over to where they were talking.

"Dania, this man needs you to act for him in the morning when you take breakfast to the woman in the house. You have to tell her something. Can you do that?"

"Yes, ma'am. I'm going to be an actress when I grow up."

"And a very good one you'll be too from what I can see," Andolar told her. "Here's the part you need to say when you see her. Tell her 'Andolar made this up special.' It's a secret message that only she will understand. Do you think you can say your line to her just like I told you?"

"Sure I can," the girl said in a louder voice. "Andolar made this up special."

Andolar and several of the women made noises at her to be quiet. Their noises were louder than the girl's talk had been. When everything quieted again, after another yell by the goblin guard, he whispered his thanks to the woman and girl.

They hadn't searched him when he came into the camp, so he still had both food and spell components. After a moment's thought, he gave the food he had to the people. He had eaten reasonably well before he came here after all. And it wasn't like he would be able to eat it in the morning with all the goblins looking on. The people left almost all of the food for the children. There wasn't enough to make much difference in the hunger of the people, but it seemed to make them feel better.

"Who are the two over by the wall?" Andolar asked them.

"Some strange people that the commander uses to work in the blacksmith shop," one of the prisoners told him. "They don't talk to us."

Andolar got up and walked over to where the two were sitting. When he got closer, he could see why the people said they were strange. He could see by the moonlight that they were much shorter than average. In fact, they wouldn't be much taller than the goblins. They were as wide through the chest as Petrion though, and their arms bulged with muscles. Working at the forge all day must have strengthened their small frames. They were also almost completely covered by hair. If it weren't for the reasonably neat way in which some of it was groomed into mustache and beard, he would have thought them more animal than human.

When he got close to where they were, one growled something to the other. They both sat up and turned to look at him. The looks from what he could see were anything but friendly. Still, he needed to try.

"I need to talk to you," he whispered to them.

They looked at each other and then back at him. He couldn't tell what they were thinking.

"Can you understand me?" he whispered with some sign language thrown in.

Apparently the sign language had helped them understand at least a little. One of them seemed to reply back in growls of some type. He accompanied the words or whatever they were with his own sign language that showed they didn't appreciate his company. At least that's what he thought a fist waved in his face meant. He moved back a little to get some room to dodge in case they decided to attack him. He also readied a sleep spell in case of emergency.

"We need to talk," he whispered slightly louder.

"Keep mouths shut," one goblin outside the pen yelled in goblin.

Andolar saw the two in front of him lay back down quickly. They must understand the goblin speech. If they understood the goblin tongue but not the human, then they could be in league with the goblins. Still, they were being kept in the pen with the others. He could at least try to talk to them in goblin.

"You and I talk," he said in Goblin as he lay down close to the creature.

It spat on the ground in front of him, and Andolar got ready to leave. The thing grabbed his arm as he started to get up though and held him to the ground. He tried to break free of the thing's grasp, but he was too strong. Andolar was getting ready to scream for help when he realized the person was talking to him in goblin.

"What you say?" he asked as soon as he could trust his voice again.

"You no leave. We talk," he replied.

"You prisoners?"

"Yes, prisoners like you."

"You want get out? Get away from goblins."

"Yes. Want get out. Go home."

"I help you."

"You no can help you. How you help us?"

"Have help. Attack comes in morning. I come here to help. I . . ."

He hadn't learned the Goblin word for *magician*. Oh well, time to improvise. He made motions trying to show things flying from his fingers. After a few seconds of uncomprehending looks, he gave up and went on with the talk.

"You no eat morning."

"Why not eat? Need food."

"You no eat morning," he repeated urgently. "You wait for attack."

He didn't want to tell them exactly what was going on in case they were friendly toward the goblins. He hadn't even trusted the regular people that far.

"What you want from *dubroty*?"

That was a new one on him. He had never heard *dubroty* used. Maybe it was the thing's name.

"Dubroty help with attack?"

Maybe the best thing they could do was to stay out of the way. They seemed to be conversing in that growling voice. The one on the far side finally nodded, and the one he had been talking to turned back around to him.

"Dubroty help," he said as he pulled what looked like a two-foot-long iron bar out of the dirt on the ground.

Andolar could see there was a shallow trench cut into the dirt. The bar was quickly replaced, and the dirt smoothed out. Andolar looked around to make sure none of the guards saw the bar. Then he realized that their bodies had blocked most of the view. It probably wouldn't have mattered anyway because the bar would have been the same temperature as the ground. Andolar turned back around after looking over the area.

"Me Andolar," he said pointing at himself then at the creature. "You dubroty."

"You human," the creature replied. "We dubroty. Me Govin. Him Duvain."

Andolar held out his hand in friendship, and almost had it hit by the spit the other fired out when he saw the hand. Well, of all the nerve, treating him like that. Apparently they would help in getting out but didn't want anything to do with humans. The dubroty turned his back to Andolar and lay back down. He should have let them be taken out by the sleeping powder as well. That's what being friendly to others got you. He returned to the humans and lay down.

CHAPTER 17

It was much too early to be getting up Andolar thought as he felt someone nudging him in the side. He tried to slap the hand away, but it persisted. Finally, he opened his eyes and saw a man in ragged clothes leaning over him. He started backing up quickly and bumped into someone else. That person promptly fell and landed in his lap.

"No time for that, deary," he said automatically to the ragged woman he was now holding.

When he looked at his surroundings, he remembered where he was. Getting up with your senses only half there was dangerous. He looked around at the other prisoners for a moment and then got to his feet as someone helped the smiling woman off of him. The goblins were herding them into the compound. The dubroty they kept a close watch on. For their part, the dubroty acted as if the goblins didn't exist as they walked across the middle of the fort. The men and boys were sent to fetch firewood for the cook stoves, while the women and girls went to the supply building for foodstuffs. There were no young women or older girls in the group.

They walked past several goblins while about their wood hauling, but Andolar saw no sign of Haslan. The men carried in an entire day's supply of firewood before going about their other duties. He felt a stinging pain in his back and dropped the load of wood he had just picked up. He was lashed several more times before he could get the wood picked up and get out of the goblin's way. He could feel what had to be blood running down his back.

"Don't stop," a man told him, "don't look around, and don't talk."

"Work, not talk," a goblin shouted, and Andolar heard the lash strike behind him.

When they finally reached the kitchen, his back was stinging worse than it had when he was struck. There were several goblins asleep with their heads on the various tables scattered throughout the room. He wasn't sure, but there was one who might be Haslan. He felt the lash again as he looked around the room. He hadn't seen a goblin that close.

"You move, or go to other camp."

Andolar left for the woodpile again. The lash cracked against his back again.

"You go get water," a goblin told him.

Andolar looked at him like he didn't understand the goblin's speech. At least he remembered that much. The goblin struck him with the lash again and pointed to a yoke with a pair of buckets on it. He started toward the yoke and hurried after he felt the lash again. The goblins sure did apply that thing freely.

Andolar got to the yoke and picked it up on his shoulders. That thing wasn't light on its own. And now he had to fill the buckets with water. His thin frame fit in well with the other people here who had thinned out from lack of food and hard work.

He hurried to the central area where he saw a pool of clear water with a wall around it. He filled the buckets and carried them into the kitchen. As he was emptying the buckets, he had a chance to talk to the women.

"Is everyone fed from the same pots?"

"No, we make a meal for the slaves in one and the good food in the others for the goblins. They don't give us much to work with for making a meal for us slaves."

"That's right, you told me that last night. I'd forgotten."

Andolar emptied the buckets, and a goblin was watching. He turned and headed out quickly to get some more water. If that little pile of meat and vegetables by the pot at the end had to do for all of the prisoners, then it was no wonder they were thinning down. You'd think the commander would take better care of the people building his fort. Of course, he used to have a steady supply of new workers, so he didn't need to worry about taking care of the ones he had. When he came back with another load, he saw much larger piles of food by the other three pots. There was also a small skillet with bacon and eggs beside it. That must be for the commander. He could smell bread baking in the ovens, and his stomach rumbled.

He emptied the water into one of the pots and turned to make another run. When he turned, he saw the small goblin working his way over to where the cooking was starting. He faked a stumble and dropped the yolk with the buckets. The guard came over with his lash raised to strike, but the little goblin stepped between them.

"Mine to hurt," the goblin said. "Get water on me."

"Move, little brat," the guard replied, "or you get what he get."

Andolar almost cried with relief when he heard Haslan's voice. He had feared deep down that he might be deserted and become a permanent slave. He probably would be anyway, but at least his squad mates were here. The guard raised the lash to strike Haslan, but Haslan punched him in the stomach. The guard folded up on the floor after backing up several steps from the blow. Several of the goblins in the room were watching now. Haslan grabbed him by the arm.

"Scream like you're being hurt," the thief whispered, "or I'll make it hurt for real."

Andolar let out a scream as the halfman's grip tightened then screamed louder when Haslan twisted his hand. That actually had hurt. This would be a good time for the halfman to take out a little bit of a grudge against him if he had one. Haslan grabbed what remained of his shirt and pulled his head down to slap him. After a couple of slaps, he pulled Andolar down to his eye level.

"You get me wet more, I hurt you more," Haslan said and then continued in a whisper. "If you have something to say, make it quick."

"Berinda is here," Andolar said, talking quickly and quietly. "Skillet is for the commander and her. I'm getting word to her not to eat. The large pot with the small amount of food by it is for the prisoners. One of the other pots is for each of the shifts in the guard. Try to spike the last ones a little heavier than the first so they all go out about the same time."

"Thanks," Haslan said as he spun Andolar around and gave him a kick as he departed.

Andolar could hear laughter behind him from the goblins as he picked up the yoke and left the building. On the next trip in, he told the cooks that he had taken care of it so that they would be able to eat. They just couldn't eat anything prepared for the goblins. He thought that was Haslan back, sitting at a table again, when he got back into the building with two more buckets of water. He hurried and dumped the buckets into the pots. It was only after four more trips that he was allowed to move to some other work.

The men had to go through and pick up the chamber pots. He almost lost the breakfast he hadn't had yet from the smell. They left the palisade under guard and went to the garden. Some of the men brought shovels and started digging a hole beside the garden. The rest of them had to go back and bring out more pots. He wished he had gotten a shovel. He ended up making three trips to the barracks and another to help carry out the pots that the prisoners used. He saw a woman carrying two pots to the pit the men had dug and figured the commander got special service there as well. The pit was finished, so they dumped the pots. He used the opportunity, like the rest of the men, to relieve himself so that they wouldn't have more to carry the next day. Then he picked up some empties and started back. It looked like that was how they increased the size of the land cultivated for the garden. After they replaced the pots, which took another trip, they got in line for breakfast. Breakfast consisted of thin soup and old bread. He managed to pass the word that they could go ahead and eat during the chamber-pot trips.

Everyone ate like they were starving, which they probably were. Some of the men commented on the recent increase in the rations they were given. Andolar couldn't conceive of this being an increase from anything. If it was an increase, then his squad was probably responsible. They had cut off the supply of new workers. The goblin food wasn't ready yet since it was a much thicker stew and had to cook longer. After they finished the meager breakfast, they were herded off to begin the real work for the day. Andolar got the job of water carrying again, thanks to the goblin that Haslan punched. The other men looked on him with some sympathy, and he really got worried. He quickly found out that his job was to carry water around all day to every place the goblins were guarding and the slaves were working. There were enough places to go that two of them were doing the work. Andolar noticed the other man was hurrying as much as possible and wondered why. When he asked, the man said that was the only way the slaves got water often enough to survive. They were only allowed to make one trip to the slaves for every two they made to the guards. The man told him that until two days before, it had been one for every three made to the goblins. It seemed strange that their attacks around Delaigamon had changed the life of the prisoners so significantly. Andolar picked up his pace as well. He was going to be paying for all of this work with sore muscles, but it was better than being beaten.

He got to see almost all the areas of the camp that morning. He visited the gardens, livestock herds, timber cutters, builders, barracks, kitchens, and blacksmith shop. The dubroty weren't any more cordial now than they had been before. It looked like they were pounding the dents out of some big pieces of armor. If he wasn't mistaken, the armor was for a horse. His father and brother had armor something like that at home. He had never taken enough of an interest in armor types to know for sure though.

"You say after breakfast," one of the dubroty said to him. *Duvain*, he thought. "It after breakfast."

"Soon now," he said before he had to move on again.

It looked like the dubroty normally made metal pieces that were used to construct the fort. There were no real weapons visible in the blacksmith shop. Of course, an iron bar made a very effective weapon even before it was converted into a sword.

His legs were already tired and sore, and it was only about an hour after breakfast. He wished they had brought more powder so the goblins would be affected sooner. It was time to fill the water barrels in the barracks again. He had already topped them off once, and the other slave had been through once as well. From the size of the wet area around the barrels, the goblins intentionally spilled some to make the slaves work harder. What kind of people were they to take pleasure in such little cruelties on people that were already slaves? He knew the duchess tried to be even-handed with all of her neighbors, including the goblins, but the goblins sure didn't act that way.

When he reached the barracks, he saw the water barrels were almost full. He also saw that nearly every goblin in the barracks was sleeping on his bunk. It was working! He had to get everyone ready to go. He dumped his buckets, not caring about what hit the floor, and returned to the kitchen. There were several goblins with their heads down on the tables. He couldn't tell if Haslan was one of them. He went to where the women and girls were cleaning the pots and crockery.

"Soon now," he told one of the women.

He noticed as he moved away that she had picked up a knife from somewhere. He saw a couple more flashes of metal from around the women before he got outside the room. Several of the guards were leaning against buildings near where the prisoners were working. Hopefully, it wouldn't take much longer.

"Work, not watch," he heard in Goblin from behind him.

He ran for the spring with the yoke and buckets. When he turned around after filling the buckets, he saw Churinius come out of the house in chain mail. He was pulling on a rope, and Berinda was tied around the neck at the other end. She looked bruised and battered. The right side of her face was almost black. He wandered if she got that in battle or if she found someone else who could beat her in a fistfight. It might be a little of both. Churinius had a small bruise on one cheek and was favoring his left side. He jerked the rope hard and continued across the fort. She had her hands tied behind her back.

It looked like he was inspecting the fort. That could be bad. The goblins straightened up when they saw him. At least the ones who were still awake did. Andolar could see three that were asleep against the buildings. Some of the archers in the towers looked like they were asleep as well. Churinius yawned heavily as he walked. He sure hoped Haslan managed to get some to the commander. Berinda looked alert enough, although it didn't appear she was in any condition to fight. Churinius yawned again and shook his head trying to clear it of sleep. He noticed the goblins then. One of the guards fell off the walkway and landed on the ground. He got up for a second after he fell then laid back down.

Churinius started yelling at the goblins to straighten up, and then he noticed how many were slumped at their posts. Just then another yawn hit him, and he ran for the spring. Andolar jumped out of the way to avoid getting trampled and spilled both buckets on the ground. Now he would have to refill them. Andolar returned to the spring and saw Churinius with Berinda in tow splashing water on his face. The commander looked close to panic when he yawned again. Leaning over to the side, he made himself vomit up his breakfast. That man was much too quick on the uptake. Andolar filled the buckets again and started toward the blacksmith shop. He should tell those creatures that things were about to break loose.

"Alarm! Alarm!" he heard Churinius yelling behind him. "We are under attack! Get up, you lazy goblins!"

Andolar saw a couple goblins come out of the kitchen, and as he watched, the trailing goblin stabbed the one in front of him. He calmly laid the dead goblin down and assumed a sleep like position beside him. Well, he found Haslan. There was still no sign of Petrion.

Churinius ran toward his house, dragging Berinda after him. Andolar was at the corner of the building now, so he decided to chance a spell. Unfortunately, by the time he had checked for observers and put down the yoke, Churinius was already in the house. Hopefully, the commander wouldn't be able to fort up and hold them off. If all else failed, he supposed, they could try and burn him out. It was likely they would lose Berinda if it came to that, but they couldn't hang around here forever.

"Children, hurry into the slave pen," he yelled when he saw several of them standing around.

They needed to be out of the way regardless of what was coming. He was surprised when they listened to him and headed for cover.

Andolar picked up the yoke and started for the blacksmith shop. The dubroty had already quit work and were ready to fight.

The men and women that were outside the fort were running back with their tools. The goblin guards were pursuing them. He cast a sleep spell, and five of them dropped. The others, realizing they had a spell caster attacking them, came toward the gate at a run instead of getting picked off at a distance.

Andolar turned, smiling at the dubroty after finally having demonstrated what he did, and saw mean looks and raised weapons. He ran.

He looked back and slowed when he saw they weren't following him.

The people ran through the gate and came to him. He wasn't sure what to do with them. Looking back to the gate, he saw the dubroty against the wall. They screamed and attacked the goblins from behind when they entered the fort. The goblins turned in a panic at the sounds.

"Get them!" Andolar yelled belatedly to the people.

They screamed and charged at the goblins and distracted them. A couple got in swings before the dubroty finished off the goblins.

The men climbed the parapet and the towers to finish off the goblins that were asleep. There were very unpleasant sounds coming from the barracks, which were soon accompanied by the butchery on the walls. They must have suffered and seen others suffer terribly to make them react like that. The work the women were doing sounded especially gruesome.

Screams started from the closest barracks, and Andolar turned to see women running in terror. Arrows started flying out at the people in the compound. One of them grazed his shoulder as it went past, convincing him that hiding might be a good thing. He hurried behind the corner of the slave pen, and heard arrows hitting the wood behind him. When he peeked out, he saw four men and two women were down from arrows. One bunch of the goblins apparently were not affected by the powder.

"You may all surrender now, and your lives will be spared," Churinius called from the building.

He didn't sound sleepy now. He must have fought off the affects. Haslan wasn't by the door anymore, and he didn't have any idea where Petrion might be. The two dubroty were hidden in the blacksmith's shop with several of the men. Andolar decided to make his way there since he had a path that was under cover for most of the distance. His dash from the edge of the slave pen to the blacksmith shop didn't draw any arrow fire. Maybe they were out of arrows. Or maybe Churinius was so sure of recapturing them that he didn't want to kill any more of his workforce. The dubroty didn't seem very happy to see him, but at least they didn't look like they were ready to attack.

Goblins ran out of the back of the barracks and began forming near the center of the fort. Fifteen goblins were in the group, and they had two women as prisoners.

"Come on out, or the women die," Churinius called. "All you need do is drop your weapons and turn over to me the ones responsible for poisoning the food, and the rest of you may live. You cannot win. You are poorly armed and unarmored. The goblins will be more than happy to destroy you at my command."

"Dubroty," Churinius called, switching to Goblin, "you no die for humans. Come out. You do more work. Live. Go free soon."

Andolar heard the two dubroty talking in their language. They obviously knew how to fight, and he surely didn't want them to go over to the other side.

"Time's up," Churinius called, and then switched to goblin. "Bring that woman forward. Get ready to kill."

"Come out, or the woman dies," he called again. "This is your last chance. If you don't come out, I'll let the goblins take turns having fun with them until they're all dead."

"We can't let them kill the women," one of the men said.

The dubroty worked their way over to where Andolar was standing.

"You tell them," Duvain said to him, "that he kill anyway. Women all die. He hurt too much by slaves. Must kill. They quit, he kill them without fight. Die fighting. Some goblins die too. Better that way."

The men were getting ready to step out. Why was everything left up to him?

"Stop people," he called out finally. "If you go out there, he'll kill them and you without a fight. We have to attack them. That way maybe some of us will get free. We still outnumber them."

What a load of crap that was. Churinius could kill every one of the prisoners without working up a sweat. One of the women in the back started crying. Andolar wondered if she had a relative out there.

"Where's your attack force?" one of the men asked.

"You've seen it," he told them. "They were all supposed to fall asleep so that you could escape."

"The commander gave those goblins something to wake them up," one of the women told him. "It was in a small vial."

"Wow, we never thought of that," Andolar said. "He had a potion to counteract the sleeping powder. And he had enough of it to revive a bunch of the goblins."

"Too late," he heard from Churinius.

"Start now," he told the goblins.

Andolar looked out, and two of the goblins were dragging a woman to the front of the kitchen. The men, from their expression, would never stand still for that. He looked around the blacksmith shop quickly and grabbed a belt that had a bag on it. The goblins were almost to the building by the time he had it fastened and stepped out.

"Wait," he called.

"You wait," Churinius told the goblins, "you get to finish her soon."

After they stopped, Churinius turned back to him.

"All of you have to come out," he yelled, "not just one."

He turned to look at the others who were standing there. He saw hope and fear on their faces. Unfortunately, he figured his only betrayed the fear. He was going to die no matter what he did, so he might as well give some others a chance.

"He just promised the goblins that they could have the woman in a little bit," he told the people before continuing. "Don't believe he'll do anything but torture and kill you."

"They aren't coming out," Andolar yelled back. "You are going to surrender or be destroyed."

"Nice bluff, slave," the commander called back. "So you're the cause of all this. Come out all of you and save yourselves."

Churinius tried to duck away from the burning streak of fire that came toward him, but it moved with him and left a deep burn mark on his cheek. Andolar tried to look confident, even though he had been aiming for the man's eye. This depended on him being able to convince the commander that he was a powerful magician.

"Next time I will use more power," he yelled. "Release the prisoners or you start dying."

The goblins looked scared enough, but Churinius didn't seem bothered. Andolar decided to preempt him with a strike at the archers. He cast the spell and four of the five archers collapsed. The goblins started to break, but a laugh from Churinius stopped them.

"Wake them," he told the goblins, "the magician only put them to sleep."

"You are not a powerful magician, are you?" Churinius taunted. "You'll have to do better than that."

Andolar dearly wanted to duck into the blacksmith's shop, but if he did, everything was going to fall apart. They could still run though. Likely he would escape. Unfortunately, the other people were in too bad of shape to outrun goblins for long, and Berinda was still a prisoner. He would have to trust Petrion and Haslan. When he looked over at the woman about to be tortured, there was only one goblin with her. Andolar could see the hilt of a dagger sticking out of the side his chest, out of the view of the other goblins. Haslan must have been one of the two goblins. He killed the other one and used one of his daggers to hold him in an upright position by the post. That meant the woman wasn't tied. Haslan was hurrying back to where the goblins were standing around Churinius.

Andolar stepped forward, and the goblins started fading back a little bit. The ones on their way to wake up the archers were backing up as well. That left him less arrows to deal with, at least for a while.

Haslan ran behind the commander, but when he got close to the man, he fell flat on his face. Churinius only spared him a slight glance as he pulled himself up using Berinda's trousers and then returned his attention to Andolar. As soon as Haslan reached his feet, Andolar began.

"No kill goblins if they run," he said in Goblin. "Show you now on commander what happen if you stay."

"Attack, magician," Churinius ordered.

The goblins started moving forward slowly, but Andolar stood his ground.

"You move, you die," Andolar told the massed goblins.

They stopped, at least temporarily, so he started his plan. He started mumbling gibberish in a loud commanding voice and made some throwing motions that he hoped Haslan saw. Churinius was shouting at the goblins now and hitting them with the flat of his sword. They started moving forward again. He pulled out some of the stuff in the pouch and started fiddling with it. It was a white powder.

The goblins were only twenty paces away and seemed to be gaining courage. Haslan finally got behind Churinius, so Andolar increased the volume of his chant. When he saw Haslan flash a dagger, he yelled out what he hoped was a suitable climax. Churinius screamed in pain, and all the goblins focused their attention on him. Andolar made the most of the opportunity and cast his last spell on the remaining archer. He also got the two who went to wake up the others. Only seven goblins were still functioning. No, make that six. Haslan was one of the original fifteen. Churinius dropped Berinda's rope at the attack, and she backed away from him.

Andolar started chanting loudly again, and the people streamed out to attack the goblins. The south gate to the fort was closed, so the goblins had no choice but to fight. They were formed up reasonably well and met the human charge, with Churinius in the back. Still, it was six against twenty. The goblin line broke, but Churinius was there to cut down two people in succession to stem the tide. One goblin went down, but they wounded six of the people in that quick exchange. The people quickly retreated. Eight were down in a few seconds, and a couple more had less serious injuries.

Andolar looked around quickly but didn't see anything of the dubroty. Maybe they decided to get out while there was still time. Churinius pulled the dagger from his back, dropping it on the ground, and walked toward Andolar at the front of his goblins. The goblins were heartened by the commander and started following. Fifteen paces. He was going to have to run for it.

He caught movement by the commander's house and saw the door closing. At the same time, he saw the dubroty come from behind the barracks and head toward the house. Petrion faded into view suddenly in front of them, holding a pair of short-hafted battleaxes and two swords. The dubroty raised their iron bars to attack him, but Petrion offered them the axes haft first. They didn't waste time in accepting the offered weapons, nor did they waste time getting into the fight. They charged right for Churinius screaming something or other as they attacked. Petrion tossed one of his swords to Berinda, who was running for the house as well. Haslan must have used his fall as a cover to cut her hands free.

Andolar breathed out a heavy sigh of relief at his narrow escape. Churinius looked back to see what the disturbance was, and Andolar ducked into the blacksmith's again. The people were staring at him as he panted and sweated, but he didn't really care. About two more steps from Churinius, and he would have been running for the gate. Churinius had been only seven paces away, and he seemed to grow larger as he got closer. People looked larger all decked out in metal armor and carrying a big weapon. He got his breathing under control as quickly as possible and stepped out again.

Petrion was gone, but Berinda was running toward Churinius with her sword. It looked like she had his dagger in her other hand.

Churinius turned quickly and engaged the two dwarfs. The last goblins formed up, with half facing the dubroty and the other half facing the prisoners. Churinius caught one ax blow on the shield and turned the other with his sword. His sword flicked back quickly and sliced open the shoulder of Govin. At least he thought it was Govin that had twin braids in his long beard. The painful wound didn't seem to slow him though. Berinda reached him, and Churinius moved closer to the barracks behind him. As soon as the commander was looking the other way, Haslan struck his neighboring goblins. A dagger thrust took one in the back, and a sword thrust quickly followed to another.

Petrion faded back into view and cut down a goblin from behind. Churinius immediately moved to get the barracks at his back when he saw he was facing three fighters and a magician with only one goblin for help. Haslan moved quickly to the building beside the enemy commander on his left side. Berinda was on that side. Churinius still managed to deliver another cut to Govin while holding off his three attackers.

Petrion blocked the remaining two goblins from following the commander. Andolar did his standard run-in-and-scare-them maneuver, but Petrion had already sliced the tip of his sword across a goblin's throat. The goblin collapsed coughing up blood.

The second goblin attacked when he saw Petrion swing at his companion. Petrion had anticipated the move, and the hit on the first goblin hardly slowed his sword. He continued the stroke, making it a head strike at the second goblin. The goblin saw the blade just in time and ducked. The sword glanced off the top of his helmet and knocked it off. The goblin backed up to get some time to recover from the blow, but Petrion pressed him hard. On the third attack, the goblin failed to deflect Petrion's thrust sufficiently. It pierced his left lung instead of his heart. The goblin fell bleeding from the mortal wound.

Petrion hurried to attack Churinius. Govin was weakening. Poor food, combined with the four cuts Churinius had delivered, was taking its toll. He had two cuts on his right arm in addition to cuts on the shoulder and left arm he had taken earlier. Petrion, moving in on that side, eased the pressure on the beleaguered dwarf. Berinda was fencing with Haslan. At least he hoped it was Haslan. Berinda was not able to attack Churinius because whoever it was there kept her engaged. As Petrion moved up, Andolar saw what the two had worked out. On Petrion's first swing, Haslan ducked low and Berinda thrust straight in and hit Churinius in the shoulder. Haslan planted Andolar's dagger solidly into Churinius's leg when he ducked. He also swung his short sword, but the sword was stopped by the commander's leg greave.

Haslan left the dagger and rolled out between Berinda and Duvain. Berinda dropped a dagger for Haslan on the ground behind her. Duvain took advantage of the new ally's move and ducked low and took a solid swing at Churinius's other leg. His greave held again, but the flesh beneath had to be injured by the force of the blow. Churinius fell against the side of the barracks. The dubroty and the fighters picked up their attacks, and four against one was odds too great even for Churinius. Petrion devoted some of his efforts to protecting Govin, but Berinda was attacking. She was too far around for the commander to be able to bring his sword to bear on her. He tried to slam her with the shield, but his injured arm couldn't put enough force in the blow to really hurt her. Berinda thrust hard again, and punctured Churinius's shield and maybe his side. Her sword snapped off at the hilt from the force of the blow. Berinda, off balance from the thrust, fell into the shield. Churinius pushed her back to get freedom to move, and he stopped Duvain's next strike at his leg.

Churinius pulled his arm from the damaged shield and grabbed something from a small case on his belt. The shield stayed pinned to the barracks wall by the sword, and Andolar saw blood streaming down the man's side. Andolar saw something sparkle in his hand but couldn't tell what it was. Haslan apparently didn't have the same problem because he threw a dagger and hit Churinius in the hand. It was a beautiful throw. The dagger went clear through the hand and shattered what must have been a glass vial. Duvain hewed at the leg yet again and, this time, penetrated the armor. Churinius stared at his hand for a second and then slid down the wall and into unconsciousness as Petrion thrust into his unprotected chest.

CHAPTER 18

Govin sat down heavily once Churinius fell, and Duvain started trying to stop the loss of blood. Petrion handed him a couple of bandages and started working with a couple more on the other wounds. Duvain looked surprised but kept working on Govin all the same. Berinda sat down for a rest as well. Someone was saying something behind him, but he couldn't quite make out the words.

"What was that?" he asked the man behind him.

"What do you want us to do now, sir magician?"

"See to your wounded first then grab some food and bedding and get ready to leave. Then go take everything of value from the goblins and bring it here."

The people hurried to do what he said. From the looks of things, most of the prisoners who were down weren't dead. He supposed they were former prisoners now. They had liberated the camp.

"See if you can find a wagon to put the wounded in while you're about it," he called after them.

Haslan was already checking Churinius's body for valuables.

"We might be able to save him," Haslan said, "if we patch up his wounds. There are a couple more potions in here that are probably healing potions. We could tie him up and give him one of them."

"What do you think, Petrion?" Andolar asked. "Should we try and take him back as a prisoner?"

"No, I don't think it's worth wasting a magic item or two just to get him to go back with us. This fellow here is in a bad way though. I don't see how he stayed conscious as long as he did with those wounds. Maybe we should see if he wants to try one."

"They speak Goblin," Andolar told him, "but not human."

"Jar, maybe heal," Petrion said to Duvain while pointing at the vials in Churinius's belt case.

Duvain just looked at him.

"You want try on him?" Petrion asked.

"Him dying. Easier die this way than from humans," Duvain said.

Andolar noticed that Duvain had dropped his ax. The dubroty must think he was a prisoner again. Andolar picked up the ax and handed it to Duvain. Then he pulled out the two vials and brought them to Petrion.

"No die," Andolar told him. "Come with us. Safe place."

"Humans kill dubroty. Duvain not kill you. You let Govin die in fight."

"We not see dubroty before," Andolar told him. "We not kill."

Andolar gave Govin one of the potions. His wounds started to close, but he was still unconscious. Andolar gave him the other one, and Govin's eye came open. The dubroty looked around to see where he was. He said something to Duvain, and they talked for a few seconds. When they were finished, Govin looked over at Andolar.

"Owe you life, *gruvot*. Debt owed must be paid. What do with Govin."

"What gruvot?" he asked the two.

Govin used the motions Andolar had made the night before when trying to tell them he was a magician. There was actually a smile on Govin's face as he taunted him. Andolar smiled back, and that seemed to surprise the two dubroty. Shaking his head, he laughed at how ridiculous he must have looked. It was good to be alive.

He got up still chuckling and followed Haslan to the commander's house. It never paid to trust a thief too far, and Haslan still hadn't returned either of his daggers. When they got to the house, they saw several weapons on the wall like those of the dubroty and four suits of plate mail in their size.

"Duvain," Andolar called, "come here."

Duvain got up and came over to the buildings. Andolar pointed out the armor to him so that he could take it. When Andolar looked around, he saw tears on the dubroty's face.

"What wrong?"

"Duvain and Govin not alone. Four five's of dubroty came out. Rest dead."

"What happened?"

"Humans attack from west, goblins attack from east. Dubroty are stuck in middle. Fight all off, but no food in mountains. Dubroty starving. Send out bands south and north. Find food. Find friends. We go south. Find more goblins. Then humans attack. Ride horses. Kill dubroty. Find out only humans south. No help for dubroty. All dubroty die."

"Not all bad. Churinius bandit."

"No lie, magician," Duvain told him. "Churinius captain in great army. He captures us. Tell us no hope."

Andolar called Petrion over because he hadn't caught all the words in that last little bit. The ranger came, and Duvain repeated it for him. Petrion translated whenever he didn't know which word Duvain was using. He also translated a few words from Andolar into Goblin.

"Churinius bandit. Duchess sends us to kill. He helps goblins kill humans."

"Humans fight great army?"

"What great army? No army here except goblins."

"Goblins this side mountains. Humans other side mountains. Humans this side mountains too."

"Humans this side mountains only kill when attacked. Even goblins. No attack goblins unless goblins attack humans. When goblins attack, humans kill. You need food. Humans have food. You fight goblins. Goblins attack humans so humans fight goblins too. We help."

Duvain looked hopeful for a few seconds, and then his features hardened.

"Human trick. Humans try before. Everyone friends. Trade goods. Humans get inside dubroty home. Humans kill dubroty. Humans kill dubroty women and children."

"You come with us. You see. No lie. No trick."

"Owe debt. We come, but you no trick dubroty."

Haslan came over with what he found. He had found a ruby ring and a gold necklace on Churinius. There were several weapons in the room that might be enchanted. And there were two chests in the back that rattled like they contained coins.

"What that?" Duvain asked, pointing to Haslan.

"That halfman," Petrion replied since Andolar didn't know the word.

"Thought he just traitor goblin. Halfmen are dead. Humans kill."

"Humans not kill halfmen," Haslan told Duvain. "Humans and us same. Work together. Fight together. Live together."

"Maybe we go and listen to you," Duvain said after a long time thinking. "Maybe Churinius trick. Let dubroty go thinking all bad to south."

"Duvain," Andolar said, "take armor and weapons. They are your size. You and Govin use."

Duvain went to the wall and started taking down all the armor and weapons. He made two trips to remove it. Haslan was working on the chest, and Petrion was gathering the remaining weapons from the walls. Berinda and Govin were stripping the armor and weapons off of Churinius.

"Petrion," Andolar said as a thought ran cold fingers of terror up his back, "could you post lookouts so that we see anyone coming before they see us."

Petrion and Haslan both looked at him and shivered. Petrion ran outside, yelling loudly for volunteers to watch for enemies. They didn't want that to happen again, especially while they were trapped with only two ways out.

Haslan went back to working on the chests after a few seconds of listening for someone to call out an alarm. He heard Haslan breath out a heavy sigh of relief as he walked away. It matched the one he had just let out.

Andolar decided to see how the packing was going. The people found two wagons and hitched horses to each. They had eight wounded that would be sitting in one of the wagons. Andolar took the two remaining horses. One of them looked like it might be a warhorse. He decided to saddle the one horse and see if Petrion wanted the other one decked out in armor. Petrion wasn't in the fort that he could see, so he took the horse to the blacksmith shop. All of the horse armor seemed to be there anyway. He put the second saddle on a table in the shop.

The people were starting to bring in everything from the goblins. Most of them were carrying something to eat. For that matter, the wounded people all had something to eat as well. Govin was walking over to him, so he stopped to wait on him.

"No leave dubroty stuff for goblins."

Andolar didn't know the word for *wagon*, so he had Govin follow him to their wagon.

"Put here. This ours. We take."

His goblin wasn't good enough to express complex thoughts. It was more like just enough to get by on. He needed to teach these dubroty the human speech. Or better yet, he could learn their language.

"Govin," he called as the dubroty was walking away, "You teach me dubroty speech. I teach you human speech."

"Govin know human speech," Govin answered.

He immediately rattled off something that sounded like a language but like nothing Andolar had ever heard. Andolar tried talking to him again in the human language. Govin shook his head that he didn't understand.

"I talk human speech. Churinius talk human speech. Churinius talk you speech too. Some others Churinius people talk both. All talk Churinius speech."

"I never hear what you call human speech before."

"We teach then. Govin get dubroty things now."

Andolar went to where the prisoners were bringing the things from the goblins. He had the children start sorting the stuff into piles: money in one pile, weapons in another, and everything else in a third. When the money started to pile up, he got barrels to put it in. There was getting to be a pile of copper. Andolar had them separate it out by type before putting it into the barrels.

Govin and Duvain loaded all the dubroty armor and weapons on the wagon and were now carrying out one of the chests. They were both wearing armor. They looked much more imposing with the heavy plate mail and battleaxes. Haslan was bringing some smaller weapons. Andolar went to see how everything was coming.

"What was in the chests, Haslan?" Andolar asked.

"One had gold," Haslan replied, "and one had silver. The chest with the gold also had a small coffer inside. The coffer held some platinum and a bar of some strange metal that Duvain grabbed. They acted like it was very valuable. Duvain almost knocked me down trying to get at it and kept saying dubroty. You might want to check into it. There also were several bottles of some kind of spirits they claimed. I packed all of Churinius's papers into a small box to put in the wagon. I can't understand the writing, but maybe someone can figure it out. I threw in some blanks and ink too in case you need it for something."

"Duvain," he called.

"Yes, Andolar?"

"Haslan say you take metal bar. Is it dubroty bar?"

"Yes, belong to dubroty. Thought Churinius send off."

"What is it?"

"It's dubroty metal. Not for humans."

"Why not."

"Humans use metal to kill dubroty."

"We humans not kill dubroty. You keep metal. Tell me about it."

"Metal makes steel strong."

"Oh."

Andolar thought quickly and decided to take a different approach to try and get some more information on the metal.

"We make good steel. Not need dubroty metal. You keep."

"It is good metal. Humans take because it make metal stronger."

"How black metal make steel stronger? Duvain trick Andolar."

"No! No trick. Here you see."

Duvain took a sword out of the wagon and had Govin hold it. He pulled out the ax he retrieved from Churinius's house. Then they swung the weapons together. The sound caused several heads to come up, but Andolar was too busy looking to see what had happened to notice. He noticed Haslan had crept up as well. The steel sword had a nick in it. The ax did too, but it was smaller.

"You see. Humans cast spells on dubroty steel. Metal helps steel take magic. Churinius armor is dubroty steel. Hard to cut."

He looked over at Churinius's body and saw his armor was gone. He saw Petrion out of the corner of his eye and hurried to talk with him. Petrion apparently didn't see him because he started walking off at an angle.

"Petrion. Petrion!"

"Oh, I was just going to look around again. What do you need, Andolar?"

"I saw horse plate armor in the blacksmith shop. I took a warhorse over there in case you wanted it. I didn't have any idea how to put it together. Oh, by the way, those dubroty have some kind of black metal that they alloy with the steel. They have a bar of it with them. Said something about it making the steel stronger, and helping spell casters enchant it further."

"Hey, that's great. That would be a big help in the war. I better go get that armor on the horse."

Andolar wondered why Petrion had such a big smile on his face. He sure didn't see any reason to smile. They were taking forever getting ready to leave.

"Don't bring out everything," he yelled at the people. "You are digging out what you want to take with you. You can't take all of that junk in one wagon. Get any valuables and some bedding. Store what you get in the wagon as you get it. Keep putting the coins in the barrels though. And put all the food you'll need in the wagon first! I don't want you starving on the way home because you loaded too much junk. In fact, just put food and blankets in the wagon with the wounded. Anything else you want you carry."

He hurried to the south gate to open it. He called to a couple of the men on the way to help him. There was a man in each of the towers acting as a guard. He wondered if they knew how to shoot the short bows they were holding. Haslan finished in the house.

"Andolar," Haslan told him, trying unsuccessfully to hide a smile, "you really should get cleaned up and find some clothes. You look a mess."

"Right," Andolar said after a look at himself. "Did Churinius have any extra clothes in there?"

"Yes, he had a closetful."

"I'll go change then. Have you checked that other barracks building over there?"

"No, it wasn't occupied."

"Well, check it anyway. Maybe that was the barracks the goblin raiders used. They could very well have left something behind."

"Yes, my lord magician," Haslan said with a mocking salute.

"Where's Berinda?"

"Staying out of your way if she knows what's good for her," Haslan said with a laugh as he headed for the barracks.

Berinda was helping Petrion put the armor on that horse. He hoped he got one of the horses. He went into the commander's house and made use of the water, towels, and clothes. The clothes were much too big for him, but at least they were clean. He hadn't any more than sat down in a very comfortable chair when Haslan came bursting into the room.

"We have trouble."

"Are more goblins coming?" Andolar asked as he jumped up.

"Not right now, but the other barracks has been in use recently. It was in use by humans. More than a score, from the number of bunks with bedding on them."

"Well go tell Petrion. Why did you come to me?"

"Uh sure. I'll tell him. By the way, with just a quick check, I found coins, gems, and jewelry over there. There's some extra clothes too if you or the prisoners want some more. You could probably find a better fit."

"I'll do that. Load the treasure in the wagon, and get ready to move. I'll talk to the prisoners while you're telling Petrion."

He went running out of the house and saw the dubroty loading the wagon with food and blankets. Govin was bringing blankets from the human barracks, and Duvain was bringing food from the storehouse. Their wagon was getting really heavy. They had armor and treasure and supplies. The former prisoners were having an even worse time. He saw Petrion hurrying them all up to get them started toward Gamalius. The size of the corral put a scare into Andolar. If the human troops were mounted, then they could catch them on the trail back.

He went to the collection area to see everything the farmers brought in. The barrel of the copper coins was almost full. There was a fair amount in the one with silver coins and a dozen golds laid out separately. The people surely wouldn't be hurting for money when they returned home. Unfortunately, none of them had homes to go to, and most of them were probably missing relatives. Money wasn't much of a substitute for all of the things in life they had lost. Andolar thought back on his own loss for a few seconds and decided things could have been much worse for him. At least he had a father come back to him and had a home and money. He shook his head. No time for those kinds of thoughts now. He had to get busy.

Petrion had the women gathering supplies and clothing. He had half of the men guarding and the other half pouring oil on the structures. They were going to burn the place down. That would send out another signal for everyone in the area that something was wrong. Andolar decided to talk to Petrion.

"You aren't starting another fire, are you?" Andolar asked Petrion in shock. "You know what happened the last time."

"Yes, as a matter of fact, I am. And this one will be much larger than the last. I'm not leaving a fortified position behind that I can destroy this easily. Do you have any idea how many lives it could cost to take this place if it was occupied again? Would you like to explain to the duchess why she lost all of those troops?"

"Oh," Andolar replied. "Well, all right then. As long as you have a good reason, go ahead and do it. We really need to get moving though."

"Someone is coming in!" one of the sentries yelled.

Petrion rushed to the wall and up a tower. Andolar was right behind him. They both stayed low.

"You realize that I have no more spells, don't you?"

"Yes, but I don't think you're going to need them. That is a group of about ten goblins with three prisoners. We can take them easily."

"While we are fighting them, we aren't getting away. All we have to do is stay pinned down here to be wiped out eventually."

"You keep the farmers moving, and I'll take out the goblins. Have them ready to leave within the half hour."

"I can do my part if you do yours."

"With those two dubroty, I think we could take out about thirty goblins. I have Berinda back now too."

"Lucky you."

"You," Petrion said to the man in the tower, "prop up the goblin bodies. Then stay down."

He ran to where the others were waiting. After collecting the fighters and the thief, again in goblin garb, he went to the south gate. Haslan was outside as the front person.

Andolar went to the people and told them they were leaving in five minutes. That way, maybe they could manage it in thirty.

"What about the cattle, sir magician?" one of the men asked.

"Take treasure instead. It's smaller, easier to carry, and won't slow us as much. The goblins will be searching for you. We have to move quickly. On second thought, get the cattle ready to move out. They can probably move as fast as you can. Why are people carrying weapons into the barracks?"

"Petrion told us to burn all the weapons we didn't take, so the goblins wouldn't have them for another attack. The fire will mess up the metal."

That ranger sure planned ahead. A hail came from around the south gate, and Andolar heard Haslan answer it. All of the people found clothes that fit them reasonably well from either the human or the goblin stores. The people had their wagon completely loaded, with the wounded sitting on top of some of the bedding. They would probably end up dumping a bunch of it before they got back to Gamalius.

"All the coins you found are yours, Divide them up evenly," he told them. "When you get back to Gamalius!" he said in disgust when he saw some of them starting to count it out. "Leave the copper if you start getting loaded down."

It looked like half of them had forgotten something they wanted to take as they scurried around with last minutes grabs of some item to add to their sacks.

"If you haven't already, each of you take a weapon of some type. You may need it."

That set off some more scrambling. He turned toward the front gate just as the goblins were entering with their three badly abused prisoners. The prisoners were coming in first. As soon as they were past, Berinda and the two dubroty jumped out and attacked. The goblins didn't even have their weapons out. Petrion faded into view behind them, and he and Haslan attacked from the back. Seven of the eleven goblins were down before they could draw a weapon to defend themselves. The other four, pressed from both sides, didn't manage to do more than die. It was all over within seconds. The thief quickly looted the bodies, and the others pulled them inside the gate. The three freed prisoners fell to weeping. Some of the others got food and drink for them.

"We're loaded, lord magician," one of the men said from behind him.

"Everyone, off the wall, we're getting out of here," Andolar yelled.

The three new prisoners were put on the wagon because they were exhausted. It was much too crowded and too heavy, but they didn't have time to sort and find things to leave behind. The men on the wall came down and grabbed packs prepared for them by the others. The wagon moved out with a woman driving and everyone else walking around it. They looked like a well-armed merchant group. With any luck, small groups of goblins would stay away from them. If the group was large enough to hit a caravan of almost seventy people, then they were lost anyway. Andolar had Berinda drive their wagon out, but not before he had to listen to a string of complaints from her. He turned around and pretended to look through the stuff while ignoring her for long enough that she got tired and left. The people finished moving the surplus weapons, and Petrion was ready to set the place on fire. Petrion told them to keep the tracks on top of each other so it looked like a single wagon. Men pushed the cattle and sheep out after the wagons, further obscuring the tracks. Andolar led one of the horses out of the fort. The warhorse was tied to the back of the wagon. It hadn't appreciated being loaded down with goods, but then neither had his horse.

When they entered the woods to the south of the fort, Petrion was going to fire the buildings. He still couldn't see any smoke rising, even when the trees were about to block the fort from view.

CHAPTER 19

When Haslan told him about the human barracks, Petrion set out to determine how many troops from the fort were out on other assignments. The humans had given him some rough estimates, but there was too much range in numbers to reassure him. He decided to see what the dubroty knew. Both dubroty seemed like trained warriors and so should have taken better note of the number and composition of the troops.

According to the dubroty, the human troops from the fort had gone with the last raiding party. One hundred goblins, twenty-three human fighters with armor and armored horse, and two human-fixing magicians the dubroty told him. His group would have been massacred if they had tried to stop the fourth raid. Unless Baron Gilbert sent a very strong force, they had been massacred.

Petrion was shocked by the numbers. Where and how had the goblins managed to recruit a large party of heavy cavalry and two healers? A desertion of that size should have been news that traveled through the realm.

Lighting off the fort would bring them quickly back if they were anywhere in the area. South was the direction they would look for the perpetrators. The prisoners and squad would need every minute they could get. Leaving the fort could cost hundreds of lives when the duchess had to take it. The only problem was the lives lost now if things went wrong were theirs. A lot of innocent people who had suffered enough were at stake as well. The fort might very well be rebuilt before the duchess could get back with troops, which would make lighting it off a useless act. He didn't really believe that though. The duchess would move quickly to gain the initiative in the coming battles.

There was an option that would take care of everything. He would stay behind and light off the fires when he saw the raiders returning. The main danger of that plan was that the raiders could cut across and intercept the wagons without returning to the fort. He should have told the others, but they might have wanted to stay. Andolar would have his spells back within a day and so would add to the defense. The dubroty were worth a lot too. Who was he kidding? If the others were anything close to Churinius or the fighter at the other camp, they would be decimated. It would take the wagons and prisoners some time to reach the border. They just couldn't move fast on foot in the condition they were in. There was no way everyone could ride even if they took nothing but food in the wagon. The prisoner's wagon was almost all essentials the way it was. He still felt guilty about loading their wagon down with the high-quality gear and coins, but leaving the stuff would have given the goblins more to fight with.

He moved about the camp, periodically going to the wall to check for approaching enemies. If they suspected something wrong, they would come in very cautiously or very quick. If they didn't suspect anything they would come in at a normal pace, whatever that was. He hated waiting. There was nothing to do but think.

He followed the trail of the wagons and finished obliterating the tracks as best he could for about two hundred paces. That occupied him for a couple of hours. Then he piled more flammable stuff on top of the captured weapons. He threw the blocks from the retaining wall into the spring to clog it. The trips to the wall slowed his progress, but not as much as being caught would. He decided to move the human bodies, except for Churinius, into the human barracks. There wasn't time to bury them, so a funeral pyre was the next best thing. That took him another hour.

Finally, he got together a couple of packs. One pack was food and water. The second pack contained a couple hundred feet of small-diameter rope, a goblin-sized ax, and ten daggers. He decided to get some sleep, since he would have to stay awake for quite a while soon. The odds of the raiders coming back during this day were remote, unless one of the goblins had been dispatched to bring them back after the attack on the other camp.

This was driving him crazy. Why did he have to think of twenty options for every single situation? He wished there was a way to turn his mind off for a while.

He couldn't find a way to turn it off, but he found a way to change its direction after a while. He thought of Lydia and the life they had planned together. The prisoner-holding pen was the least likely spot for them to search. He went there to sleep so they wouldn't find him before he woke and made sure he was cloaked. He sat down and leaned against the inside wall to rest. Thinking of Lydia was a pleasant way to take that rest. There had been too little time for thinking of pleasant things lately.

❧

Petrion woke to the sound of movement and voices nearby. He carefully opened his eyes and looked around at ground level so his cloak concealed his face from other eyes. It was night, but the gold moon was bright again and the silver one was helping some. He could just make out a figure with him in the pen by the light of the moons. It was a human, and he thought it was a woman, standing just inside the pen, looking out. He got up as quietly as he could and went to the gate. Goblins were conversing in front of the entrance. At night, he couldn't look at the goblins at this range, except from the back. His eyes, according to ranger training, showed up more than the rest of his body to the heat vision of the goblins. The rangers practiced ways of defeating the goblin heat vision, and one of the most common mistakes they talked about was peeking out of a good hiding place. He drifted quietly to the side until he could look out at their feet and count them. His cloak gave him that advantage over normal hiding at least. They had to be looking at the same angle he was looking to see his eyes.

There were three goblins, and they were quietly discussing the empty fort.

"All dead."

"Churinius dead too."

"All prisoners gone. All treasure gone. All everything gone."

"Oil all over everything too. Ready for fire."

"Waiting for someone to drop torch to burn fort down."

"Need to tell Glurius. He needs to know what happen."

"Someone will need to tell the king too. He will be plenty mad about this."

"He will want to kill. He might kill one who brings news. I'm not going."

"He might reward someone if he brings news quick. I will go."

"I will tell Glurius."

"I will stay here with woman."

"You will not stay. I will get Glurius. Budorf will tell king. You will follow humans."

"We can't leave the woman here. She will get away."

"We can't take her. She will slow us down."

"We will have to kill her. She is about dead anyway."

"Yes, not much more fun. Some maybe. We will see before we go. Then kill her."

Petrion had heard all he needed or cared to hear. His teeth were locked together so tightly that his jaw was starting to ache. He moved away from the door along the wall of the pen so that the goblins wouldn't bump into him by accident. The door to the pen opened, and he saw the feet of the three goblins as they came after the woman. She was so far gone that she didn't try to get away.

The goblins were too intent on the woman for their own health. Petrion slid cautiously to the gate. He could see them for their entire length since he didn't have to worry about their seeing him. Two of the goblins had swords, and the third had a short bow and dagger.

The rasp of his sword being pulled could warn them that trouble was nearby. Petrion turned his back to the goblins as he drew his sword, so that a chance look wouldn't expose him early while the gap in the cloak was there. Turning his back on goblins was a very hard thing for him to do in spite of the cloak. When he turned back, he was behind the goblins and in perfect position. They hadn't noticed the slight noise he made. His only consideration was making sure his swings were shortened enough not to endanger the woman.

Petrion swung with all of his strength in a flat arc. He took the head from the shoulders of the left goblin and sent it rolling across the pen. The body collapsed into the dust. The other two goblins stared stupidly at the rolling head, and then turned to look at the collapsing body of their companion. Both caught sight of Petrion as they turned and grabbed at their weapons. Before the two could draw weapons and turn, the second was down from shoulder and lower back wounds. The third goblin got set enough to fence with him but wasn't that good of a fighter. Petrion patiently fought him, never taking a chance on being injured. His first blow that got through sliced the goblin's cheek. He winced a little at the thought of his own recent injury. He feinted to the goblin's shield side high, quickly redirected the blade and brought it in low toward the goblin's ankles. The goblin brought his sword over to help block. Petrion changed directions from the second feint and brought the sword quickly across the front to lay open the goblin's sword arm from wrist to elbow. The goblin's sword dropped, and Petrion thrust with his own sword into the goblin's stomach.

The stomach wasn't the best place to strike because it left an opponent alive long enough to kill you. In battle, you took what was offered. Petrion walked toward the woman as the goblin watched his little bit of remaining life pour out of his arm and his stomach. Petrion didn't even turn when he heard the goblin fall behind him.

"You're safe, ma'am," Petrion said to the woman.

She looked at him uncomprehendingly for a couple of moments and then started walking calmly toward the gate of the slave pen. Petrion stooped over the nearest goblin to see if he had any valuables. He dropped and rolled away from the gate when he heard the sound of a weapon being drawn. He hadn't thought to check the rest of the compound for more returning raiders. He had just assumed the three he heard talking were all there were. Now the woman was in worse danger than before. How stupid could a guy be? He desperately turned and got his feet under him after the roll.

When he scrambled into the guard position, all he saw was the woman standing close to the gate with a dagger sticking out of her chest. Petrion watched as she slowly sank to the ground. He swallowed hard at the sight and turned his head quickly to keep it from burning into his memory any deeper. He regretted then that the duchess hadn't set out on a plan to rid the north of goblins, regardless of the cost in money and lives. These particular goblins at least didn't deserve to live.

Not all goblins were bad though. He remembered hearing in ranger school that when the humans first entered this area, some goblins accepted them. Some even wanted to try the human way of life. Most of them were women since many times, the males dominated them to the point of brutality. They set up a few small villages at the edge of human lands. Other goblins had come one night and kidnapped or killed them.

More goblins had come over to the humans in the following years, although the numbers had decreased each year. They were resettled on lands further to the south, away from their vengeful kin. The last goblins to come over had been about five years before as the war ended.

He had to get out of the slave pen and away from the woman's body. He quickly made a circuit of the fort, looking for other returning goblins. When he didn't find anything else alive, he climbed onto the walkway of the fort. Walking the walls and sharpening wooden stakes kept him awake and away from the sights and memories of the slave pen.

By the time morning was well along, the stench in the fort was becoming unbearable. So was the sound of the various carrion birds which he constantly disturbed as he walked around the fort.

Petrion suddenly felt like an idiot. If the returning raiders could see smoke from a fire during the daylight, they could surely see vultures winging in the sky above the fort. The smoke would be visible farther away probably, but the circling birds would be visible from a distance too. The raiders might not return to the fort, except to scout from a distance. He could be sitting here waiting for them to return while they were heading off in a different direction maybe to attack his people.

He made the decision to light off the fort and head south. If he didn't have a good lead on the raiders, they might get around him before he could catch up with the squad. That wasn't part of his plan at all.

He entered the slave pen and quickly moved the woman's body in with the other humans. Then he started setting fire to the north wall. By the time he reached the south wall, the smoke and heat were becoming unbearable. He had no idea how far the waves of heat coming off of the fort could be seen at night. Surely not farther than the smoke could be seen during the day. He hurried into the surrounding woods. He felt the heat from the fort on his back for some distance. It comforted him a little at least.

When he reached the point where the wagon tracks started again, he slowed and looked for spots to place traps. He rigged three traps in the area using sharpened sticks and bent limbs. The real trick was to make the traps invisible to people coming from the north but noticeable to people coming from the south. The duchess would have ranger scouts in front of her army if she came this way, but he still didn't want to take a chance on one of his traps hurting a comrade. The small-diameter rope he brought could be concealed easily in the heavy debris on the forest floor. The first trap he set on the wagon path. There was a low spot between the ruts that would allow enough movement on the rope that it could pull out a pin when stepped on. A low limb, which he bent back, would then spring across the path. He fastened a half dozen ten-inch sharpened stakes to the limb. The few wood chips he hid under the leaves. The best height for the traps was he figured about three feet. That way it would hit goblin or human. The other two traps were off of the path of the wagons. He wanted them to know that no place was safe around his group's trail.

He finished the trigger on the last of the three traps and got ready to move on. Then he spied some low-hanging branches a little ways ahead over the trail of the wagons. Just the sort of branches someone on a horse would brush out of the way when riding through. Maybe a fourth trap wouldn't be a bad idea. He set up another one at the height of a man riding a horse and put the trigger in the limbs above the path. The wooden stakes most likely wouldn't be effective against a man in armor, but you never could tell. Even if they weren't hurt, the traps should make them wary. That would buy the group some extra time.

After setting the fourth trap, he hurried south again. The heavy growth of the forest eventually cut off the sight of the burning fort. What he had seen since coming north seemed to age him. Getting to destroy the fort took away some of the sting of the last few days.

The path taken by the wagons wouldn't be hard to follow even in the night. The ruts from the wheels cut so deeply into the forest floor that even the cattle following behind didn't obscure them significantly. He alternated between a slow walk and a fast walk for the rest of the morning. The sky was bright, and the sun about to the middle of its path when he caught up with his wagon. The other wagon was there too.

Haslan was on guard, so he called out to the thief before pulling back the cloak and moving into camp.

"What's going on?" Petrion asked. "You didn't make more than four miles. It's still eight miles to the border. And everyone is still in bed. You should have been moving by now."

"The people were moving very slow, and we caught up with them. They are exhausted from the bad treatment and then everything that went on yesterday. We moved all during the daylight yesterday and in the dark for as long as we could."

"If the raiders kept to their old schedule," Petrion said in desperation, "they hit the farm on their raid yesterday afternoon. They will probably try and get back to their camp today or early tomorrow at least. It will only take them a little more than a half a day to reach the border on foot. That's when we'll get there at this rate. If one of the goblins gets word to them about what happened, they could easily be at the border waiting on us when we get there."

"We can make better time if you want," Haslan said, "but they can't. Believe me, they are more motivated than you are to get away. They went on till they could hardly move. Any reserves they had were used yesterday. They may make less distance today."

"We can't leave them behind," Petrion said in frustration. "Let's find a way to hitch the other two horses to our wagon. Then we can let the people ride in shifts on our wagon as well. That might add a little bit of speed."

"I'll start packing the stuff around so people can sit more comfortably," Haslan said.

"I'll get Andolar and start rigging a harness out of ropes and blankets," Petrion added.

Haslan ran off toward the wagons, while Petrion woke Andolar and explained what he wanted to do. Andolar got up stiffly but hurried to help. The magician was anxious to be home. He had given himself up for dead once. Now that hope was back he must not want to lose it again.

The former prisoners were much harder to rouse. They were running on fear and hope all the previous day, and they were just plain exhausted now. Petrion piled all of their goods, except for their weapons, into the wagons. Then he assigned the five weakest a place on top. Having a disorganized large group like this meant additional time was needed to get going. Their first meal of the day was a long drawn-out affair that had Andolar running all over the camp checking on problems and assigning work. After breakfast, it took more time to pack everything, and then they had to select which people would be riding for the first part of the day. It was almost an hour after midday before they started the wagons moving.

CHAPTER 20

Berinda hurried along beside the wagons. She was glad she had her headband back. Haslan had slipped it to her when he cut the ropes at the goblin camp. She wanted to try sparring with one of the dubroty after they made camp last night, but she couldn't make them understand her. They looked like they had a lot of strength in those short heavy limbs. They had been very efficient with those axes as well.

These stupid farmers were slowing them down. And she was getting heartily sick of them deferring to Andolar all the time. That lord magician stuff was more than a little bit ridiculous. He should put a stop to it. There it came again. Another farmer was asking the lord magician what to do. It seemed they needed someone to tell them when to relieve themselves. Andolar was eating up all the attention too. She wandered over to where he was.

"Andolar," she asked him, "why don't you tell them to stop that lord magician stuff?"

"Because," he told her quietly, "about the only thing keeping these people's hopes up enough to go on is that they have a powerful group protecting them. With a group of people this size, if someone didn't take charge, it would be more wasted time."

"Yes, but what about that lord stuff? You don't have to be a lord to control farmers. They grovel to anyone around."

"I suppose that's one way to term what they do. Another is that they have a desire to have someone to follow. According to my father, many people like to have someone to follow. They would find someone on their own eventually who would lead them, but I come ready made without all the maneuvering. And that maneuvering would go on until everyone was assigned tasks and responsibilities. This way, I can just tell people what to do, and they do it. And since I had to learn leadership skills, I can get the job done more efficiently than anyone they could come up with. Besides, people have always called me my lord. My father is titled, you know."

Well, the insolent little mongrel. She'd like to wipe that silly grin off his face. She could never seem to get anywhere with the magician in a verbal argument. Fists would be another matter entirely. Of course, if she challenged him, he might just decide to use magic. That would put the odds heavily in his favor. She turned to get away from the magician. One of these days, the people would be deferring to her.

"Berinda," Andolar called over, "as soon as the people are on board the wagon, get it moving."

She just growled at the pompous fool and went to the wagon. They had completed the first rotation of who was riding. All of the squad members except Petrion were walking, but she was the only one in armor. Petrion hadn't roused from sleep even with all the noise of the stop.

They would make better time alone. They should leave the others to fend for themselves. The duchy had more than enough farmers anyway. They all seemed to breed like rabbits. Her family had been a good example of that—growing up in a small house without enough room for the family they had and her mother having more children. She was constantly taking care of kids.

She looked back to see how their wagon was doing. The warhorse had finally quieted down. He hadn't minded the harness probably because he was used to all the trappings of armor and rider. The horse had rebelled strongly when they tried to get him to help pull. Andolar ended up leading the horse for the first half of a mile until he quieted down. Once he started pulling, he did more work than two of the other horses. Warhorses had to be large and strong to carry around all that weight.

An hour later, she didn't think they had covered a mile. The farmers were tired and moving slowly. There were two less of them now. Two had died from wounds during the night. It had been all Andolar could do to get them to leave the bodies behind. They had absolutely insisted on burying them. Haslan was scouting the trail ahead with the two dubroty, while she and Andolar made up the rear guard. It was much different traveling with wagons. Small obstacles became major blockages, and larger obstacles were impassible areas. Haslan was out trying to find the best path south. He marked it as he went, and the dubroty did what was necessary to make it passable for the wagons. They had actually volunteered for the duty. Petrion put in tools for clearing a path through the forest. They had four axes, four picks, six shovels, two brush blades, and two tree saws. The dubroty took some of the tools with them. They had only been delayed three times so far while the dubroty worked, and all of the delays had been relatively short. Maybe they could move even faster when Petrion got up and did the scouting.

The wagons started again after changing riders. Some of the ones who had been walking all afternoon were having trouble keeping up, although they seemed better for a while because of the short rest. They had another rest and passenger change forty-five minutes later when they had to wait while the dubroty finished cutting a stream bank down. It was their first long delay because of terrain. Petrion woke up but promptly went back to sleep. They lost additional time getting across the stream because the streambed was soft. Andolar took the team off the squad wagon to help pull the farmer's wagon and then pulled the squad wagon across. The dubroty were already long gone toward the next obstacle. Andolar at least utilized the necessary stop to squeeze in a meal for everyone.

Later in the afternoon, another of the injured women died. She had relatives among the folks who survived the goblin raids, and they were crying at losing her so close to safety. She wasn't sure any of them were that close to safety. Having the healers along would have been wonderful. Hopefully, they escaped from the goblins. They would need those two in the future if the duchess kept them working together. The people wanted to stop for another burial, but Andolar kept them moving. They could bury the woman at the next rest stop.

Having a position in the Rogue's Squad would be good for her, Berinda thought as she walked behind the wagon. It got her away from the rigid confines of the regular army that had not accepted her. She also got the chance for more accelerated advancement and notoriety. And besides all that, there was almost no one to tell her what to do. The income was much better than the regular army. She hadn't seen inside the chests, but they were heavy. While loading the wagon, she had lifted them to check the weight. It was a very satisfying lift. The only problem was dealing with a couple of shortsighted men who didn't recognize her potential. Her thoughts became less pleasant when she recalled that one of those shortsighted men was dead now. Of course, he could have stayed alive if he had run like Petrion told him. That was no place for an archer. For that matter, if Petrion had given them a better idea of what he was planning on doing, they both could have gotten away without the additional trouble. She had just stayed behind to take out that horseman.

Of course, if she hadn't been captured, then they wouldn't have gone to the fort. And if they hadn't gone to the fort, then they wouldn't have all the wealth. They also wouldn't have rescued the prisoners. That alone should assure her a noncommissioned officer's rank in the army when she eventually left the squad.

They were really going to have a good time when they returned to civilization with all of that money. She could dress up and go into all the good places. Servers and even owners would defer to her.

Oh blast! She hadn't been watching the path and had stepped into a pile of horse manure. Hopefully, they would cross another stream soon so she could clean off her boot. She looked around to see what Andolar was doing. One laugh out of him, and he would find himself on the ground, lord or not. Fortunately, he was looking the other way and was coughing hard. She hoped he hadn't caught something while among the goblins and slaves. The last thing they needed was to have sickness sweep through the group. He must have just gotten choked because the coughing stopped after a while.

Andolar would be the perfect one to go out with when they got back. His lordly attitude was a real bother on the trail, but in the city, it would be a different situation entirely. He would surely know the best places to stay and eat. And he would also know the best wines. He would have all of that information that it took a lifetime of being pampered to learn. Once they learned he was Lord Andolar of Brighthome, they would really get preferred treatment. He wasn't all that far down in the succession to the duchy itself. She might even let his name slip herself when it came right down to it. Everyone would naturally assume she had rank too since she was with a lord of the land. She would have to suggest it to the magician.

"Andolar."

"Yes."

"You know, I was thinking we ought to go out and have dinner together when we get back to a city."

Maybe he was getting sick. He was coughing again. He had to stop and lean against a tree for a while to get his breath back. The wagons were almost thirty paces ahead by the time he recovered.

"Are you all right?"

"Yeah," he said in a wheeze, "I think so. Something didn't sit right in my throat. What was that you said?"

He took a long drink to clear his throat.

"With all that money we have, I think we should celebrate."

"Oh sure. We'll all go out and celebrate when we get back."

"Oh, I'm sure we'll do that, but I thought you and I might go out together for dinner."

"You want to go out with me for dinner?" Andolar said in surprise.

"Sure. You're a nice-enough fellow for a magician, so I wouldn't mind doing something with you. We always have something to talk about."

"I suppose we do. You'd have to let me pick the place though. The last place we were together was a bit hostile toward me."

"Sure. I'd like you to pick the place."

"You would!"

He acted surprised that she trusted his judgment. She had always thought of him as very self-confident. Maybe it was just an act he put on for people. She'd better reassure him before he panicked.

"I trust your judgment in things like that, Andolar," she told the magician. "I'm sure we'll have a good time together. At least as long as you don't add something extra to my drink this time."

"Your drink?" Andolar asked as he put a little more distance between them.

"Oh come on, Andolar. I figured it out the next morning. I know how I am before I pass out. Everything felt different that night. You probably gave me the same stuff Haslan gave those goblins."

"Well," he said in close to a panic, "there wasn't anything else I could think of to do. And if you were arrested or came to Gilbert's attention, then our mission would probably have been over. And we surely didn't want to go on the mission without you. It wasn't like I would have a chance of winning a fistfight with you. That was the only other thing I could think of."

"I understand," she said quietly. "You would stand no more chance against me in a fistfight than I would against you in a magic duel. That's what you always have to do when confronted by superior strength. Resort to trickery."

"Then you're not mad!"

"No," she said as she smiled at the magician, "I wouldn't try that little trick again though. Now what about the meal and drink?"

"I've been thinking about giving up drinking," he replied quickly, "uh…for obvious reasons."

"The duchess is liable to keep us extremely busy when we get back too," he said after a short pause. "Full war will almost surely break out now. She'll be grabbing every person capable of fighting, if I know her. I think we might not have time to work it in."

"Oh, Andolar. They can't work us all day every day. There's bound to be a few evenings we can go out together in Delaigamon or Gamalius."

Andolar mumbled something that she didn't quite catch.

"What was that you said?"

"I said…uh…that's a real…uh…city."

"Which one? Delaigamon?"

"Oh, uh…no. I was thinking of Gamalius. Delaigamon is more of a provincial capital than a real city. Brighthome is considerably bigger than Delaigamon. That's what we should do. Wait till we get to Gamalius! There are a lot of superb restaurants that I know about in the city. It would be no trouble at all to find one. That's what we should do. Go out for dinner in Gamalius. Of course, my father will want to join us."

"I like the city of Gamalius better too, and dinner with your father would be fine. We will surely be there sometime as well, so that's a great idea. We'll do dinner in both cities. I've been looking forward to some relaxation."

"So had I."

"Great. It's settled then. Since we don't know which day it will be, I'll see when we're both off and let you know."

"Yeah, just catch up with me after we get to town. Well, I better check to see how the other wagon and the people are doing," he told her as he hurried forward. "If you don't watch carefully, something always goes wrong. It's been interesting talking to you."

"It's been interesting talking to you as well. Bye."

That was so funny—a wealthy son of a lord embarrassed by a woman. She just assumed that he was more experienced. Maybe it was just that not too many women had made the first move with him. Men were funny that way sometimes.

"You stupid horse!" she yelled at the back of the wagon.

Several of the people turned around to see what was going on. She had been daydreaming again and stepped in some more horse droppings. At least it was the same boot, so there wouldn't be any more to clean.

There were a lot of limbs and briars piled off the path. The dubroty had been working hard since early morning and were still going strong. They hadn't had any more stops except the three to change riders, although at the first one, they lost some time burying the woman. It was about four hours after midday.

She noticed that the unattached farm folk were starting to pair off into groups. They seemed to be deciding on whom they would pick to live with from their fellow captives. She supposed there wouldn't be much demand out there for women who had been held prisoner by goblins. Probably, these men were the only ones who would have them. Some of them also appeared to be getting into multiple family groups and planning what to do. More people at a place would mean a better defense, and that would be very important with war about to break out. It would also spread out the work that had to be done before winter.

Oh well. What did she care about what peasants did anyway. She had her own life to think about. There were always opportunities for rapid advancement during a war. Commanders were almost as favorite a goblin target as spell casters. The large loss rate meant a large promotion rate. Of course, generals and such wouldn't be mixing in the actual battles much, so there was a limit to how far you could rise. Most of them were old anyway. She would still be young when she reached the middle ranks of the military, so she could afford to wait a little while till the old people retired.

She moved off the path cut by the dubroty when the surrounding area was clear enough. The clearness didn't last long though. Soon the thorns and brush forced her back into the path of the wagons.

Petrion was still sleeping. Maybe when he got up, they could get this thing moving faster. He had roused from his sleep on the last two passenger changes but promptly rolled over and went back to sleep. She would feel safer with him scouting the rear.

"You on the back of the wagon," she called out.

"Yes, ma'am," one of the women replied.

"I want you to keep a watch to the back," Berinda told her. "You're higher than the rest of us, so you might be able to see goblins or horsemen coming sooner."

All of the people turned and started staring back toward the goblin fort. The conversation between them turned to whispers.

Andolar halted the group and was making his way toward the back, telling everyone to fix something to eat. This was going to be the next meal stop. He was strolling along and talking to the people as if nothing was wrong, and many of them smiled back at him. At least they did until those from the back wagon got among the group. Then everyone was whispering and looking back up the trail. Andolar had to get them moving on the meal again. Once the people were working, he came to the back where Berinda was.

"I figured," Andolar told her, "that they would eventually realize what the goblin raiders would do when they found the fort burned. I hoped it would be longer though. They've had a hard time, and hope is about the only thing keeping them going. If they lose hope, then they'll move slower than ever."

"Is there something wrong up front, Andolar?" Petrion said from the top of the wagon.

"Yes," Andolar replied. "Haslan came back and said the way ahead was completely blocked by a ravine. He is scouting for a better way to the east, and Duvain is scouting to the west. Govin started working on the best spot right ahead in case they can't find anything better. They were planning on going about a quarter hour out to see what they could find."

"I'll go back and check our trail while we're stopped," Petrion said as he jumped down from the wagon. "How far have we come?"

"I have no idea," Andolar told him. "I can't judge how fast these wagons are moving."

"I hope we can reach the border today," Petrion said.

"Me too," Andolar added from the heart.

"How far behind us do you think they are?" Berinda asked the ranger.

"There are too many things it depends on for me to even guess," Petrion replied. "It could range all the way from them waiting for us at the border to having clear passage to Delaigamon."

"I'll vote for the latter," Andolar said.

"I wish I could help up front, but I really need to scout behind us. I also need to leave a few surprises for anyone following. But

I can scout the front more than twice as fast as Haslan and speed up our progress. What do you think, Andolar?"

"You already know what you need to do, Petrion," Andolar replied.

"And what's that?"

"Haslan is doing a good job up front. So far, over a full day of traveling, we have not lost any time because of slow scouting. We were due to stop for another meal now anyway. On the other hand, no one else can do the job in the back."

"Thanks. It's always nice to get a confirming opinion. Besides," he said with a slight smile, "I didn't know how the wagons had been moving."

"Oh yeah. I guess that's right."

"I'm going to look over our back trail now," Petrion told them, "and see what I can do to discourage pursuit."

Petrion shed his chain mail and grabbed some trail rations and a pair of water skins off the wagon. Then he picked up the pack he brought and tied on a shovel and ax. He pulled the pack on his back and pulled his cloak over it. It bulged weirdly in the back. When all of his preparations were done, he jogged out of the camp to the north and quickly disappeared from sight. Berinda looked around to say something to Andolar, but the magician was already gone. She moved around the wagon looking for him and finally saw him walking quickly south toward the ravine that was blocking their progress. He even had a shovel over his shoulder. That was really odd.

Well, she supposed that left her in charge of this ragged group. Now maybe they could get things moving along. A couple of the farmers were looking around for Andolar. Finally, they stopped looking and started in her direction. She waited for them to come over.

"Excuse me, ma'am," the man said, "could you tell me where you want the fire placed and the waste pit dug?"

"What?" she exclaimed. "Just clear a spot somewhere and build a fire. And go out into the woods downwind to dig the pit."

The man had a hurt expression on his face as he walked off. Well, he deserved to be called down for asking such a simple question. There was a woman still there trying to attract her attention. She had hoped they were together.

"What were you wanting?"

"Sorry to bother you, ma'am," the woman stammered. "I was just wondering if you knew what the lord magician wanted us to cook for lunch."

"What he wanted for lunch! You know more about cooking than I do. For that matter, you know more about cooking than the 'lord magician' will ever know. Just fix something that tastes good and that will give everyone energy."

"Yes, ma'am."

The woman hurried off even faster than the man had. Two more men were heading her way. She was beginning to understand now why Andolar headed down the trail. Couldn't these people do anything on their own? She started digging around in the wagon for a shovel. All she found before the men got to her was a pick. It would have to do. She pulled it out of the wagon as she turned around. The two men were standing there waiting to speak, and another man was on his way over.

"Pardon us, ma'am," the smaller of the two men said. "Where should we go to fill up the water barrels? The lord magician gave us the job of keeping them full."

"Is there water around here somewhere?"

"That's what we were asking, ma'am."

"I don't know. I haven't been out scouting. How much water do we have left?"

"Three and a half barrels out of the four we started with."

"Ma'am," the man who had just walked up said, "these two wouldn't let me water the horses until they talked to you about the water supply. The lord magician told me and Shuvar over there to make sure the horses were watered and fed at every meal stop and watered at every stop. Can I go ahead and get some water?"

Snap!

She looked down at her hands and saw the handle on the pick had broken. All three of the men jumped at the sound. They were staring at her hands now and the two pieces of the pick. She had forgotten about having on the headband. She quickly tossed the broken piece of the handle into the woods. The smaller man of the first pair swallowed a couple of times before continuing.

"We didn't know, since there was no water here to refill the barrels, if you wanted to go ahead and give water to the horses."

"Yes, the water is for the horses and for you," she said in a low growl. "That is why we brought the barrels along—so we can all have water to keep up our strength when there is none around."

The man responsible for the horses went hurrying off to water them. The other two were still standing there, looking at her. Finally, the bigger of the two spoke.

"Ma'am, do you want us to look for water?"

"No," she said, with the growl in her voice rising a notch, "Wait till we stop at a stream crossing and then fill them up. There are streams all over this country."

"Then what do you want us to do now?"

"I don't care!" she told them. "If you can't find something useful to do, then just sit down and rest!"

"Yes, ma'am," the smaller man squeaked out as they both turned and almost ran to get away from her.

She wondered what their problem was. There was another woman coming over, but she took one look at Berinda and hurried away. Now what was the matter with her? She started to put the broken pick back in the wagon and suddenly figured out what bothered the farmers. She had bent the pick heads around till they almost touched. She was getting ready to toss it into the woods when she heard a whistle nearby. She turned quickly at the sound and saw Haslan and the dubroty staring at her. Andolar was just coming around the wagon. It looked like he was trying to stay out of sight of the farmers.

"What did the poor pick ever do to you?" Haslan asked in a mournful tone while trying to hold in his laughter.

"It was in the area when the farmers came looking for advice, I'd say," Andolar said quietly from beside the wagon. "Do you think I could borrow that headband for a while later?"

Berinda managed a small grin at the overdone pleading in the magician's voice. Haslan laughed outright, and the farmers looked over to see what was going on. They immediately went back to talking softly between themselves.

The dubroty were speaking together in their heavy language. Finally, one of them said something to Andolar and Haslan in what sounded like Goblin. Govin came over and held out his hand for the pick.

"He wants to look at it," Andolar told her. "They were arguing about the quality of the metal."

She passed Govin the remains of the pick. He grabbed the two bent ends and started pulling to straighten it out. The ends moved some, but not more than about an inch. Duvain tried but was unable to move it anymore. He handed the pick back to her and made a motion of pulling it apart. She took the pick and managed to get the points out somewhat where they were supposed to be. The dubroty again talked for a while, and then shaking their heads, they started toward where lunch was being served. Andolar caught up with them, and they talked together in Goblin on the way to the fire.

"What are you talking about?" Berinda asked the magician as she caught up with them.

"We were discussing your strength," Andolar answered her. "The goblin commander beat them, and the goblin commander beat you. Then you show strength that is even greater than theirs. It worried them somewhat that you were so much stronger than they. And that Churinius was stronger than you. They weren't sure they really wanted to deal with humans if there was that much difference in abilities."

"What did you tell them?"

"That your strength was magically enhanced," Andolar replied, "and that Churinius was much more skilled than you. I told him that we did have people the equal of Churinius in combat but that we were a relatively inexperienced group."

"Do you think they needed to know all of that?"

"Actually, yes I do," he told her. "The duchess will almost surely try and recruit them as allies. I want them to trust us. To do that, we have to trust them. I'll let them look at my dagger, too, once I get it back."

They sat down to eat, and the farmers brought them all bowls of a thick stew with lots of meat. It was surprisingly good food, and they all ate heavily. The other people were eating more sparingly probably because they were near exhaustion.

"After lunch," Andolar announced, "I want everyone to rest for an hour. It will make the evening easier. It will also give the workers a chance to get further ahead of us. With an extra lead, they can save us some stops later."

Nobody questioned him about the coming goblins.

CHAPTER 21

Petrion took off on their back trail. The wagons hadn't come more than four miles while he was sleeping. That left them at least four miles from the border and only eight miles from the fort. If the raiders hadn't reached the fort yet, then the wagons would surely be able to reach the boundary of Gamalius safely. But if he went to the fort, it would leave the wagons with fewer defenders for the rest of the day and part of the night.

If the raiders were already on their trail, then he would have all he could do to stay ahead of them. He decided to range a couple miles behind the wagons, setting traps to cause trouble among any pursuers.

When he was about a mile along the back trail, he found a perfect setup for a deadfall. A tree close to the path taken by the wagons was lightning struck. A large section of the tree was hanging across the path. If he could cut it loose at both ends, then he could rig it to fall with a trip line. He climbed the tree and reached the base of the broken section. This end could certainly be rigged. He looked around from his higher vantage point to make sure no one was in the area. The sound from the ax would carry a long way in the forest.

He tied himself off on the side of the tree away from the break and started working. He cut for about ten minutes and then rested his arm while he tied a piece of his rope around the limb and over a crotch in the tree. He went down the tree to secure the line around a root. The other end of the limb was in a tree on the other side of the trail. He climbed that tree and got ready to cut the top loose from the section he wanted to fall on the raiders. He drove a small wooden spike into the tree just back of the cut location to hold up the log when he cut the top off. Next he secured the top of the limb to three places on the tree where it was lying. Because of his awkward position, it took him fifteen minutes to cut through the limb.

He climbed back down and took a moment to drink some water and rest. His arm was getting tired. When he rested for five minutes, he pulled his rope tight and made a trip-cord trigger. Then he climbed back up the tree to finish cutting loose the base of the limb. This was the most dangerous part, because if the rope didn't hold, then the limb could jerk the tree and dislodge him. As he worked, he could see the rope gradually stretching as it absorbed more of the weight. Finally, he finished cutting the limb free. The end dropped about six inches as the rope stretched but held. He waited a few more seconds to make sure before he climbed down.

He carefully hid the wood chips, and the traces of his movement around the trees. The trigger was very tight and had pulled about half loose when the rope took the weight. He was very careful as he covered the rope with leaves. The last of the wood chips he took up the trail about thirty feet and spread out. There weren't many, but the bright white of the newly cut wood would attract attention. With any luck, expecting a trap around the tree further up the trail would keep them from seeing the one in this tree.

He moved on, looking for other places to rig traps. He found three more places where he could rig ground-level spring traps with sharpened stakes. At one place, he found a perfect location for a horseman trap. Two heavier limbs crossed an opening beside the trail. He bent them back, and using the same kind of hidden trigger that he used on the last trap for a horseman, he armed it. Two of his daggers were attached to each limb. The limbs had the strength to drive them through armor.

He wished the place was on the trail so there would be a better chance of them riding through it. After some thought, he decided to move some of the cut brush over the trail at that location. He didn't leave any other obvious signs, hoping that it being in the trail would be sufficient to make them think there was a trap. That might get them into his trap. Half of the work in setting traps was figuring out how your enemy would react to the things you did.

He reached the place where the group stopped, but they were gone. From the looks of the tracks, they hadn't been gone long. When he got to the ravine crossing, he saw the first wagon was just starting up the other side. All of the horses were attached to the lead wagon. This was when having all of the treasure on the wagons worked against them. Most times, the wagons didn't slow them. The cattle and sheep were already across with their tenders. He saw Andolar standing on the other side of the ravine, directing the people in various jobs. Berinda was down in the ravine, leaning against the squad's wagon. He needed to rig some kind of trap on both sides of the ravine. It was a natural choke point on the raiders.

He walked to the wagon and threw the tools he was carrying into the back. Berinda almost came out of her armor.

"It's just me, Berinda," he told her.

"You could at least open that cloak before coming up!" she growled down at him.

He opened the cloak, and her searching eyes finally focused on him as he faded back into view. A quick turn of his head hid the smile that he hadn't been able to help. That jump and the expression on her face made him feel he'd gotten a little bit of revenge for all of the trouble she caused him.

"How are things going?" he asked her. "I expected you to be further along than this."

"Andolar," Berinda replied, "told the farmers to lie down and sleep for a while after the meal to regain some of their strength. He let them sleep for about two hours. He told them that would give Haslan and the dubroty time to scout ahead for better paths."

"Both the scouting and the rest will probably help in the long run," Petrion told her, "but I begrudge every single minute of delay."

"We could have been across the border now," Berinda said, "if we weren't following the farmers. We could still let them take care of themselves and get out of here."

"So they could be taken prisoner again?"

"If the raiders catch us, we will all be dead or prisoners, except possibly for you with your vanishing cloak. You can get away any-time you want."

"Yes," Petrion told her with more than a little annoyance, "and I still stayed and worked out a way to free you instead of leaving you for the goblins in spite of you disobeying my orders. Why should I treat these people worse?"

"These people are just farmers," she replied after an embar-rassed look around. "Our being here won't help them if they're attacked. We could break free and do damage against the goblins some other time. These people will never do anything against the goblins."

"Except feed all of the army while it is out fighting," Petrion said with a shake of his head. "How long do you think the army would last without food?"

"The duchess can always find people to be farmers," Berinda replied. "She has to train people to be warriors. That means the warriors are more valuable in the scheme of things. Like the duchess said, if she loses her warriors, then the goblins win and the whole area will be lost."

"These people have held off the goblins as much as the army has," Petrion told her. "By settling on and maintaining the land at the edge of Gamalius, they have limited goblin movements south of the border. They also help keep the area cleared so that the army has a better chance at getting the goblins in battle where we have the advantages. Open areas."

Berinda turned away, apparently unconvinced, but without any more arguments to offer. She walked to where Andolar was directing the people. Govin was still there to help with moving the wagons. Berinda pitched in from behind and helped push the wagon forward. It finally cleared the top of the ravine, and they brought the horses back to the second wagon.

Petrion went to the north side of the ravine and started working on traps again. He managed to set four traps in the cutaway where the wagons went down. By the time he finished, the second wagon was up the other side and on its way. He didn't waste time putting traps on the other side of the ravine. After so many traps on the north side, they would spend a lot of time looking on the south side. They might even look longer if it wasn't trapped, figuring he had concealed it very well. They also might bypass it and save themselves the trouble. He caught up to the wagons again. Berinda was walking in the back and Andolar in the front.

"Berinda," Petrion called, "I'm going to take a look ahead and see what we have to look forward to. You keep a watch on the rear."

"Sure, Petrion," Berinda replied. "Just make sure you're around if we need you."

Petrion waved and started south. The farmers with the first wagon waved to him as he went by. He smiled and waved back as he was passing. It might be a good idea to scout ahead as well as behind to make sure there wasn't an ambush waiting somewhere. They didn't need the odds more against them than they already were. He also needed to range out a little to the east periodically just to check.

He told Haslan on the way by that he was scouting ahead and would leave markers, so the halfman could help elsewhere. Haslan passed the bag of cloths to Petrion, after explaining the marking setup they agreed on, and headed toward the wagons. Petrion started off at a light jog to the south. The ground he scouted was good for wagon travel. The only stream he found on his trek had relatively low banks and a gravel bottom. After about two miles of travel, he came to an open area with grass and water. It would be past dark when the wagons got there, but they could make it. Petrion took the time to gather some wood for fires to speed up the camping process.

There wasn't much after that for him to do, so he started back toward the wagons. When he got back, Haslan was with the dubroty, helping clear the trail. He told the thief that he marked out a campsite with water, wood, and some concealment. Then he started to the east to check the flank. After going about a half mile to the east, he cut to the northwest to check on their back trail. He finally worked his way to the ravine before deciding to go back to the wagons.

He didn't know exactly what caught his eye. He only knew that he almost missed seeing the goblin lying at the top of the north side of the ravine. He went down the bank, using the footprints left earlier in the day to disguise his movement in case someone was watching. Having a footprint suddenly appear in the loose dirt would be almost as bad as yelling out that he was there. He saw several goblin prints in the dirt of the ravine but didn't stop to try and figure out the number of goblins. When he reached the north ridge, he cautiously looked over the top. He looked around for a couple of minutes before moving. The goblin body was there, with spikes from two of his traps sticking out of him. The first trap had knocked him into the trigger of the second. Petrion took a couple minutes to investigate the north edge of the ravine for goblins still lurking around.

From the tracks, the goblins had no horsemen with them. That meant the cavalry hadn't returned or that they were taking another route to cut them off. There were more than twenty goblins in the group from the number of footprints around. When he didn't find any enemies close by, he decided to drag the goblin into the ravine and reset the two traps.

Without the human fighters, a goblin group this size could be handled. Slowing the human fighters, if they were coming, was more important than intercepting the goblins right away. It had only been about a half hour since they had been through, judging by the still-drying blood on the dead goblin. He could easily catch them before they reached the wagons, unless they were running. He moved the body and started working on the traps. He had to make two new wooden stakes to replace broken ones.

He didn't cover the area as well as he had the previous time because time was starting to weigh heavily on him. He kept seeing in his mind the goblins attacking the wagons from ambush and killing everyone. Petrion hurried to the south at his best possible speed for distance and concealment.

After walking fast for about a half hour, he had to slow down and regain his breath. These last few days had really sapped his strength. He was lying near death only a few days before and had fought in two battles since. He had also covered many miles of territory on foot while getting considerably less than a good sleep every day. He chewed on trail rations and drank plenty of water while he moved.

The sun was halfway below the horizon when he sighted the goblins following the trail of the wagons. He didn't know how far ahead the wagons were, but he hoped they had already reached the campsite. It was only about a mile ahead of where he was now. If the goblins were planning on moving through the night, they could attack the camp in no time at all.

As he closed the distance to the goblins, he saw two of them were wearing bandages. Apparently, the goblin at the ravine wasn't the only one to stumble into his traps. He hoped they hadn't tripped the rider traps.

Petrion continued to follow at a safe distance, and he got more worried by the minute. The goblins were moving much faster than the prisoners could hope to. They continued south even after the sun went down. The wagon tracks weren't hard to follow.

As it started to get truly dark, the goblins stopped and began to set up camp. Petrion heaved a silent sigh of relief at the narrow escape. Another half hour of traveling would have brought the goblins within sight of his group. Petrion closed in on the goblin camp under the covering noise, and listened in on their conversations for a while. As near as he could tell, these goblins were part of the force Churinius led in the counterattack on the supply camp. He sent them south looking for the remaining squad members and any escaped prisoners. They sent runners to the raiders and to Durp when they returned and discovered the ruined fort.

There was some talk of turning back, with a lot of references to the traps. The majority of the goblins were in favor of continuing so they could link up with the raiders and share in the loot. They thought the raiders should be able to reach them by noon the next day.

Petrion didn't waste any more time but moved away from the camp quietly until he could run. Of course, Baron Gilbert might have destroyed the raiders when they entered Gamalius. It was doubtful though. It would have taken a large force to win against them on even terms. Since they had humans along to help scout and investigate the setup, he doubted if the army would be fighting on even terms. He could imagine how they would have reacted if a large well-armed force of men had come riding through the ambush area. They would have welcomed their help in the coming battle. Then when the goblins struck, their human allies would have been in perfect position to destroy the defenders.

It took him about an hour to reach the campsite. It was farther away than he thought. He was tired enough that his idea of distance was getting distorted.

The cooking pots were already out and simmering. Andolar was directing the people about their tasks, and Haslan and the dubroty were cleaning off the day's dirt. He almost ran into Berinda as she came out from behind a tree on her rounds. She must have heard something, probably his heavy breathing, because she was closely scanning the ground. He pulled back the cloak and faded into view in front of her.

"What is it?" she asked when she saw the expression on his face.

"We have company behind us," he told her breathlessly. "Twenty-nine goblins are only a short distance back on the trail."

"Do we set an ambush for them in the morning?" Berinda said with open enthusiasm.

"Not this time," he told her.

He ignored her disappointed look and told her to get the rest of the group together to talk. He really didn't want to explain this several times, and he didn't want the people to hear. A panic was the last thing they needed. Berinda went off in a huff to get the others.

"Don't say anything about what I told you," he whispered to her urgently from behind.

She just nodded her head and continued on. It would have been just like her to go announce that they had thirty goblins behind them, and Petrion was calling a meeting to deal with the matter. When the squad members and the dubroty arrived, he told them the news.

"We have almost thirty goblins closing in behind us," he said.

The faces of the dubroty lit up as much as Berinda's had when he repeated the message in goblin. Andolar looked like he was about to be sick. He couldn't read anything from Haslan's expression.

"We aren't going to attack them," he continued. "From what I overheard of their conversation, the group is some of those who attacked us at the first camp. They have been hunting prisoners. They saw the fort and sent runners to Durp and to the raiders. They are expecting to link up with the raiders at the border at noon tomorrow."

Andolar sat down heavily on the ground. Even Berinda and the dubroty looked concerned.

"We have to keep moving tonight, so we can get to the border well ahead of them," Petrion told them. "I know everyone is tired, but right after we eat, we are moving again. I'll take the lead, and Haslan will bring up the rear. You need to be in goblin disguise, Haslan. That way if they do decide to come ahead instead of stopping for the night, you can blend in. Tell them you were tracking the wagons."

"What do I do then?" Haslan asked. "They're going to want to include me in the attack."

"I don't think so," Petrion replied. "They know we destroyed the fort. They probably want the raiders to join them before they attack. If they do decide to attack, then do what you do best. Stay out of the way of the fighters though. A night attack is no time to be trying to sort out one halfman from among a group of goblins. You, on the other hand, should be able to distinguish the humans and dubroty easily."

"Where do you want the rest of us?" Andolar asked.

"Andolar, you stay close to the wagons. Berinda, you go to the front," Petrion ordered. "Govin, protect back wagon," he continued in Goblin. "Duvain, protect front wagon."

"What about the farmers?" Andolar asked. "What do you want them to be doing?"

"Tell them to keep their weapons handy as always in case of trouble," Petrion told him. "We may need their help since we are spread out to cover the front and back. Tell them not to fire arrows in the dark. They could hit one of us."

"Sure, Petrion," Andolar replied in that same fatalistic voice he used before the attack on the goblin fort. "I'll go take care of it now."

Petrion watched him get up and go to the former prisoners. He looked worried, and Petrion didn't blame him in the least. Their luck had been holding good for a while recently. Just like it had at first. Then the bad luck had come streaming in. The group coming now was bigger and more dangerous. Besides that, they would be primed for a fight. It would be hard to ambush them. And even if they did manage the ambush, the fight was still heavily weighted against them.

He heard Andolar giving instructions to the people in that steady voice of his. The people seemed to accept the instructions even though they had to be exhausted. For that matter, Andolar and Berinda were probably the only ones who weren't exhausted. Then again, maybe they were too. Andolar had been hauling water, and Berinda had received a serious beating recently. They would make do somehow. There wasn't any other choice.

"Duvain," Petrion said in Goblin, "I mark path with cloths. White means 'follow.' Red means 'follow but needs work.' You see red cloth, go ahead and fix path."

"Take Govin too?"

"You look first. You need Govin, then get Govin."

"I understand."

He decided that he needed to move out immediately, so he went to the cook fires for his supper and wolfed it down. He grabbed some additional travel rations and a new water skin and set out on the path to the border. This was going to be a very long night for everyone.

Petrion moved slowly into the night, conserving his strength in case he needed it later. It would be a while before the group moved on, giving him a substantial lead. He picked up the bag of torn white and red cloths that Haslan made to mark their path. They would have to carry torches to see the markers, but that was better than wandering around aimlessly. He tied one about every fifty paces. They weren't hard to follow since they were in as straight a line south as he could make them.

He came to the first obstacle after a half hour of walking. It was another small stream. This was a very well-watered country. Livestock or crops, either one would do well on this land if some of the trees were cleared.

He tried west first. If they had to move out of line, he would rather it was away from the raiders. The difference in the time at which the raiders caught them would be next to nothing, but every little bit helped. After moving two hundred and fifty paces to the west without seeing a good crossing, he went back to the east. He went about two hundred paces to the east, but there was still no good crossing. He went to the best spot he saw and hung up a white marker. Then he went into the stream to make sure the bed was solid. It was some kind of soft rock, but should hold the wagons. He hurried back the equivalent of a fifteen-minute walk and tied a red marker beside one of the white. That would give Duvain a chance to work on the banks before the wagons got there. He had already used his lead time, so he hurried back to the south. He had trouble seeing his markers without a torch even though he knew where he placed them. He finally reached the stream again and crossed. His legs were already tiring, and the night had just begun. He was the only one who could remain concealed if he stumbled on enemy border patrols, and they were entering the patrolled area of the border.

An hour later, he was trudging to where he was going to tie the next marker when he glimpsed the white stones of the border beneath his feet. If he had been alert, he would have seen them sometime before in the moonlight. He decided not to tie a marker here in case the raiders happened by. It would draw their attention to the wagons that much quicker. He would need to obliterate their trail as much as possible through this area to slow pursuit. Once they were out of sight of the border, they should be safe. The goblins wouldn't cross into the human territory without a plan of some type. The humans had taught them the dangers of that many times over. Of course, lately the goblins had been teaching the humans they could raid whenever they wanted. They didn't have Churinius now though, and the patrol schedules had hopefully been changed. Of course, the goblins and their human allies might not know that the schedules were different. Besides that, the group that was coming might be able to destroy a reinforced patrol.

He crossed into Gamalius, and using a wide back-and-forth pattern, he covered the area east of the crossing point and then west. As far as he could tell in the dark, the way was clear. He started working his way back toward the wagons. He took down the first white marker he came to and tied two red marker cloths by the second.

By the position of the stars, it was only two hours before sunrise when he sighted the light of torches leading the wagons. The wagons were still a ways from the border and moving slowly. They were past the stream that was the only bad spot he found during his scouting. When he was within twenty paces of Duvain, he called out.

"Duvain," he called softly, "Petrion is coming in."

"Good," the dubroty replied, "you come in."

Petrion spoke softly, so the sound of goblin speech wouldn't send the people into a panic. From the looks of them, he didn't need bother. Those still walking were dragging slowly along. He saw two people fall from exhaustion while he watched but get back to their feet. Andolar had piled people onto the wagons, into the driver's seats, and even a few on top of the horses pulling the wagons. Many of them were sleeping. He had a great need for sleep himself. He must have covered many times the distance these people had.

He pulled back his cloak so he would be easier for people to see and made his way past the wagons. When he reached Berinda, he spoke louder so that all of the people who were awake could hear.

"Only a little ways to the border, Berinda," he said with a cheerfulness he didn't feel.

She only stared at him and continued walking along. The fighter hadn't had the benefit of curing like he had, and the effects must finally be catching up with her. The bruises on her face were still mostly dark, although they were starting to lighten up around the edges. None of the other people reacted to his announcement either. They were moving at not much better than a crawl. The horses were about done as well. They had transferred some of the items from their wagon to the other as the volume of food steadily decreased. Both loads were still heavy, especially with the large number of people piled on.

"Come on!" he called out. "We're almost to the border. When we get across, we'll have us a long rest."

The people on the wagons started waking up to find out what was going on, and the others told them the news. At last, some excitement started to come over the people. Andolar was hurrying in from the back to see what the excitement was all about. Haslan was not far behind.

"What's going on?" Andolar called out. "What's all the fuss about?"

"We're only a mile from the border!" Petrion replied with all the energy he could summon. "Once we cross the border, we'll be safe and we can rest."

"Do you hear that, folks?" Andolar called. "Only a little further to the border. Everyone get down and lighten the load on the horses so we can hurry and see the sun rise in our own land this morning."

A ragged cheer erupted from the people at Andolar's words. They started climbing down from the wagons and off of the horses. Calling up reserves of energy from somewhere, they started forward at the almost steady pace they had used when they left the goblin fort. Andolar walked up beside him. Some of the people were even singing a song about coming home from a long journey. Petrion felt new energy flowing into his weary body as well. The enthusiasm seemed contagious. Andolar stood waiting with him as the wagons got further ahead.

"Good thought," the magician whispered even though the people were far away. "They were about to give up regardless of the cost. That little lie about the border brought their spirits back. We should at least be able to get a little ways into Gamalius before they give out."

"What lie?" Petrion said in astonishment. "The border isn't far."

"No," Andolar said with a ghost of a smile under his torch, "I meant the one about…you really meant it, didn't you?"

"What are you talking about? Meant what?"

"They aren't going to stop at the border, Petrion," Andolar told him seriously. "They won't even slow down. They can't. Their whole strategy to this point has been to push the humans into starting a war. Right now, we have the only evidence it was war. The three prisoners the goblins brought in the other night could be all that were still alive. Those poor people couldn't outrun goblins that were fresh, healthy, and well fed. That just leaves Korin and Florine if they managed to escape. If they did escape, they are just fugitives who have been raiding in goblin lands, and as such are subject to goblin justice for their crimes if caught. The goblins can even justly show where we raided into their lands in violation of the treaty. These prisoners are the only thing linking a major goblin force to the raids. Otherwise, it's just goblin thieves who need to be brought to justice. Even the fact that there were several groups will be written off by the goblins if the king has an advisor worthy of the name. If they can wipe us out, then they can continue as before."

"Why would they want the humans to declare war?" Petrion asked. "It doesn't make sense."

"I don't know, but that seems to be their plan. We are the only thing between them and continuing the plan. Even if they come into human territory after us, they can argue they were pursuing robbers and murderers. All they have to do is kill all the prisoners and get their bodies out of here."

"Then when can we stop?"

"When we reach a major force that they can't overcome. I doubt if a patrol would be sufficient."

"That could be several days' journey," Petrion said in anguish.

"Yes, but we will have one advantage once we cross the border. They will have to be on the lookout for patrols. That will make them slow and send out flankers and scouts to keep from being ambushed."

"They will be able to run us down easily," Petrion said with despair. "The inhabited area is five miles beyond the border. There is no way we can cover even that distance before they catch us. They move at several times our speed."

"That means you have to cover our tracks so they can't follow us."

"I can't cover wagon ruts well enough to fool anyone for more than a few minutes. They make too much of an impression on the ground. The cattle are leaving an easy trail too."

"Oh, then I guess you'll just have to think of something else," Andolar replied. "Maybe you and Haslan can set some traps or a false trail to slow them down."

"Not for long enough," Petrion stated simply. "Those cost minutes, and we need hours."

"Well," Andolar said in reply without looking at him, "there must be something we can do. For now you need to get up on a wagon and get some sleep. We need you thinking clearly come tomorrow morning. Or I guess this morning since it's only a little while till daylight. I'll keep them moving till we're hidden in the trees on the other side."

"All right, I do need some sleep."

"Good night, Petrion," Andolar said softly.

Petrion heard him mumble something about dreaming a way out of this mess as he moved away. It was obvious that what Andolar said was true. He had just been too tired to work it all out.

He caught up with their wagon and found a comfortable spot on top of the goods. He reached for a blanket but wasn't sure if he got it or not.

CHAPTER 22

After Petrion went to sleep on the wagon, the job of scouting fell back to Haslan. The thief moved out with his small lantern, finding the trail markers. The lantern gave much better light than a torch, and could be shielded quicker. He widened his lead to almost a hundred paces. Petrion hadn't mentioned any more serious obstacles on the way to the border, but it wouldn't hurt for him to be prepared. It would be so nice to set foot on Gamalius soil again. They wouldn't be able to relax completely, but at least they shouldn't have to worry about running into stray patrols of goblins. He pulled his hood up so that he looked more like a goblin in case he came upon a patrol.

He hoped the duchess didn't have any patrols working this area, or they might shoot him before he had a chance to explain. The cloak was definitely coming off when they reached Gamalius. The dubroty would have to stay with the wagons to keep anyone from reacting wrong when they first saw one of them. People tended to be a little bit strange around things that were new to them. They might think those short hairy people were relatives of the goblins in some way. That would really make them unpopular among the locals.

The singing had slowed down some, but the people were still pushing themselves hard. Sunrise was only a few moments away when he saw the white and double red cloth markers. Petrion had used a different sign here. Maybe they were near the border. Haslan took down the markers and worked his way ahead quickly. The first sunlight struck then across the open area where the boundary stones lay. Gamalius was in sight.

Haslan started to run forward and then caught himself. It wouldn't do to come this far and give way to carelessness. He started moving as silently as possible from tree to tree as he approached the border.

There was no sign of anyone, so he crossed the open ground to see what happened. Once he was deep into the trees inside Gamalius, he circled east and moved back to the north. That might draw out anyone who was skulking along the border. As he cautiously approached the edge of the trees again, he didn't see any movement. He decided to wait in Gamalius for the group to cross. He moved back toward the crossing spot that Petrion picked out for them.

It was a measure of how tired everyone was that he gained distance on them even with his scouting. He noticed the sounds of singing again before the group came in sight. He watched the area up and down the border carefully for any sign of movement. When the wagons and cattle reached the border would be the perfect time for an ambush by mounted troops. There was still no movement that he could detect, and the group could be seen at the edge of the open area. He wanted to quiet them down, but they would still make enough noise to alert anyone in the area, and they would be visible down the border farther than they could be heard.

With another ragged cheer, the first of the former prisoners crossed the white border stones into Gamalius. Haslan just kept watching both ways for an ambush to happen. He was sweating heavily even though the day wasn't all that warm. Now would be the optimum time to attack. The prisoner's wagon crossed next, followed by the group wagon. Finally the herders brought the livestock across on the path of the wagons. Haslan breathed a slight sigh of relief. He still waited and watched the border region until Govin entered the woods and disappeared from sight.

The crossing was easy to see even for an inexperienced tracker like him. The raiders would find them easily. He wondered how long they could push themselves, the slaves, and the horses until everyone gave out. He wished he could set some traps along the border to slow pursuit, but there wasn't a good place. The duchess limited those opportunities along the border for obvious reasons. With a heavy sigh, he ran after the wagons. Actually, in his condition, it was more like a tired hobble. It still didn't take him long.

He saw Govin first then Berinda. Petrion was still sleeping on their wagon, along with six of the farm folk. The other wagon had ten people crammed in it sleeping. What he wouldn't give to join them. Instead, he hurried as much as possible past the wagons and up by Duvain.

"All quiet?" he asked the dubroty.

"Yes, Haslan," Duvain answered, "all quiet. Humans tired. We stop soon?"

"Yes. I go find place to stop."

The dubroty nodded his head as Haslan moved off. *Humans tired, huh. This halfman was tired as well*, Haslan thought. Come to think of it, the dubroty did look like they were in better shape than anyone else, and they had done more over the last few days than anyone, except maybe Petrion. And Petrion was sleeping it off in the back wagon. They were prisoners too and were walking around in full armor. The dubroty must have incredible endurance and must have been treated better than the other prisoners besides.

The ground ahead looked much like what they had been passing over, except there was more space between the trees. It was almost ten minutes of walking before he found a small clearing with water nearby. This would be a good place to camp. The only problem was that they were only a few hundred paces from the border. According to Petrion, the raiders were supposed to meet the goblins at the border at about noon. The ranger hadn't had much more than a nap, but Haslan was going to wake him when the wagons arrived regardless. They had to do something about the coming trouble.

He sat down to wait but had to get up to keep from falling asleep. The wagons finally arrived, and most of the people simply collapsed on the ground wherever they happened to be. Andolar went around and covered some of them with blankets. Berinda unhitched the horses and led them to water. They were about dead on their hooves as well. Haslan helped with the horses until they were picketed on the grass and then went to a watch post to the north. The two dubroty were already there.

"You sleep," Govin told him. "Govin and Duvain take turns watching."

Haslan was too tired to argue and went back to the wagon to lie down. As he walked toward the wagon, he remembered that he was going to wake Petrion. He climbed up beside the ranger and, after some difficulty, roused him from sleep. Petrion tried to rub some of the sleep from his eyes but looked like he was only partially successful.

"It's morning, Petrion," Haslan told him quietly, "and we've set up camp. The people were completely done in and have fallen asleep wherever they were. The dubroty are going to take turns guarding the north while the rest of us sleep. I just thought you might like to know."

"Over the border?" Petrion said. "What time are we attacking the goblin fort?"

"Petrion!" Haslan said. "Wake up. We're back in Gamalius, in our own country. We have the farmers with us and the wagons."

Petrion blinked a couple of times and then started really looking at the surrounding.

"Back in Gamalius," he said with relief. "What time is it?"

"Maybe an hour and a half after sunrise."

"How far are we from the border?"

"Not far," Haslan replied. "Only a few hundred paces. The people were lucky to make it this far."

"Farmers and wagons."

"What was that"?

"You said farmers and wagons," Petrion said quickly. "Where's the saddle for that warhorse? He should be in the best shape."

"What are you talking about?"

"Farmers and wagons. We are only five miles from farmhouses and maybe even a small village. They will have horses and wagons. I can get some of them back here before the raiders if I hurry. We might be able to get enough wagons to load everyone on. At the least we can get some fresh horses. I've got to get going."

Petrion started throwing stuff around in the wagon until he dug out the saddle, blanket, and bridle and threw them to the ground. He followed the stuff down, but his legs gave out on him when he hit, and he rolled. He limped his way to the warhorse and led the animal back to start saddling him.

"Andolar!" Petrion called, "Get over here now!"

"What is it, Petrion?" the magician answered around a yawn.

"Write me out an official-looking order to commandeer wagons and horses," Petrion told him, "with appropriate compensation for the owners. Put some official-sounding title at the end that I can use if the promise of money fails me. Make yourself the official."

"Sure, Petrion," Andolar said. "Wagons and horses, of course." He murmured as he turned, "He did dream up something."

Andolar ran to the wagon as fast as Petrion left, dug through the box of Churinius's papers until he found a blank sheet, and dug out the small bottle of ink and pen that Haslan included. Haslan peered over the side of the wagon to see the magician's work. He had excellent handwriting and signed the document with a flourish. Andolar blew on the document for a few moments to dry the ink then folded it and grabbed a leather pouch out of the wagon. He emptied out the coins that were in the pouch and inserted the folded order. Petrion had the horse saddled and was waiting for Andolar to hand him the message. He caught the pouch of gold Haslan threw to him and tied it tightly to the pommel. As soon as Andolar's message was in his hand, he sunk his heels into the horse's side and left the camp at a trot. The horse quickly picked up speed though, and before he was out of sight in the trees, he was close to a gallop.

Haslan went back to preparing his bed. Tired as he was, he had trouble getting to sleep. He felt every single item piled under him sticking up through the sacks. There were fewer blankets on top of the pile now since the people were sleeping. He finally got himself situated with reasonable comfort and relaxed for sleep. His thoughts followed Petrion on his ride for some time.

⚜

Petrion admired the horse that was carrying him south. Churinius hadn't picked the horse just for show. It had great stamina as well. The horse did try to slow down after about a mile, but Petrion kept kicking it to get more speed. The magnificent animal would have to be left behind on the return trip. He just hoped it wouldn't be injured by his use.

Petrion paid special attention to the terrain he was passing over. He tried to find the route that would give him the best speed with the wagons when he returned. Even at best speed, he had probably two hours before he could get back to the camp.

He wished he had thought of this sooner. Of course, he couldn't have left much sooner without endangering the group. He kicked the horse again as he felt it begin to slow its pace.

"Just a little further fellow," he whispered in the horse's ear.

The horse wiggled an ear at him and continued to run. At least he wasn't carrying as much metal as he usually did. Petrion thought about dropping his leather padding to lighten the load further, but it would cost more time. Time was the most precious thing in the world right now.

"Come on, boy, we have to make it."

There was a stream ahead, but as he closed on it he saw a ford that should be passable for the wagons. He splashed through the stream and up the south bank. The bottom felt solid under the hooves of the horse. The animal tried to pull up for a drink, but Petrion didn't allow the stop. He fought the bit for a while after that, trying to turn around and get to the water. Petrion just kicked him to get more speed. He was getting heavily lathered. Heavy warhorses weren't ridden hard for long distances. They were used for short runs and long walks carrying a lot of weight.

With four miles behind him, the horse started to lose speed. The land was opening up, and Petrion was able to see for a goodly distance around him. He crested a long slow hill on his exhausted horse, and could see four farms and a small village in the distance. Turning the horse toward the village to the west, he kicked it up to speed again. The animal was absolutely magnificent. He would have to make sure and get him as part of the spoils that came as his share.

As he neared the village, he started yelling as loud as he could.

"Come out! Come out!"

Some of the people heard him and came into the street. He saw three wagons sitting in the street and another one in the yard of what must be the stable. He rode to the stable and pulled up at the alarm bar that always hung there. He beat the bar frantically until he had a good-sized crowd gathered around.

"Listen, people," he called, pulling the message out of the pouch, "I have an order here from Andolar of Brighthome, magician of the army. I am hereby authorized to take wagons, horses, and drivers to help me bring back a group of refugees stranded near the border."

A couple of the people started edging away, probably hoping to escape getting pulled in to this mess.

"Stop," he called. "All of you will comply with this order. Many lives are at stake."

"You don't have any right to do that, young fellow," an old man called from the back.

"Yes, I do, and your compliance will be enforced by the army if necessary. This is a military emergency and as such takes precedence over other matters."

There was a lot of angry muttering going on in the crowd now.

"As compensation for your lost time and trouble, I am authorized to pay three gold for every wagon and five silvers for every horse used in this effort. We will return here to this village by the end of the day."

That turned the muttering into smiles and willingness.

"It is critical that we leave quickly," he called and the crowd quickly quieted, "as there are injured people that need this transport. Everyone who is ready to go in five minutes will receive an additional two gold as a bonus. Also…"

He was only speaking to himself then, as the people scattered to do and get whatever they could to contribute to the effort. Petrion dismounted and led the poor tired horse to the stable while he talked to the hostler. There was another large wagon in the barn and ten draft horses. The two men in the stable were already getting the harnesses for the two wagons. He went back outside and found a boy who wasn't too busy to take care of his horse for him. Then he pulled off the saddle and went in and saddled the best horse in the stable. It wasn't as good as the one he was leaving behind, but none of them were.

"To whoever owns the horse," he said, flipping the hostler a gold piece from the pouch he had transferred to his waist.

He rode the horse out of the barn and into the street. Three light wagons were already there as well as a man with a string of four horses. He could see dust trails going out of the town in both directions. People were heading for their farms to get their wagons. He tossed the boy with his horse a silver piece and watched his face light up.

"That's for telling the next three drivers with wagons to follow our trail to the north. Don't let the horse drink too much and walk him around for a while to cool him off."

Petrion rode into the barn and saw the first wagon was ready and moving toward the door. He got out of the way and went to where the hostler was saddling his horse. The extra six riding horses that were in the barn were already tied together to the back of the first heavy wagon.

"Do you have two more harness sets for four horse teams?" he asked the hostler.

"Sure do," the hostler answered. "One of them is kind of old, but it's still strong enough to use."

"Throw them in as well, and I'll throw in an extra gold for you. Throw in any extra saddles you have too."

The man quickly gathered the additional gear. When the second wagon was driven through the barn, he stopped it and loaded the harnesses and saddles. Petrion hurried outside to where the people were waiting.

"We need to make a quick trip," he yelled out. "So everyone who makes the camp, which is just over five miles away, in an hour will receive an additional gold piece. Just follow me."

With that, he started them to the north at a rapid pace. He scouted the route ahead for evenness, to ease the wagon's passage as much as possible. He saw the wagons again as they crossed the ridge of the hill. The drivers were bouncing around in their seats because they were moving so fast. He didn't give them any time for rest during their trek to the north. Once off to the east, he saw a horseman speeding south. It didn't look like he was wearing heavy armor, so maybe it wasn't someone attached to the raiders. Of course, if someone was scouting for them, he wouldn't wear metal armor. Maybe one of the patrols sighted their group and was sending for help. A normal patrol would have small chance of defeating the incoming force, even with their help. They needed to reach a defensible town before the raiders caught up with them.

Of course, Andolar could be wrong about their reactions. It did seem like good reasoning though. Why were they so interested in having the humans start the war? If they could catch his squad and dispose of the former prisoners, they would have their fabricated proof. Of course, three bands of raiding goblins should be enough evidence of goblin hostility for the duchess to say the goblins started it.

They had covered half the distance when another farm wagon caught up with them. The driver looked like he had been out in a serious windstorm. That made six wagons and twelve spare horses. They could make do with this. The heavy wagons of the hostler were much bigger than the others, and would hold more. They were each pulled by four horses.

He didn't let them stop at any of the streams to water their horses. They could get water at the camp when they reached it.

The five miles to the border took an hour and fifteen minutes to cover. The trip back wouldn't be nearly so fast with the wagons loaded heavy and the horses feeling tired. Better that they run unloaded than loaded though.

He heard a call ahead of him and saw Duvain step out from a behind a tree and wave.

"I have wagons," he called in goblin. "Get ready leave."

"We go, good"

Duvain hurried back to the camp fortunately before any of the farmers saw him. He would be easier to explain if there were humans standing around. Petrion waited till the wagons caught up and then motioned them to pull in on the south side of the camp.

When he entered the camp, he saw the people getting wearily to their feet. A wounded man had died. The dubroty were already digging the grave. Some of the people from the village looked at the dubroty with suspicion, but the humans moving unconcerned around them eased their fears.

"People," he called out, "get food and get into a wagon. Spread—"

Another pair of wagons came flying into the clearing and barely got stopped without causing an accident. He breathed a sigh of relief at avoiding a mishap. He motioned the wagons over with the others and continued, "Spread yourselves out among the wagons. Hostler, bring your wagons over by these two so we can spread out the load. Hook the spare horses to these two wagons. Let's make it quick. We're too close to the border for real safety."

"That's right," Andolar said. "Everyone, take your personal goods and get into a wagon."

"But, my lord magician," one man said pleadingly, "what about the cattle and sheep?"

"They can't keep up," Berinda yelled at the man. "They'll have to stay here."

"But they mean a new start for us," the man replied.

"Well," Andolar said quickly when he saw people gathering around, "I suppose everyone that wants can stay here and try to drive the cattle and sheep on at the slower pace."

"Or," Petrion said catching on, "we could scatter them out when we go. That way, you could come back later and find them when the danger from the goblins is less."

That last bit made them forget about the livestock and really got them moving. Andolar gave him a nod for helping out and then started calling out orders to get stuff moving quicker. It was still a half hour later before the last wagon was ready to move out. Petrion used the time to get back into his armor in case they had to fight. Andolar sent the light wagons on as they filled with people, with Berinda riding along as the leader. Their two wagons and the two from the hostler were slower in getting going since they were redistributing the weight and harnessing the teams. It was another ten minutes before those wagons moved out, with Haslan and the two dubroty riding with the drivers. Andolar and Petrion were on horses alongside.

"Quickly, quickly!" Petrion called to the hostler and his other driver. "We have to get away from here."

The drivers cracked their whips over the horses and got the teams moving a little faster. Petrion rode up beside the hostler who was in the first heavy wagon so he could talk with him.

"Excuse me, sir," he told the man in a low voice not meant to carry to the people riding in the wagon, "but you really need to hurry."

"We're going along pretty good for the load we're carrying," the man replied in a tone that implied others shouldn't tell him how to run his business. "And you ran my horses pretty hard getting here."

"Sir," Petrion replied in the same tone, "we expect a hundred and forty goblins with more than a score of mercenary cavalry in heavy armor to come over the border soon to wipe out our little group. And they could do it easily. You see, we know they have been organizing all the raids into human territory lately. If they can keep us quiet, they can keep on raiding and killing along the border. That means they aren't going to stop at the border."

The man turned white and cracked a whip above the heads of the horses to get them moving quicker. His man driving the other of his wagons followed his boss's lead, and the other two wagons followed him. Their wagons were driven by the man who brought the four horses and by one of the former prisoners. The five tired horses were tied to the back of the last wagon. Petrion hated to think about it, but if the raiders caught up, they would have to leave the wagons and try to get away. They would have no chance against the raiders, and alive, they might be able to do something to get the people back.

Petrion used his horse to drive the livestock deeper into Gamalius as they went, letting them break off and scatter as they willed. It took them twenty minutes to catch up to the other wagons, and Petrion let the heavy wagons take the lead. That way, he wouldn't have to tell the other drivers about the trouble they were in. They would just follow the lead of the first wagon. The dubroty objected because they wanted to be close to where the fight happened if it did. Petrion ignored their protests and continued riding. The drivers should know the way well enough, having just covered it, to get back to the village without his help. From there, they would work their way to Delaigamon. Of course, that would leave an almost defenseless village in the path of the raiders. When did the greater good matter more than the good of an individual? That was a question he didn't want to answer.

He decided to scout along their trail and see what was happening at the border. It was a little past midday.

He told Andolar what he was planning, grabbed a few supplies and his trap pack, and headed back. He needed to find out if and when the raiders followed them. They almost had to stay with the wagon tracks to be sure they caught up. He wondered what their reaction would be to the addition of several wagons. The wagons changed the situation from an almost assured catch to a race that depended on the difference in speed between goblin runners and wagons. The raiders might decide not to risk what would become a deep incursion into Gamalius.

The wagons were only about a mile from the border when he left and a little more than four from the village. They had many more miles after that before they reached Delaigamon. Petrion figured the raiders would head for home instead of following if they hadn't caught up by the time they reached the inhabited lands. A large force couldn't be dismissed as random raiders or a pursuit force for a small band of human brigands.

He started to set some traps along the way but figured he better save that for the trip back. After fifteen minutes of relatively easy riding, he reached the clearing where they had camped. He was taking it slow to make sure he didn't run into any unwanted company. The area was quiet. He was halfway across the clearing before he realized it was too quiet. A glint of sunlight off of metal was his only warning, but he turned the horse quickly to run.

He felt a sharp pain in his shoulder as the horse turned and noticed an arrow sticking out. His horse accompanied him in a cry of pain as they turned and headed south as fast as they could go. He changed directions suddenly and frequently as he crossed the clearing, hoping to avoid the arrows that were coming his way. His horse screamed in pain again as it galloped, and Petrion looked to see how badly it was hurt. It had taken two arrows in the side and another in the rump. The horse was losing a lot of blood and wouldn't last long. Petrion booted it to get all the speed and distance possible out of the mount before it collapsed.

An arrow struck him in the back but didn't penetrate his armor. Then he was weaving between the trees and no longer a good target. When he glanced back at the clearing, he saw goblins flooding out with heavy cavalry among them. The raiders had crossed the border.

The humans charged their horses after him, but they were more heavily encumbered with metal. He could have outdistanced them easily on a healthy horse. As it was, they would catch up to him in a matter of minutes.

He pulled the arrow out of his shoulder while he was riding. He probably made the wound worse, but now he could put a bandage on it to stop the bleeding. It was awkward trying to tie a bandage one handed while riding on the back of a speeding horse and holding a shield, but he finally managed to get it tight.

He rode the injured horse for five harrowing minutes before he felt its steps start to falter. As the horse fell, he kicked loose of the stirrups and rolled with the fall. The pursuit was out of sight momentarily, so he pulled his cloak around himself, grabbed his saddlebags, and hurried south. He stopped for a moment to adjust the bandage on his shoulder when he felt blood running down his arm. At least he had the forethought to bring along a few supplies. He heard the jangle of armor behind him and saw some of the cavalry searching the area around the horse. They scanned the woods but couldn't see him because of the cloak. The four riders who were chasing him fanned out and started working their way south along the path taken by the wagons. They were moving slowly enough that the rest of their group should be able to catch up with them. He was too close to try and set a trap for the raiders. He hurried south to get some more distance, but he realized he wasn't gaining ground on the enemy, and he wasn't sure how long he could continue. Without a horse, the best he could do was get back to the wagons at the same time the raiders did. His shoulder was aching from the wound, and the pound of his footfalls weren't making things any better.

The raiders were blocked from his sight by the trees after about five minutes, but he still kept up his pace. It seemed like he had been running forever, and he was already having pains in his side. He wanted to throw away his armor, but that would mark his trail and leave him vulnerable. He could probably move off the path a ways and let the raiders go by while he hid in his cloak.

It was an appealing thought, but he needed to help the others. He hoped they were making good time.

Suddenly he heard the sound of hoof beats coming up the trail behind him, and he dodged quickly to the right. A pair of horsemen galloped down the path of the wagons. There was no way he could keep up with running horses. Even increasing his speed a little proved to be impossible as he started south again. He stopped for a few moments and leaned against a tree to catch his breath. He allowed himself five minutes to rest. His run was becoming more of a shuffle. He hoped the two riders were only going to scout. If they were good fighters, they could probably defeat the entire group at the wagons. Of course, they wouldn't know that.

CHAPTER 23

This time, Petrion saw the riders in the distance before he heard them. Their armor sparkled from the sunlight about a hundred and fifty paces to the south. They weren't traveling as fast on the return trip, letting their group close the distance to keep down the fatigue of their horses. That meant he had a few seconds of time before they reached him. He quickly tied a line between two of the trees as high as he could reach. His cloak was a real help when it came to working in secret. He finished while they were still a good distance away.

Hurrying behind the closest tree, he pulled back his cloak to make himself visible. Then he entered the path at a tired run, not all of which was an act, and headed south. The men in armor quickly noticed him and drew their swords to attack. He stopped and pretended to just notice them. After a second of delay, he turned quickly and started at a broken run back to the north. He kept looking over his shoulder to make sure they stayed lined up on his trap. If they missed the line, or if it broke before they were unhorsed, then he would be in trouble and need to hide quickly. Petrion saw the line ahead and checked behind to see if his timing was right. He had to be close to the line when they hit or his chance for a horse would be gone.

The man on the left was leading, so Petrion cut to the right a bit to draw him closer to the other rider as he got to the line. Suddenly the man was knocked back, taking his horse down with him. The second rider dodged the first but still hit the rope. He lost hold of the reins and fell free from his horse.

The horse came running toward Petrion.

Petrion ran for the horse as it went by, caught the reins, and was almost pulled off his feet by the animal as it went past. He had a couple of frantic moments as he tried to get control of the animal, but he finally managed to get hold of the pommel and mount. Then the horse didn't want to turn around. When he finally got the horse under control, he was a hundred paces from the line. He turned the horse and started it running back the way he had come. One of the men was on his feet with a sword out, so Petrion didn't take any chances and left the path. The man tried to cut him off but couldn't outmaneuver the horse while wearing plate mail. He finally gave up and made his way back to his companion. That man had a leg trapped under his downed horse. Petrion rode south at full speed for the second time that day.

He received a lot of curious stares when he rode up to the wagons a little later on a strange heavily armored horse. There were also a lot of stares at the bloody bandage on his shoulder. The rest of his squad were trying to sleep in the wagons, so he didn't bother them. It would take goblins some time to catch up, and when they did, the squad would need to be rested. The goblins could, if they ran, move about twice as fast as the wagons were going. The group had about a thirty-minute lead. That meant more than an hour till they were run-down, unless the humans left the goblins and rode on to attack. When the raiders came within sight of the group, the horsemen could still speed ahead to stop them while the goblins caught up. But through the woods, they would probably let the goblins run ahead to spring traps.

The village was probably more than an hour away. That meant they would reach the village at the same time the raiders reached them. They would either have to bypass the village and try to draw off their pursuit, go into the village and try and defend it, or run and leave all the farmer folk to worry about the problem. They had enough horses to get away if they had to. He wondered if the duchess would consider the remnants of the Rogue's Squad and a couple of dubroty as an adequate exchange for a village, several farms, and over a hundred people. He sure wouldn't if he was doing the figuring. Maybe they could take one or two of the prisoners along to prove what the goblins were doing. Proof of full military cooperation in the raids might be enough to warrant them losing a village.

If the raiders decided to attack the village, then all of the villagers and probably some of the surrounding farmers would be taken captive. Of course, since they'd be in a hurry to get back across the border, the goblins might just kill the people instead of taking them along. The question was, could the squad defend the village?

The village might be a match for the goblins, with the addition of the Rogue's Squad and the surviving prisoners. The problem would be the cavalry. Maybe, if the men sent the goblins in first, they could deal with the goblins and then make the men attack on foot. Then if they could scatter the enemy horses, the people could get away on foot and in wagons. There were too many things that had to go exactly in their favor for that to ever work. Maybe Andolar or one of the others could come up with something he hadn't thought of.

Petrion decided that a couple more traps could buy them some time. He set up two rider and two foot-soldier traps along the trail of the wagons. He cut ranger marks nearby to warn others of danger. Hopefully, the enemy wouldn't see the warning and the traps would slow them down.

Fifty minutes later, he was still trying to figure out a plan. He woke the other members of the squad and had them start thinking about what they could do. Andolar and Berinda took time to mount horses when he woke them. They weren't really rested but weren't in too bad of shape. They ranged out slightly from the wagons. Andolar went to the west, which was the area least likely to face a direct assault. Berinda went to the east, and Petrion stayed at the back to guard the north.

Petrion finally saw the clearing before the village opening in front of them. He had been expecting the raiders to show up behind them for the last half hour, but there was still no sign of them. Maybe they had turned back or hadn't been able to keep the goblins running. He couldn't very well ride back again and take a chance on being ambushed.

The group reached the edge of the clearing and the light of the early afternoon sun warmed him after the cool of the woods. The grass was thick and still mostly green, and the horses had to be continually prodded to keep them from stopping to eat. The long hill rose slowly, and at the bottom of the other side of the hill was the village.

Petrion urged his horse to more speed and caught up to the last wagon about halfway up the hill. The other side descended more steeply, so they had less than half a mile to the village. Maybe they would have some time to prepare a few surprises for the raiders.

He looked back. Well, maybe they wouldn't have time. Goblins were at the edge of the clearing, and he could see the glint of sunlight off of metal armor further back in the trees. The goblins screamed when they caught sight of the wagons and charged. The cavalry stayed with the goblins but were behind them. He supposed that allowed them to get into the fight without being cut off or trampling any of their troops.

Reactions among the drivers varied. The hostler had been expecting this for some time. He had been glancing back over his shoulder every few seconds since Petrion talked to him. He turned and instantly whipped his horses into a run. The drivers of the other heavy wagons joined him. The farmers in the light wagons were looking around stunned.

"*Move, you idiots!*" Petrion yelled at the top of his lungs. "*Get to the village, or they'll kill you!*"

That spurred the rest of them into motion. They whipped all the horses into a run, and the passengers were bouncing around all over the place. He thought they would lose some of them several times in the next few seconds before they were able to get secure holds. Andolar and Berinda met him as he closed the distance to the wagons again.

"What now?" Andolar called when he got close.

"Get to the village as fast as you can," Petrion called back. "We have to set up some kind of defense before they get there. We'll use the houses, wagons and anything else we can find to give us some cover."

"They'll run right over us!" Andolar exclaimed. "These people couldn't hold off the goblins, let alone heavy cavalry."

"The riders will have to dismount and attack buildings on foot," Petrion replied. "That will even up the odds."

"Then we'll be fighting heavy infantry," Andolar retorted. "You can't be fool enough to think we have any chance at all of defeating them. They'll cut through us like a fish through water."

"Maybe these aren't as skilled as the two we fought earlier," Petrion said, trying to calm the magician. "They may be no better than we are."

"You don't believe that any more than I do," Andolar yelled back. "And besides that, even if they are only as good as we are, they still outnumber our fighters by four or five to one. Do you honestly think you can hold off five people who are more heavily armored than you are and have healer support? Our only chance of living is to run. Remember what my father said when we were outnumbered. We run."

"Andolar," Petrion said quietly in spite of the closing goblins, "if we run, the villagers will be raped, tortured and murdered. If we stay, there is at least a chance they won't be. I'm going to give them that chance. You do what you want, but the odds of winning are much less without you. Besides, the longer we hold the enemy here, the less likely they are to escape to attack again."

Andolar turned his horse and kicked it quickly into a gallop. Petrion looked back and was surprised at how much distance the goblins had covered during the short conversation. Petrion kicked his horse into a gallop as well, following Berinda, who was following Andolar. The last of the wagons were almost to the top of the hill. Unfortunately, the goblins were about halfway up. The three members of the Rogue's Squad were in the middle but were closing the distance to the wagons rapidly. The wagons were gaining ground on the enemy, but not much.

He expected the enemy cavalry to try and cut them off, but they seemed content to follow the goblins. They must be very assured of victory and didn't want to take a chance on any of them being injured. That comforted Petrion not at all.

Petrion saw the wagons would reach town only minutes before the goblins. He needed to catch up with the first wagons to get them to move quickly into position. He had already figured out which group of houses to defend, but they had to throw together some walls between the houses so that all the groups could support each other. He also needed to warn the villagers as quickly as possible.

His horse was a better animal than those ridden by Berinda and the magician, so he closed quickly on Berinda and passed her. Andolar maintained his distance. His horse was carrying much less weight than the other two. Andolar crested the hill and disappeared from view. Petrion looked back to get a good idea of the situation behind him as he got to the top. The goblins were slowing down some from the incline, and the wagons should be picking up speed on the downhill slope.

They would have perhaps two to five minutes to prepare a virtually undefended village to receive the attack of a hundred and fifty goblins as well as heavy human cavalry. No problem.

The drop as he crossed the hill scared him by leaving him above his saddle for a moment. He grabbed on tight to the horse and leaned onto its neck. Berinda crossed the hill behind him. He turned to see how far ahead the wagons were and almost fell out of his seat again.

Spread out before him at the base of the hill and in front of the town was an army. It was a big part of the northern army of Gamalius by their pennants. Cavalry units were moving out on the flanks as he watched. There was a large gap in the center for the wagons to get through to the town. The first wagons were about halfway to the battle line. There had to be almost two thousand troops in the force. Heavy infantry was holding the center, supported by medium infantry with spears. Bowmen were in formation behind the lines. The cavalry units on the flanks were light units. Petrion didn't see any medium or heavy cavalry except for the personal guards of the force commander. He was sitting on a fully armored warhorse with a dozen other officers or guards. Several messengers on light horses were waiting beside the commander. A couple others were moving behind the lines of the army. A ranger came riding hard from the east side to the commander as he watched.

Petrion heard Andolar whooping for joy and waving his arm in the air as he galloped his horse down the hill toward the gap in the line. Petrion looked back and saw a big smile on Berinda's face. They were saved. He felt tears of relief rolling down his cheeks. The people and the squad were going to be safe.

They were nearly down the hill when the goblins reached the crest. Petrion grinned in satisfaction as they stopped and stared at the sight before them. There had to be close to a hundred and fifty of the little brigands, but now they faced many times their numbers of men in battle formation on an open field. The goblins knew as well as he did what odds like that meant. He saw the goblins turn to run but then stop again with cries of dismay. Anything that made a goblin unhappy was good news to him. The enemy cavalry came over the crest of the hill and rode at a measured pace toward the village. Petrion could see them conversing as they rode. The commander must have stationed forces behind them to cut off retreat. He remembered the rider he saw earlier. They might have been the bait to draw in the rat all along. Whatever the reason, he was glad to see them.

He smiled and waved at the rows of infantry and got waves and thumbs-up signals in return. He wished he had enough money to buy them all a drink. In fact, he might have enough. He whooped for joy as he passed between the lines.

Berinda was the last one through. The line closed quickly behind her. Haslan and the two dubroty were already on the ground. He pulled up and dismounted too. Andolar looked like he had just been reprieved from a death sentence, which was just what had happened. The magician was leaning against one of the wagons, trying to catch his breath.

The goblins decided to follow the cavalry down the hill. When they had covered about three quarters of the distance, a line of medium and heavy cavalry crested the hill. No surprise the goblins were moving. The cavalry would chew them to bits. The enemy cavalry pulled up about ten paces from the line of infantry.

"I wish to speak to the commander of this force," the leader of the human raiders called out.

The troops started yelling back ideas on what the man could do with his wishes. The guard commander came over with his escort to just behind the lines and raised his hand for silence among his troops.

"I am the commander," he yelled back once the line quieted down. "You will drop your weapons and surrender to me, or we shall kill you. You are illegally on the property of the Duchy of Gamalius in the Great Realm with an armed force of goblins. If you surrender, we may be able to save your lives."

"We have no quarrel with you," the raider called back, "and meant no invasion of your sovereign territory. We are merely here to retrieve our two prisoners who were stolen by some of your people."

"Who are these prisoners?"

"They are the two short hairy ones you just let through your lines," the raider replied. "We were holding them in a goblin encampment while we were out securing supplies. We have a peace treaty with the goblins, so they allowed us to stay there. While we were out buying supplies, this group attacked and took our prisoners with them. They are of a degenerate breed, and there was a bounty offered on them because of their depredations."

"I have heard of no such bounty," the commander replied.

"The bounty is in our lands," the raider told him. "There is a human kingdom to the north of the goblin lands."

"And what about the goblins you brought into our lands?" the commander prompted. "Our treaty with them forbids their entering the duchy under arms."

"The prisoners were their responsibility," the raider explained, "since they were left in the goblins' care. Therefore, by our treaty with the goblins, they were obligated to help us retrieve them."

"What a load of horse manure!" Petrion yelled out.

He turned away embarrassed when the commander looked his way, but many of the soldiers were voicing supporting opinions. The guard commander raised his hand again for quiet. It took several seconds for the murmurs to quiet.

"If you have come on a peaceable mission," the commander said finally when quiet was restored, "then drop your weapons and surrender. The duchess will hear your case and decide it at her convenience."

"But—"

"No buts," the commander said interrupting. "Surrender now, or I will order my troops to attack."

"I shall have to confer with my comrades," the leader of the raiders replied. "This decision affects all of us."

"You have one minute," the commander called back.

Petrion roughly translated the conversation to the dubroty while the two leaders were speaking. Both dubroty listened in silence.

The men shifted around to talk. The goblins stopped between the two groups of cavalry. Finally, after what Petrion felt was more like five minutes than one, the man came out from among his comrades.

"Your time is up," the guard commander called. "Drop your weapons and surrender, or you will be killed."

The cavalry charged, and because of their shifting to talk, they were in a wedge formation.

CHAPTER 24

The goblins, after a couple moments' hesitation, followed the cavalry in the attack. Petrion heard screams behind him as the farmers fled the area. The raiders were coming right at them. The commander immediately yelled orders to the various groups, and the lines of infantry tried to react. There wasn't time to get set properly. The infantry in front of the horsemen braced their spears, while those to the side hurried to thicken the line. The heavy cavalry of Gamalius, on the slope of the hill, was moving quickly to get into the battle. If he wasn't badly mistaken, the leader of the heavy cavalry was a woman. That narrowed it down to three people.

The sound of impact was horrendous. The shriek and clash of metal combined with the screams of the wounded and dying. The first man in the raider formation went down with two spears in him and two in his horse. The next two men jumped their horses over their fallen comrade and closed with the infantry. One of them was speared, and the other went down as a soldier with a sword opened the belly of his horse. The next three men in the triangle reached the infantry line since their comrades broke the nearby spears. The men at the front desperately tried to get out their swords but were sent flying by the heavy horses. The horses made it through the two ranks of heavy infantry and into the medium infantry behind. One of the men from the second line fell when a sword took off his arm. Another went down under the steel-shod hooves of the trained warhorse.

The raider spurred his horse through the gap he created in the line but went over backwards as a succession of arrows and bolts pierced his armor at short range. The gap in the line was made though, and the raiders came flowing through as best they could. Five of them fell to the spears and swords of the infantry on the sides, while three more went down from arrow fire. Two healers were in the middle of the formation casting spells as quickly as they could to slow the losses. At a command of some type, the remaining raiders dismounted toward the center of their formation and used the horses to shield themselves from the spears and arrows of the infantry. The horses themselves were still inflicting injuries on the army by battling with the infantry. The raiders moved through the gap and were definitely coming toward the squad.

"Escort, close the gap," the commander called. "Infantry kill the horses. Keep the raiders surrounded."

His guards were moving before the order because the commander was heading into the battle. The warhorses were taking a toll on the closely pressed infantry but were falling rapidly themselves. The raiders ran for the line of archers—the only thing between them and the squad—and the line shattered. Light armored archers were no match for the heavily armored and skilled raiders. Many of them didn't get their short swords drawn before they were cut down. The raiders were trying to kill the squad before dying.

"Form up!" Petrion called. "Andolar, get behind the fighters. Haslan, do what you do best. Berinda, support Govin, I'll support Duvain." He called in Goblin to the dubroty, "Govin, help Berinda. Duvain, help me."

The fighters deployed in twos. Andolar was behind them, readying a spell of some type. Petrion could see the duchy's heavy cavalry closing rapidly on the breach. They had lances down but couldn't charge. The goblins would be to the infantry by the time they arrived. A few of the goblins were trying to surrender. He turned his attention back to the immediate problem.

A fighter with three arrows in his shield and two more in his armor was the first to reach the squad. He aimed a strong overhand swing at Duvain, which the dubroty deflected with his shield. Petrion swung in from the right, and the raider took the blow on the shield. At the same time, Duvain cut up between his legs with his ax. The heavy ax split through the armor and into his groin. He fell dying to the ground. He saw out of the corner of his eye that Berinda and Govin were embattled as well but didn't have time to determine anything more. Another pair of fighters engaged them.

One of the fighters had no shield but replaced it with a dagger. The second carried a hand-and-a-half sword and shield. Both aimed attacks at Duvain. Duvain blocked the hand-and-a-half sword with his shield, but the force of the blow moved him sideways toward Petrion. The swing of the long sword he caught between the spike and blade of his ax. The raider used the sword to push the ax sideways and drove in with the dagger in his left hand. Petrion swung at the hand and severed the fingers holding the dagger. The raider cried out in pain as he lost the dagger and held his maimed hand against his side to slow the loss of blood. The other raider got a swing past the guard of the beleaguered dubroty, whose armor only partially stopped the blade. Duvain surely had a cut on his shield shoulder.

Neither of the raiders had tried a swing at him. All they were concerned about was killing the dubroty. Anything they wanted was something Petrion opposed.

He thrust hard at the fighter with the maimed hand and forced him a step away from Duvain. Then he swung wildly across at the other raider to distract him. The swing rang off the raider's shoulder armor and didn't penetrate, but it did give Duvain a moment's rest in which to get set again. Both raiders immediately renewed their assault on the dubroty. Petrion was forced to fight defensively for Duvain. His sword helped turn swings, and his shield helped cover Duvain's body. The shielded raider finally called something to the other, and the man switched his attack to Petrion. Petrion stayed totally defensive in his maneuvers. Time was completely in his favor. If he could hold out, then the raiders would be dead in a matter of seconds. Seconds could last forever in a battle though.

A fire dart flew over Petrion's shoulder and impacted on the nose of the man in front of him. Petrion quickly used the distraction as the fighter blinked to clear his eyes to take a swing at his throat from the shield side.

His opponent had tricked him. The man hadn't been distracted as much as he pretended and used Petrion's move for a thrust of his own. The sword penetrated his right shoulder and almost made him lose his grip on his own sword. He was bleeding badly from the wound. He changed quickly back to defensive tactics, but the shoulder wound slowed his responses. He was quickly hit twice more for minor wounds. Why couldn't he learn from his mistakes? Baron Gardoney had done the very same thing to him.

The other fighter was pressing Duvain hard. He was going to lose this fight if he didn't do something quick. Desperation made him resort to the trick Berinda had shown him. The next time he was cut, he closed his eyes and fell toward the raider.

He expected to land on the raider and was ready to react. Unfortunately, the man moved out of the way in time to avoid his fall. He hit the ground hard and rolled over. The man ignored him once he was out of the way and attacked. Petrion rolled over and hooked the man's leg with his own. He pulled back hard with his foot as the man lifted it off the ground. The raider lost his balance and fell, spoiling an attack from his companion.

Petrion got to his knees, feeling dizzy. He stabbed forward with all the strength he could manage, driving his sword at the back of the standing soldier. He didn't know Petrion was there so didn't dodge the blow. The sword drove through the armor and into the man's back. He collapsed quickly as the sword hit his spine, taking Petrion's sword with him. The other fighter never got back to his feet. Duvain, relieved of pressure to the front, made an overhand swing and split the raider's head in spite his armor.

With no more enemies immediately in front of him, Petrion looked to see how the battle was going. The commander of the duchy forces was dueling with the last standing raider, the spokesman—from his decorated armor. A fighter and healer lay on the ground in front of Berinda and Govin. Berinda was dripping blood from a cut on her sword arm and from one in her leg too, if the cut in her armor was any indication. That reminded him of his own wound. He grabbed a bandage from his belt and fumbled to get it on his shoulder.

Unfortunately, his legs wouldn't support him anymore, and he sat down heavily. His side felt like it was completely soaked with blood, and he could feel consciousness slipping away. He needed a rest anyway.

"Here, let me take care of that."

He turned his head to see who was talking to him, but the effort was too much, and he fell to his side and then to his back and lay looking into the sky.

"Korin!" he said in surprise as the familiar face came into view. "You escaped!"

"Sure did," the healer replied in a steady voice. "So did you. We can catch up later. Right now, hold still. I have a lot of other injuries to attend to."

"Is Florine safe too?" Petrion asked as he tried to sit up to talk to the kneeling healer. "We really missed you."

"Yes," he said in exasperation as he held the ranger to the ground. "Now hold still and let me work."

The healer quickly chanted a healing spell and a second and then finished with some bandages and an arm sling and then went to work on Duvain. The dubroty's appearance didn't have any visible effect on the healer as he tended his wounds.

He turned his head slightly and saw the commander had finally disarmed the raider facing him. As he stepped forward to take the man prisoner though, the raider pulled a knife and plunged it into his own chest. He stood for a couple more seconds before collapsing. Not one of the raiders appeared to be conscious.

Petrion got unsteadily to his feet and looked around to see what happened to the goblins. They were littering the ground in front of the army position, most with arrows sticking out of them. It looked like only a few made it to the lines of the infantry. The commander surveyed the scene and shook his head. At least twenty of his infantry were on the ground. Many of them would probably never get up.

Petrion felt tears in his eyes again, but of sadness instead of joy. Those brave troops had welcomed them to safety just moments before and had paid for the squad's lives with their own.

The heavy cavalry of Gamalius arrived at the line, though too late to join in the battle. They had a few goblins who surrendered.

The soldiers were doing what they could for their comrades, but magic would be needed for many of the wounded. There were three other healers running over. He also noticed that the force commander was coming their way.

"You," the commander called, pointing at Petrion, "come here."

Petrion looked around quickly to see if there was someone else the commander was talking to. When he saw there wasn't, he walked over. When he was five feet away, he halted and came to the best attention he could in his present condition. It should be Baron Gilbert, whom he had met, but with the visor on his armor down, Petrion couldn't be sure. It was possible it was one of his high officers.

"Yes, sir."

"Who and what are those two people that these men were so determined to kill?" the commander asked him.

"They are dubroty, sir," Petrion replied, "and they were indeed held at a goblin fort across the border, along with many human prisoners taken on raids into Gamalius."

"Dubroty huh," the commander said. "I've never heard of them before. Do you know where they come from?"

"They said they live in the mountains, sir," Petrion answered. "They don't speak our language, but they both speak Goblin and another language that was used by the human raiders that we just killed. They told me they were sent south to look for allies in their fight against the goblins and the humans on the other side of the mountains. Their column was destroyed, and they were taken prisoner. They were working in the goblin fort as black-smiths when we rescued them."

"You say they spoke the language of these raiders?"

"Yes, sir."

"What are their names?"

"Duvain and Govin."

"Could you ask them to come over here?"

"Yes, sir."

Petrion hurried and brought the two dubroty back with him. Both of them looked a lot worse than they had at the start of the battle in spite of getting help from the healers. Both had several gashes in their armor. The raiders had been doing their best to kill them, and their best had come close to being enough. Those were some tough people though.

The commander motioned for Petrion to stay behind and for the two dubroty to follow him to a tent he had ordered set up. He said something to one of his messengers, and the messenger rode quickly to the cavalry commander. It was really hard to tell anything about what was going on with everyone wearing full helms. You couldn't judge facial expression, and the metal distorted the voice.

Petrion turned to look at the battle scene again while the messenger was riding to the cavalry. He counted twelve dead among the troops on the ground. Twelve people who had given their lives so he and his companions could live. Several more had serious wounds that would be a long time healing without magical assistance. Apparently, only three of the human raiders were still alive, and it looked like the commander had ordered that they stay alive. He probably wanted to question them.

Petrion doubted that he would have much luck getting information from people who would charge to certain death to accomplish a mission and fall to the last person. All of their horses were down as well.

Looking at the carnage around him, Petrion realized how quickly they would have fallen without the army. It would have been a foolish gesture on his part to try to stop the raiders with just the villagers for help. The only thing the squad would have done is add a few more bodies to the pile of dead. He also had a terrible insight into the costs of the war that had just started.

Petrion returned to the infantry line to see if there was anything he could do. Korin and Florine were both there and working on the wounded. He was five paces away when he was told to go find something useful to do. They didn't need someone with only one good arm. He wandered back to where the rest of the squad was standing.

He supposed this was a very minor conflict as far as battles with the goblins went. He remembered when he and his mother heard that his father wouldn't be coming home. He was with his aunt and uncle when the news of his mother's death reached him. War was always ugly. He pitied the twelve families that would have to be informed about the loss of a son, brother, or father.

It had been male infantry units in this part of the line. The duchess had always segregated the men and women in the main army into different infantry, cavalry, and archery companies, until they got to the command level. She did that to cut down on relationships.

The women's companies also used smaller armor, shields, and weapons, so keeping everyone of the same sex together insured that people would have usable weapons and armor in the area during battles if they lost or broke their own. Ration packs, camp tools, and tents were all sized differently as well, meaning the women's packs could be more appropriate to their size.

The cavalry commander followed the messenger to the tent and dismounted to go inside. The infantry commander spoke to the two guards standing at the entrance and then closed the flaps. Almost immediately, the sound of armed conflict erupted from inside.

CHAPTER 25

Petrion hurried over to help, but two guards blocked his way. They quietly refused him permission to pass. Another half dozen heavy infantry and cavalry officers were coming to the area as well as more guards. He heard a sharp intake of breath from one of the men at a particularly loud exchange of blows. Petrion turned to get the rest of the squad, but they were already behind him. No wonder more guards were coming. Even Korin and Florine had come over with the rest to support him. A warm feeling came over him. You didn't find that many true friends in life. Even Andolar had come. The magician looked uncomfortable at the situation he was in, but he was there.

An ax blade came slicing through the side of the tent as the fight continued to rage. Finally it occurred to Petrion that the commanders must not be fighting to kill the dubroty. He had handled the commander of the raiders without difficulty, and the other raiders had been more than a match for any of them.

Duvain flew out the front entrance of the tent and went charging right back in. He had lost his ax. The next time Duvain appeared was through the hole the ax made in the side of the tent. This time, he sat working his jaw back and forth with his hand. The clash of metal finally stopped. The cavalry commander stuck her head out of the rent and said something he couldn't understand to Duvain. Duvain got up and made his way unsteadily back inside. The infantry commander stuck his head out the front and said something to one of the guards. The guard jumped at the sound but quickly recovered and motioned for Petrion to enter. Petrion shrugged his shoulders at the other squad members and went.

Govin and Duvain were sitting on camp chairs in the tent, and opposite them were the Duchess Eviola and Baron Gardoney with their visors open. Petrion's mouth dropped open at the sight, and it took three times of the baron saying something to him before it registered.

"Petrion! Please take a seat. We have a lot to talk about."

He saw, as he made his way to the seat, that both of the dubroty were going to have some really astonishing bruises on their faces by morning. They were sitting rather sullenly and threw Petrion a look of betrayal as he walked to the other seat. Petrion had no idea what was going on, but Baron Gardoney started explaining as soon as he was seated. The duchess translated the language the baron was using for Petrion's benefit. The baron was apparently speaking in the language the human raiders used. He could see why the dubroty were upset. They probably thought Petrion brought them to another group of enemies to betray them. He had to quit thinking and start listening as the story unfolded from Baron Gardoney.

Baron Gardoney put a map of the Great Realm on the small table in the middle of the room and started explaining about the realm. The northern details ended not far after the border with the goblin kingdom. The rest of the realm was drawn out with as much of the adjacent area as had been explored. He noticed there was a considerable area in the lands of the Barbarians that was mapped out in the area of The Pass.

The baron told the dubroty about the great wall at the choke point of The Pass that kept the barbarians away from the Great Realm. The Pass was the only passage through the mountains that could be used by an army. The High Range Mountains narrowed there, and a low area coincided with the narrowing. That was The Pass. The rest of the range was too rugged and high for any but a very experienced climber to cross. Many of them had failed in the attempt.

After he finished talking about the geography of the region, he went on to tell the story about how they came by the details of the land of the barbarians. The baron explained how as a young fighter he and a group of adventurers, including the duchess, had disguised themselves as barbarians and made their way into the enemy lands to find out what they could. They put on the garb of the enemy and during the confusion of a battle joined with the enemy forces in retreat. Once they were clear of The Pass, they slipped away from the army and made their way into the countryside.

They found a poor peasant who needed the money they could provide and stayed with him, working around the place to help the man so they wouldn't look suspicious. The peasant taught them the language for a couple of months until they were fluent. Once they had a good grasp of the language, they paid the peasant and moved around the land collecting information. They also did as much covert damage to the war effort of the barbarians as they could. They had plenty of the money used in that country, taken from the bodies of the many soldiers who had died trying to force a way into the Great Realm.

Finally after a year and several harrowing adventures, they attached themselves to the army again as a portion of it moved to assault The Pass. When they reached The Pass, they again slipped away from the army and crossed to their own side. It took some time for them to convince the guards on the wall to let them through, but they finally got lifted to safety. They watched the next morning as the barbarians were driven back again.

After the battle, they went to the High King and reported their findings. The barbarians had a much larger military than the Great Realm's. In fact, from the information they gathered, the barbarians were fighting on several fronts at once and winning. They also had cities that would number many times the population of any of the cities of the Great Realm. It appeared that the people of the Great Realm were the barbarians, instead of their attackers. The name had been used for so long though that it was never changed. The wall and the defenders of The Pass were the only thing that prevented the barbarians from overwhelming the Great Realm.

Gardoney paused for a moment to take a drink from the glass that the duchess handed him. She had filled one for each of the dubroty, Petrion, and herself as well. The chest she got the drink and glasses from had a couple of hack marks in the lid and another on the side.

Petrion focused back on the baron as he told the dubroty about the current situation. The barbarians had been attacking hard at The Pass for the last twelve years. The Great Realm was being gradually worn down by the constant conflict. The wall across The Pass was being destroyed faster than it could be fixed. Things were bad enough that a second wall was being erected behind the first. It would be longer than the first, which was at the narrowest part of The Pass and harder to defend. Losing the current wall would probably mean losing the war eventually.

The Duchy of Gamalius had, in former years, supplied a lot of seasoned troops to the defense of The Pass but had been forced to quit because of the goblin wars. The Pass would hold for another six to ten years at the current rate of attack. The second wall would have a life of about ten years.

Baron Gardoney stopped talking and waited for the dubroty to speak. Petrion had learned more about his world during the last few minutes than he had ever heard before. He could see why people weren't told about it. How would people feel if they knew their country would be taken over by the barbarians at sometime in their life?

Duvain looked over at Govin, and Govin nodded his head that Duvain should go ahead and talk. The dubroty showed the approximate location of their kingdom in the mountains beyond the area explored in goblin lands. He recounted how his people were trapped between enemies on both sides—and were starving—and explained how his band had been sent looking for allies and were assaulted by Churinius's people. The dubroty told about his time as a prisoner waiting for Churinius and his people to free them or for a chance to escape. The commander had promised they could go free as soon as their people surrendered their caverns, which crossed under the mountain range. They had never associated with the human prisoners at the fort because they were told the prisoners were low-society criminals from Churinius's own people. Andolar was the first they could communicate with until Petrion and Haslan arrived. Finally after another look and nod from Govin, he told about the metal the dubroty mined, its properties when mixed with steel, and the barbarians' lust to get the mines. He pointed to the ax the baron had and told him that the ax was made with such steel.

The baron tried out the ax on the table and then called for his guard to fetch someone called Fleinsir. A few moments later, a magician stepped into the tent. Gardoney asked permission from Duvain to do an experiment on the axes. Duvain nodded to the baron, and Gardoney handed them to the magician.

"See if they can be enchanted, Fleinsir," Gardoney told the magician.

"My lord," the magician said pleadingly after he recovered from his surprise, "there would be only an extremely small chance

of an enchantment taking and holding on a weapon under conditions like these. You know how few times we succeed when all of
the conditions are right in one of our magic rooms. Why waste
the power?"

"Fleinsir," Gardoney said with impatience, "just do it. Report
back to me on your results within an hour."

"Yes, my lord."

The magician turned and left with the axes, and Gardoney
continued his talk with the dubroty. Petrion was starting to get
bored and stopped listening to the flow of the conversation about
road conditions and distances. The duchess had joined directly in
the conversation rather than translating for him. He must have
just been brought in to reassure the dubroty as much as possible.

Baron Gardoney suddenly stood up. He was looking at the
dubroty strangely. That got Petrion's attention.

"*Durragar?*" he said in a questioning tone.

The duchess looked at him puzzled, but his attention was
totally fixed on Duvain. Duvain replied something, and Petrion
heard the word *durragar* used again.

Petrion fell backward off his seat when the baron jumped up
in the air with a loud whoop. He was back on the ground quickly.
You don't get very high in the air jumping in full plate mail.
Petrion picked himself up off the ground and checked to see how
many new dents would have to be worked out of his armor.

"What is it, Gardoney?" the duchess asked in their
own language.

"Some really good news for a change," the baron said joyfully.
"Good news for us and maybe for the Great Realm if it's not too
late. Don't you recognize the name Durragar?"

"No," she replied. "Is there some reason I should?"

"Not particularly," the baron told her in a rather self-satisfied
voice. "You remember that I did some recreational reading when
we were in the land of the barbarians. You know how you said
that it was a waste of time and that I should be helping plan more

attacks. You remember how every time I bought another book how you…"

"*Get on with the story!*" the duchess snapped at him.

"Yes, your ladyship," the baron said, and the smile never left his face. "Some of the stories I read concerned a people called the Durragar. They related to fables in our own lands. They were a people of legendary prowess in mining, blacksmithing, and stonework."

"Dwarves?"

"Yes, your ladyship," Baron Gardoney said with a laugh. "We have found the fabled dwarves, and they are looking for an alliance."

"The barbarians," the duchess said in surprise. "They were doing everything in their power to keep us from linking up with the dwarves to our north. They were also trying to convince these dwarves that the humans to the south were every bit as bad as the humans to their west so they wouldn't look south for allies. They were probably planning on letting them escape after a time to report back. They also kept the border area stirred up in case some managed to sneak past them. We would be expecting enemies when we saw each other and likely would have attacked. Baron! Tell them what's happening. And if they starve the dwarves into submission, then they have a highway under the mountains to bring their troops over."

"Yes, your ladyship."

The baron started talking in the other language again, and the dwarves started out looking disbelieving and ended up looking as surprised and happy as the baron. Then Fleinsir came running back into the tent.

"My lord," he called breathlessly, "my lord. This is unprecedented. I cast an enchantment on the weapon, and it took on the third try. I think that has only happened so soon twice before in my twenty-two years of casting, and those were under ideal conditions. I thought it the best of luck, wishing I had been at a chancery by the way, and tried for a second enchantment. I exhausted my magic without getting a second enchantment to take, but it felt like it almost did. It was a most unusual sensation. The metal seemed to want the enchantment. The second ax enchantment took on the eighth try by Erianna. What is this ax made from?"

Baron Gardoney apparently put the question to the dwarves because Duvain brought out the block of metal that they said they used to alloy with steel. The baron took the metal and passed it to the magician. The magician handled it carefully and started what appeared to be an enchantment of some type. He broke off suddenly, looking up at the baron in wonder.

"It's almost as if the metal were pulling the enchantment in because it wanted to be strengthened," the magician said in awe. "What is it called?"

The baron conversed with the dwarves quickly and then turned back to the magician.

"It appears we have found two legends in one day, sir magician," the baron said with a smile. "The dwarves say this metal is adamantine. It's the metal that makes steel virtually unbreakable. He said that the unbreakable part is an exaggeration, but that it does strengthen the steel and makes it easier to enchant for more strength."

"Dwarves? Adamantine?" Flensir said in shock.

The baron took the bar away from the magician with everyone looking on and handed it back to Duvain. Then he took the ax from the magician and with a light swing sliced the corner off of the camp table. Duvain and Govin were as surprised as Petrion. The duchess, the baron, and the magician were positively glowing with smiles. The baron passed the axes back to the dwarves, which seemed to surprise them even more. Duvain took the metal bar out and handed it to the baron. The baron wouldn't accept the bar and said something to the dwarf. The dwarf put the metal bar in his pack and extended his hand to the baron and then the duchess. Govin did the same.

"You can leave now, Petrion," the duchess told him.

Petrion got up to leave, but the baron stopped him before he got out of the tent.

"Would you please send my son in to me, Petrion?" the baron asked.

"Of course, sir."

"Oh, and don't tell him it's me in here," the baron said with a smug smirk. "Tell him the force commander is demanding to know who this Andolar of Brighthome is and what gives him the right to issue orders."

"Yes, my lord," Petrion said with a smile.

The baron clapped him on the back as he left the tent. The old fighter must really have been worried when the healers returned from the north alone. Andolar was the least likely to survive stuck out in the wilds. He had probably almost given up hope. Petrion left the tent and quickly killed the smile on his face as he made his way to where the squad members were standing.

Andolar was waiting with most of the others when Petrion came out of the tent. Florine and Korin had gone back to tending the wounded. They had waited just long enough to make sure there wasn't going to be any trouble.

Petrion had something between a fearful and guilty look on his face. It looked almost like a smile tugged at the corners of his mouth a couple times too, but the smile didn't fit with the other expressions. The ranger stopped in front of the magician and kept his head down.

"Uh, Andolar," Petrion stammered out, "the force commander wants to see you in the tent."

"What for?"

"You know what," Petrion said hurriedly, "those two dubroty are dwarves. That's the way their name translates into Goblin. Isn't that wild? The commander said that dwarves were masters at metal working, mining, and stone work."

"Petrion," Andolar said again, "what does the commander want to see me about?"

"Well, Andolar," Petrion said while still looking down, "he wants to see whoever wrote that order."

"What order?"

"The one that conscripted citizens of the duchy without lawful permission, took them into a battle area, and also promised them a ridiculously high reward from the army for doing it."

"You told me to write that note!"

"Well, yes. But the commander didn't ask about that. He just asked to see this Andolar of Brighthome, magician of the army."

"Thanks a lot, Petrion," Andolar said in disgust. "Maybe I can do something for you someday."

"Hey," Haslan added in, "you can't say you're of Brighthome anymore. Your father disowned you. That means you're guilty of impersonating a noble. Doesn't that carry a fairly severe penalty? I seem to remember that from my study of the law."

"And thank you for your support too, thief."

He started slowly toward the tent. He heard whispering behind him as he walked and turned to see the others huddled together chuckling. For some reason, he felt a little betrayed. He could hear a conversation being carried on as he approached the tent but didn't recognize the language. The guards waved him in as he drew near. He stopped at the flap to catch his breath, but the guard on the right went ahead and pulled it open. He ducked below the height of the flap and entered the tent. The commander was standing at the back of the tent, talking with the dubroty. His back was turned, so even though his visor was up, Andolar couldn't tell how upset he was.

"Andolar of Brighthome reporting, sir," Andolar said in what he hoped was a somewhat military manner.

"I don't recognize that person," the commander said in a low voice. "As I recall, Baron Gardoney has only a single son, and his name is not Andolar."

"But, sir—" Andolar stammered out before being cut off.

"I also don't think that you have any position in the army," the commander said, growing louder all the time, "that allows you the privilege of conscripting citizens of the duchy. I know you are not empowered to make promises of payment from the army to those citizens!"

"Excuse me, sir, but we intended to pay them ourselves," Andolar said as humbly as he could. "We liberated a considerable treasure from the goblin raider's camp."

"*That does not excuse your irresponsible actions!*" the commander boomed out.

"Father?"

"Oops, you've heard me say that before, haven't you?" Baron Gardoney said as he turned to face his son.

"It is you, Father. What's with the act?"

"Just returning a little of the worry and frustration you've given me over the years, my son."

"Thanks a lot, Father."

"No problem at all," the baron replied. "I was more than happy to do it. It's good to see you back safe, son."

"Yeah, no thanks to you," Andolar replied angrily. "Do you have any idea what I've had to go through the last couple of weeks? Do you have any idea how many times I've come close to being killed"?

"Yes, I'm sure I do," Gardoney replied quietly. "After all, I've been there many times myself. I'm glad you've come back to me, my son."

"Oh right, and—" Andolar stopped his tirade for a moment. "Did you say 'my son'?"

"Well, yes," Gardoney said, "I believe I did."

"Thank you, Father."

"You didn't lose anything of your mother's, did you?" his father asked anxiously.

"No," Andolar replied, "but Haslan has almost permanently borrowed one of her daggers. He has used it well though."

"All right," his father said, "as long as he doesn't forget who it belongs to. How did you come out in the goblin lands?"

"We lost Lecik, Father," Andolar said with a trace of sadness.

"The archer, huh. He was a good person and a valuable member of the Rogue's Squad. Only nineteen years of age and lost in the goblin wars. There will be a lot more young men and women lost in this war before we're done, I'm afraid. You'll have to tell me all about what happened."

"Maybe later." Andolar heard from the other side of the tent.

The duchess was sitting there. He hadn't even noticed her, what with all the worrying about what was going to happen to him.

"Greetings, your ladyship," Andolar said with the formal bow his father had taught him.

"Someday, Gardoney!" she said to his father, who had a strange smirk on his face while looking at him.

"What, your ladyship?" Andolar asked her.

"Nothing, Andolar," the duchess replied. "We have some important matters to discuss right now. We'll catch up on all the details of your attacks on the goblins and their attack on you later. I'm especially interested in the details of the treasure."

"Yes, your ladyship."

Andolar turned to leave the tent and had taken a step that way when his father called out to him.

"Andolar!"

Andolar turned around only to be caught in a hug by his father.

"I am very glad you are back safe, son," the baron said, and Andolar saw the tracks of tears on his cheeks. "Take care, and we'll talk later."

"Yes, Father, we will. Ouch. You can't get near that armor without getting pinched."

His father chuckled and let him go. Andolar saw a tear running from his father's eye as he turned back to the dubroty, or dwarves, he supposed. His voice betrayed no sign of emotion though as he started conversing with the dwarves again. The duchess gave him a wink as he left the tent.

All of his squad mates were standing around with smiles on their faces, waiting on him to reappear. Petrion looked especially smug. Andolar wiped some moisture out of his eye before he started over to them.

"Very funny, Petrion," Andolar said. "Maybe you should be in entertainment."

"Sorry, Andolar," Petrion replied. "Actually I guess I'm not sorry. Besides, it was orders. I can't go against official orders."

The others laughed at that as well, and he found himself laughing along with them. It was so good just to be alive and safe that he couldn't help but be happy.

"Now," Haslan said, "let's go and see exactly what we came away with as treasure. I've been dying to count it."

"Hey, I'd almost forgotten about that," Andolar said. "Let's go."

"We still have to settle up with the villagers," Petrion reminded them. "It's worth it though. Without them, we wouldn't have made it, let alone made it with treasure."

"What treasure?" Korin asked.

That started the stories going about what they had done while they were apart. Andolar and Petrion did most of the talking. Petrion glossed over the details of who caused Lecik's death. In fact, he acted as if Berinda hadn't been acting rashly. Andolar was about to say something when he remembered what Petrion had chosen to overlook with respect to his own conduct. Humiliating

Berinda wouldn't do any good for Lecik now. They would just have to hope that she learned from the mistake and didn't repeat it. His father always said it was more important to fix the problem than to fix the blame. He figured there was not a big chance of her reforming. She was as stubborn and self-centered a person as he had ever seen.

Oh no! He had been so concerned with staying alive that he had forgotten they had an outing together planned. No, not *they*—that bully had virtually ordered him to go out on a date with her. He'd never survive the evening. There was absolutely no way he could manage to keep his mouth under control around her for an entire night. He might as well plan on waking up in a room somewhere with a mild concussion. He groaned at the thought.

"Are you hurt, Andolar?" Florine asked concerned. "If you are, I can help you."

"He's fine, Florine," Berinda said testily from the other side of the group. "I kept the raiders away from him in the battle. You don't need to help him. Did I tell you all about how I finished off that healer?"

"Yes," Petrion said with an amazingly neutral expression, "but only three times so far. Maybe we can hear it again later."

Petrion continued updating Korin and Florine on what happened at the fort in spite of Berinda's fuming. By the time they got to the point where they were telling about the treasure, they were sorting through it.

They paid off all the villagers from the chest of silver. It was still about a quarter full, so in a fit of generosity, they split the rest between the former prisoners. They gave the silver taken in their other battles to prisoners as well. The people now had enough money to make a good start on a new life. Besides, they did still have a lot of gold.

"That's my favorite position to be in," Haslan said after Andolar had voiced a comment about the amount of gold.

Andolar was surprised at how many of the unpaired prisoners were now paired up with someone else from the fort. All of the women appeared to be taken, and all the orphans had families to look after them.

After the goods were divided, the prisoners sought places to lie down and rest. He wondered if they would ever manage to forget their time with the goblins. He didn't think he ever would.

Now they were left with the gold, platinum, gems, and jewelry. And that didn't include the armor and weapons they had. One of those items might even be enchanted. That would really add to the value. Churinius's armor was enchanted if what the dwarves said was true. Andolar planned to check for enchantments on the items after he rested.

The fighters and healers counted out the gold while he counted the platinum. Haslan spent the time appraising the gems and jewelry. At the final tally, they had a total of four hundred and thirty-seven gold and ninety-three platinum. They had four pieces of jewelry and twelve gems, of which Haslan estimated the total value to be slightly over eleven hundred in gold. Haslan took out the most valuable of the gems and gave it to Andolar, with the permission of the other squad members, to add to his belt stash against an emergency. Haslan estimated he could get somewhere around a hundred and forty gold for the stone.

Andolar removed the storage buckle and added the ruby to his diamond. It was a tight fit. The others were inquisitive about the device, and Haslan related how the potion his father hid in the device saved Petrion's life. Haslan also took the opportunity to look at the other gem in the device and decided it was worth about two hundred and fifty gold. It was an extremely nice stone.

Korin and Florine, on their part, related what had befallen them and the duchy after Churinius attacked them at the camp. They had trouble controlling the horse but finally got it to go in the direction of their horses. It had taken some distance to get the horse stopped once they reached the horses. They had to drag the horse back and get everything ready to go. By the time they were mounted, the goblins were in sight and closing. They followed the group plan and headed south. Korin had suggested that since they had so many riderless horses, they could cut a little to the west and try and pick up the prisoners. They managed to find several of the people before the goblins closed, but they missed at least four or five.

Petrion let out a strange noise when Korin said that. The two healers stopped talking, and everyone looked at Petrion. The ranger, apparently for the first time, related the story of the goblins at the fort. How he had fallen asleep but still ambushed the goblins and killed them. Then he finally told about how the woman captive had taken her own life.

The squad sat silently for a while. Korin seemed especially hurt because they failed to find her.

Finally Florine began their story again. They returned to Gamalius without incident and went immediately to Delaigamon instead of waiting at the rendezvous. They used the contact at the wine shop to get an urgent message to Baron Gilbert. The baron immediately sent word to the south of the size of the goblin force and also sent a relief force to the east in case the band he sent to intercept the raiders was in trouble. Gilbert had sent word south earlier that the Rogue's Squad had defeated raiders operating in Gamalius. Baron Gardoney had immediately forwarded the message to the duchess and headed north with all the troops he had in the training camp. The duchess followed as soon as possible with the rest of the troops that could be spared from other duties.

Baron Gilbert also formed up all the local members of the guard into an army and sent out all of the rangers to track the enemy movement and determine if they were in or coming in to Gamalius territory. From the conversations they overheard, Baron Gilbert figured on going into goblin territory with the army to attack the raiders.

Baron Gilbert lost all but two warriors out of a band of nearly fifty at the site of the ambush. The two warriors were ranger scouts. One of the rangers met the relief force on the way and told what happened. The human raiders came into the area where the forces of the duchy were waiting on the goblins. They mixed in with the troops and attacked without warning as the goblins were coming into range. The raiders were more heavily armored and in better position than their opponents and destroyed the troops without a single loss of life. From the damage to their armor seen later by the scouts, the healers were needed to keep the loss of life to zero. The scouts were following the goblins to keep them from escaping, and the battle was over when they arrived, so they turned to the west.

One of them decided to shadow the raiders to keep track of them, while the second went for help. The relief force gave a fresh mount to the ranger and sent him to Delaigamon. When the ranger arrived in Delaigamon, he found Baron Gilbert preparing for war. Korin and Florine's report was enough to have him place every army unit in the area on alert. They moved out within a day of when the healers arrived. The ranger scout found them in camp a short way from the city.

Baron Gardoney with his cavalry caught up the next day. The baron was outraged at the story the healers told and had pushed the troops hard to get them into striking position. When they started north, Korin and Florine went along to lend what assistance they could. The duchess joined them on the march with more cavalry. The rest of the infantry hadn't caught up yet. The scouts reported the movements of the raiders, and the army moved accordingly.

They finally had the break they were looking for when some scouts investigated the sudden leaving of a bunch of wagons from a small village at the edge of the inhabited area. A ranger scout brought back news that a man named Andolar of Brighthome had requisitioned wagons from the village to bring wounded back from the border. The army was close to the village already. From the number of wagons taken, they decided the squad had liberated a lot of prisoners. The army moved at maximum speed to the village. Ambush preparations were quickly made, and the rangers continued to track the movement of the wagons and to make sure the raiders followed, but not too closely. Some traps and arrows along the way helped slow their movements. At the same time, the duchess took most of the cavalry north to get behind them and cut off their escape.

Finally the word came that the wagons were close with the raiders close behind. It was a closer pursuit than the commanders wanted but was still workable.

The squad members breathed a sigh of relief again as they thought about coming over the hill and seeing the army of Gamalius in full-battle array in front of them. Then they each told their view of the battle when the raiders breached the line to kill the dwarves. Berinda got to tell her part of the story yet again. Andolar certainly hoped he didn't have to spend an entire evening listening to how she won every battle they were in with her exploits. He would definitely end up making a sarcastic comment.

The duchess still had Baron Gardoney and the dwarves in the new command tent. They erected that one shortly after Andolar came out. The first one had a bit too much breeze for their liking, apparently. They had been talking for about an hour.

Yawns were coming quickly to all but the healers, so the conversation stopped. The squad wearily collected their things and got ready to catch up on some sleep. They constructed a lean-to off the wagons they captured and laid down. Andolar felt like he could sleep for a week straight.

CHAPTER 26

The army was going north as soon as the rest of it came and as soon as the supply lines could be guaranteed. The squad members, except for the healers, had slept around the clock. All of them were famished when they woke. It was almost like old times to have Korin working over a fire getting together a meal for the squad. Andolar supposed they could have joined one of the military groups to eat. However, the food they prepared was not likely to come up to the standards of Korin's cooking. The only thing missing was Lecik's voice.

That evening, he saw his father and the duchess coming to their wagons, along with the dwarves. Mythical beings come to life. His father used to tell him stories about the dwarves and their treasures when he was growing up. It would be a good idea for him to pick up their language. While he was at it, he could learn the language of the barbarians if he could talk his father or the dwarves into teaching him.

"Hello, your ladyship," Andolar called. "Hello, Father."

Most of the others mumbled some words of greeting and looked a bit nervous. Berinda, on the other hand, looked like she thought they were about to receive military honors from the duchess. The duchess walked right up to the wagon and started looking at their treasure and the other goods they had taken from the camp of the raiders.

"You did well for yourselves," the duchess said.

"Yes, your ladyship," Petrion replied. "We also destroyed the fort Churinius built for a base."

"Very good, Petrion," the duchess told him. "That will be a help when we invade."

"We are invading, your ladyship?" Petrion asked.

"We have been attacked," she replied, "and no one comes into my country with an army and gets off without being punished. I think the best punishment for Durp would be to lose some more territory."

"Yes, your ladyship."

"How much money did you take in?"

"In total," Petrion said, "we have nearly five hundred and fifty gold and a hundred platinum. We also captured some gems and jewelry. Oh, did Baron Gilbert deal with the goblin merchant that was working to the west?"

"Yes, he did," she replied, "and brought in a bit of treasure that will help the army prepare for the coming war. Some of it paid the others in the area for their losses of livestock."

"There was quite a bit of treasure there if I remember correctly, your ladyship," Haslan said.

"Yes," she told the squad, "and most of it made from the coins of the goblins. Speaking of which, we need to discuss the amount of taxes you owe on what you found."

"Taxes!" Haslan said. "Why do we owe taxes? This wasn't money from the duchy."

"Well," she replied, "everyone has to pay taxes. I think, on a fortune like this, you'll have to pay 75 percent. That will be 75 percent of the total, including what you gave away. Baron, you must remind me to collect some extra taxes from this village as well since they have profited so much recently. I will also need the money I loaned you returned since you are self-supporting now. Then there is the matter of your enchanted items. I will need those back. It's too bad you aren't in the army."

Many of the villagers drifted over to see what was going on. When the duchess mentioned collecting more taxes, they started fading back again. However, curiosity got the better of them, and they were back in moments.

"I thought we were in the army," Petrion said.

"You were in the army when this was taken," the duchess asked quietly. "Is that the way you thought it was?"

"Andolar," his father called, "I don't think oof —"

The duchess elbowed his father at a joint in his armor without looking around to aim.

"Sure," Petrion answered, "that's what we thought. We were acting on behalf of the duchy after all."

"Well, if the duchy was paying your expenses, then everything you collected, except for a small finder's fee, is the property of the duchy."

"What?" Haslan yelled. "You can't do that!"

"What did you say?" the duchess asked in a dangerous tone.

Andolar saw his father waving at him, trying to tell him something, but the baron was forced to dodge another elbow. Andolar wondered what his father wanted. Suddenly he remembered some of the stories his father told them while he and his brother were growing up. There was nothing much that Eviola hated more than being told there was something she couldn't do. He cut in quickly to stop any trouble.

"Very good, your ladyship," Andolar told her quickly. "What percent of the money do we receive as this finder's fee?"

"Percents are such a bother," she said. "I was thinking something in the range of a hundred gold."

"That seems a bit inadequate even as compensation for the coins," Andolar replied quickly, "and there are gems and jewelry too. We also brought back armor, weapons, livestock, and imprisoned citizens of the duchy. In addition to the material goods that we have brought to add to your ladyship's wealth, we also thwarted several raids against your people and sacked two goblin encampments. One of those was a fortress which you would have needed to destroy before pressing the invasion. We also killed the human strategist supporting the goblins, killed several hundred enemy soldiers, and led a large number of the enemy into an ambush. We exposed a goblin trader, leading to the acquisition of more goods for the realm, increased safety for the people of that area, and a reduction in the war material available to the goblins. And finally, we brought back extremely valuable allies against the goblins and the barbarians."

Andolar had to stop for a moment to let some scattered applause die down. The duchess was frowning at him, so he continued quickly.

"Now let's see," the magician continued. "One hundred gold will cover your financing of our squad. That would leave us something in the neighborhood of eight hundred gold in coin and about a thousand gold in gems and jewelry according to Haslan. I think his opinion on these matters should be adequate. I think two hundred gold is less than we deserve for obtaining the wealth. But the realm is at war, and wars are expensive, so we can let it go at that."

He saw shocked looks all around as he stated the sum he wanted. Even the duchess looked surprised. She expected to be asked for much more than that. She would be asked shortly.

He hoped no one in the squad mentioned that he hadn't counted the gem they already stashed away. After all, it was emergency money. More of the villagers were gathering around to see what was going on. It was time to enlist some support in their cause.

"As for the armor and weapons," Andolar continued, "I think we should be allowed first choice of the items and a 10 percent bonus on everything that we do not keep to continue the fight. As for saving citizens of the duchy, that was our pleasure. We don't want any compensation for bringing safely home some of the loyal citizens who support our armies. No true citizen of the duchy could do less when his fellow citizens are held in such deplorable conditions, being tortured and worked to death. That was our duty."

Andolar bowed to the former prisoners as he spoke and received cheers from the farmers now returned to their homeland.

"We also don't want compensation for destroying the three raiding parties," Andolar said to the crowd. "We just happened to decipher the pattern for the raids before your strategists."

He received some more applause from the farmers and villagers for that, but he also got some hard looks from some of the military people that were in the crowd. He made a mental note to talk up the army later, but now it was time to get on to the good part.

"I think that a hundred gold each is adequate compensation for destroying a major fortification as well as its supply camp. I think that is in line with precedent," Andolar said as he smiled, thinking how some of the tiresome information his father had forced him to learn was helping now.

"And taking out the enemy commander who, by your own words, would aid the goblins significantly in any battle against the troops of the duchy would rate another hundred and fifty," he continued. "Yes, even though that action could save the lives of hundreds of our soldiers and more of our citizens, we think that small compensation is fair."

Andolar saw the duchess take a breath to say something in response, but he continued quickly to keep her from being able to counter. Being on top of the wagon gave him a small tactical advantage over her, and he stood up to make the most of it. More soldiers were working their way over, so he needed his voice to carry better because he was playing to them too.

"For exposing a merchant selling arms and supplies to the goblins for raids into our home land, I think a hundred gold is all we should take. We all need to do everything we can to support the brave soldiers who protect us from harm. All of the dwarf armor and weapons should be left in the keeping of the dwarves even though our squad captured the goods. They are our allies and our friends. We have fought side by side to end the scourge of these raids into the peaceful lands of Gamalius."

He had to stop another moment to let a few cheers die down.

"Finally, for bringing such staunch allies as the dwarves to join with us against the goblins and the barbarians…"

He made his voice swell in volume and, by design, was forced to interrupt his speech because of the applause from the now-large crowd of villagers and soldiers. The yells continued for a while, apparently to the delight of the dwarves, for whom his father was translating all that was said.

"Thank you, my good friends," he said, trying to make himself seem more a part of the group. "Your kindness is worth more than gold."

The startled look on the face of the duchess at his ploy was intoxicating.

"Even though the worth of this last deed is enormous," Andolar continued after the applause again died, "with the potential to change the course of both our wars, we think three hundred gold is adequate compensation. After all, we are all fighting for the common good."

More applause and cheers accompanied the conclusion of his speech. Wow, did he feel good. The subtle pulling in of the attention of the crowd was exhilarating. Working the emotions of the group was in its own way as delicate a task as crafting a magical spell. The duchess didn't appear at all pleased by his work though. His father was smiling and talking quietly with the dwarves, at least until the duchess started to speak.

"Right you are, Andolar," Eviola began. "Six hundred gold is less than you could have asked for all of the things you have done for the duchy. Therefore, I am also going to reward you in another way. It is a way that is fitting for such an effective group as the Rogue's Squad. You are hereby appointed our ambassador to the dwarf kingdom, with the rest of the squad as escort."

The cheers began again, and Andolar was forced to smile and accept the cheers of the crowd. Dueling for the emotions of the crowd appeared to be dangerous as well as difficult. He hadn't stopped to consider that the duchess had many more years of experience swaying crowds to her words than he did. He remembered another thing his father said about the duchess many times. She hated to lose.

"Thank you, your ladyship," Andolar said with a bow. "Giving us six hundred gold for our deeds, along with the three hundred and fifty for adding so much money to your coffers, is agreed since we are being given first choice of the enchanted items.

He wanted the terms clearly defined before he lost the crowd for support.

"As for the position," he continued, "I am afraid I must decline this generous offer. I regret that my abilities as a speaker are such that I could not do your realm justice as an ambassador. I appreciate the honor but feel that the position requires someone with more experience in these types of affairs than I have."

Oh no. She had a very self-satisfied smile on her face. That could not be a good sign.

"I appreciate your concern for the good of the realm, sir magician," the duchess said to the crowd. "I wish that all of my citizens would put the good of the duchy ahead of personal gain as all of you here today have done. However, after talking with these good dwarves, we have come to the conclusion that a trained diplomat would not be the best choice. Dwarves are not fond of the vague words and shadowed meanings that are the strong point of every diplomat. Rather they appreciate someone who speaks directly to a matter. I wish I had visitors from other lords who would do the same."

A round of polite laughter circulated through the crowd at her words and sorrowful look. She nodded to the people and smiled at them before continuing. The people loved her.

"You have also suffered and fought for these dwarves," the duchess continued. "That devotion to members of another race without thought of gain shows the dwarves that humans on this side of the mountains are trustworthy. You are also the son of the highest-ranking baron in the duchy, which will show the dwarves how important their friendship is to us. In short, Andolar of Brighthome, magician of the army, you are the very best person to help bring about an alliance as soon as possible for the good of the duchy, the dwarves, and the realm."

The cheers came loud and long, and Andolar knew he was being ordered to take the position. It would be best if he conceded defeat and worked on what he could get out of the situation. Like time off, salary, extra benefits, and things like that. Unfortunately, the duchess started talking again before he could get started.

"What is the name of this town?" she called out.

"Erbos," said several of the people at the same time.

"Know this, good people," she continued in a loud voice, "this battle will be called the Battle of Erbos. It will be considered the start of this goblin war, when the people of Gamalius refused to allow attacks on their territory. It will be the start of a move to push the goblins so they will never endanger the duchy again."

The crowd really loved that little speech. The villagers had obviously decided they would be permanently famous. Some others were apparently happy to have the goblins punished and the lands of the duchy expanded. Andolar turned back to the duchess from looking at the crowd so he could get his concessions. She wasn't going to let him have another chance at using the crowd to get something because she was already walking away. His father noticed his glances and shrugged his shoulders at Andolar.

"Don't worry about it, son," the baron said when they got close enough to be heard over the crowd. "You didn't do badly against her ladyship. Most people, when dealing with her, immediately give up on winning and start trying to minimize their losses. If I know her, she'll have you over later to tell you some things you missed."

"Thanks for the encouragement, Father," Andolar said. "You really shouldn't give up on a battle until it's been fought. You never know when or how the tides of battle will change."

"A good tactician also has to know when victory is no longer possible," his father replied. "Still you have a good point. If you think you've lost, you have."

The dwarves were waiting to talk to them, so his father decided to stay and serve as translator.

"Thank you for allowing us the goods of our dead," Duvain said through the baron. "I am also glad you will be accompanying me back to the dwarf lands."

"What will you do with the armor and weapons?" Gardoney asked the dwarves while translating for the squad.

"Return them to their families if possible," Govin said with sadness. "Right now, our families have many war items with no one to use them."

"Would it be possible for some of these to be remade into something sized for humans?" Gardoney asked. "We could trade something for the privilege if that is appropriate."

"The adamantine does not work well for one unskilled in its properties," Govin told them. "Dwarf smiths must practice for years to learn its tricks."

"Petrion said you were working as smiths in the goblin camp," Gardoney said. "Do either of you have the knowledge to do this work?"

"Yes," Duvain replied, "most dwarves learn the art of smithing and stonework even if they do not intend to become masters at the crafts. Govin is very skilled with the hammer and metal of the smith."

"Then maybe Govin could stay in the duchy," Gardoney suggested, "using his skill to remake half of the items. In exchange, the duchess could commission the enchantment of the rest to aid the dwarves until our forces can join."

"It is a good plan," Duvain agreed, "although Govin may not like to be separated from his homeland."

"I will endure that and more for the good of our people," Govin immediately countered.

"Then that is what we will do if your duchess agrees," Duvain said. "I will travel with Ambassador Andolar to the dwarf kingdom while Govin stays here as ambassador. Govin can also use the bar of adamantine to create new weapons."

"Duvain," Andolar cut in, "could you teach me the language of the dwarves and of the humans on the other side of the mountain?"

"Of course, Andolar," Duvain replied. "I would have suggested it even if you had not. It is always best to speak the language wherever you go. That is why we both learned the human speech. We were planning on learning your speech as well."

"I think the duchess wants to see us," Gardoney said in both languages. "Here comes her favorite messenger."

His father was right. The duchess summoned them to her tent. His father got the fun job of translating again.

"I am going to send a wagon train of supplies along with our new ambassador to the dwarf kingdom," the duchess began after they were all seated. "The squad will serve as escort."

"Your ladyship," Gardoney interrupted, "Govin has consented to stay and rework half of the dwarf armor and weapons into items usable by humans. He has also agreed to serve as temporary ambassador on behalf of the dwarves. In exchange, I ask that we attempt to enchant the remaining items and send them with the supply train. In this way, both armies will be helped in their wars."

"Very good, Baron Gardoney," the duchess told him. "See to the details of making it happen."

"Yes, your ladyship," the baron replied.

"Govin," the duchess continued, "how much food do your people have remaining, how much do they eat over a time period, and what food items are in shortest supply?"

The dwarves exchanged a look and some speech in the dwarf language before answering the questions.

"Duchess," Duvain said finally, "we must ask that this information not leave the group here. If the enemy finds out our true condition, he can gauge his attacks accordingly. We cannot say unless we have your word that the information will not leave this group."

The duchess and then the other people in the tent nodded their acceptance of Duvain's terms. This seemed to satisfy the dwarves. They were probably extremely prickly about promises.

"Our people were on half rations when we left," Govin said. "By the time schedule that the king set up, they would go on quarter rations two months later. Two months after that, there would be quarter rations only for children and warriors, with eighth rations for everyone else until the food runs out. When they reach that final state, it is merely a waiting until everyone starves. Heavy losses from attacks would slow down the rationing process. We left our home about two months ago. Fruits and vegetables are in the shortest supply naturally since they are harder to preserve for long periods of time. Meats are next, with grains being the most plentiful. A dwarf will eat about two-thirds of what a human would consume. When we left, there were about eight thousand adults and five thousand children."

His father let out a long whistle at the numbers. The duchess apparently hadn't expected such large numbers of dwarves either because it looked like she was doing some calculations in her head.

"Thirteen thousand," the duchess said shaking her head. "That is more people than we expected. I wanted to give the food to your people as a gesture of friendship, but that amount of food is more than I could buy and still run my duchy."

"Are there other places where we could purchase the food, Duchess?" Duvain asked with some disappointment.

"Purchasing food is not a problem, Duvain," the duchess said quickly, "but the money to purchase it is. We are draining our coffers to build the army for the war. I can sell you all the food you need because then I can buy more from my neighbors. But I am not able to give you that much food."

"Selling is fine, Duchess," Govin replied. "We would not wish to come to you as beggars."

"Allies are never beggars, good dwarf," she replied. "If we have your promise of eventual payment for the food, then I will go ahead and get the arrangements started on credit. I can give you the current prices here and in neighboring areas as well as tell you about what you will have to pay for shipment and financing."

"I have seen that your people use gold, silver, platinum, and gems for trading," Govin said. "Do you also think they will take steel, steel alloys, and crafted goods from the dwarves?"

"Most assuredly, Govin," Eviola told him. "A permanent trade in goods is what we want. We can start working out the details later. Right now, I think we should focus on getting the first of the food to your people."

"The biggest problem is that a large shipment of supplies traveling through enemy territory should have an army to force it through and protect it," Gardoney told them. "The army needs to attack elsewhere to have the most impact. It will also take us some time to get the amount of supplies you are going to need in the long term here and ready to go. We have already brought most of the quickly available stores along with the army. The army needs most of that to take the war into goblin territory.

"We could give up twenty wagons safely and have them ready to go in two weeks," Gardoney concluded after thinking for a few moments. "We could also have the Dwarf items enchanted in that time."

"Very good then," the duchess said looking at the squad members. "I will have your wagon train waiting at the location of the goblin merchant in two weeks. The squad will serve as escort. Duvain will go along to support and guide you. I will assign drivers to you who are trained soldiers, two for each wagon. You may continue to use the enchanted items in your possession if they are needed. If you find replacements among the goods of the barbarians, then I shall want these items back."

"Us and forty soldiers to guard twenty wagons," Petrion said in disbelief. "We had trouble as a mobile force that could strike at will. With wagons, the enemy will be able to ambush us. We need more troops."

"The smaller the group," the duchess replied, "the more likely you are to slip through. You have already proven yourselves resourceful. In two weeks time, the army will be deep into goblin territory. That is information also that is not to leave this tent. The goblins will be pulling in forces to try and stop us, leaving you a relatively clear path to the dwarves."

"How long will it take us to get there?" Andolar asked.

"About four and a half weeks from what the Dwarves told us," Gardoney replied.

"A month of moving deeper into goblin territory with a fifty person escort for twenty wagons of supplies!" Haslan said in terror. "We will be ambushed and killed."

"I'll try and come up with a couple more people," the duchess said. "It will help that other humans are moving freely through goblin lands. You must make sure Duvain arrives safely at the dwarf kingdom. From what he told us, if you show up without a dwarf in your company, you are likely to be attacked."

"Another bonus to the trip," Haslan said sarcastically.

His father translated everything that was said, and Haslan's comment drew chuckles from Govin. Duvain apparently didn't see the comment as quite so funny.

"Can we get replacements for the potions we used, your ladyship?" Petrion spoke up quickly to head off any trouble. "We used a neutralized poison and an enhanced healing potion during the attack at the first goblin camp."

"And two healing potions at the fort," Haslan added.

At least Petrion managed to control his features at that last addition. It was true after all. The potions just hadn't been in their possession at the start of the mission.

"Where did you get a potion of enhanced healing?" Eviola mused. "Ah, the buckle. I hadn't noticed you weren't wearing it, Gardoney. Of course, the replacements will cost you."

"Could you put those on my account, Duchess?" Govin asked. The healing potions were used on me. The debt is ours."

"Oh, very well," the duchess said. "Gardoney will see to it that they are replaced at no cost from the stores of the army. If there's nothing else, you are all free to go.

"We have two wagons of our own, your ladyship," Andolar added quickly. "They could also be used to help transport goods to the dwarves."

"Capacity isn't the problem, Andolar," the duchess replied. "Getting the goods to fill the wagons is the problem."

"With your ladyship's permission," Andolar answered, "we will see what we can do to fill them before we go. We should be able to purchase enough."

"Thank you, Andolar," the duchess replied with a smirk at his scheme. "You can help your father as he organizes your wagon train. And try not to offend anyone in the dwarf kingdom while you're trying to make a profit. Is there anything else?"

"No, your ladyship," all of them said at about the same time.

"Your squad will stay together as a group until you are ready to depart for the dwarf kingdom," the duchess continued. "Duvain will accompany you, so you can all become better acquainted. That will also give all of you more time to learn each other's languages. I encourage all of you to learn the dwarf, goblin, and barbarian languages as well as you can. The knowledge will be critical. Oh, by the way, Petrion, I have arranged to have a story passed around that you were framed so we could use you for a secret mission. You are now returning from that very successful mission. I believe there is someone in Gamalius that is anxious to see you. Please don't say anything to contradict the stories. And don't say anything about your future mission. That's all. You may go."

They left the tent and returned to their wagons with Duvain trailing along. Govin would now be in the company of her ladyship most of the time, working out the arrangements of the treaty between the two peoples.

Andolar was already starting to pick up some of the dwarf language. With two weeks to work on it before they left and another few weeks on the trail, he should be getting reasonably good by the time they arrived. "Ambassador Andolar." It sounded good. So did "Andolar of Brighthome."

"We got to keep almost all of the coins," Haslan said, interrupting his thoughts, "and a very nice gem. You did a good job, Andolar."

"Thank you, Haslan," Andolar replied, "I consider that high praise coming from you. Oh, there is one more thing I wanted to mention. Since I greatly increased the value of the treasure we received, I think I should receive an extra share of the increase. After all, that's what Haslan gets, and he didn't increase the value nearly as much as I did."

"All in favor of an extra share for the magician," Petrion said, "raise your hand."

Everyone in the squad raised a hand—even Berinda and Haslan. Wow, he had been almost joking, figuring there was no way they would give him any extra.

Now he could buy more goods that he could sell to the dwarves for a profit. This ambassador job could have some substantial fringe benefits.

"We are going to have a really good time," Berinda said then. "We can stop for a bit in Delaigamon and then go on to Gamalius. After that, we'll have to head for Omnirus's old house. We should still have a couple days of free time."

"That's right," Andolar said with a forced smile, "though we will have to spend quite a bit of that time preparing for our journey."

"That's right," Petrion said, "but we'll still have some free time. I'll make sure of it."

He would never avoid Berinda for two whole weeks. She was already talking to Petrion about evenings off, and they were going to Delaigamon and Gamalius. He might have to spend a night out alone with Berinda twice. Florine appeared to be interested in him as well. That was sure to cause problems if he was any judge of people. And there was still Quilonia in Delaigamon. It would, he supposed, be good practice for his diplomatic duties.